Iris Murdoch was born in Dublin of Anglo-Irish parents. She attended Badminton School, Bristol, and read classics and philosophy at Somerville College, Oxford. During the war she was an Assistant Principal at the Treasury, and then worked with UNRRA in Belgium and Austria.

She held a studentship in philosophy at Newnham College, Cambridge, for a year, then in 1948 returned to Oxford where she was for many years a Fellow and Tutor in philosophy at St Anne's College. In 1956 she married John Bayley, professor and critic in the field of literature.

For her highly acclaimed novel, *The Sea, The Sea*, Iris Murdoch won the Booker Prize in 1978.

By the same author

Novels

*Under the Net*
*The Flight from the Enchanter*
*The Bell*
*A Severed Head*
*An Unofficial Rose*
*The Unicorn*
*The Italian Girl*
*The Red and the Green*
*The Time of the Angels*
*The Nice and the Good*
*Bruno's Dream*
*A Fairly Honourable Defeat*
*An Accidental Man*
*The Black Prince*
*The Sacred and Profane Love Machine*
*A Word Child*
*Henry and Cato*
*The Sea, The Sea*
*Nuns and Soldiers*
*The Philosopher's Pupil*

Plays

*A Severed Head* (with J. B. Priestley)
*The Three Arrows*
*The Servants and the Snow*

Philosophy

*Sartre, Romantic Rationalist*
*The Sovereignty of Good*
*The Fire and the Sun*

IRIS MURDOCH

# The Sandcastle

TRIAD
PANTHER

Triad/Panther Books
Granada Publishing Ltd
8 Grafton Street, London W1X 3LA

Published by Triad/Panther Books 1979
Reprinted 1980, 1982, 1985

Triad Paperbacks Ltd is an imprint of
Chatto, Bodley Head & Jonathan Cape Ltd and
Granada Publishing Ltd

First published in Great Britain by
Chatto & Windus Ltd 1957
Copyright © Iris Murdoch 1957

ISBN 0-586-04914-2

Printed and bound in Great Britain by
Collins, Glasgow

Set in Intertype Lectura

*To*
**JOHN BAYLEY**

# CHAPTER ONE

'Five hundred guineas!' said Mor's wife. 'Well I never!'

'It's the market price,' said Mor.

'You could articulate more distinctly,' said Nan, 'if you took that rather damp-looking cigarette out of your mouth.'

'I said it's the *market price*!' said Mor. He threw his cigarette away.

'Bledyard would have done it for nothing,' said Nan.

'Bledyard is mad,' said Mor, 'and thinks portrait painting is wicked.'

'If you ask me, it's you and the school Governors that are mad,' said Nan. 'You must have money to burn. First all that flood-lighting, and then this. Flood-lighting! As if it wasn't bad enough to have to see the school during the day!'

'Shall we wait lunch for Felicity?' asked Mor.

'No, of course not,' said Nan. 'She always sulks when she comes home. She wouldn't want to eat anyway.' Felicity was their daughter. She was expected home that day from boarding-school, where an outbreak of measles had brought the term to an early conclusion.

They seated themselves at the table at opposite ends. The dining-room was tiny. The furniture was large and glossy. The casement windows were open as wide as they could go upon the hot dry afternoon. They revealed a short front garden and a hedge of golden privet curling limply in the fierce heat. Beyond the garden lay the road where the neat semi-detached houses faced each other like mirror images. The housing estate was a recent one, modern in design and very solidly built. Above the red-tiled roofs, and over the drooping foliage of the trees there rose high into the soft mid-summer haze the neo-Gothic tower of St Bride's school where Mor was a housemaster. It was a cold lunch.

'Water?' said Nan. She poured it from a blue-and-white porcelain jug. Mor tilted his chair to select his favourite from the row of sauce bottles on the sideboard. One advantage of the dining-room was that everything was within reach.

'Is Donald coming in this evening to see Felicity?' asked Nan. Donald was their son, who was now in the Sixth Form at St Bride's.

'He's taking junior prep,' said Mor.

'He's taking junior prep!' said Nan, imitating. 'You could have got him off taking junior prep! I never met such a pair of social cowards. You never want to do anything that might draw attention to you. You haven't taken a vow of obedience to St Bride's.'

'You know Don hates privileges,' said Mor briefly. This was one of the points from which arguments began. He jabbed un-enthusiastically at his meat. 'I wish Felicity would come.'

'I've got a bone to pick with Don,' said Nan.

'Don't nag him about the climbing,' said Mor. Donald wanted to go on a climbing holiday. His parents were opposed to this.

'Don't use that word at me!' said Nan. 'Someone's got to take some responsibility for what the children do.'

'Well, leave it till after his exam,' said Mor. 'He's worried enough.' Donald was shortly to sit for a Cambridge College entrance examination in chemistry.

'If we leave it,' said Nan, 'we'll find it's been fixed. Don told me it was all off. But Mrs Prewett said yesterday they were still discussing it. Your children seem to make it a general rule to lie to their parents for all your talk about truth.'

Although he now held no religious views, Mor had been brought up as a Methodist. He believed profoundly in complete truthfulness as the basis and condition of all virtue. It grieved him to find that his children were almost totally indifferent to this requirement. He pushed his plate aside.

'Aren't you going to eat that?' said Nan. 'Do you mind if I do?' She reached across a predatory fork and took the meat from Mor's plate.

'It's too hot to eat,' said Mor. He looked out of the window. The tower of the school was idling in the heat, swaying a little in the cracked air. From the arterial road near by came the dull murmur, never stilled by day, of the stream of traffic now half-way between London and the coast. In the heat of the after-noon it sounded like insects buzzing in a wood. Time was longer, longer, longer in the summer.

'You remember how poor Liffey used to hate this hot weather,' said Mor.

Liffey had been their dog, a golden retriever, who was killed two years ago on the main road. This animal had formed the bond between Mor and Nan which their children had been unable to form. Half unconsciously, whenever Mor wanted to placate his wife he said something about Liffey.

Nan's face at once grew gentler. 'Poor thing!' she said. 'She used to stagger about the lawn following a little piece of shadow. And her long tongue hanging out.'

'I wonder how much longer the heat wave will last,' said Mor.

'In other countries,' said Nan, 'they just have the summer-time. We have to talk about heat waves. It's dreary.'

Mor was silent while Nan finished her plate. He began to have a soporific feeling of conjugal boredom. He stretched and yawned and fell to examining a stain upon the tablecloth. 'You haven't forgotten we're dining with Demoyte tonight?'

Demoyte was the former headmaster of St Bride's, now re-tired, but still living in his large house near to the school. The Mors had continued their custom of dining with him regularly. The sum of five hundred guineas, which had so much scan-dalized Nan, was to be paid for a portrait of him which the school Governors had recently commissioned.

'Oh, damn, I had forgotten,' said Nan. 'Oh, what a blasted bore! I'll ring up and say I'm ill.'

'You won't,' said Mor. 'You'll enjoy it when you're there.'

'You always make that futile remark,' said Nan, 'and I never do. Will there be company?' Nan hated company. Mor liked it.

'There'll be the portrait painter,' said Mor. 'I gather she arrived yesterday.'

'I read about her in the local rag,' said Nan. 'She has some pathetically comic name.'

'Rain Carter,' said Mor.

'Rain Carter!' said Nan. 'Cor lumme! The daughter of Sidney Carter. At least he's a good painter. Anyway, he's famous. If you wanted to waste money, why didn't you ask him?'

'He's dead,' said Mor. 'He died early this year. His daugh-ter's supposed to be good too.'

'She'd better be, at that price,' said Nan. 'I suppose I'll have to dress. She's sure to be all flossied up. She lives in France. Oh dear! Where is she staying, by the way? The Saracen's Head?'

'No,' said Mor, 'Miss Carter is staying at Demoyte's house. She wants to study his character and background before she starts the picture. She's very academic about it.'

'Demoyte will be delighted, the old goat!' said Nan. 'But what a line! I like "academic"!'

Mor hated Nan's mockery, even when it was not directed against him. He had once imagined that she mocked others merely in order to protect herself. But as time went on he found it harder to believe that Nan was vulnerable. He decided that it was he who needed the consolation of thinking her so.

'As you haven't met the girl,' he said, 'why are you being so spiteful?'

'What sort of question is that?' said Nan. 'Do you expect me to answer it?'

They looked at each other. Mor turned away his eyes. He suffered deeply from the discovery that his wife was the stronger. He told himself that her strength sprang only from obstinate and merciless unreason; but to think this did not save him either from suffering coercion or from feeling resentment. He could not now make his knowledge of her into love, he could not even make it into indifference. In the heart of him he was deeply compelled. He was forced. And he was continually offended. The early years of their marriage had been happy enough. At that time he and Nan had talked about nothing but themselves. When this subject failed, however, they had been unable to find another – and one day Mor made the discovery that he was tied for life to a being who could change, who could withdraw herself from him and become independent. On that day Mor had renewed his marriage vows.

'Sorry,' said Mor. He made it a rule to apologize, whether or not he thought himself in the wrong. Nan was prepared to sulk for days. He was always the one who crawled back. Her strength was endless.

'In fact,' he said, 'according to Mr Everard she's a very shy, naïve girl. She led quite a cloistered life with her father.' The Reverend Giles Everard was the present headmaster of St Bride's, generally known as the Revvy Evvy.

'Quite cloistered!' said Nan. 'In France! As for Evvy's judgment, he casts down his eyes like a milkmaid if he meets a member of the other sex. Still, if we have this girl at dinner we shall at least escape Miss Handforth, on whom you dote so!' Miss Handforth was Mr Demoyte's housekeeper, an old enemy of Nan.

'I don't dote on Handy,' said Mor, 'but at least she's cheerful, and she's good for Demoyte.'

'She isn't cheerful,' said Nan. 'She just has a loud voice – and she expects to be in the conversation even when she's waiting at table. I can't stand that. There's no point in having servants if you abandon the conventions. There's ice cream to follow. Will you have some? No?'

'She keeps Demoyte's spirits up,' said Mor. 'He says it's impossible to think about oneself when there's so much noise going on.'

'He's a morbid old man,' said Nan. 'It's pathetic.'

Mor loved Demoyte. 'I wish Felicity would come,' he said.

'Don't keep saying that, darling,' said Nan. 'Can I have your ice-cream spoon? I've used mine to take the gravy off the cloth.'

'I think I ought to go into school,' said Mor, looking at his watch.

'Lunch isn't over,' said Nan, 'just because *you*'ve finished eating. And the two-fifteen bell hasn't rung yet. Don't forget we must talk to Felicity about her future.'

'*Must* we?' said Mor. This was the sort of provocative reply which he found it very hard to check, and by which Nan was unfailingly provoked. A recurring pattern. He was to blame.

'Why do you say "must we?" in that peculiar tone of voice?' said Nan. She had a knack of uttering such a question in a way which forced Mor to answer her.

'Because I don't know what I think about it,' said Mor. He felt a cold sensation which generally preluded his becoming angry.

'Well, I know what I think about it,' said Nan. 'Our finances and her talents don't leave us much choice, do they?' She looked directly at Mor. Again it was impossible not to reply.

'I suggest we wait a while,' said Mor. 'Felicity doesn't know her own mind yet.' He knew that Nan could go on in this tone for hours and keep quite calm. Arguments would not help him. His only ultimate defence was anger.

11

'You always pretend people don't know what they want when they don't want what you want,' said Nan. 'You are funny, Bill. Felicity certainly wants to leave school. And if she's to start on that typing course next year we ought to put her name down now.'

'I don't want Felicity to be a typist,' said Mor.

'Why not?' said Nan. 'She could have a good career. She could be secretary to some interesting man.'

'I don't want her to be secretary to some interesting man,' said Mor, 'I want her to be an interesting woman and have someone else be her secretary.'

'You live in a dream world, Bill,' said Nan. 'Neither of your children are clever, and you've already caused them both enough unhappiness by pretending that they are. You've bullied Don into taking the College exam and you ought to be satisfied with that. If you'd take our marriage more seriously you'd try to be a bit more of a realist. You must take some responsibility for the children. I know you have all sorts of fantasies about yourself. But at least try to be realistic about *them*.'

Mor winced. If there was one thing he hated to hear about, it was 'our marriage'. This entity was always mentioned in connection with some particularly dreary project which Nan was trying to persuade him to be unavoidably necessary. He made an effort. 'You may be right,' he said, 'but I still think we ought to wait.'

'I know I'm right,' said Nan.

The phrase found an echo in Mor's mind. He was perpetually aware of the danger of becoming too dogmatic himself in opposition to Nan's dogmatism. He tried to change the subject. 'I wonder if Felicity will mind your having changed her room round?'

Nan liked moving the furniture about. She kept the rooms in a continual state of upheaval in which nothing was respected, neither one's belongings nor the way one chose to arrange them, and thereby satisfied, or so it seemed to Mor, her desire to feel that all the things in the house were her things. He had become accustomed, after many years, to the perpetual flux, but he hated the way in which it hurt the children.

Nan refused to leave her point. 'You're so simple-minded, Bill. You think that reactionaries consider all women to be stupid, and so progressives must consider all women to be clever!

I've got no time for that sort of sentimental feminism. Your dear Mr Everard has got it too. Did I tell you that he wants me to make an after-dinner speech at that idiotic dinner?' There was to be a ceremonial dinner, at a date not yet arranged, to honour the presentation to the school of the portrait of Mr Demoyte.

'Yes, he told me,' said Mor. 'I hope you will. You'd make a good speech.'

'No, I wouldn't,' said Nan. 'I'd just make myself and you look ridiculous. I told Evvy so. He really is an ass. Men of his generation have such romantic ideas about female emancipation. But if his idea of the free society is women making after-dinner speeches, he'd better find someone else to co-operate with. He told me to "think it over". I just laughed at him. He's pathetic.'

'You ought to try,' said Mor. 'You complain about the narrowness of your life, and yet you never take the chance to do anything new or different.'

'If you think my life would be made any less, as you charmingly put it, "narrow" by my making a fool of myself at that stupid dinner,' said Nan, 'I really cannot imagine what conception you have of me at all.' The two-fifteen bell for the first afternoon lesson could be heard ringing beyond the trees.

'I wish you hadn't stopped your German,' said Mor. 'You haven't done any for months, have you?'

Mor had hoped to be able to educate his wife. He had always known that she was intelligent. He had imagined that she would turn out to be talented. The house was littered with the discarded paraphernalia of subjects in which he had hoped to interest her: French grammars, German grammars, books of history and biography, paints, even a guitar on which she had strummed a while but never learnt to play. It irritated Mor that his wife should combine a grievance about her frustrated gifts with a lack of any attempt to concentrate. She deliberately related herself to the world through him only and then disliked him for it. She had few friends, and no occupations other than housework.

'Don't go out of your way to annoy me,' said Nan. 'Haven't you got a lesson at two-fifteen?'

'It's a free period,' said Mor, 'but I ought to go and do some correcting. Is that Felicity?'

13

'No, it's the milkman,' said Nan. 'I suppose you'd like some coffee?'

'Well, maybe,' said Mor.

'Don't have it if you're indifferent,' said Nan; 'it's expensive enough. In fact, you weren't really thinking about my German. You're still stuffed up with those dreams that Tim Burke put into you. You imagine that it's only my narrow-mindedness that stops you from being Prime Minister!'

Tim Burke was a goldsmith, and an old friend of the Mor family. He was also the chairman of the Labour Party in a neighbouring borough, where he had been trying to persuade Mor to become the local candidate. It was a safe Labour seat. Mor was deeply interested in the idea.

'I wasn't thinking about that,' said Mor, 'but you *are* timid there too.' He was shaken more deeply than he yet liked to admit by his wife's opposition to this plan. He had not yet decided how to deal with it.

'Timid!' said Nan. 'What funny words you use! I'm just realistic. I don't want us both to be exposed to ridicule. My dear, I know, it's attractive, London and so on, but in real life terms it means a small salary and colossal expenses and absolutely no security. You don't realize that one still needs a private income to be an M.P. You can't have everything, you know. It was your idea to send Felicity to that expensive school. It was your idea to push Don into going to Cambridge.'

'He'll get a county grant,' Mor mumbled. He did not want this argument now. He would reserve his fire.

'You know as well as I do,' said Nan, 'that a county grant is a drop in the ocean. He might have worked with Tim. He might have knocked around the world a bit. And if he learns anything at Cambridge except how to imitate his expensive friends—'

'He'll do his military service,' said Mor. In persuading Donald to work for the University Mor had won one of his rare victories. He had been paying for it ever since.

'The trouble with you, Bill,' said Nan, 'is that for all your noisy Labour Party views you're a snob at heart. You want your children to be ladies and gents. But anyhow, quite apart from the money, you haven't the personality to be a public man. You'd much better get on with writing that school textbook.'

'I've told you already,' said Mor, 'it's not a textbook.' Mor was writing a book on the nature of political concepts. He was

14

not making very rapid progress with this work, which had been in existence now for some years. But then he had so little spare time.

'Well, don't get so upset,' said Nan. 'There's nothing to get upset about. If it's not a textbook, that's a pity. School textbooks make money. And if we don't get some extra money from somewhere we shall have to draw our horns in pretty sharply. No more Continental holidays, you know. Even our little trip to Dorset this year will be practically ruinous, especially if Felicity and I go down before term ends.'

'Oh, for Christ's sake, Nan,' said Mor, 'do shut up! Do stop talking about money!' He got up. He ought to have gone into school long ago.

'When you speak to me like that, Bill,' said Nan, 'I really wonder why we go on. I really think it might be better to stop.' Nan said this from time to time, always in the cool, unexcited voice in which she conducted her arguments with her husband. It was all part of the pattern. So was Mor's reply.

'Don't talk that nonsense, Nan. I'm sorry I spoke in that way.' It all passed in a second.

Nan rose, and they began together to clear the table.

There was a sound in the hall. 'Here's Felicity!' said Mor, and pushed quickly past his wife.

Felicity shut the front door behind her and put her suitcase down at her feet. Her parents stood looking at her from the door of the dining-room. 'Welcome home, dear,' said Nan.

'Hello,' said Felicity. She was fourteen, very thin and straight, and tall for her age. The skin of her face, which was very white but covered over in summer with a thick scattering of golden freckles, was drawn tightly over the bridge of her nose and away from her prominent eyes, giving her a perpetual look of inquiry and astonishment. She had her mother's eyes, a gleaming blue, but filled with a hazier and more dreamy light. Nan's hair was a dark blonde, undulating naturally about her head, the ends of it tucked away into a subdued halo. Felicity's was fairer and straighter, drawn now into a straggling tail which emerged from under her school hat. In looks, the girl had none of her father. It was Donald who had inherited Mor's dark and jaggedly curly hair and his bony face, irregular to ugliness.

Felicity took off her hat and threw it in the direction of the hall table. It fell on the floor. Nan came forward, picked up her hat, and kissed her on the brow. 'Had a good term, dear?'

'Oh, it was all right,' said Felicity.

'Hello, old thing,' said Mor. He shook her by the shoulder.

'Hello, Daddy,' said Felicity. 'Is Don here?'

'He isn't, dear, but he'll come in tomorrow,' said Nan. 'Would you like me to make you lunch, or have you had some?'

'I don't want anything to eat,' said Felicity. She picked up her suitcase. 'Don't bother, Daddy. I'll carry it up.'

'What are your plans for this evening?' said Nan.

'I've just arrived,' said Felicity. 'I haven't got any plans.'

She began to mount the stairs. Her parents watched her in silence. A moment later they heard her bedroom door shut with a bang.

# CHAPTER TWO

It was a fine clear evening. Mor closed the door of the Sixth Form room and escaped down the corridor with long strides. A subdued din arose behind him. He had just been giving a lesson to the history specialists of the Classical Sixth. Donald, who was in the Science Sixth, had of course not been present. It was now two years since, to Mor's relief, his son had ceased to be his pupil. Mor taught history, and occasionally Latin, at St Bride's. He enjoyed teaching, and knew that he did it well. His authority and prestige in the school stood high; higher, since Demoyte's departure, than that of any other master. Mor was well aware of this too, and it consoled him more than a little for failures in other departments of his life.

Now, as he emerged through the glass doors of Main School into the warm sunshine, a sense of satisfaction filled him, which was partly a feeling of work well done and partly the anticipation of a pleasant evening. On an ordinary day there would be the long interval till supper-time to be lived through, passed in reading, or correcting, or in desultory conversation with Nan. This was normally the most threadbare part of the day. But this evening there would be the strong spicy talk of Demoyte and the colour and beauty of his house. If he hurried, Mor thought, he would be able to have one or two glasses of sherry with Demoyte before Nan arrived. She made a point of arriving late, to the perpetual irritation of Handy. Then there would be wine with the meal. Nan never drank alcohol, and Mor did not usually drink it, partly as a lingering result of his teetotaller's upbringing and partly for reasons of economy, but he enjoyed drinking occasionally with Demoyte or Tim Burke, though he always had an irrational sense of guilt when he did so.

Demoyte lived at a distance of three miles from the school in a fine Georgian house called Brayling's Close, which he had acquired during his period of office as Headmaster, and which he had left to the school in his will. He had crammed it with treasures, especially Oriental rugs and carpets on the subject of which he was an expert and the author of a small but definitive treatise. Demoyte was a scholar. For his scholarship Mor, whose talents were speculative rather than scholarly, admired him without envy; and for his tough honest obstinate personality and his savage tongue Mor rather loved him; and also because Demoyte was very partial to Mor. The latter often reflected that if one were to have him for an enemy Demoyte would present a very unpleasant aspect indeed. His long period as Headmaster of St Bride's had been punctuated by violent quarrels with members of the staff, and was still referred to as 'the reign of terror'. A feeling of security in their job was a luxury which Demoyte had not had the delicacy to allow to the masters of St Bride's. If the quality of an individual's teaching declined, that individual would shortly find that Demoyte was anxious for his departure; and when Demoyte wanted something to occur it was usually not long before that thing occurred.

Demoyte had not been easy to live with and he had not been easy to get rid of. He had persuaded the Governors to extend his tenure of power for five years beyond the statutory retiring age – and when that time was up he had only been induced to retire after a storm during which the school Visitor had had to be called in to arbitrate. Ever since Mor had come to the school, some ten years ago, he had been Demoyte's lieutenant and right-hand man, the intermediary between Head and the staff, first unofficially, and later more officially, in the capacity of Second Master. In this particular rôle, Mor was sincere enough to realize, he had been able to experience the pleasures of absolute power without remorse of conscience. He had mitigated the tyranny; but he had also been to a large extent its instrument and had not infrequently enjoyed its fruits.

Demoyte would have liked Mor to succeed him as Head; but St Bride's was a Church of England foundation, and at least a nominal faith of an Anglican variety was required by the Governors in any candidate for the Headship. This item Mor could not supply; and a storm raised by Demoyte with the purpose of changing the school statutes on this point, so as to allow Mor to stand, failed of its object. Demotye himself, Mor supposed, must originally have conformed to the requirement; but by the time Mort first met him his orthodoxy had long ago been worn down into a sort of obstinate gentlemanly conservatism. Under the Demoyte regime not much was heard at

St Bride's about Christianity, beyond such rather stereotyped information as was conveyed by the Ancient and Modern Hymnal; and the boys had to learn about religion, much as they learnt about sex, by piecing together such references to these blush-provoking topics as they could discover for themselves in books. What Demoyte cared about was proficiency in work. This his masters were engaged to produce and sacked for failing to produce; and during his period of office the yearly bag of College scholarships by St Bride's rose steadily and surely. As for morality, and such things, Demoyte took the view that if a boy could look after his Latin prose his character would look after itself.

Very different was the view taken by Demoyte's successor, the Reverend Giles Everard, whom Demoyte regarded with unconcealed contempt and always referred to as 'poor Evvy'. The training of character was what was nearest to Evvy's heart — and performance in Latin prose he regarded as a secondary matter. His first innovation had been to alter the school prospectus, which had formerly reflected Demoyte's predilection for star pupils, in such a way as to suggest that *now* St Bride's was concerned, not with selecting and cherishing the brilliant boy, but with welcoming and bringing to his humbler maturity, such as it was, the mediocre and even the dim-witted. Demoyte watched these changes with fury and with scorn.

Nan had never taken to Demoyte. This was partly because Demoyte had never taken to her, but she would have disliked him, Mor thought, in any case. Nan hated eccentricity, which she invariably regarded as affectation. She did not, it seemed to Mor, care to conceive that other people might be profoundly different from herself. Nan had, moreover, a tendency to be hostile towards unmarried people of either sex, regarding them as in some way abnormal and menacing; and in Demoyte the sort of bachelor behaviour which made Nan particularly uneasy had developed, through age and through the long exercise of tyrannical power, to the point of outrage. Demoyte was overbearing in conversation and rarely sacrificed wit to tact. Although he was a Tory by habit and conviction, there were few institutions which he took for granted. Marriage was certainly not one of these. In the sacred intimacy of the home Nan was often pleased to refer to 'our marriage'; but she did

19

not think that this was a subject which, either in particular or in general, could be discussed or even mentioned in the company of strangers – and everyone beyond the family hearth was to her a stranger. Demoyte felt no such delicacy, and would often embarrass Nan by outbursts on the subject of the married state. 'A married couple is a dangerous machine!' he would say, wagging a finger and watching to see how Nan was taking it. 'Marriage is organized selfishness with the blessing of society. How hardly shall a married person enter the Kingdom of Heaven!' And once, after an occasion when Mor had sharply defended Nan from one of Demoyte's sarcasms, he had almost turned the pair of them out of the house, shouting, 'You two may have to put up with each other, but I'm not bound to put up with either of you!'

After that Mor had had great difficulty in persuading Nan to accompany him to Demoyte's dinners. But he knew obscurely that if it ever became established that he went alone, Nan's hostility to Demoyte would take a more active form and she would seriously endeavour to bring the friendship to an end. As it was, Nan worked off her spleen on each occasion by making bitter comments to Mor as they walked home. With these comments Mor would often weakly concur, excusing his disloyalty to himself on the ground that he was thereby averting a greater evil. Nan was prepared to tolerate Demoyte on condition that he was judged finally by Mor and herself in unison; and to placate her Mor was prepared to allow the judgment to seem final, and to keep his private corrections to himself.

On this occasion as Mor walked across the asphalt playground in the direction of the bicycle-sheds, averting his eyes automatically from the windows of classrooms where lessons were still in progress, he remembered with a small pang of disappointment that tonight Demoyte would not be alone. Mor would sometimes cycle over to Brayling's Close in the late evening after supper – but there was something especially sacred about the short encounters before dinner, when the glow of Demoyte's drawing-room came as a sharp pleasure after the recent escape from school. Mor was glad when Demoyte had guests, but he liked to see the old man alone first, and as he tried to arrive soon after five-thirty he was usually able to do so. This evening, however, the portrait-painter woman, Miss Carter, would of course be present. Mor had a vague curiosity about this young woman. When her father had died some months ago the newspapers had been filled with obituaries and appreciations of his work which had contained many references to her. She was supposed to be talented. Concerning her personal appearance and presence Mor had been able to obtain only the vaguest account from Mr Everard, who, as Nan had remarked, was not generally to be trusted in summing up the opposite sex. Mor's thoughts touched lightly on the girl and then returned to Demoyte.

In spite of the difference in their political views Demoyte had, somewhat to Mor's surprise, been very much in favour of Tim Burke's plan to make Mor a Labour candidate. 'You won't do us any harm,' he told Mor, 'since whatever else you'll be doing at Westminster you certainly won't be governing the country – and you may do yourself some good by getting out of this damned rut. I hate to see you as poor Evvy's henchman. It's so painfully unnatural.' Mor was of Demoyte's opinion on the latter point. As far as this evening was concerned, however, Mor was anxious to warn Demoyte not to mention the matter in Nan's presence. Demoyte's approval would merely increase her opposition to the plan.

The masters' bicycle-shed was a wooden structure, much broken down and overgrown with Virginia creeper, and situated in a gloomy shrubbery which was known as the masters' garden, and which was nominally out of bounds to the boys. Beside it was a stretch of weedy gravel, connecting by a grassy track with the main drive, on which stood Mr Everard's new baby Austin and Mr Prewett's very old enormous Morris. Mor found his bicycle and set out slowly along the track. He bumped along between the trees, turned on to the loose gravel of the main drive, until he reached the school gates and the smooth tarmac surface of the arterial road. Fast cars were rushing in both directions along the dual carriageway, and it was a little while before Mor could get across into the other lane. He slipped through at last and began to pedal up the hill towards the railway bridge. It was a stiff climb. As usual he forced himself at it with the intention of getting to the top without dismounting. He gave up the attempt at the usual place. He reached the summit of the bridge and began to free-wheel down the other side.

Now between trees the Close was distantly in sight. At this

place on the road it seemed as if one were deep in the country. The housing estate was momentarily hidden behind the bridge, and the shopping centre, which lay on a parallel road on the other side of the fields, had not yet come in sight. Demoyte's house stood there, stately and pensive as in a print, looking exactly as it had looked when company had come down in coaches from London, across heaths infested by highwaymen, to report to their friends in the country what was Garrick's present rôle and what the latest saying of the Doctor. Mor waited again for a gap in the traffic to get back across the road, turned into Demoyte's drive, and cycled up the untidy avenue of old precarious elm trees. These trees had long ago been condemned as unsafe, but Demoyte had refused to have them cut down. 'Let Evvy do it when I'm gone,' he said. 'I don't grudge him that pleasure. He has so few.'

The house was long in the front, built of small rose-coloured bricks, and arching out in two large bow windows. A wide door with a stone pediment faced the avenue across a square of grass. The main garden lay at the side. Mor cycled between two pillars and skirted the grass. He left his bicycle leaning against the wall of what had once been a coach house and made his way on foot towards the front door. He felt that he was being watched, and looked up to see Miss Handforth gazing at him out of the window above the door. He waved cheerfully at her. He was one of Handy's favourites.

Miss Handforth met him in the hall, sweeping round the white curve of the staircase with a vehemence which made the house shake. She was a stout powerful middle-aged woman with a face like a lion and a foot like a rhino. She had once been an elementary school teacher.

'Hello,' said Mor. 'How goes it, Handy? How's his Lordship?'

'No more lazy and troublesome than usual,' said Miss Handforth in ringing tones. 'You've arrived early again, but I don't suppose it matters.' Handy never addressed people by their names. She coughed unrestrainedly as she spoke. 'I've got a most awful cold, though how I could have caught it in this weather's a regular mystery. It must be hay fever, only the hay's in, I don't know if that makes any difference. If you want to wash, go straight through, you know the way, the downstairs toilet this time, if you please. The boss is still getting up from lying down, but Miss Thing is in the drawing-room if you want to be polite. Otherwise go and knock on the dressing-room door. I must go and look at the dinner.'

Miss Handforth went away, coughing and sneezing, through a green baize door in the direction of the kitchen. Mor went through to what she called the downstairs toilet and tried to wash his hands. They were blackened, as usual, by the ancient rubber grips on the handle-bars. Soap made little impression on the dirt, although plenty came off on the towel. Mor, who had deduced from Miss Handforth's tone that she was hostile to Mr Demoyte's other guest, decided that he would not be, as she put it, polite, and instead he mounted the stairs and knocked on the door of Demoyte's dressing-room. A growl came from inside.

'May I come in, sir?' said Mor.

'No,' said Demoyte's voice. 'Go away. You're infernally early. Three minutes ago I was asleep. Now I have to make a decision about my trousers. I'm not going to receive you in my shift. There's a charming lady down in the drawing-room.'

Mor turned away and went slowly downstairs again. Half thoughtfully he straightened his tie. As he made for the drawing-room door he saw through a vista of passages straight into the kitchen; the figure of Handy was discovered in a listening attitude. Mor made an ambiguous gesture of complicity. Handy replied with another gesture and a resounding snort. Mor was not sure what she meant. He went into the drawing-room and closed the door softly behind him.

The room was full of yellow evening light and its three tall windows were wide open on to the garden. It faced the side of the house, overlooking a long enclosed lawn which was separated from the front drive by a brick wall. Beyond the lawn was a thick dark yew hedge cut in the centre by a stone archway beneath which an iron gate led into a second garden which was invisible from the windows. This garden consisted of another lawn, with a wide herbaceous border at either end. Beyond it and at a higher level lay a third garden which was reached by a flight of stone steps. On either side of the steps were two clipped holly bushes, and on either side of these a low box hedge which grew on top of the flower-hung wall which marked the difference of level between the two gardens. This last one was the rose garden, a triangular strip ending in an

23

avenue of mulberries which led towards the farthest tapering point of Demoyte's estate. After that there were taller trees through which in winter were revealed the red roofs of the housing estate, but which in summer enclosed the horizon except where at one place their line was broken by the upwardly pointing finger, just visible from the house, of the neo-Gothic tower of St Bride's.

The drawing-room was empty. Mor felt some relief. He fingered his tie again, and sat down quietly in one of the chairs. He loved this room. In his own home, although there were few ornaments, and such as there were chosen carefully by Nan to harmonize with the curtains, no part of it seemed to blend into a unity. The objects remained separate, their shapes and their colours almost invisible. Here, on the contrary, although the room was overcrowded and its contents extremely miscellaneous, all seemed to come together into a whirl of red and gold wherein each thing, though contributing to the whole, became more itself. A rich Feraghan carpet covered the floor, almost entirely obscured by equally splendid rugs which lay edge to edge over its surface. Pieces of furniture stood about, without plan or pattern, their only obvious intention being to provide as many smooth surfaces as possible upon which might be placed cups, bowls, vases, boxes, together with a variety of smaller objects made of ivory, jade, jet, glass and amber. *Petit-point* cushions crowded so thick upon most of the chairs that it was quite hard to find anywhere to sit down. The walls were papered in a gold-and-white pattern, but were rarely visible between the most splendid of the rugs which hung upon them, stretched at various angles between the floor and the ceiling, and glowing there with silky vitality like the skins of fabulous animals. Mor half closed his eyes and the forms about him became hazier and more intense. He let the colours enter into him. He rested.

Then suddenly with a strange shock of alarm he realized that upon a table at the far end of the room a very small woman was kneeling. He had not noticed her as he came in, since the colours of her dress faded into the background, and he had not expected to see her at that point in space. She had her back to him, and seemed to be examining one of the rugs which hung on the wall behind the table.

'I'm so sorry!' said Mor, jumping up. 'I didn't see you!'

The young woman turned abruptly, tilted the table with her weight, tried to spring off it, and then fell on the floor. Mor ran forward, but she had recovered herself before he reached her.

'You frightened me,' she said. 'I didn't hear you come in.'

They looked at each other. Mor saw a very short youthful-looking girl, with boyishly cut dark hair, and darkly rosy cheeks, wearing a black cotton blouse, an elaborately flowered red skirt, and a necklace of large red beads; and he became for an instant acutely aware of what the girl was seeing: a tall middle-aged schoolmaster, with a twisted face and the grey coming in his hair.

'I am Rain Carter,' said the girl.

'I am William Mor,' said Mor. 'I'm so sorry I alarmed you.'

'That's quite all right,' said Miss Carter. 'I was just looking at this rug.' She spoke in a slightly prim way.

'That's one of Mr Demoyte's treasures,' said Mor. 'I believe it's a Shíraz.' He thought, how very small she is, and how like a child. Perhaps Evvy was right after all. Her eyes were dark brown and fugitive, her nose rather broad and tilted. A not unpleasant face.

'It *is* a Shíraz,' said Miss Carter. 'Do you notice how mysteriously the colours behave here? Each piece has its own shade, and then there is a sort of surface colour which the whole rug has which is different, a sort of blush.' She spoke with a pedantic solemnity that Mor found touching and absurd. He found himself wondering if she could really paint. He stretched out his hand to touch the rug, and as he moved it its lustre changed. The surface was extremely close and smooth. He caressed it for a moment.

Before Mor could think of a suitably impressive answer to Miss Carter's remark, Demoyte came in. Mor turned about, and looked at Demoyte with some surprise. At this time in the evening the old man was usually to be found wearing a frayed velvet jacket, of a tobacco-stained red colour, and a rather limp bow tie. This evening, however, he was wearing a grey lounge suit, which Mor had rarely seen, and an ordinary tie. He had put a clean shirt on. He came in with head thrust forward and bore down upon them. Though he stooped now, he was still a tall man and with a head only just not grotesquely large for his body. His nose seemed to have grown bigger with age. His eyes were blue and looked out between many ridges of almost white

25

dry skin. Scant white hairs still clung in a gentle film to his bulging skull.

'What!' shouted Demoyte, 'you haven't given Miss Carter a drink! Mor, you are only fit to be a country schoolmaster. Excuse our provincial habits, Miss Carter, we don't know any better. You will have some sherry?' He began to pour it out.

'Thank you,' said Miss Carter, 'but do not blame Mr Mor. He has only this moment seen me. He thought I was part of a rug.' As Miss Carter replied to Demoyte her primness became coyly animated. Mor looked at her again. Although she had no accent, she spoke English as if it were not quite her native tongue. He remembered that her mother had been French.

'And so you might be, my dear,' said Demoyte; 'a flower, a bird, an antelope.' He handed her the glass with a flourish.

Miss Handforth was discovered leaning in the doorway. 'The dinner's ready,' she said, 'but I suppose you aren't.'

'Go away, Handy,' said Demoyte. 'You're far too early. You all seem to want to get the evening over quick. Mr Mor's better half is still to come.'

'Well, what am I to do about the dinner?' said Miss Handforth. 'Spoil it by over-cooking, or let it get cold? I don't mind which it is, but just let me know.'

There was a knock on the outside door, and then Nan stepped into the hall. Mor saw her head appear suddenly behind Miss Handforth.

'Nan!' he said, as if to protect her from the hostility of the house against her. He went to help her off with her coat, a service which it never seemed to occur to Demoyte or Miss Handforth to perform, and then led her back into the drawing-room, holding her by the hand. Nan had made what she herself would call a real social effort, and was dressed in a smart well-fitting black dress with which she wore a pearl necklace which Mor had bought once from Tim Burke at a reduced price as a wedding anniversary present. Her wavy hair, glossy and impeccably set, framed the pale oval face, smoothly powdered and unmarked by wrinkles, the long mouth and the shrewd eyes, intelligent, practical, reliable, full of power. She looked a tall handsome woman, well dressed and confident. Mor looked at her with approval. In any conflict with the outside world Nan was invariably an efficient ally.

'Nan, may I introduce Miss Carter,' said Mor, since Demoyte said nothing. 'Miss Carter, my wife.'

The women smiled and greeted each other, and Nan as usual refused the glass of sherry which Demoyte as usual poured out and offered to her.

'As I said before, the meal is ready,' said Miss Handforth, who was still standing in the doorway. 'If the ladies want to go upstairs first, they know the way. Meanwhile I shall be bringing in the soup.'

'Oh, shut up, Handy,' said Demoyte. 'Give us a moment to finish our sherry, and don't rush the ladies.'

Nan and Miss Carter took the opportunity to withdraw, and Miss Handforth stumped away to the kitchen. Mor turned to Demoyte and looked him over. Demoyte peered at Mor, his eyes gleaming and his nose wrinkled in what Mor had learnt to recognize as a smile. Demoyte's heavy sardonic mouth did not follow the usual conventions about smiling.

'Why the fancy dress, sir?' said Mor, indicating the lounge suit.

'Not a word!' said Demoyte, conspiratorially. 'Am I to be summed up by a slip of a girl? You don't know what I've suffered in these last twenty-four hours! She wants to see pictures of my parents, pictures of me as a child, pictures of me as a student. She wants to know what I've written. She practically asked if I kept a diary. It's like having a psychiatrist in the house. Her sense of vocation is like a steam hammer. You wouldn't think it to look at her, would you? But I'm going to lead her up the garden. I've got her thoroughly foxed so far. She shan't know what I'm like if I can help it! These clothes are part of the game. Ssh! here she comes.' They all went in to dinner.

They had reached the dessert. Nan was methodically eating a pear and Miss Carter was picking daintily at a branch of very small grapes. Mor was enjoying the port. Demoyte sat at the head of the table and Mor sat at the foot with the ladies between them. As Nan had predicted, no place had been set this evening for Miss Handforth. This person towered over the table, often leaning upon it as she made a remark, sneezing from time to time, and breathing down the ladies' necks.

Demoyte said, 'I asked old Bledyard to come to complete the

party, but he made some excuse, obviously false. Miss Carter hasn't met our Bledyard yet.' Bledyard was the art master at St Bride's, an eccentric.

'I look forward to meeting him,' said Miss Carter. 'I have seen some of his work. It is good.'

'Really?' said Mor. 'I didn't realize Bledyard ever actually painted anything!'

'He used to, certainly,' said Miss Carter. 'I have seen at least three good landscapes. But I gather now he has theories which interfere with his painting?'

'His head is full of cant,' said Demoyte, 'which he employs to excuse the fact that he can't paint any more. That's how I see it. But at any rate Bledyard is a man. He's got some stuff inside him. Not like the pious dolls poor Evvy will fill the place with before long. You'd better start clearing out, you infidel,' he said to Mor.

Mor, who was anxious to skirt the dangerous subject of his clearing out, said quickly, 'I believe we are both to lunch with Mr Everard on Thursday, Miss Carter. I think Bledyard has been invited too.' He regretted this change of subject at once, since it struck him that Everard had as usual blundered in inviting him and failing to invite Nan. This aspect of the matter had not struck him when Everard had mentioned the lunch that afternoon. Nan put down her fruit knife noisily and drank some water.

'You'll get nothing to drink with Evvy,' said Demoyte. 'Better stoke up now. Have some more wine, Miss Carter. Can't I persuade you, Mrs Mor? See, Miss Carter is drinking like a fish, and is more sober than any of us.' Mor had noticed this too.

Miss Carter did not rise to this quip. She said rather solemnly. 'I have only met Mr Everard once. I look forward to seeing him again.'

'Impossible!' said Demoyte. 'What did you think of poor Evvy? Let's hear Evvy summed up!' He winked at Mor.

Miss Carter hesitated. She cast a quick suspicious look at Demoyte. 'I think he has a fresh and gentle face,' she said firmly. 'He seems a man without any malice in him. That is both rare and good.'

Demoyte seemed taken aback for a moment. Mor taunted him with his eyes. 'Little puritan!' said Demoyte. 'So you reprove us all! Let me fill your glass yet again.'

'No, thank you, Mr Demoyte,' said Miss Carter. 'Of course, it takes a long time to know a man, and this is only an impression. What do you think, Mrs Mor?'

Mor held his breath. He thought the question rather bold. He hoped that Nan was not going to dislike Miss Carter.

'Well,' said Nan, 'I think fundamentally Mr Everard is a fool, and if someone is a fool, especially if he's in a position of authority, this spoils his other good qualities.'

'For once,' cried Demoyte, 'I find myself in complete agreement with Mrs Mor. And now, dear friends, it's time for coffee.'

Coffee was taken in the library. Mor loved this room too. It lay above the drawing-room and had the same view, but it was a longer room. There were the three tall windows, corresponding to the ones below, and then an extra piece on the front side of the house giving to the library one of the big bow windows which faced the drive. Directly below this, cut off from the drawing-room, was a little room which Miss Handforth, making what was always supposed to be a joke, would call her boudoir. The bow window on the other side of the hall belonged to the dining-room, and above, to Demoyte's bedroom. Next to the library at the back of the house was a guest bedroom, which also enjoyed a view of the lawn, and through whose other window could be seen, once it had grown dark, a reddish glow which showed, at a distance of some twenty miles, where London lay.

Demoyte's books were all behind glass, so that the room was full of reflections. Demoyte was a connoisseur of books. Mor, who was none, had long ago been barred from the library. Mor liked to tear a book apart as he read it, breaking the back, thumbing and turning down the pages, commenting and underlining. He liked to have his books close to him, upon a table, upon the floor, at least upon open shelves. Seeing them so near and so destroyed, he could feel that they were now almost inside his head. Demoyte's books seemed a different kind of entity. Yet he liked to see them too, elegant, stiff and spotless, gilded and calved, books to be held gently in the hand and admired, and which recalled to mind the fact of which Mor was usually oblivious that a book is a thing and not just a collection of thoughts.

The others sat down near to one of the lamps. Mor wandered

about the room. He felt free and at ease; almost, for the moment, happy. He looked out of the windows. The Close was never silent, since day and night there could be heard the hum of the traffic along the arterial road and the distant thunder of trains and their sad piping cries. Headlights of cars swept by perpetually in the middle distance, revealing trees and the scored surface of sandy embankments. Mor turned back into the room. He surveyed the group by the lamp. His eyes still full of the night, he felt detached and superior. Miss Carter was sitting with her legs drawn up under her. Her skirt spread in a big arc about her, and the lamplight falling upon the lower half of it made it glow with reds and yellows. She looked, Mor thought, like some small and brilliantly plumaged bird. He felt he was being rude, and turned to one of the bookcases.

'Keep your paws off those books!' called Demoyte. 'Come and drink your coffee, or Handy will remove it. You know she only allows seven minutes for coffee.'

Miss Handforth appeared. She was wearing a rather grubby apron and was clearly in the middle of washing-up.

'Can I take it now,' she said, 'or have I spoken out of turn?' She sneezed. Nan ostentatiously averted her head while Handy busied herself pulling the curtains. Mor gulped his coffee down and the tray was removed.

Mor joined the conversation. He could see Nan looking restless and knew that she was now calculating how soon she could decently rise to go. He could almost hear her counting.

'I think we ought to be starting for home,' said Nan, after some little time. She looked at Mor.

'Yes, I suppose so,' said Mor. He did not want to go yet.

Nan rose with determination. Demoyte did not try to detain her. The company began to drift in a polite group towards the door.

'I asked Handy to cut you some roses,' said Demoyte, 'but I have an uneasy feeling she's forgotten. Handy!' He shouted over the banisters, 'Roses for Mrs Mor!'

Mor was touched. He knew that the roses were really for him, in response to his having, a few days ago, expressed admiration for the rose garden.

Miss Handforth appeared from the kitchen with a loud clack of the green baize door. 'I didn't get down the garden today,' she announced.

'Well, get down *now*,' said Demoyte in an irritated tone. He was tired of the evening.

'You know I can't see in the dark,' said Miss Handforth, well aware that Demoyte was not serious. 'Besides, the dew is down.'

Nan said simultaneously, 'Don't bother, please. They would have been *lovely*, but now don't bother.' Mor knew that she was not interested in the roses. Nan thought on the whole that flowers were rather messy and insanitary things. But she was quite pleased all the same to be able to underline that Handy was in the wrong.

'Let me go!' said Miss Carter suddenly. 'I can see in the dark. I know where the roses are. Let me cut some for Mrs Mor.' She ran ahead of them down the wide staircase.

'Capital!' said Demoyte. 'Handy, give her the big scissors from the hall drawer. You go with her, Mor, and see she really knows the way. I'll entertain your lady. But for Christ's sake don't be long.'

Miss Carter took the scissors and vanished through the front door. Mor ran after her, and closed the door behind him. The night was cool and very dark. He could not see, but knew the way without sight to the wooden door in the wall that led into the main garden. He heard the door clap before him, and in a moment he felt its surface under his hand, cool and yielding. He emerged on to the quiet dewy lawn. He heard the distant traffic and saw the interrupted flashes from the headlights, but all about him was dark and still. He blinked, and saw ahead of him the small figure hurrying away across the lawn.

'Miss Carter!' said Mor in a low voice, 'wait for me, I'm coming too.' After the brilliance of the house the garden was strange, pregnant with trees and bushes, open to the dew and the stars. He felt almost alarmed.

Miss Carter had stopped and was waiting for him. She seemed less tiny now that there were no objects with which to compare her. He saw her eyes glint in the darkness. 'This way,' she said.

Mor blundered after her. 'Yes, you can see in the dark,' he said. 'I wish I could.' They went through the yew hedge under the archway into the second garden.

They walked quietly across the lawn. Mor felt strangely breathless. Miss Carter was laying her feet very softly to the

31

earth and made no sound at all as she walked. Mor tried to step softly too, but he could feel and hear under his feet the moisture in the close-cropped grass. An intense perfume of damp earth and darkened flowers surrounded them and quenched the noises of the world outside. Mor could see very little, but he continued to follow the dark moving shape of the girl ahead. He was still dazed by the swiftness of the transition.

They reached the steps which led up into the third garden. Miss Carter went up the steps like a bird and for a moment he saw the pallor of her bare arm exposed against the black holly bush as she turned to wait for him. Mor plunged forward, his foot seeking the lowest step. He stumbled and almost fell.

'Here, come this way,' she said from above him, 'this way.' She kept her voice soft, compelled to by the garden. Then she came back down the steps and he realized that she was reaching out her hand. Mor took her hand in his and let her guide him up the steps. Her grip was firm. They passed between the black holly bushes, and released each other. Mor felt a strong shock within him, as if very distantly something had subsided or given way. He had a confused feeling of surprise. The moon came out of the clouds for a moment and suddenly the sky was seen in motion.

The rose garden was about them now, narrowing towards the place where Demoyte's estate ended in the avenue of mulberry trees. Mor had never seen it by night. It looked different now, as if the avenue were immensely long, and Mor had a strange momentary illusion that it was in that direction that the house lay, far off at the end of the avenue: Demoyte's house, or else its double, where everything happened with a difference.

'*Quelle merveille!*' said Miss Carter in a low voice. She took a few quick steps across the grass, and then stopped, lifting her face to the moonlight. A moment later she began to run and threw her arms about the trunk of the first mulberry tree of the avenue. The branches above her were murmuring like a river.

Mor coughed. He was slightly embarrassed by these transports. 'You know, we mustn't be too long,' he said.

'Yes, yes,' said Miss Carter, detaching herself from the tree, 'we shall pick them very quickly now.' She began to run between the beds, picking out the buds which were just partly open. The scissors snicked and the long-stemmed roses were cast on to the grass. The moon whitened the paler ones and made the dark ones more dark, like blood. Mor tried to pick a rose, but as he had nothing with which to cut it he only pricked himself and mangled the rose.

'Leave all to me,' said Miss Carter, coming to snip off the dangling blossom. 'There, that should be enough.'

Mor was anxious to get back now. He had a vision of Nan and Demoyte waiting impatiently in the hall. Also, there was something which he wanted to think over. He hastened ahead down the stone steps, his eyes now accustomed to the dark, and ran noisily across the lawn to the yew hedge. Here he waited, and held the iron gate open for Miss Carter. It clinked to behind them, and now they could see the lighted windows of the house where already Miss Handforth had drawn back the curtains in preparation for the night. They passed the wooden gate, and in a moment they were blinking and rubbing their eyes in the bright light of the hall. Miss Carter clutched the great armful of roses to her breast.

'What an age you were,' said Nan. 'Did you get lost?'

'No,' said Mor, 'it was just very dark.'

'Here are the roses,' said Miss Carter, trying to detach them from where they had pinned themselves to her cotton blouse. 'What about some paper to put them in?'

'Here, have the *Evening News*,' said Demoyte, taking it from the table. 'I haven't read it, but to the devil with it, now the day is over.'

Nan spread out the paper on the table and Miss Carter laid the roses upon it, trying to order them as she did so. 'How beautiful!' said Nan. 'Miss Carter must have one, don't you think?' She selected a deep red rose and held it out graciously to Miss Carter, who took it and fumbled awkwardly to fix it at her bosom. She failed, and held it in her hand, against her skirt.

'Now take your flowers and be off with you,' said Demoyte, who was yawning and clearly wanted to be in bed. 'Good-night!'

'Good-night, sir,' said Mor, 'and thank you. Good-night, Miss Carter.'

'Good-night,' said Nan. 'Thank you for the roses.'

'Good-night,' said Miss Carter.

Nan and Mor were out on the gravel outside the front door. The house glowed at them for a moment from within, and they saw the figures of Demoyte and Miss Carter waving them off. Then the door shut and the light above it went out. Demoyte did not believe in seeing his guests off the premises. Nan waited while in darkness Mor found his bicycle. They started down the drive, Mor pushing the machine. Nan took hold of his arm.

'Thank heavens that's over!' she said, 'it was rather grisly, wasn't it?'

'Yes,' said Mor.

'What did you make of Miss Carter?' said Nan.

'Not much,' said Mor. 'I found her a bit intimidating. Rather solemn.'

'She takes herself seriously,' said Nan. 'But she's really a little clown. She obviously gets on swimmingly with Demoyte when no one else is there.'

'Maybe,' said Mor, who hadn't thought of that.

'You were ages in the garden,' said Nan. 'Whatever happened?'

'Nothing,' said Mor, 'absolutely nothing.'

They walked on in silence and turned on to the main road. Mor was reviving in his mind the curious feeling of shock which he had experienced at the top of the stone steps. He found it hard to interpret.

# CHAPTER THREE

'Rigden,' said Mor.

A long silence followed. Mor was taking the Fifth Form Latin class, a chore which sometimes came his way during the absence on sick leave of Mr Baseford, the classics master. The day was the day after Mr Demoyte's dinner party. It was a hot afternoon, the first period after lunch, a time which Mor hated. A fly buzzed on the window. Twenty boys sat with the Elegies of Propertius open before them. Rigden clearly could make nothing of the line in question.

'Come on, Rigden,' said Mor rather wearily, 'have a bash. You can translate the first word anyway.'

'*You*,' said Rigden. He was a slight crazy-looking boy with a small head. He idolized Mor. His inability to please him was one of the tragedies of his school days. He leaned intently over his book.

'That's right,' said Mor, 'and the second word.'

A yell of uncontrolled laughter went up in the next room. That was Mr Prewett's mathematics class. Prewett was unhappily quite unable to keep order. Mor knew that keeping order was a gift of nature, but he could not but despise Prewett a little all the same. Mor himself had but to look at the boys and they fell silent.

'*Only*,' said Rigden.

'Yes,' said Mor, 'now go on.'

Ridgen stared wretchedly at the page. '*While it is permitted*,' he said.

'*Lucet*, you juggins,' said Mor, 'not *licet*. Carde?'

Jimmy Carde was one of Mor's enemies. He was also the bosom friend of Mor's son Donald. Mor never felt at ease with Carde.

'*While there is light*,' said Carde. He spoke in a casual and superior way, scarcely opening his mouth, as if it were a concession on his part to support these absurd proceedings at all.

'That's right,' said Mor. 'Now, Rigden, you go on.'

Rigden was beginning to look desperate. He gazed into the book, biting his lip.

'Get a move on,' said Mor, 'we haven't got all day.' He sighed, hearing the traffic which murmured away sleepily in the distance. There came back into his consciousness the thought, which had not been far absent from it throughout the lesson, that at a quarter past three he was to meet the portrait painter, Miss Carter, and show her round the school. A note from Mr Everard, waiting in his pigeon-hole that morning, had conveyed the request; and since its arrival Mor had had little time for reflection. He had felt only, for some reason that was obscure to him, a slight feeling of disappointment and irritation that his next meeting with Miss Carter was not to be at Mr Everard's lunch party, which he had fixed in his mind as the next occasion when he would see her.

'*Lives do not desert the fruit,*' said Rigden in desperation, throwing caution to the winds.

'No,' said Mor. 'Did you prepare this, Rigden?'

'Yes, sir,' said Rigden, not raising his eyes, and trying to invest his voice with a tone of injured innocence.

'Well, you'd better stay behind afterwards and talk to me about it,' said Mor. 'Our time's nearly up. Could somebody finish translating? Carde, what about you, could you do the last six lines for us?'

Carde sat quietly looking at the poem. He was a good performer, and he was in no hurry. Carde was efficient, and Mor respected efficiency. In the moment of renewed silence he looked again at the poem. He had chosen it for them that morning as a piece of prepared translation. Perhaps after all it was too hard. Perhaps also not quite suitable. His eye passed over the lines.

*Tu modo, dum lucet, fructum ne desere vitae.*
*Omnia si dederis oscula, pauca dabis.*
*Ac veluti folia arentes liquere corollas,*
*Quae passim calathis strata natare vides,*
*Sic nobis, qui nunc magnum speramus amantes,*
*Forsitan includet crastina fata dies.*

Carde cleared his throat.

'Yes?' said Mor. He looked at his watch. He saw that the

period was nearly ended, and a slight feeling of uneasiness came over him.

'While the light remains,' said Carde, speaking slowly in his high deliberate voice, 'only do not forsake the joy of life. If you shall have given all your kisses, you will give too few. And as leaves fall from withered wreaths which you may see spread upon the cups and floating there, so for us, who now as lovers hope for so much, perhaps tomorrow's day will close the doom.'

'Yes,' said Mor, 'yes. Very nice, Carde. Thank you. Now you can all go. Rigden, wait a moment, would you?'

An immediate clatter broke out, and amid a banging of books and desk tops there was a rush for the door. Carde was first out. Mr Prewett's class was evidently up at the same moment, and there was a confluence of din outside. The admonishing of Rigden took but little time, and Mor strode into the musty corridor to disperse the riot. A moment later he emerged from the centre door of what was gracelessly called Main School into the sunshine and looked about him.

The chief buildings of St Bride's were grouped unevenly around a large square of asphalt which was called the playground, although the one thing that was strictly forbidden therein was playing. The buildings consisted of four tall red-brick blocks: Main School, which contained the hall, and most of the senior classrooms, and which was surmounted by the neo-Gothic tower; Library, which contained the library and more classrooms, and which was built close against Main School, jutting at right angles from it; School House, opposite to Library, where the scholars ate and slept; and 'Phys and Gym' opposite to Main School, which contained the gymnasium, some laboratories, the administrative offices, and two flats for resident masters. The St Bride's estate was extensive, but lay along the slope of a hill, which created notorious problems upon the playing fields which lay behind Main School, stretching away towards the fringes of the housing estate and the maze of suburban roads in the midst of which Mor's house lay. The playground was connected with the main road by a gravel drive which ran through a shrubbery, past the masters' garden; but the largest section of the grounds lay farther down the hill, below the Library building. Here there was a thick wood of oak and birch, dense with fern and undergrowth, and cut by many winding paths, deep and soft with old leaves, the paradise of the younger boys. On the fringe of this wood, within sight of the Library, stood the Chapel, a stumpy oblong building of lighter brick and more recent date, looking not unlike a water works. Beyond this, hidden among the trees, were the three houses to which the boys other than the scholars belonged, where they lived and took their meals and, if they were senior boys, had their studies. These were Mor's house, Prewett's house, and the third was under the aegis of Mr Baseford, then on sick leave. The houses dully bore the names of their housemasters, and a keen rivalry between them was continually fostered by the teaching staff. Beyond the wood, alongside the arterial road, which skirted the school grounds on that side, lay the squash courts and the swimming pool – and upon the other side, upon the edge of the housing estate, were the music rooms and the studio. At the bottom of the hill was a ragged lawn, a half-hearted attempt at a flower garden, and beyond these a white stucco Victorian house inhabited *de officio* by Mr Everard. This ended the domain.

Mr Everard's note to Mor had said that Miss Carter would be waiting in the playground at the end of the first afternoon period. Mor looked quickly about, but could not see her. The strong sun was slanting in between the Library and the Phys and Gym, gilding the dark knobbly surface of the asphalt. Warmth arose from it, and the air quivered slightly. What Mor did see, at the corner of the playground near the far end of the Library, was his son Donald. Towards Donald, across the sunny asphalt, Jimmy Carde was making his way by a series of spectacular skips and jumps. He reached Donald and made violent impact with him like a bouncing ball. They spun round gripping each other's shoulders. From a distance Mor saw this encounter without pleasure.

Mor began to walk across the playground in the direction of Library. He looked about him for Miss Carter, who was not to be seen, and kept the still rotating pair in the corner of his eye. As Mor neared the main door of Library he saw that Donald and Carde had noted his approach. They drew apart, and in a moment Carde had sped away back across the open space, leaping as he did so madly into the air and spreading out his arms with palms and fingers extended until at last, capering grotesquely, he disappeared through the door of School House.

Carde was a scholar. Donald was left standing alone at the corner of the Library building. He was clearly uncertain what to do. He would have liked to slip away, but now that his father patently had him in his field of vision, it seemed improper to do this. On the other hand, Donald had no intention of making any approach to his father. He stood perfectly still, clutching his book and watching in a glassy way to see whether Mor would go into Library or pass round the far side of the building.

Mor also hesitated. Random encounters between himself and his son during school hours embarrassed both, and Mor avoided them as far as possible. However, he felt that he could not ignore Donald. This might hurt the boy even more. So he turned towards him. Rooted to the spot, Donald awaited his father.

'Hello, Don,' said Mor, 'how goes it?'

Donald looked at him, and looked away at once. He was tall enough now to look Mor in the eyes; indeed, there was scarcely an inch between them. His resemblance to his father was considerable. He had Mor's crisp dark hair, his crooked nose and lop-sided smile. His eyes were darker though, and more suspicious. Mor's eyes were a flecked grey, Donald's a brooding brown. The black points upon his chin portended a dark and vigorous beard. His face was soft, however, still with the indeterminacy of boyhood. His mouth was shapeless and pouting, not firmly set.

Donald was long in growing up – too long, Mor felt with some sadness. He could not but grieve over his son's strange lack of maturity. At an age when he himself had been devouring books of every kind in an insatiable hunger for knowledge, Donald appeared to have no intellectual interests at all. He worked at his chemistry in a desultory fashion, sufficiently to keep himself out of positive disgrace; but apart from this Donald seemed to do, as far as Mor could see, nothing whatever. He spent a lot of time hanging about, talking to Carde and others, or even, what seemed to Mor odder still, alone. He was to be seen for half an hour on end just leaning out of his window, or else sitting on the grass in the lower garden beyond the wood, his arms about his knees, doing absolutely nothing. This mode of existence was to Mor extremely mysterious. But he had not yet ventured to chide or even question Donald concerning the employment of his time. Donald's reading, such as it was, seemed to consist mainly of *Three Men in a Boat*, which he read over and over again, always laughing immoderately, and various books on climbing which he kept carefully concealed from his mother. During the holidays he was a tireless and indiscriminate cinema-goer. As Mor looked at him now, at his suspicious and sideways-turning face, he felt a deep sadness that he was not able to express his love for his son, and that it could even be that Donald did not know at all that it existed.

'All right,' said Donald. 'I'm just off down to the nets.' Donald was a fanatical cricketer.

'You're in the house team, aren't you?' said Mor. Donald was in Mr Prewett's house.

'Yes, sir,' said Donald. 'I was last year.'

He half turned, not sure if it was now proper for him to go away.

But Mor wanted to keep him there, to keep him until something had been said which would be a real communication between them. He wished that Donald would meet his eyes. He hated his calling him 'sir'.

'Carde translated well in my Latin class,' said Mor. He felt anxious to say something nice about Carde.

'Ah, yes,' said Donald.

Mor wondered whether Donald would tell Carde that he had said that, and whether it would please Carde to be told. How little he knew about them. He looked at the book under Donald's arm. He knew from experience that the boy hated being asked what he was reading. But curiosity overcame his judgment. 'What's the book, Don?' he asked.

Donald passed it over without a word. Mor looked at the title. *Five Hundred Best Jokes and Puzzles*.

'Hmmm,' said Mor. He could think of no comment on the book. He gave it back to his son.

At that moment Mor saw, over Donald's shoulder, a small figure approaching. It was Miss Carter. Mor saw at once, with some annoyance, that she was wearing trousers. Donald half turned, saw her, and mumbling an excuse retreated rapidly and took to his heels, running in the direction of the playing fields.

'I'm sorry to be so late,' said Miss Carter, 'and I hope I didn't disturb you just now. One of your pupils?'

'My son,' said Mor.

Miss Carter seemed surprised. She looked at Mor curiously. 'I did not think you could have a son so old,' she said, her odd precise voice lilting slightly.

'Well, you see I can,' said Mor awkwardly. He wished that she had not made herself conspicuous by wearing trousers. They were close-fitting black ones, narrow at the ankles. With them Miss Carter wore a vivid blue shirt, blue canvas shoes, and no other adornments. She was slim enough; but all the same she looked in those garments, Mor thought, rather like a schoolchild dressed to impersonate a Paris street boy.

'It must be a wonderful thing to have a grown-up son,' said Miss Carter.

'It is good,' said Mor, 'but it has its stormy moments. Shall we go this way?' They began to walk along towards the main door of Library.

'I can see that you are irritated by my trousers,' said Miss Carter, 'and if I had thought more I would not have worn them. But I have them for working in, and it didn't occur to me to change. I will next time.'

Mor laughed, and his irritation vanished completely. He led her up the stairs to show her the Library. As they walked in silence between the tables, now loaded with books over which the senior boys were bent at their work, Mor found himself wondering whether Miss Carter remembered with any sort of interest that in the garden last night she had taken his hand in hers. He did not imagine that she did. The speculation came quite quietly into Mor's mind, and he entertained it without emotion. As they descended the stairs, he forgot it again.

They crossed the playground towards Main School. Mor thought he would show Miss Carter the hall next. They found it empty, its rows of windows open wide to show a slope of pine trees and a distant view of the playing fields. It was melancholy with summer. High in the rafters a few butterflies flitted to and fro. The velvet curtains on the stage swayed in the light breeze from the windows. Their feet echoed on the boards.

'This is the hall,' said Mor. He looked at it gloomily. It was deplorably familiar.

'You must tell me all about Mr Demoyte,' said Miss Carter suddenly.

'What do you want to know?' said Mor. He felt that he had

41

half expected this. They walked back slowly into the open air.

'Well, everything,' said Miss Carter, 'as much as you know. As you will realize, painting a portrait is not just a matter of sitting down and painting what you see. Where the human face is concerned, we interpret what we see more immediately and more profoundly than with any other object. A person looks different when we know him – he may even look different as soon as we know one particular thing about him. And in any case there are simpler problems. A choice must be made about the clothes which the person is to wear in the picture, the posture which he is to hold, the expression on his face, the background, the accessories. A consideration of all these things will then affect one's methods and one's technique. It is impossible to be in a hurry.'

Mor smiled inwardly at this speech, which had been delivered in a slightly pompous and didactic tone. They were now walking across the playground in the direction of the Gym. He wondered if this was Miss Carter's own voice or the voice of her father. Partly to try her, he said, 'Why should you want to learn more about Demoyte? Who knows what view of him is the right one? Perhaps you, meeting him for the first time, and knowing no more than what you see, will see him more truly than we who have known him for so long.'

'I am a professional portrait painter,' said Miss Carter rather primly, 'and I am employed to paint *your* Mr Demoyte, not *my* Mr Demoyte.'

Mor whistled to himself. He now saw what Demoyte had meant when he said that she had a sense of vocation like a steam hammer. They entered the Gymnasium. It was full of juniors, who were dangling on ropes, curling over bars, springing over the horse, or otherwise bouncing about on the floor after the rather frog-like manner of small boys. Mr Hensman, the gym instructor, smiled and waved to Mor. Mor liked him. He was one of Donald's well-wishers.

Miss Carter looked a while at the pullulating scene. Then she said, as they turned away, 'Of course, what I said just now was pretentious nonsense. What Mr Demoyte would call cant. At least I know him well enough to know one of his favourite words. I want to paint a really good likeness. We all think that there is something which is what a person is really like, and that this takes some time to learn. I think you

42

know what Mr Demoyte is really like, and I want to find out.'

They walked across the playground again, and entered School House. Mor felt a new respect for Miss Carter, and it occurred to him for the first time that he liked her. He wondered where she had been educated. He supposed in a French *lycée*. He would have liked to ask her, only it would have been too forward.

'Well, I shall do what I can for you,' he said. 'Here is one of the main scholars' dormitories.' He opened the door and showed the long double line of iron beds, all with their blue coverlets. Beside each bed stood a white chest of drawers, on top of which each boy was allowed to place no more than three objects. Between the beds were white curtains which were pulled back in the day time.

This spectacle seemed to interest Miss Carter more than the Gym and the hall. 'It looks Dutch,' she said. 'I wonder why? So much white material, and the light— Does your son sleep here?'

The question disturbed Mor. 'My son isn't a scholar,' he said. 'Anyway, only the younger boys sleep in dormitories. The older ones sleep in their studies.'

'There's something very touching about a dormitory,' said Miss Carter. 'I have seen graveyards which are touching in the same way.'

They began to descend the stairs.

'I have the impression, for instance,' said Miss Carter, 'that Mr Demoyte is deliberately trying to deceive me about certain things. Since I arrived I am quite sure that he has been wearing clothes that he does not usually wear. I think this is not only because of the smell of mothballs but because of the way the clothes look on him.'

Mor laughed. He felt no obligation to keep Demoyte's absurd secret. 'You're right!' he said. 'Demoyte hardly ever puts on a suit. He usually wears corduroys and a sports coat during the day, and black trousers and a velvet smoking-jacket in the evening. And a bow tie, of course.'

'I suspected the bow tie,' said Miss Carter, 'because of a certain gesture he makes as if to adjust one. Yes. Why should he want to deceive me?'

43

'He doesn't want to be summed up by a slip of a girl,' said Mor. He glanced sideways at her.

Miss Carter smiled faintly. 'But I *will* sum him up,' she said. 'I *will*!'

Not her father's voice, thought Mor. Herself. They began to walk down the hill, across the ragged slope of grass which separated the Library building from the first trees of the wood. 'Would you like to see the Chapel?' he said.

'No, thank you,' said Miss Carter firmly. 'Not dressed like this. I might offend someone. Tell me, has Mr Demoyte ever published a volume of poems called *Falling Flowers*?'

Mor stopped and went into a peal of laughter. 'No!' he said. 'Did he try to tell you those were his?'

'Yes,' said Miss Carter. 'When I asked to see all his published works he offered me the poems, and said he'd get the others in a day or two.'

'He's probably inventing something even more fantastic,' said Mor. 'It's almost a shame to spoil his fun. *Falling Flowers* is an early effort of Mr Everard!'

Miss Carter laughed. 'Mr Demoyte is enjoying himself,' she said. 'I'd better rely on you instead. Could you please get me all his books? Can I trust you, I wonder?' She spoke with a cool peremptory air which Mor might have resented.

'Yes!' said Mor fervently. He did not resent it. 'I'll get you what he has written. There isn't much. The book on Oriental rugs, some articles on rare editions, and a volume of sermons preached at School Services. That was published very long ago. Demoyte would be furious if he knew I'd given it to you.'

'It shall be a secret between us,' said Miss Carter.

Mor felt at once a little uneasy at the thought that he was going to deceive the old man; but he wanted to please Miss Carter, and he thought her wishes were reasonable.

'What would you like to see now?' he said. 'What about the studio? There's an exhibition of the boys' art that was put on for Speech Day. I think it's still there.'

'Oh yes, please,' said Miss Carter. 'I love children's art.'

It seemed to Mor a little quaint that she should refer to the boys as children. It occurred to him that he was regarding Miss Carter as being in some way more youthful than his own pupils. They walked out of the sun on to one of the shadowy paths of the wood, the ground underfoot crackling with twigs and leaves and scattered with patches of golden light.

'But won't we meet Mr Bledyard?' said Miss Carter.

'Would you mind?' said Mor. 'In fact, he's hardly ever there on these sunny afternoons. He takes the boys out sketching.'

'I haven't met him yet,' said Miss Carter, 'and I feel a bit nervous.'

'He's quite harmless, our Bledyard,' said Mor, 'only a little odd. He's a sort of primitive Christian, you know. His views on portrait painting are connected with that. He thinks we ought to get back to Byzantine styles or else not paint at all.'

They approached the studio. It was a long rambling building which incorporated an old barn that had been standing there before. The music rooms were in a jumble of Nissen huts which were just visible farther on through the trees. Scattered sounds of a piano and of wind instruments were borne on the summer air. Miss Carter shivered and stopped in her tracks.

'What is it?' said Mor. He was surprised at her emotion. 'Don't be afraid. I can see from here that there's no one in the studio.'

They came down the grassy path, stepping on the withered leaves of ferns, and crossed a cobbled yard towards the door. Mor stepped inside first. A strong smell of paint greeted him, the clean self-assertive smell of art, after the woodland perfumes of nature which had drifted with them down the hill. There was no one within.

'Come on, the coast's clear!' he called to Miss Carter, who was still standing on the cobblestones and looking as if she was ready to run. She entered slowly, leaning warily round the side of the door.

Once she was well inside her attention was caught by the paintings which were pinned on to tall boards which leaned against the walls all round the room. She began to look at them. Through the high windows the golden lights of the afternoon came benevolently down, and gave to the studio something of the air of a modern church. For the first time that day Mor felt himself at leisure to observe his companion. He sat down on one of the stools and watched her as she moved from picture to picture. She looked like a child's picture herself, extremely gay and simple. Her dark hair, which was jaggedly

45

cut, arched at the crown and crowded on her brow. Mor observed the youthful fullness of her face, pouting with concentration – and as he watched her he reflected to himself how rarely it was now that he met a woman.

'How wonderfully children observe!' said Miss Carter in an excited tone. 'Look at this scene – it's so dramatic. A grown-up artist would not dare to be so dramatic. Indeed he could hardly do it without being sentimental.'

Mor looked at the picture. It represented a young girl stepping on to a train, while a young man offered her a rose with a gesture of despair. Before Mor could think of a comment, Miss Carter had moved on to another picture, and another, making enthusiastic exclamations. At the end of the row lay a pile of white paper and some poster paint ready mixed. When she reached the last picture Miss Carter twirled on her heel, seized one of the brushes, and drew in paint an almost perfect circle on one of the sheets. She did this so quickly that Mor had to laugh.

'You know the story about Giotto,' she said, 'that when some grand people came to commission a picture, and wanted a specimen of his work, he just drew a perfect circle for them with his brush? He got the job. That impressed me somehow as a child. I used to practise it, as if it were a guarantee of success.'

'Is it hard?' said Mor.

'Try,' said Miss Carter, handing him the brush, still full of paint.

Mor balanced the unfamiliar object in his hand, and drew a very shaky oval shape upon the paper. 'Hopeless!' he said, laughing. The two figures intersected. 'I think we ought to go,' said Mor. He had promised to deliver Miss Carter back for a late tea at Brayling's Close, and he began suddenly to be uneasy about the time.

'Oh dear,' said Miss Carter. 'Now I don't want to go. The smell of paint makes me feel quite strange.' She began to wander between the rows of stools and easels, sniffing the air and spreading out her arms. 'Where does that lead to?' she asked, pointing to a wooden ladder which led upward to a trapdoor in the ceiling of the studio.

'This is an old barn, you know,' said Mor. 'That leads to the loft. It's quite well lighted. The near part of it is a pottery room, and the far part has been made into a sort of flat for Mr Bledyard.'

'He lives up there?' said Miss Carter.

'Yes,' said Mor.

'I want to see!' she said, and before Mor could stop her she was running up the ladder and pushing at the trap-door.

'Wait a moment!' cried Mor, and began to climb after her. The trap-door yielded and he saw the canvas shoes flapping to reveal the soles of her feet as she pulled herself up into the loft above him. When he reached the top Miss Carter was running about between the potter's wheels which stood at intervals about the floor. Mor was reminded of the scene in the rose garden. He began to feel nervous.

'I think we'd better go,' he said. 'Mr Bledyard might come back and find us here.'

'I should like to see his room,' said Miss Carter. 'Is it in here?' She went to the far end of the loft and opened a door. Mor followed her.

The big space, stretching the width of the loft, with the roof sloping on both sides, and well lit by skylights, was Bledyard's bed-sitting-room. His kitchen and bathroom were in an out-house below, which was reached by a wooden stair. Mor, who had only once before beheld this room, looked at it with a little awe. It was extremely bare and colourless. The floor was scrubbed and the walls whitewashed. No picture, no coloured object adorned it. The furniture was of pale wood, and even the bed had a white cover.

Miss Carter stared about her. 'No colours,' she murmured. 'Interesting.'

'Well, now you've seen it, let's go down,' said Mor.

'I must just try the bed,' said Miss Carter, 'to see how hard it is!' She skipped across to Bledyard's bed and subsided on to it, reclining there with her head propped on her arm and her black trousered legs outstretched on the counterpane. In the chaste scene she looked as dusky as a chimney-sweeper's boy. She peered up at Mor.

Mor was irritated and slightly shocked. He checked a comment, and deliberately withdrew his attention from her as from a child that shows off. It was not clear to him just how spontaneous these antics were. He went back to the trap-door,

47

meaning to descend again into the studio, but as he looked down through the square hole into the well-lighted room below, he saw with a slight thrill of alarm that the studio door was opening. The foreshortened figure of Bledyard, his chin sunk upon his breast as usual, appeared slowly round the door. He seemed to be alone. He began to poke around, looking for something. As he was so intent upon his search, and as his lank and longish hair fell well forward on either side of his cheeks like blinkers, it was unlikely that his gaze should be attracted to the trap-door. He continued to potter. Mor watched him, feeling the curious guilt which attaches to seeing someone unseen from above: and the moment somehow passed at which he could call out to him in a natural way. He hesitated, trying to think of something to say to Bledyard which would at the same time warn Miss Carter to rise from her ridiculous pose and set the bed to rights. However, before he could speak, Bledyard had turned about and left the studio, and his footsteps were to be heard pounding across the cobbles and into the wood.

'What is it?' asked Miss Carter. She was still stretched out on the bed, watching Mor intently through the bedroom door.

He came back and stood over her. He did not want to raise his voice. 'Bledyard!' he said. 'But he's gone now.'

Miss Carter sprang up and began to smooth down the counterpane. She was extremely flurried and apologetic. 'Oh dear,' she said. 'He didn't see us, did he? I *am* so sorry.'

Mor told her it didn't matter, and then led her away quickly down the back stairs. He felt annoyance with himself for not having spoken at once to Bledyard and with the girl for the thoroughly silly way in which their afternoon had ended. Here, it seemed, was another foolish small secret between them. Mor disapproved of secrets.

# CHAPTER FOUR

Nan never managed to look like anything in her outdoor clothes. She could look handsome and well got-up at an evening party – but her coats and hats never looked quite right. Mor could see her now, as he gazed over the heads of his audience, sitting near the back with a slightly superior smile on her face. She wore a rather characterless felt hat, and although it was a warm evening, a coat with fur on the collar.

Mor was giving his WEA class. The evening was nearly over. He often wondered why Nan insisted on coming and what she made of those performances. She was not on easy terms with Tim Burke, who always acted as chairman and entertained them afterwards, and Mor could hardly believe that she came to hear him talk. In any case, she never referred later to anything that he had said. If she ever asked a question, it was a simple and sometimes a stupid one. Mor felt that she did it merely for appearances, and wished that she wouldn't.

Donald Mor was also present, not sitting with his mother, but in a seat at the side near the front, leaning his back against the wall, one long leg crossed over the other. He had a special dispensation from St Bride's to attend these sessions. Marsington was three stops along the railway, and just inside the London area, but a fast train would bring the boy back to school well before midnight. Why Don came was no mystery to Mor. He came for the sake of Tim Burke, whom he adored, and from whom he scarcely took his eyes throughout the evening. Mor doubted whether Donald listened to a single word that was said.

Mor was answering a question. 'Freedom,' he said, 'is not exactly what I would call a virtue. Freedom might be called a benefit or a sort of grace – though of course to seek it or to gain it might be a proof of merit.'

The questioner, a successful middle-aged greengrocer, who was one of the props of the local Labour Party, was hanging grimly on to the back of the chair in front of him, whose occupant was leaning nervously forward. The greengrocer who had made the remark that surely freedom was the chief virtue, and wasn't it thinking so that differentiated us from the Middle Ages? stared intently at Mor as if drinking in his words. Mor thought, he is not really listening, he does not want to hear what I say, he knows what he thinks and is not going to reorganize his views. The words I am uttering are not the words for him.

He felt again that sad guilty feeling which he had whenever he caught himself going through the motions of being a teacher without really caring to make his pupils understand. How well he knew that many teachers, including some who got high reputations by doing so, contented themselves with putting up a show, often a brilliant one, in front of those who were to be instructed – and of this performance both sides might be the dupes. Whereas the real teacher cares only for one thing, that the matter should be understood; and into that process he vanishes. Mor hated it when he caught himself trying to be clever. Sometimes the temptation was strong. An adult education class will often contain persons who have come merely to parade a certain viewpoint, and with no intention of learning anything. In response to this provocation it was tempting to produce merely a counter-attraction, a show, designed to impress rather than to make anything clear. But to make anything clear *here*, Mor felt with a sudden despair – how could it be done? With this feeling he irreverently remembered Tim Burke's moving proposition, and felt a sudden shame at this evening's efforts.

'I'm sorry, Mr Staveley,' said Mor, 'I've said nothing to the purpose. Let me try again. You say surely freedom is a virtue – and I hesitate to accept this phrase. Let me explain why. To begin with, as I was saying in my talk this evening, freedom needs to be defined. If by freedom we mean absence of external restraint, then we may call a man lucky for being free – but why should we call him good? If, on the other hand, by freedom we mean self-discipline, which dominates selfish desires, then indeed we may call a free man virtuous. But, as we know, this more refined conception of freedom can also play a dangerous role in politics. It may be used to justify the tyranny of people who think themselves to be the enlightened ones. Whereas the notion of freedom which I'm sure Mr Staveley has in mind, the freedom which inspired the great Liberal leaders of the last century, is political freedom, the absence of tyranny. This is the condition of virtue, and to strive for it is a virtue. But it is not itself a virtue. To call mere absence of restraint or mere kicking over the traces and flouting of conventions a virtue is to be simply romantic.'

'Well, what's wrong with being romantic?' said Mr Staveley obstinately. 'Let's have "romantic" defined, since you're so keen on definitions.'

'Surely, isn't love the chief virtue?' said a lady sitting near the front, and turning round to look at Mr Staveley. 'Or does Mr Staveley think that the New Testament is out of date?'

I've failed again, thought Mor, with the feeling of one who has brought the horse round the field a second time only for it to shy once more at the jump. He felt very tired and the words did not come easily. But he was prepared to go on trying.

'Let's leave "romantic",' he said, 'and stick to one thing at a time. Let me start again—'

'I'm afraid,' said Tim Burke, 'that it is time to bring this stimulating session to a close.'

Confound him, thought Mor. He's ending early because he wants to talk to me about that other matter. Mor sat down. He felt defeated. He could see Mr Staveley shaking his head and saying something in an undertone to his neighbour.

Tim Burke stood up and leaned confidentially forward across the table in the manner of one pretending to be a public speaker. Mor knew his timidity on these occasions.

'I am sorry, friends,' said Tim Burke, 'to terminate this most educational argument so abruptly, but time, as they say, waits for no man. And Mr Mor will, I am sure, not be offended if I say that we shall all appreciate a short spell in the adjacent hostelry during which his words of wisdom may be digested together with a pint of mild and bitter.' The termination of the meeting well before closing time was one of the few matters on which the Marsington WEA was in complete agreement.

'And with this,' said Tim Burke, swinging back upon his heels, 'we terminate yet another series of profitable talks from Mr Mor; talks, I may safely say, from which we have all profited one and all, and which will stimulate us, I have no doubt, to private studies and reflections in the months that lie ahead, before our class reassembles here in the autumn. And by which time, if I may be so indiscreet, we all have hopes that Mr

Mor will have been persuaded to fill another and a more exalted post for which the people of Marsington think him to be most eminently fitted. On which delicate topic I say no more – and close proceedings with a request that you express your grateful thanks to Mr Mor in the customary manner.'

Loud and enthusiastic clapping followed, together with cries of 'Hear, hear!' Damn! thought Mor. He could see Nan clapping daintily, her eyes cast down. Mor disliked Tim Burke's public eloquence in any case, and his *persona* of a student of politics in particular. When he encountered Tim in the context of the WEA he was made aware of him as an awkward half-educated man, ill at ease and anxious to impress. Mor was fond of Tim, there were even things about Tim which he wished to admire, and he was hurt for him by these appearances. He preferred to see his friend relaxed in a pub, or business-like in a committee, or best of all talkative and serene in the dark encrusted interior of the jeweller's shop. But it was a sad paradox of their relationship that Tim was continually trying to please Mor by a parade of his scanty learning. To instruct him was difficult; to have checked him would have been unthinkable. So Mor continued to be irritated. He had not, however, expected this evening's indiscretion. Just when Nan needed to be handled especially carefully, Tim had elected to put his foot in it. Now she'll think I've arranged everything with Tim behind her back, thought Mor.

The meeting was breaking up. Mor rose to his feet and stretched. He felt only tired now, his eagerness dissipated. He hoped that he would be spared a private interview with Mr Staveley, and moved nearer to Tim Burke for protection. Tim was gathering up the papers with which he felt it part of his duty as chairman to strew the table. Tim was an old friend of the Mor family. They had met through Labour Party activities, when Mor had been teaching in a school on the south side of London, and Mor and Nan had to some extent taken Tim, who was a bachelor, under their wing. They saw less of him now than formerly, but Mor still counted Tim as one of his best friends. He was a trifle older than Mor, a lean pale man with a pock-marked face and large white hands and rather thin pale hair of which it was hard to say whether it was yellow or grey. He was distinguished chiefly by his eyes, of a flecked and streaky blue, and by his voice. Tim Burke had left Ireland when he was a

52

child, but there was no mistaking his nationality, although long residence in London and the frequenting of cinemas had introduced a Cockney intonation into his brogue and a number of Americanisms among the flowery locutions of his Dublin speech. He was an accomplished goldsmith and could have been richer if he had wished.

'Take it easy, chief, we'll get you out of this if it's the last thing we do!' said Tim, casting a wary eye at Mr Staveley, who was standing by himself in brooding meditation.

The meetings took place in the Parish Hall, an exceptionally featureless building whose bright unshaded electric lights had just been turned on. The evening was still blue and bright outside and through it a large part of the audience were already making their way towards the Dog and Duck. The rest stood about on the bare boards, between trestle tables and tubular chairs, talking or listening or casting uneasy glances towards the speaker, wondering if they dared to ask him a question and whether they could make their question sound intelligent. Nan was pulling her gloves on in a very slow way which Mor knew she adopted when she wished to detach herself in a superior manner from the surrounding scene. Mor had hoped that Nan might make some friends at this class, and had originally imagined that perhaps this was why she came. But Nan had steadfastly refused to get to know anyone or to pay any attention at all to her fellow-students. If Mor ever referred to a member of the class she would be unable, or profess to be unable, to remember who it was. She behaved as one surrounded by her inferiors.

Nan came slowly down the room. Donald had already come forward and was holding on to the table while Tim Burke gathered up his things. At such moments Donald seemed to attach himself directly to Tim as if invisible threads joined their bodies. In passing between them, as he moved now past Tim in the direction of the door, Mor felt a shock. He stopped close to his son, but he knew that it was Tim only that Donald was aware of, Tim's gesture and Tim's voice for which he was waiting. Don's admiration for his friend was another thing which irritated Mor. It was so totally non-rational. He could not conceive why it should exist at all.

It was customary after these meetings for Tim to carry off the Mor family and take them down the road to his shop, where he would offer them refreshment until it was time to take the train. Tim held, and Mor agreed, that it was not necessary for Mor to run the gauntlet in the Dog and Duck. Tim now took a quick look at the scene. Mr Staveley was lifting his head. A look of renewed determination was on his face.

'Out the back!' said Tim, and in a moment he had shepherded them out through a kitchen and an alleyway and round into the road. Marsington was an old village with a fine broad main street with grassy cobbled edges. The fields about it had long ago been covered with the red-roofed houses between which the green Southern Region trains sped at frequent intervals bringing the inhabitants of Marsington and its neighbouring boroughs to and from their daily work in central London. The main street now carried one of the most important routes to the metropolis, and its most conspicuous features were the rival garages whose brightly lit petrol pumps, glowing upon ancient brick and stone, attracted the passing motorist. The traffic was incessant. For all that, in the warm twilight it had a remote and peaceful air, the long broad façades of its inns and spacious houses withdrawn and reassuring.

Tim Burke's shop was a little farther down, in the middle of a row of old shops, dark below and white above. A black sign swung above the door. *T. Burke. Jeweller and Goldsmith.* Tim stood fumbling for his keys. Mor leaned against the wall. He felt relief at having escaped, mingled with uneasiness at the presence close beside him of Nan, who was probably angry and preparing for a sulk. He cast a quick glance sideways at her. Her lips were pursed. A bad sign. The door gave way and they all stepped into the shop, and stood still while Tim turned on a lamp in the far corner.

Mor loved Tim's shop. The wooden shutters which covered the shop windows at night made it quite dark now within and in the dim light of the lamp it looked like some treasure cave or alchemist's den. Near the front there was a certain amount of order. Two large counters, each in the form of a glass-topped cabinet, faced each other near to the street door. But beyond these the long shop became gradually chaotic. Loaded and untidy shelves, from floor to ceiling, ran round the three walls, well barricaded by wooden display cases of various types which stood, often two or three deep, in front of them. Between these, and in the rest of the available space, there were small tables, some of them also topped with glass and designed for display purposes. The more precious jewellery, such of it as was not behind the bars of the shop window, or hidden in safes in the back room, was laid out in the glass-topped cabinets, and ranged in fair order. Tim, when he tried, knew how to display his wares. He loved the stones, and treasured and displayed them according to his own system of valuation, which did not always accord with their market prices. This week, Mor noticed, one of the cabinets was given over to a display of opals. Set in necklaces, ear-rings and brooches they lay, black ones and white ones, dusky ones flecked with blue or grey patches, and glowing water opals like drops of water frozen thick with colour. The other cabinet was full of pearls, the real ones above, the cultured ones below, and worked golden objects, seals, rings and watches. Mor had learnt a certain amount about stones during his long friendship with Tim. This had been somewhat against his will, since for reasons which were never very clear to him, he rather disapproved of his friend's profession.

The front of the shop was orderly. But the cheaper jewellery, which lay behind, seemed to have got itself into an almost inextricable mess. Within the squat glass-topped tables especially, ropes of beads were tangled together into a solid mass of multicoloured stuff, and bold was the customer who, pointing to some identifiable patch of colour, said 'I'll have *that* one.' Heaped together with these were clips and ear-rings, their fellows often irrevocably missing, brooches, bracelets, buckles and a miscellany of other small adornments. Tim Burke was not interested in the cheap stuff. He seemed to acquire his stock more or less by accident in the course of his trade and dispose of it without thought or effort to such determined individuals as were prepared to struggle for what they wanted, often searching the shop from end to end to find the second ear-ring or the other half of the buckle. The remoter parts of the shop were also found to contain other objects, varying in value, such as snuff boxes, pieces of embroidery, foreign coins, pewter mugs, fans, paper-weights and silver-hilted daggers – concerning all of which Tim Burke would declare that really he had no idea how the creatures got there for he couldn't for the life of him remember buying them.

Tim Burke brought chairs and his guests sat down in the

main part of the shop between the counters, while he disappeared into the back regions to fetch glasses and biscuits and the milk which he would offer to Nan and Donald and the whisky which he would offer to Mor and himself. Behind the shop was Tim's workshop and his kitchen, and a whitewashed yard with a single sycamore tree in it. Above was the small cottage bedroom with its tiny windows looking on to the street. Mor spread his legs. He was always a bit excited at finding himself inside a closed-up shop. There was something privileged and unnatural about it. On these occasions he noticed a similar excitement in his wife and son. In Tim Burke's shop they were always agitated and restless. They would not sit down for long, but soon would be roaming about, opening cases and fingering objects. This behaviour made Mor uneasy. It was as if he were watching his family stealing. It never failed, however, to delight Tim Burke, who urged them on.

Tim returned with a large tray, which he set on the counter. He stirred some Ovaltine into a cup of cold milk for Nan, and set the biscuits at her elbow. He said to Mor, 'What about giving the boy a shot of whisky this week?' Tim always said this.

Mor replied, as he always did, 'Well, not yet I think. What do you say, Don?'

'I don't want any,' said Donald crossly. Tim passed him the milk.

Mor sat swishing his whisky round thoughtfully inside a cut-glass tumbler. He had decided to outstay his family and return on the midnight train. He wanted badly to talk with Tim alone. He settled down to wait with impatience.

Nan had got up, and holding her mug of Ovaltine in one hand, began to wander about in the back of the shop, picking up objects here and there. Mor watched her uneasily, Tim Burke with a curious half-concealed satisfaction. The single lamp in the corner cast a golden glow upon the worm-eaten oak shelves, and Nan's face was bright and dark by turns as she roamed to and fro. Tim Burke, his head turned back, and the darkened side of his face towards Mor, was marked by a golden line down his brow and nose. Donald turned his face into the light, wistful and restless. He rose too and began to walk about, crossing the path of his mother. The whisky bottle gleamed upon the tray and the glasses flashed intermittently in the hands of the two men – while here and there in the shop the glow of the lamp had found the surface of a precious stone which transformed it and tossed it back as a glittering splinter of light.

Nan had opened one of the cabinets and was picking over a heap of necklaces. She seemed unusually gay and animated. Donald was now at the very back of the shop and had mounted on a chair to examine some shelves. Mor wished that they would stop. He looked at his watch. It was still early.

Donald had found something. He got down and came rather shyly towards Tim Burke with an object in his hand. It was a small ivory box. 'You still haven't sold this box, Tim,' said Donald.

Really! thought Mor, doesn't Don know how Tim always responds to any remark of this sort – and if he does know, why does he make it?

'What, that old thing still there?' cried Tim. 'You have it, my boy, it's no use to me. No, of course you can't pay for it, the tuppenny ha'penny thing it is, I got it in a job lot, I daresay, and it cost me nothing. You'll please me by keeping it.'

'What do you want that box for?' said Mor sharply. 'Whatever will you use it for?' He immediately regretted these words. Nan turned quickly towards him, Tim Burke averted his face, and Don blushed scarlet.

'It's a nice box,' Don said, 'I shall keep things in it.' He sounded childish in his reply.

Mor wished he could blot out his words. Donald suddenly looked to him extremely young and touching. If he had been a small child Mor might have taken him in his arms to erase the words. As it was, there was nothing to be done, and the words had to stay, wounding both of them. Mor was silent.

Tim, wanting to smooth things over, got up and took his keys and began to open the drawers at the back of the counter. Tim loved showing things. Usually he had his waistcoat pockets full of little knick-knacks, rings, cigarette lighters, watches and such, which he would produce and place suddenly in the hand of his interlocutor. Mor had often seen him do this in a pub. Now Tim began to rifle the drawers and show-cases, keeping up a continuous patter as he did so. 'See these pearls, the rosy sheen is best, from the Gulf they came, the Persian Gulf – and see how different they look from the cultured ones, your cultured pearl won't last so well anyhow, though these are good ones indeed – and here, how are these things for colour, a pair of sapphires as blue as a cornflower, and if it's green you want, a fine emerald – a fine emerald is the king of gems, an emerald does your eye good, they say, and it will blind a snake. There are no snakes on the Emerald Isle, just paradise without a serpent – and now will you just cast a look at these rocks, how's that for rocks?'

Tim lifted up a diamond necklace and swung it gently to and fro, holding it by one end. With a rippling movement the stones flashed. 'Look at the light of it!' he said. 'It needs a fine woman's neck to show it off. Let me put it on your wife.'

Mor disliked this. It was something Tim often did, and Nan never protested. She came forward now with docility and took off her coat. She was wearing a round-necked summer dress. Tim fixed the diamonds round her neck and stood back to look. The necklace was impressive, but Mor thought it looked out of place. Nan hurried forward to look at herself in the mirror which was fixed behind one of the counters.

'Diamonds have no mercy,' said Tim, 'they will show up the wearer if they can. But you have nothing to fear from them. A queen is the one who can wear them, and a queen you are.' He was looking over her shoulder into the mirror. He often talked in this flowery strain to Nan, but Mor suspected that he was more aware of the jewels than the woman.

'They are dazzling!' said Nan. She took the necklace off and held it in her hand. Then that excitement began to take hold of her which Mor had seen come upon her in the past in Tim Burke's shop. An animation which he himself could never seem to inspire glowed in her whole person. She wound the diamonds loosely round her wrist like a bracelet, and began to skip about the shop, picking up tiny things, trying on an earring and running to see how it looked, disentangling a string of beads, spreading a fan and fanning herself ostentatiously. Donald had resumed his prowling in the back regions. Tim Burke was still rifling the forward cases, drawing Nan's attention to rings and brooches. The pinpoint fire of jewels lit up here and there throughout the shop, like stars that appear and disappear upon a cloudy night.

'It's time you two went,' said Mor.

'Ah, it's early yet,' said Tim.

'If you don't want to rush, you should leave now,' said Mor. 'I want to stay and talk shop with Tim.' It irritated him to see Nan so gay, and he was aggrieved that he had offended Don and no way had been allowed him to repair his fault.

'Don't bother to see us to the station,' said Nan. 'Donald will protect me. Don't let Bill miss his train.' Serenely she passed into the street. Donald followed, still clutching his box. Mor contrived to touch his shoulder as he went by, but got no answering look. The door closed behind them.

'Have some more drink, then,' said Tim Burke.

Mor handed over his glass. The diamond necklace was lying in a heap on one of the tables. Mor picked it up and put it back into the drawer. 'You're very casual with these valuable things, Tim,' he said. 'How much is that worth?'

'Oh, I don't know,' said Tim carelessly. 'These values are so artificial. Maybe five hundred guineas.'

The thought of Miss Carter flashed immediately into Mor's mind. He had not thought of her all the evening. With extreme vividness there was present to him again the absurd scene of the previous day in Bledyard's bedroom. The memory was disturbing. He wondered if he would tell Tim Burke about it, and decided not to. He also remembered that it was tomorrow that he was to have lunch with Mr Everard, in the company of Miss Carter and Bledyard. Mor felt interest at the thought of this meal, which was bound to offer some curious features. The mood of gloom and emptiness which had possessed him earlier in the evening seemed to be lifting. Once more he felt a sense of purpose and direction, a sense of the future.

He was about to speak to Tim Burke about the matter which was to be settled between them when Tim said, 'I wish you'd take something for the wife. No, don't take on, I'll not offer you the diamonds! What about these ear-rings? She cared for them, I could see. She put them on herself this time, and last time too. And they become her. Why not take them? They're but cheap things that I'll never sell. I'll wrap them up for you now.'

The ear-rings were blue, as far as Mor could see of lapis lazuli, and did not seem to him to be especially cheap. He checked Tim, who was producing tissue paper and a little box.

'You're too good to me. No,' said Mor.

'It's your wife I want to be good to!' said Tim.

'Well, no, you mustn't really,' said Mor. 'We've already taken one thing off you this evening. Another time, Tim. Now, listen, we must talk business.'

'All right,' said Tim, reluctantly replacing the ear-rings. 'Is it yes or no?'

Mor sat forward stiffly in his chair. In the face of this rather fierce question he suddenly realized that he was, that he had been perhaps for some time, in the position of the coy maiden who has made up her mind but who puts up a show of resistance merely in order to be persuaded. Mor hated vain shows. He felt that his wishes had crystallized. He felt it with a certain surprise and with an intimation of joy. He said, 'The answer is yes, of course. But there are a number of difficulties.'

Tim turned on him. 'Yes, is it?' he cried. 'Holding out on us, were you? And I thought you would surely say no, and no again for the next months!'

'You seem disappointed!' said Mor, smiling faintly.

'Disappointed!' cried Tim. 'I could embrace you! Here, have some more whisky, and if I could dissolve a pearl in it I would!'

'Not so fast,' said Mor. 'I want to carry out this plan, and I have now, I must say, absolutely no doubt but that I will carry it out. All the same, to throw up my job and be a parliamentary candidate at my time of life – it's not all that simple. I suppose there's no doubt I'd get in?'

'None, me boy,' said Tim Burke. 'Ten thousand majority last time. Saint Francis wasn't a surer candidate for heaven than you for Westminster.'

'Well, then,' said Mor, 'there are a lot of financial considerations. I won't bother you with these just now. And St Bride's must be squared. I'm not giving them much notice. But that leaves the gravest thing of all, and that's my wife. You know that Nan is very much opposed to the idea, she won't even hear it spoken of.'

Tim looked grave. 'I'd gathered,' he said, 'that she's against it. But she'll come round surely.'

'I suppose she will,' said Mor. 'She'll have to. But it won't be easy. Why did you mention it tonight, by the way, you fathead? Nothing annoys Nan as much as the notion that people are making plans without consulting her. I'd hoped you might have some influence on her – only now she'll think we've been plotting this for months. Do you think it would be any use if you talked to her alone?'

Tim looked down. 'No,' he said, 'it would be no use. You must handle it. But, as you say, she will agree because she must. I'm glad to hear at last that courage in you. If you really will a thing, Mor, that thing will be. We shall all support you in every way possible. But this thing you must do for yourself alone.'

'Well, it will be done,' said Mor. He felt deeply encouraged by Tim Burke. 'Only not a word about this to anyone for the moment. I shall have to discuss my resignation with Mr Everard. And I shall have to persuade Nan. When that's done I'll let you know and then you can tell the Party and the Press.'

'Splendid!' cried Tim Burke, his eyes shining, his glass held aloft. 'When shall I see you?'

'We'll talk of it again,' said Mor, 'when, now? What about the day of the House Match – you're coming over then, aren't you? It's my house against Prewett's this time.' Invited originally by Donald, Tim Burke usually came over to St Bride's for the final summer House Match, which was also something of a social occasion. 'I hope I'll be able to give you the all clear,' said Mor, 'and we can go ahead. But till then, not a word!'

'You must go for your train,' said Tim Burke. 'I'll see you down the road.'

'You know,' said Mor, 'perhaps after all I'll take those ear-rings for Nan. Only you must let me pay something for them.'

'I'll not hear of it!' said Tim. 'You oblige me by taking them. Here, I'll pack them up nicely, handy to give. Now please me, Mor, in this way too.'

Mor protested, smiled, and finally put the ear-rings in his pocket. They left the shop together.

# CHAPTER FIVE

When Mor awoke next morning he found, with his first consciousness, that he felt extremely light-hearted. It was as if a good angel had passed in the night. For a while he lay marvelling vaguely at his condition. Then it came back to him that of course he had now at last *decided*. In the light of the actual decision the moves necessary to carry it out seemed very much easier. What was necessary was possible. Recalling the previous evening, and asking himself what exactly had happened, it seemed to Mor that Tim Burke had suddenly been able to communicate to him a new sort of confidence. He wondered why. His thoughts switched to Miss Carter, whom he would be seeing at lunch-time today; and then it seemed to him that in some strange way it was Miss Carter who had been responsible for his ability to decide, having given him, by her mere existence, a fresh sense of power and possibility. Mor mused for a while upon this mystery. Eccentric people, he concluded, were good for conventional people, simply because they made them able to conceive of everything being quite different. This gave them a sense of freedom. Nothing is more educational, in the end, than the mode of being of other people.

The morning passed quickly, and a little before one o'clock Mor set out on his bicycle for Mr Everard's luncheon party. In the bicycle basket he had placed a small packet which contained the complete works of Demoyte and which in accordance with his promise he was taking to Miss Carter. A cycle track, for the use of masters only, led down the hill through the wood towards the neglected garden of the Headmaster's house. As Mor free-wheeled through the trees, his bicycle bumping about agreeably on the undulating track, he experienced a profound sense of well-being and general benevolence. The weather was still extremely sunny, but today there was a soft breeze which seemed to bring, from not so very far away in the south, the freshness of the sea.

Benevolently Mor thought about Mr Everard. There came back to him the remark which Miss Carter had made about his having no malice in him. It was true. Evvy had no malice. In some sense of the word Evvy was undoubtedly a good man. He was well-intentioned and unselfish; indeed he seemed utterly to lack the conception of getting anything for himself. Evvy's life was not constructed, it seemed to Mor, in such a way as to leave any place in it where he could store things for himself. Most people's lives had a sort of bulge or recess in which they piled up their selfish acquisitions, their goods, their fame, their power. Evvy had no such private place. He lived in the open, with simplicity, seeming to lack altogether the concepts of vanity or ambition, weaknesses which he was equally incapable of harbouring within himself or of recognizing in others. If he hurt people, it was through indecision or sheer obtuseness and not through any preference for having things his own way, since his own way was something which had never really developed.

Doubtless such a character ought not to be in a position of power. All the same, it occurred to Mor more forcibly than ever before, there was something impressive about Mr Everard. And he wondered, too, how it was that while Mr Everard was so gentle and unselfish, and Mr Demoyte so much the reverse, he felt deep love and tenderness for Demoyte and could hardly summon up any affection at all for poor Evvy. Mor wondered whether this reflected badly on his own character. Here was another mystery. He seemed to be surrounded by them. As Mor thought this, he found that it was rather a pleasant thought; and as he sailed on down the hill the soothing sense of mystery became transformed into the more precisely pleasurable anticipation of meeting Miss Carter again.

The approach to Mr Everard's house was by a gravel drive, which connected with the main road, and on to which the cycle track eventually emerged at right angles. Mor dismounted at the drive, as the coarse gravel was not pleasant for cycling on, and pushed his bicycle up towards the white house. The yellow gravel expanse in front of the house was dotted with concrete tubs which contained geraniums and between which visiting cars had to pick their way. Mor saw that a car was standing at the door. He saw as he drew closer that it was a long dark green Riley. He looked at it with desultory admiration. Mor had never been able to dream of affording a car. He took his bicycle round to the side of the house, and then came back into the entrance hall. He hung his coat up on a peg and mounted the stairs to the big room which served Mr Everard as both drawing-room and dining-room.

As he entered, Mor saw that Bledyard and Miss Carter had both arrived. He was sorry at this, as he would have liked to have witnessed the encounter. They were both standing about in silence, Miss Carter leaning against the mantelpiece and Bledyard looking out of the window. Mr Everard was not famous for putting his guests at their ease.

He came forward now to welcome Mor. 'Bill, I'm so glad you've come. Now we can have some lunch. I believe you know Miss Carter, and here is Mr Bledyard. You left your coat downstairs? Good, good.'

Mr Everard had a plump healthy face of the kind which passes imperceptibly from boyhood into middle age without any observable intermediate phase. He always wore a tweed suit and a dog collar. His expression was habitually gentle, his eyes doe-like. His hair was light brown and rather fluffy and unruly. As a boy he must have been pretty; as a middle-aged man he appeared candid and disarming to those who did not see him as looking stupid.

'Hello, sir,' said Mor. 'Sorry I'm a bit late.' Evvy had once tried to persuade Mor to call him by his Christian name, but Mor could not bring himself to do so.

Mor cast a quick glance at Miss Carter, and she nodded to him. She was wearing a close-fitting blue silk dress which made her look smarter and more feminine than Mor had yet seen her look. She seemed very preoccupied. Clearly what preoccupied her was the presence of Bledyard. Mor observed this with an unpleasant pang which he was surprised to identify as a sort of jealousy. He would have liked Miss Carter to have shown more interest in his own arrival. His mind reverted again to the odd scene in Bledyard's room. He felt uneasy, and turned towards Bledyard, who still presented his back to the company.

'Come along now, lunch-time!' said Evvy. He had a rich deep public school voice which could make any statement seem portentous. He began to usher his guests down the room towards the dining-table, which was laid at the other end. In Demoyte's day things had been far otherwise; but now the furry den-like interior had gone, and the room seemed longer and lighter, and prints of the French Impressionists hung upon the walls from which Demoyte's rugs had been stripped.

'Mr Bledyard, you sit here,' said Evvy. 'Oh, Miss Carter, please you here, and Bill by the sideboard. You can help me with the plates, Bill.'

Mr Everard believed keenly that the servants should be spared. He had introduced the policy as far as he could in the face of protesting parents into the school régime: caféteria lunches, and the boys to make their beds, clean their shoes, and wash up twice a week. In his own household Evvy was able to proceed unchecked, especially as he had refused to draw the considerable entertainment allowance which Demoyte had established as part of the Headmaster's emoluments. Except for extremely ceremonial occasions, there was no waiting at Mr Everard's table. His daily help, who disappeared shortly before one, left behind such hot or cold offerings as she thought fit for his guests to consume, and Evvy presented these as best he could. The offering today, Mor saw with some relief, was cold. One blessing was that meals with Evvy were at least brief; no dawdling with sherry beforehand, or lingering over wine or liqueurs, prolonged the episode which proceeded usually with a consoling briskness.

Evvy handed the plates of cold meat and salad from the sideboard, and Mor distributed them, and then poured out water for the guests. Miss Carter seemed a little paralysed. Bledyard sat as usual quite at his ease in saying nothing, moving his large head gently to and fro, as if he had just had it fixed on and was trying to see if it was firm. Bledyard's age was hard to determine. Mor suspected him of being quite young, that is in his thirties. If he had not looked quite so odd he might have been handsome. He had a great head of dark hair which was perfectly straight and worn a little long. It soughed to and fro as he moved or talked. He had a large moon-like face and a bull neck, big luminous eyes like a night creature, and a coarse nose. His mouth was formless and sometimes hung open. His teeth were good, but were usually concealed behind the massy flesh of his lips. He rarely smiled. His hands were big too, and moved about in slow gestures. Bledyard had an impediment in his speech which he had partly overcome by the expedient of repeating some words twice as he talked. This he did with a sort of slow deliberation which made his utterance ludicrous. It had long ago been discovered that a lecture from Bledyard reduced the whole school to hysterical laughter within a few minutes – and, rather it seemed to Bledyard's chagrin, he had been rationed to one art lecture a year, which he gave annually late in the summer term.

Evvy, whose ability to think of only one thing at a time made him far from ideal as a Headmaster, having satisfied himself that each of his guests had a plate of food and a glass of water, addressed himself to conversation. 'Well, Miss Carter,' he said, 'and how are we getting on with the picture? Soon be done, will it?'

Miss Carter looked very shocked. 'Heavens,' she said, 'I haven't started yet. I've made some pencil sketches of Mr Demoyte, but I haven't yet decided what position to paint him in, or what clothes or expression to give him. Indeed, I am still quite at a loss.' Her shyness made her seem foreign.

'What would you say, sir,' said Mor wickedly, 'was Mr Demoyte's most typical expression?' He wanted to incite Evvy to be malicious for once.

Mr Everard considered this, and then said, 'I would say a sort of rather suspicious pondering.'

This was not bad, thought Mor. Accurate and not uncharitable. His opinion of Evvy went up a point. He glanced at Bledyard. Bledyard was sitting abstracted from the scene, as if he were a diner at a restaurant who had by accident to share a table with three complete strangers. He got on with his meal. Mor envied Bledyard's total disregard of convention. He agreed with Demoyte that Bledyard was undoubtedly a man. There was something exceedingly real about him. He made Evvy seem flimsy by comparison, a sort of fiction. Miss Carter was very real too. Am I real? Mor wondered with a strange pang.

Mr Everard was now touchingly anxious to make conversation. His forehead wrinkled with the effort, and he turned a worried face towards Miss Carter between every mouthful. 'I believe you have lived abroad a great deal,' he said, 'and that you are quite a stranger to this island, Miss Carter?'

'Yes, I have lived mostly in France,' said Miss Carter. 'I was brought up in the South of France.'

'Ah, the shores of the Mediterranean!' said Evvy, 'that "grand object of travel", as Dr Johnson said. You were fortunate, Miss Carter.'

'I don't know,' said Miss Carter, turning seriously towards him. 'I am not sure that the South of France is a good place for a child. It is so hot and dry. I remember my childhood as a time of terrible dryness, as if it were a long period of drought.'

'Ah, but you were by the sea, were you not?' said Evvy.

'Yes,' said Miss Carter, 'but a melancholy sea as I remember it. A tideless sea. I can recall, as a child, seeing pictures in English children's books of boys and girls playing on the sand and making sandcastles – and I tried to play on my sand. But a Mediterranean beach is not a place for playing on. It is dirty and very dry. The tides never wash the sand or make it firm. When I tried to make a sandcastle, the sand would just run away between my fingers. It was too dry to hold together. And even if I poured sea water over it, the sun would dry it up at once.'

This speech caught Bledyard's attention. He stopped eating and looked at Miss Carter. For a moment he looked as if he might speak. Then he decided not to, and went on eating. Mor looked at Miss Carter too. She seemed to be overcome with confusion, either at the length of her speech or at Bledyard's attention. Mor was both touched and irritated.

Mr Everard pursued his conversational way relentlessly. 'You are an only child, I believe, Miss Carter?'

'Unfortunately, yes,' said Miss Carter.

'And did you always live with your father? You must have led quite a social existence.'

'No,' said Miss Carter, 'my father was rather a solitary. My mother died when I was very young. I lived alone with my father, until early this year, that is, when he died.'

There was a silence. Evvy toyed with the remains of his meal, trying to think what to say next. Mor stole a glance at Miss Carter, and then sat petrified. She had closed her eyes, and two tears had escaped from them and were coursing down her cheeks.

Mor was pierced to the heart. How little imagination I have! he thought. I knew she had just lost her father, but it didn't even occur to me to wonder whether she was grieving. He also tried to think, in vain, of something to say.

Bledyard saw the tears and threw down his knife and fork. 'Miss Carter,' said Bledyard, leaning forward, 'I am a great admirer admirer of your father's work.'

Mor's heart warmed to Bledyard. Miss Carter dashed away the tears very quickly. Evvy hadn't even noticed them. 'I'm so glad,' she said. She sounded glad.

'Did your father teach you to paint?' asked Bledyard.

'Yes,' said Miss Carter, 'he was quite a tyrant. I feel as if I was born with a paint brush in my hand. I can't remember a time when I wasn't painting, with my father standing beside me.'

Evvy had taken advantage of this shift of the conversational burden to rise and remove the plates. Mor helped him. It was stewed fruit and ice cream to follow. The ice cream was rather melted.

'In fact, you can't teach teach children to paint,' said Bledyard. 'They already know how to paint. It is the only art that comes naturally to all human beings.'

'What about music?' said Mor. He wanted to get into the conversation.

'I know,' said Miss Carter simultaneously. 'My father didn't teach me in that sense till I was quite old. But then he was very severe. I can remember being made to paint the same thing again and again.'

'But they forget it later,' said Bledyard. It was characteristic of Bledyard's conversation that he did not always attend to remarks made by his interlocutor, but pursued his own train of thought aloud. This was sometimes confusing until one got used to it. 'They forget how forget how to paint at about the time when they lose their innocence. They have to learn all over again after that. What does that prove? Painting is man's most fundamental mode of apprehension. We are incarnate incarnate creatures, our mode of knowledge is sensible, and vision is sovereign over the other senses. Before man could speak he could draw.' It was also characteristic of Bledyard that whereas he might sit completely silent for long periods at a social gathering, if once he did start to talk he would dominate the conversation.

Miss Carter was not embarrassed by Bledyard. She watched him with lips parted. She clearly found him fascinating. Mor set aside his plate. The ice cream was tasteless. He hated ice cream anyway.

'If you will excuse me,' said Mr Everard, 'I will start making the coffee. It takes a little time to prepare in my special coffee-machine. No, no, stay where you are. You haven't finished your fruit, I see. Cheese and biscuits are on the table, so do help yourselves if you want any. I shall just be getting the coffee quite quietly.'

Evvy escaped from the table. He had lately acquired a coffee-machine, from which Mor had had great hopes; however, since Evvy never put even half of the correct amount of coffee into the machine, the results were just as deplorable as before.

'You think we give significance to the world by representing it?' said Miss Carter to Bledyard. 'No, thank you,' she said to Mor, who was offering her a biscuit.

Mor gloomily undid the silver paper from a limp triangle of processed cheese.

'Representation is an ambiguous word,' said Bledyard. 'To represent something something is a task which must be under-taken with humility. What is the first and most fundamental truth which an incarnate being must realize? That he is a thing, a material object in space and time, and that as such he will come to an end. What is the next next truth which he must realize? That he is related on the one hand to God, who is not a thing, and on the other hand to other things which surround him. Now these other things things,' Bledyard raised his spoon to emphasize his words, 'are some of them mere things, and others of them God-related things like himself.'

Over by the hearth, Mr Everard seemed to be having some trouble with the coffee-machine. Mor saw with foreboding that he seemed to be pouring in a lot of water at the last moment.

'Shall we repair?' said Evvy. 'The coffee is almost ready.' Bledyard, Mor and Miss Carter rose from the table.

'It is distinctly indicated indicated in the Bible,' said Bled-yard, 'that the works of nature are placed upon this earth for the benefit of man. Is that not so, Mis-ter Ever-ard?'

Evvy jumped at being suddenly appealed to. 'That is so, Mr Bledyard,' he said. 'Er, Miss Carter, pray sit here. Do you take milk in your coffee?'

'Yes, please,' said Miss Carter.

'It is also the case,' said Bledyard, 'that the Bible commands commands us to abstain from the creation of graven images.'

'I hope you don't mind the milk being cold, Miss Carter,' said Mr Everard. 'This is rather a bachelor establishment, I'm afraid.'

'Thank you,' said Miss Carter, 'I like it better like that. Only a little, please.'

'So that we would expect,' said Bledyard, 'to find the early Church the early Church in two minds upon the matter of religious painting and sculpture. However, it seems to be the case that the fathers felt no special impediment impediment to representational art, and very soon in the history of the Church we find worship and praise naturally taking the form of representation, as in the noble mosaics at Ravenna.'

'Ah yes, how very fine they are!' said Mr Everard. 'Have you been to Ravenna, Miss Carter?'

'Yes, I often went there with my father,' said Miss Carter. 'I know the mosaics very well.'

'The early Church the early Church,' said Bledyard, accepting his coffee-cup from Mr Everard, 'does not seem to have made any distinction distinction between the representation of the works of nature and the representation of human forms. So near so near in time to the source of light, their vision was informed by a reverence which penetrated even their method of depicting the human face. However, when we are overtaken by the secular spirit of the Renaissance, we find we find a more exclusive interest in the human shape as such, conjoined alas with a total loss of that insight and that reverence.'

'What do you think of the coffee this time, Bill?' said Mr Everard. 'A bit better, isn't it?'

'It's very good, sir,' said Mor, pouring the insipid stuff hastily down his throat.

'Are you suggesting,' said Miss Carter to Bledyard, 'that we should treat the representation of the human form in some way quite differently from the representation of other things?'

'As you know,' said Bledyard, 'we find it natural to make the distinction. Only we do not make it absolutely absolutely enough. When confronted with an object which is not a human being we must of course treat it reverently. We must, if we paint it, attempt to show what it is like in itself, and not treat it as a symbol of our own moods and wishes. The great painter the great painter is he who is humble enough in the presence of the object to attempt *merely* to show what the object is like. But this *merely*, in painting, is everything.'

'How I agree with you!' said Miss Carter. Distantly from the school the two-fifteen bell was heard ringing.

'But,' said Bledyard, 'when we are in the presence of another human being, we are not confronted simply by an object—' He paused. 'We are confronted by God.'

'Are you teaching the first period, Bill?' said Mr Everard. 'I'm sorry, I should have asked you earlier.'

'No, I'm not, in fact,' said Mor.

'Do you mean that we ought not to paint other human beings?' asked Miss Carter.

'Each must find out his own way,' said Bledyard. 'If it were possible, ah, if it were possible to treat a head as if it were a spherical material object! But who is great enough to do this?'

'I don't see why one should attempt to treat a head as a spherical material object,' said Mor. 'We know what a head is, and we know what it is to understand another person by looking into his eyes. I don't see why the painter should be obliged to forget all this.'

'Who is worthy to understand another person?' said Bledyard. He spoke with no more and no less intensity than at the start. He answered Mor's words, but his eyes were fixed upon Miss Carter. 'Upon an ordinary material thing we can look with reverence, wondering simply at its being. But when we look upon a human face, we interpret it by what we are ourselves. And what are we?' Bledyard spread out his two hands, one of which held the untasted cup of coffee.

'I agree with much of what you say,' said Miss Carter, speaking quickly before Bledyard could interrupt her. 'Our paintings are a judgment upon ourselves. I know in what way, and how deplorably, my own paintings show what I am. But still I think—'

'It is a fact,' said Bledyard, 'that we cannot really observe really observe our betters. Vices and peculiarities are easy to portray. But who can look reverently enough upon another human face? The true portrait painter should be a saint – and saints have other things to do than paint portraits. Religious painters often understand this obscurely. Representations representations of Our Lord are usually not presented as if they were pictures of an individual. Pictures of Our Lord usually affect us by the majesty of the conception, and not by any particular expression or gesture. Where the picture is individualized, as in Caravaggio's rendering of Christ at Emmaus,

71

we are shocked. We should be equally shocked at any representation of a human face.'

Mr Everard was looking at his watch and shifting restlessly. He began to say something, but Miss Carter got in first. 'What you say is so very abstract, Mr Bledyard. One might think beforehand that it is impossible to depict a human face with sufficient reverence – and perhaps in some absolute sense *sufficient* reverence there never is. But if we consider paintings by Rembrandt, by Goya, by Tintoretto, by—'

Miss Carter's voice was rising higher. She was becoming extremely excited. Bledyard tried to interrupt her. Mr Everard uttered some half-articulate sound.

Mor, speaking very loudly, managed to drown them all. 'I've got to go now, I'm afraid.' A sudden silence followed.

Bledyard laid his cup down and stood up. He turned to Mr Everard. 'Thank you,' he said, 'for a very pleasant lunch, Mister Ever-ard. I have enjoyed meeting Miss Miss Carter. I hope I have not stayed stayed too long.'

Miss Carter stood up. She was looking flushed and agitated. She said, 'Thank you very much indeed – it was so kind of you. I have enjoyed it.'

Evvy was looking ready to drop with exhaustion. They all walked down into the hall. As Mor descended the stairs he saw the little packet of books which he had left on the hall table. He pounced on it and took the opportunity to hand it quickly to Miss Carter. 'The books I promised you.'

Miss Carter took them distractedly and said, 'Oh, thank you,' hardly looking at him. Mor cursed Bledyard. They all came out on to the gravel in front of the house. The blazing heat of the afternoon rose from the earth in waves.

'Oh, Bill,' said Evvy, 'do make my apologies to your wife. I quite meant to invite her, I really meant to, but you know how inefficient I am. At this time of term my memory quite goes. But do tell her, will you, and make my excuses.'

'I will certainly,' said Mor, who had no intention of passing this idiotic apology on to Nan. He knew how it would be received.

'And don't fail to persuade her to make that little speech for us at the dinner,' said Evvy.

'I'll try,' said Mor. He put his hand up to shield his brow from the sun.

'Well, I'm so glad you came,' said Evvy, 'it was so nice. Now I really must get back to my tasks. End of term in sight, you know. Good-bye, Miss Carter, we shall meet again soon – and thank you so much for coming.' He retreated quickly into the house and shut the door.

The three guests stood for a moment undecidedly in the drive. Mor thought, if Bledyard says another word I shall crown him. Miss Carter was evidently thinking the same. She scraped the gravel with her feet and said hurriedly, 'I must be going too. I suppose I can't give either of you a lift back to the school?' The invitation did not sound very whole-hearted.

Mor realized with a shock of surprise that the big green Riley which stood at the door must belong to Miss Carter. It seemed to him amazing that such a small woman should own such a large car. The next moment it seemed to him delightful.

Bledyard said at once, 'No, thank you, Miss Carter. I have my bicycle here. I shall go on that. So I shall say good-bye.' He disappeared abruptly round the side of the house.

Mor was left alone with Miss Carter. He thought very quickly. He was suddenly overwhelmed by a most intense wish to ride away in Miss Carter's car. He said, 'Yes, please, I'd be very grateful for a lift.'

He opened the door for her, and then jumped in himself on the other side. Miss Carter stowed the parcel of books in the back seat. Then she put on some dark glasses and wrapped a multicoloured handkerchief round her head. After that she started the engine. As they began to move slowly forward a curious apparition passed them. It was Bledyard, riding his own bicycle and pushing Mor's. He went by at speed, with head down, and turned off the drive on to the cycle track that led back to the school.

The impudence of him! thought Mor. He hoped that Miss Carter would not realize the significance of the spectacle. He feared that she would. Then suddenly he began to laugh aloud.

'What is it?' said Miss Carter.

Mor went on laughing. 'What a droll fellow Bledyard is!' he said.

The car gathered pace.

# CHAPTER SIX

The Riley turned on to the main road.

'I'm so sorry,' said Miss Carter, 'if I sounded rather short when I offered you the lift. I was afraid Mr Bledyard might accept. I really couldn't have endured his company for another moment.'

'That's all right,' said Mor. 'The first hour is the worst. One does get used to him in time. There's something very remarkable about Bledyard.'

'He is certainly remarkable,' said Miss Carter, 'but infuriating. I'm sure he isn't mad – but he has a characteristic of mad people. He argues insistently and coherently and with the appearance of logic – but somehow it's just all wrong, there's some colossal distortion.'

'I know,' said Mor, thinking suddenly of his wife. 'Yet Bledyard commands respect. One has to ask oneself now and then whether it isn't one's own vision that's distorted.'

'Yes,' said Miss Carter. 'Oh dear!' She stopped the car abruptly. They were almost outside the main entrance to the school. 'Do you mind if we talk for a minute or two? I seem to have brought you back already. I really feel knocked out by that conversation. It's a great relief to be able to talk to you.'

'Not at all,' said Mor. 'I'm in no hurry. I haven't anything special to do this afternoon.' He felt pleased at what she had said.

'Well, in that case,' said Miss Carter, 'perhaps we could drive on a bit. I know it's very naughty, and I ought to be working, but I really must have some air. I expect you need some too. I'll bring you back almost at once.' She let in the clutch and the Riley glided off again.

Mor immediately began to feel guilt. Although he was not actually teaching, there were in fact a lot of things that he ought to be doing that afternoon. All the same, it was so delightful to fly along in the car, the still summer air changed to a warm breeze, and the noisy menacing main road to an open obedient highway that for once really led somewhere. Mor saw that they had crossed the railway bridge without his even noticing the hill. All this was good for him, he felt, after the strained atmosphere of Mr Everard's drawing-room. It would be all right to go a little way.

'I'm really upset by that man,' said Miss Carter. She was very serious. It was clear that she could think about nothing but Bledyard.

'Well then, confound him!' said Mor, laughing, 'if he upset you!'

'No, no,' said Miss Carter, 'as you said yourself, he may be right – or rather, I don't actually think he's right, but it all comes as a sudden – reproach. I take my art very seriously. Indeed *now* it's all I have. I know I'm quite good. I believe I shall be better. But this man makes me feel that everything I do must be rotten. In a way it is – rotten, rotten, I know.' She said the word as a foreigner would say it, giving it significance. She was speaking excitedly again, her small hand gesturing above the steering-wheel. And as she spoke she accelerated. The sandy edges of the main road flashed madly past and a number of cars were left behind. In a moment the speedometer was at seventy. Miss Carter seemed scarcely to notice. Mor held on to his seat.

'Look,' he said, 'and do slow down. I don't often travel in cars. As Bledyard said, each must find his own way. And as you said, his remarks are too abstract. The answer to him is the works themselves. And your answer is your work. When you're not distracted by theories, when you're alone with the work, you know what you have to do, and at least in what direction perfection lies.' Mor spoke earnestly. He felt that here too was something to be taught, something to be understood. And he too had something which he must try to understand. He wanted to continue the conversation.

'I'm so sorry,' said Miss Carter. She put the brake on, and they proceeded for a little way in silence. By this time they had reached the outskirts of Marsington. The car stopped at the traffic lights.

'Turn left here,' said Mor. 'Let's get off the main road.' He didn't want to go past Tim Burke's shop.

They turned, and in a moment or two they were in a country lane. The murmur of the traffic diminished to silence. The leaves met over their heads. Miss Carter slowed the car down. 'This is a surprise,' she said, 'that to escape is so easy. I wonder if there is a river anywhere near here? I feel so hot – it would be wonderful to see some water. I suppose it's too far to go to the sea?'

'Oh, much too far!' said Mor, scandalized. 'It's rather a dry country about here, but I expect I could find some sort of little river for you. Let me see. Yes, if you drive on another few miles there should be one. Drive on anyhow, and I'll recognize the way when I see it.'

'Are you sure I'm not keeping you from anything?' said Miss Carter. 'You must say as soon as you want to go back. Or perhaps I could take you somewhere, or go and collect something for you? I believe you said you hadn't got a car.'

'I haven't,' said Mor, 'and in fact you could help me by dropping me in a little while quite near here. There's someone I ought to see, and since we're so close I might as well go this afternoon. It'll save me a railway journey. But let's find your river first. It had occurred to Mor that since he was practically in Marsington he might call again on Tim Burke. In his exalted state of mind of the previous evening he had failed to have a sufficiently precise conversation with Tim. He ought to be, Mor thought, more fully briefed about the financial aspect of the enterprise before raising the question with either Nan or Evvy. Nan would be certain to make some objections on the grounds of finance – and in order to convince her his answers must be exact. Another talk with Tim would be exceedingly useful.

'Good,' said Miss Carter. The road opened before them and she let the car take it at a rush. Mor's recent nervousness was clearly far from her mind. From the expression on her face he suspected she was still thinking of Bledyard's reproach. He saw her eyes side view behind the dark glasses and they were large with thought. She held the steering-wheel lightly with one small hand, and the other arm lay along the edge of the window. A grove of pine trees swept past behind her head, and an odour of sand and resin filled the car. It was indeed a dry country.

It occurred to Mor that he had told Nan he would be back for tea. He said to Miss Carter, 'Would you mind stopping if you see a telephone-box? I must just ring my wife to tell her what time I'll be back.'

'Certainly,' said Miss Carter. A telephone-box appeared very soon, and she stopped the car.

Mor went into the box and fumbled for his sixpence. A curious stillness surrounded him after the sound of the engine. Out of this, in a moment or two, came Nan's voice speaking. She always sounded apprehensive when she picked up the telephone. 'Hello.'

'Hello, Nan,' said Mor. 'It's Bill. I just thought I'd ring to say I won't be home for tea. I've got one or two things to do, and then I have to go and see Tim Burke about a Labour Party thing.'

'That's all right,' said Nan. 'When will you be home?'

'Oh, about five-thirty, I expect,' said Mor. 'Maybe sooner. Cheerio.'

He put the phone down. Then he stood quite still in the telephone-box and a strange cold feeling came over him. Why on earth had he done that? Why had he told Nan a lie? Why hadn't he said that he was out with Miss Carter in the car? He hadn't even reflected about it, he had told the lie immediately, without even thinking. Why? He supposed it must have been because he was vaguely aware that Nan would be very sarcastic and unpleasant about his wasting the afternoon in this way. But this wasn't a reason for telling her a lie. Anyhow, it was so idiotic. Anyone might have seen him and Miss Carter in the car together. But that wasn't the point. He ought not to have lied to Nan. He came slowly out of the box.

'What's the matter?' said Miss Carter. 'You look very strange. Are you all right?'

'Yes, fine,' said Mor. 'I'm just feeling the heat a bit. I'll be better when the car's started.'

Miss Carter gave him an anxious glance and they set off.

Here I am telling another lie, said Mor to himself. Suddenly he said to Miss Carter, 'I'm sorry, that's not true. The fact is that, I don't know why, I didn't tell my wife that I was with you in the car – which was very foolish of me.'

Miss Carter turned to look at him. Her eyes were hidden behind the dark glasses. Now she'll despise me, thought Mor. She'll despise me for telling the lie, and she'll despise me for telling her that I told it.

'Oh dear,' said Miss Carter. 'You'll have to tell her when you get back. She won't mind much, will she? But I expect she'll be cross with me.'

Mor felt a sudden relief and an enormous liking for Miss Carter. Of course, it was straightforward enough, and not much harm would be done. He would have a nasty half-hour with Nan, that was all. He was grateful to Miss Carter for the simple way in which she had dealt with it, and he was glad now that he had told her.

'You're perfectly right, of course,' said Mor, 'and naturally I shall tell her when I get back. She'll be cross with me, quite rightly, but she won't be cross with you – I'll see that she isn't. I'm so sorry about this. I really am a fool.'

The car had been speeding along as they talked. 'Where are we now?' said Miss Carter.

Mor wasn't quite sure. 'Drive on a bit,' he said. 'We may have missed the turning. I'll recognize something in a moment.' He felt that this last exchange had broken some barrier between himself and Miss Carter, and he found himself now more at ease in her presence. For a moment he was almost glad of his foolishness.

Miss Carter slowed the car down and Mor began to study the countryside. By this time they were deep in the ragged coniferous Surrey landscape which lies between the fanned-out lines of the great main roads out of London: the region where the escaping Londoner, alone of city-dwellers to use the word in quite this way, says a little doubtfully, 'Now at last we are really in *the country.*'

Mor decided that they must have passed the turning he had in mind, but he felt sure that if they continued they would find their way to the river all the same. He was determined, after that unpleasantness, not to fail Miss Carter in the matter of the river. He owed her a service. Meanwhile the afternoon was growing hotter and the woodlands thicker, more immobile, and more heavily perfumed. They drove on.

With a simultaneous cry they greeted what now appeared quite suddenly upon the road before them. Miss Carter braked violently, and approached at a walking pace. She said, 'How strange, I thought at first it was a mirage.' She stopped the Riley within a few feet of the ford.

The water ran twinkling across the road in a wide steady

78

sheet. They could hear it running. For a while they sat in an entranced silence listening to its noise. Then Miss Carter let the car come very slowly forward until the front wheels were dipping into the water. She turned to Mor with a look of triumph.

Mor was glad at her joy. He looked about him to each side. The water emerged from the wood under concrete shelves, the tops of which were covered with earth and grasses. Beyond this the trees were thick and it was impossible to see what happened to the little river. Mor looked across the water. A short way beyond the ford there was a turning to the left. 'Let's just go down there,' said Mor, pointing to it. 'We might be able to reach the bank of the river farther along.'

Miss Carter looked at him a little anxiously. 'Are you sure you have time?' she said. 'I don't want to keep you. My pranks have caused you some trouble already.'

'Nonsense!' said Mor. 'Nothing was your fault, my dear child. I've still got some time in hand. If you'd like to go— We won't spend more than a moment looking.'

'I'd love to!' said Miss Carter promptly, and the car went through the ford with a gentle swish and sailed round the corner. Here once more the trees met overhead and there was a diffused green light. Miss Carter took off her glasses.

After about a hundred yards they saw that the little road was bearing to the right, away from the direction where the river must lie. The wood was still far too thick for them to see what was there, although when the car stopped and Miss Carter switched off the engine a murmuring sound of water was distantly audible. Straight in front of them, however, was a white gate, and beyond it was a gentle green bridle path which curved away to the left between ferns and brambles under a close continuous archway of oaks, birches and conifers. It was tempting. They looked at each other.

'Let's leave the car,' said Mor. 'We could walk down there in a moment and find the river.'

'No,' she said, 'why walk? We can ride.' And she had leapt out of the car and was unfastening the gate. A minute or two later the Riley was lurching gently along the bridle path.

'To drive a car along a path like this,' said Miss Carter almost in a whisper, 'is like sailing a boat along a street. It is an enchantment.'

Mor was silent. It was so. The engine was almost noiseless

79

now and above it rose the massed hum of the woodland on a summer afternoon, a dazing sound that confounded itself with silence. It was as if since they had passed the white gate they had entered another world. The spirit of the wood pressed upon them, and Mor found himself looking from side to side expecting to see something strange. The path was well kept and closely covered with fine grass, and someone had cut the bracken back on either side. All the same, the ferns and the wild flowers were close enough to the wheels of the car to touch them as they passed, and Mor saw gorse and ragged robin and ladies' lace banked and swaying slightly on either side of the path ahead. Here and there came a deep vista into the wood, down leaf-strewn alleys lighted by a brown light. There was still no sign of the river. Miss Carter stopped the car suddenly. She still spoke in a low voice. 'Would you like to drive?'

Mor was startled. It was nearly fifteen years since he had driven a car, and he had never possessed one of his own. 'I haven't driven for a long time,' he said, 'and I don't know whether I could now. Anyway, I haven't got a driving licence.'

'That doesn't matter,' said Miss Carter, 'no one will know — and we're not in a real road anyway. Would you like to?'

'I might harm your beautiful car,' said Mor. But he knew that he would like to, he would like to very much indeed, drive the Riley. Before he could say any more Miss Carter skipped out of the car and they changed places. She seemed very elated and watched Mor with delight as he looked doubtfully at the dashboard. He could remember nothing. 'How do I start it?' he asked.

'There's the ignition, it's switched on, there's the starter, there's the gear lever. You remember how the gears go? There's the clutch, the foot-brake, the accelerator. The hand-brake's in front here.' Miss Carter was perched sideways in her seat with the gleeful air of a little boy who sees his father about to make a mess of things.

Mor felt large and awkward. He fiddled a little with the gears. He began to remember. He started the engine. Then gingerly he put the car into first gear and released the clutch. With a jolt the Riley leapt forward. Mor immediately put his foot on the brake and the engine stalled. Miss Carter rocked with laughter. She had drawn her feet up and clutched her skirt about her ankles.

'Damn!' said Mor. He tried again and was more successful. The Riley glided very slowly forward and Mor navigated her round a turning in the path. A tree brushed the roof. Almost silently they sailed on through the thickest part of the wood. Miss Carter was grave now, she was looking ahead. As he felt the big car purring quietly along under his control Mor felt like a king. He experienced a deep and intense joy. His body relaxed. He was continuous with the car, with the slowly moving woodland, with the thick green carpet of the unrolling bridle path. They drove for a minute without speaking.

Then Mor saw the woodlander. He was lying very close to the path in a little clearing where the trees receded and left a wide bare space which was covered with fallen leaves. All round the edge the flowers and brambles were festooned in a thick palisade, at the farthest point of which a triangular cleft led far back into the wood and was lost in darkness. The man lay on his side in the dry leaves and seemed to be playing a game with some brightly coloured cards. Most of the cards were in his hand, but some half-dozen were laid out upon the ground. He was a short broad man, dressed in shabby blue cotton trousers and a blue shirt. The clothes had something of the air of a uniform, without being of any identifiable kind. Near by, beneath the brambles, could be seen a bundle and what looked like the handle of some tool. The man's face was half turned towards them, his eyes cast down, and the peculiarly dark bronze of his cheek suggested that he might be a gipsy. His hair was tangled and black.

Involuntarily Mor stopped the car. They were within a few feet of the man. A moment passed. The reclining figure did not look up. He continued to stare at the row of cards that lay upturned before him. He paid not the slightest attention to the watchers in the car. Mor felt Miss Carter touching his arm. He started the engine again and they drove on. The man was lost to view in the trees.

Mor turned to look at his companion. Miss Carter was pale and had covered her mouth with her hand. 'Don't be frightened,' said Mor.

'I am frightened,' said Miss Carter. 'I don't know why.'

The car bumped quietly along. The path seemed endless.

Mor was a bit frightened too, he didn't know why. He said, 'He was probably one of those nomadic woodcutters that work for the forestry commission. They live in shacks, or tents in the wood.'

'He looked to me like a gipsy,' said Miss Carter, 'and I'm sure they never work for anyone. I wonder if we should have given him money? Do you think so?'

Mor cast a quick glance at her. He was unnerved by her agitation. 'Much better not,' he said. 'Sometimes they are very proud, those people.' He realized as he said this that he would have felt timid at having to address the man.

'Did you notice that those weren't ordinary playing cards?' said Miss Carter.

At that moment they came round another bend in the bridle path and there before them was the river. The path turned along the bank, transforming itself into a wide lawn, and between waving banks of bullrushes, willow herb and meadow sweet the river ran strongly, its surface glossy and brilliant. A few late forget-me-nots still lingered, their stems submerged, at the edge of the reed-bed. There was a smell of water.

Mor stopped the car and they both got out. They went forward to the edge and stood for some time in silence. The scene was so like a garden that Mor glanced about him, half expecting to see a house nearby. But there was nothing to be seen except the river, which disappeared again on both sides into the thick wood. He looked at Miss Carter. She was standing deep among the tangle of leaves and flowers on the river bank. She had a drugged entranced look upon her face. As if blindly, her hands reached out into the foliage. She plucked a leaf, and conveyed it to her mouth, and chewed it thoughtfully, her eyes upon the water.

Mor turned about and walked a little way along the grassy lawn. Here was the real country where the seasons' change is marked by minute signs. Blackthorn gives way to hawthorn and hawthorn to elder. How rarely he came here. He drew the branches aside, and then saw that the river widened into a pool, hidden under a low roof of spreading leaves. The bank shelved gently here, and met the water in a pebbly beach. Beyond it the stream seemed to be deeper, striped upon one side with lines of white crows' feet, which lay thickly beneath the far bank, but clear in the middle. A white swan's feather scudded lightly upon the surface. Mor turned to convey this discovery to his companion, but found her there already beside him.

'Oh,' said Miss Carter, 'I must swim! Do you mind? I must! I must!'

Mor felt a little alarmed and shocked at this suggestion; but he felt too that his permission was being asked and he could hardly say no. He was silent.

'Oh, please I *must* swim,' said Miss Carter again. Mor saw the wild light in her eye. He was reminded suddenly of the rose garden, of Bledyard's room.

'Of course, swim if you want to,' said Mor. 'I only hope nobody comes. I'll stay well away here on the bank and watch for intruders.'

'No one will come,' said Miss Carter, 'no one will find this place. Yes, you go down there. I'll undress here, on the far side of these bushes. I won't be a moment. But I *must* get into the river.'

Mor went out again into the sunlight and walked away, his feet dragging through meadow sweet at the river's brim. He felt uneasy. The sun was intensely hot. The perspiration was running steadily like tears down the side of his face. The river was very inviting indeed. Mor turned his head the other way. He sat down where a gap in the reeds showed him a small section of water. Here the bank was high and steep and the river flowed past, three or four feet below him. Gorse bushes on the far side of the water emitted their strong coconut perfume. A large dragon-fly hovered for a moment and then whisked into invisibility. No birds sang. The heat had silenced them.

Mor kept his back turned to the place where the low spreading trees concealed from view the weedy pool and Miss Carter. In a moment or two he heard a vigorous splashing sound, and then a triumphant cry. 'It's wonderful!' cried Miss Carter from behind him. 'It's marvellously warm. And the water is so clear. And do you know, there's water cress growing?'

'Be careful,' said Mor. 'Don't get caught in those weeds.'

The splashing continued.

Mor felt very uneasy indeed. He suddenly began to wish that he had not started on this silly expedition at all. He began to think about Nan, and his optimistic idea of the earlier afternoon now seemed futile. He had thought that no great harm would be done. But how did he know this? He had no precedents for episodes of this kind. Mor had never deceived his wife, except for very occasional social lies, and one or two lies about his health. These were all of them occasions which Mor never forgot. Never before had he had to offer to Nan the sort of confession which he would have to present tonight. He had not the slightest idea how she would take it. Of course, nothing very terrible could happen. Once the truth was told, they would both just have to digest it somehow. But he did not know exactly, or even roughly, how it would be, and he felt a deep anguish.

He wondered if he should tell Nan about Miss Carter's bathing. Probably he ought to have told Miss Carter not to bathe. Yet somehow that would have been cruel. He had better tell everything, Mor thought. If he was to take refuge in the truth, and indeed that was his only possible refuge, it had better be the whole truth. Of course, he would call on Tim Burke on the way home, and that would make at least part of his story true. Or would this be deceitful? Perhaps he had only decided to see Tim Burke as a sort of device to allow himself to spend a longer time with Miss Carter? He wasn't sure. It occurred to him that after tonight he had better see to it that he did not meet Miss Carter again except in so far as this was inevitable. Not that it mattered specially. How foolish that lie had been. It had made something very simple and trivial into something that appeared important. Mor stared at the river. A water vole swam slowly across and vanished into the reeds on the far side. Mor did not see it. He felt a black veil of sadness falling between him and the warm late afternoon. He looked at his watch.

It was a quarter past five. Mor jumped up. How the time had fled! He must think about getting back at once. He turned towards the pool and saw Miss Carter's blue silk dress spread out on a gorse bush and her very small golden sandals perched on a tuft of grass. He turned quickly away again. 'Miss Carter,' he called, 'I think we ought to go fairly soon. I'll just turn the car round.'

Miss Carter said in a clear voice from somewhere very close to him, 'Are you sure you can manage?'

'I can manage,' said Mor. He climbed gloomily into the Riley and started the engine. How could he have been such a fool as to get himself into this idiotic situation? Tonight all would be plain and clear again. Nan would be hurt and angry. But at least he would be out of the tangle. He hated deeply the feeling that at this very moment he was deceiving her. He put the car into reverse and began to swing it round. He backed it for a little distance along the bank of the river. The Riley moved fast. Mor put the brake on and engaged the first gear. He released the clutch slowly. Nothing happened. He tried again, accelerating slightly. Still nothing happened. The car did not move forward. Mor's attention came sharply back to the present scene. He checked the hand-brake and went through all the movements again, accelerating hard this time. The car remained where it was, and he could hear a sinister whirring sound as one of the back wheels turned vainly in the undergrowth of sedge and willow herb.

Miss Carter came towards him across the lawn, taking small steps. She had resumed her slightly prim appearance, although the silk dress seemed now to cling even more closely to her body. She was barefoot, carrying her shoes and stockings. 'What is it?' she asked a little anxiously.

'We seem to be stuck for the moment,' said Mor. He got out.

'You're sure you haven't got the hand-brake on?' said Miss Carter.

'Sure,' said Mor. He walked round to the back of the car. The back wheels were extremely close to the edge of the stream and had entered a thick mass of matted weeds and grasses. The bank fell away here and the undergrowth overhung it in a deceptive manner. Under the canopy of green the earth was damp and sticky. The bank then fell steeply to the water, some feet below. Mor stepped waist deep into the patch of willow herb and saw that the off-side wheel was almost clear of the ground, protruding into the greenery that hung down from the bank towards the water. The other wheel appeared to have sunk into a rather muddy hollow. The front wheels were a foot or two away from the river bank.

'How's the situation?' said Miss Carter. She followed him barefoot, and as he bent forward he saw her small white feet appear in the grass near to his heavy shoes.

'Mind the nettles,' said Mor. 'It's all right, I think I see what to do. This wheel is almost at the edge, I'm afraid. But we could move if the other wheel would bite. That one's stuck in a patch of mud. If we just put some grass and branches underneath it, that should do the trick. Look, I'll rev the engine again, and you watch the back wheels.'

'No, I'll rev the engine,' said Miss Carter. 'Perhaps the car will move for me.' She got in and went through the motions. The same thing happened. The engine roared in vain. Mor could see the back wheels turning, one in the patch of mud. Miss Carter switched off and got out again.

'Lots of grass and twigs is what we need,' said Mor. He ran to the edge of the wood and began to pluck armfuls of bracken and tall grass. Miss Carter went a little farther into the wood and gathered small twigs and branches. As she returned Mor saw that her legs were bleeding. They knelt together beside the wheel. Miss Carter smelt of river water. From the wet ends of her hair, as she leaned forward, a little water trickled down towards her bosom. She helped Mor to strew the foliage under the wheel from both sides. With his hand Mor scooped the mud out from under the tyre, and packed in a compact bunch of twigs and ferns.

'There!' he said. 'We ought to get away now. Will you take her, or shall I?'

'I will,' said Miss Carter. 'You watch what happens.'

Mor squatted near the wheel while Miss Carter got in again and started the engine. Breathlessly Mor watched the wheel begin to rotate. It was all right. It was biting well upon the dry bracken. Mor was about to call out, when suddenly something happened. There was a violent jolt, and the car stopped again. Mor saw with surprise that the wheel had risen clear of the ground and was turning in the air. He jumped up.

'What's happened now?' said Miss Carter. She sounded alarmed. The car was tilting towards the river.

Mor ran round the back of the car. He looked at the other back wheel. A section of the bank had given way under it, and it hung in mid-air above the water. The Riley seemed to be resting now upon its back axle, straddled across the bank.

'Get out of the car,' said Mor.

'No, let me try again,' said Miss Carter.

'Get out,' said Mor, 'at once.'

She got out and joined him. When she saw the position of the back wheels she gave a gasp of distress.

86

'I am *extremely* sorry,' said Mor. 'This is all completely my fault. But apologies aren't much use. The thing is to decide what to do.'

'Supposing,' said Miss Carter, 'we were to wedge something under the inside back wheel, and you were to push hard from behind, we might get her to jump forward.'

'I don't think so,' said Mor. 'We'd have to raise the axle somehow. The car is tilted too much already.'

'Suppose we jacked her up,' said Miss Carter, 'and got her on an even keel, and then lowered her slowly again.'

'We wouldn't be able to jack her up,' said Mor. 'The jack would just sink into that muddy ground. Anyhow, as we lowered her she would just sink into the same position.'

Miss Carter was worried, but by no means distracted. She was thinking hard. Before Mor could stop her, she was crawling underneath the Riley.

'*Don't* do that, Miss Carter,' said Mor sharply. 'With the car tilting like that it's not safe.'

Miss Carter emerged. Her knees and the hem of her dress were covered in mud. She had thrown her shoes and stockings away into the grass.

'I wanted to see what exactly the axle was doing,' she said. 'In fact it's resting on a stone. What I suggest is that we put something large and firm underneath the other wheel, and then dig the stone away. Then the car will be resting on three wheels again.'

'It's no use,' said Mor. 'What we need now is a tractor.'

'Well, let's try this first,' she said firmly, and already she was running away into the wood. Mor followed her. He felt nothing now except an almost physical distress about the car.

Miss Carter soon found a flat mossy stone and Mor helped her to carry it back towards the river. It was very heavy. Mor took off his coat and rolled up his sleeves. They began to introduce the stone underneath the wheel. It became very muddy and slippery in the process.

'This is a crazy proceeding,' said Mor. He squatted back on his heels and looked at his companion. Miss Carter was very flushed. There were patches of mud on the dark red of her cheeks. Her dress was hitched up, and one knee and thigh were embedded in the muddy ground. She looked like something from a circus.

'We must be careful,' she said, 'to see that the stone is tilting from the inside of the car outwards. Then when it takes the weight the car won't slither any farther towards the river.'

Mor sighed. He could not desert her. He helped her to complete the operation.

'Now,' said Mor, 'the question is, how are we to dig out the stone from under the axle without the whole thing coming down on top of us?'

'We'll use the starting-handle,' said Miss Carter. She was not calm, but intent and fervent. She fetched the starting-handle from the back of the car.

'Give it to me,' said Mor. 'You keep clear, and don't whatever you do get into the car. When it does rest on three wheels again I'll try to drive it out.'

Mor got into the Riley for a moment and engaged the handbrake and the first gear. Then he went behind the car and lay down close to the wheels. He could see the inside back wheel touching the stone which he and Miss Carter had put in place, and the axle resting upon another stone nearer to the river bank. He reached underneath with the starting-handle and began to undermine the stone on which the axle rested, digging hard at its base. Miss Carter came and sat near him, almost invisible in the long grass.

It was easier than Mor had expected to undermine the stone. Perhaps, after all, he thought, this mad plan will work. He felt the stone give slightly and begin to sink. In another moment it would be clear of the axle and the car would be resting upon its three wheels. Mor gave a final dig and drew sharply back.

With a roar of grinding tyres and tearing undergrowth and crumbling stones the Riley lurched over madly towards the river. Mor saw it rise above him like a rearing animal. He rolled precipitately back into the grass and came into violent contact with Miss Carter's knees. They both staggered up.

'Are you all right?' she cried.

Mor did not answer. They ran forward to see what had happened to the car. Another large section of the bank had given way, and the car had slid down and was now balanced with one back wheel and one front wheel well over the edge of the bank. Below it the river, foaming and muddy with the recent avalanche, swept on its way carrying off long reeds and tufts of grass and broken blossoms of meadow sweet.

'Hmmm,' said Mor. 'Well, now I think it's time to go and get the tractor.'

'It's too late for the tractor,' said Miss Carter in a steady voice.

Mor looked. Then he saw that it was indeed too late.

'It's going to turn right over into the river,' said Miss Carter.

They watched. Very very slowly the big car was tilting towards the water. There was a soft gurgling sound as pieces of the river bank descended and were engulfed. Mor took Miss Carter by the arm and drew her back. There was a moment's pause, during which was audible the steady voice of the stream and the buzz of the surrounding woodland. The car was poised now, its inside wheels well clear of the ground, its outside wheels biting deep into the soft earth half-way down the bank. Then slowly again it began to move. Higher and higher the wheels rose from the ground, as the roof of the car inclined more and more sharply until it stood vertically above the water. Then with a grinding crash of buckling metal and sub-siding earth the car fell, turning over as it went, and came to rest upside down with its roof upon the bed of the stream.

The moment immediately after the crash was strangely silent. The woodland hum was heard again, and the murmur of the stream, now slightly modified as the water gurgled in and out of the open windows of the Riley. The stream was very shallow, and the water did not rise above the level of the windows. The reeds were swaying in the warm air and the dragon-flies darting among the sharp green stems. Everything was as before, except for the dark gash of the broken bank and the spectacle of the Riley lying upside down in the middle of the river, its black and sinister lower parts exposed to the declining sun.

'Oh dear,' said Miss Carter.

Mor turned to comfort her. He saw that she was starting to cry.

'My poor Riley,' said Miss Carter. And she wept without restraint.

Mor looked at her for a moment. Then he put one arm round her and held her in a very strong grip.

In a moment Miss Carter recovered and disengaged herself quickly from Mor's hold. Mor offered her a handkerchief.

'Look here,' he said, 'all we can do now is go and find a garage with a breakdown unit and let them deal with this scene. In fact the car isn't badly damaged – it's just a matter of pulling it out. It'll need a crane, but it won't be difficult. I suggest you go home now in the bus, Miss Carter, and leave me to arrange the rest. I'm deeply sorry about this, and needless to say I'll pay all the bills. You go home now and have a good rest. I'll see you as far as the main road.'

'Oh, don't be silly,' said Miss Carter in a tired voice. 'I'm not going to leave the car. You go and find the breakdown people. I shall stay here.'

'I don't like leaving you alone in the wood,' said Mor. He thought of the woodcutter.

'Please go,' said Miss Carter. 'I'll stay here. I'd much rather stay with the car.' She spoke as if it were a wounded animal.

Mor gave up trying to convince her. It was clear to him that she really wanted him away. He turned back on foot along the grassy bridle path, and as he passed the clearing he saw that the man had gone. He passed through the white gate, and almost at once was able to hail a car which took him to a nearby garage. Less than half an hour later a small lorry mounted with a crane conveyed him once more to the river, ripping the ferns and the branches on either side as it bumped along the track.

Miss Carter was standing knee-deep in the water beside the Riley. When she saw them coming she scrambled out. She came straight up to Mor.

'Listen,' she said, 'please go home now. It wasn't your fault, this thing. It was all my fault for taking you away. Please go home. Your wife will be very worried.'

'I must wait and see that everything is all right,' said Mor.

Miss Carter put her hand on his arm. 'Please, please go,' she said. 'Please, please, please.'

At last Mor allowed himself to be persuaded. The breakdown men seemed to think that it would not be difficult to lift the Riley; and Miss Carter seemed intensely anxious for his departure. So in a little while Mor turned away and went back alone to the road. When he came in sight of the ford he saw that there was someone there. It was the man from the clearing, who was standing with the water covering his shoes and lapping round his trouser ends. When he became aware of Mor he moved on a step or two into the deepest part of the ford and stopped again, but without looking round. Mor watched him for a moment. Then he turned and began walking in the other direction along the road. It was not long before he met a car which was able to give him a lift as far as the main road. There he caught a bus.

As the bus conveyed Mor along the noisy road towards the outskirts of the housing estate he felt as if he were emerging from a dream. It was only a few hours ago that he had risen from Evvy's lunch table. What world had he entered in between? Whatever the region was, Mor thought, in which he had been wandering, one thing was certain, that he would never visit it again. At this reflection he felt a mixture of sadness and relief. He looked at his watch. It was after eight. Nan would indeed be worried. He ought to have telephoned her. But somehow it had not occurred to him, so completely insulated had he been by the strange atmosphere of that other world. He shook himself and looked to see the familiar streets appearing. He got off the bus and began to walk quickly past the rows of semi-detached houses towards his own.

As Mor came to the corner of the road where he lived he suddenly paused. A familiar figure had come out from under the shadow of a tree and was hurrying to meet him. It was Tim Burke.

Tim came up to Mor, took him by the wrist, and turning him about began to lead him quickly back the way he had come.

'Tim!' said Mor. 'Whatever is it? We can't talk now. Look, I must get home. I'm in an awful fix.'

'You're telling me you're in a fix!' said Tim. He took Mor's arm in a wrestling grip and began to urge him back along the road. 'I had to wait there, I wasn't sure which way you'd come. I don't want Nan to see me.' They turned down another road.

'What is it, Tim?' said Mor, freeing his arm. They stopped under a tree.

'Nan rang me up,' said Tim.

Mor thought, of course, it hadn't occurred to him, but naturally Nan would have rung up Tim to ask why he was so late. 'What did she say,' said Mor, 'when you said I hadn't been with you?'

'I didn't say that,' said Tim.

'What?' said Mor.

'I didn't say it,' said Tim. 'I said you'd been with me most of the afternoon and that just then you'd gone over to the committee rooms and that you'd been delayed and you'd probably be back a bit later.'

Mor put his hand to his head. 'Tim,' he said, 'for heaven's sake, what put it into your mind to invent all that?'

Tim took hold of the hem of Mor's jacket. 'I saw you down at the traffic lights at Marsington,' he said, 'in a car with a girl.'

Mor leaned against the tree. It was a plane tree with a flaky piebald bark. He pulled a piece of the bark off it. 'I see,' he said. 'I'm afraid your Irish imagination has carried you away a bit, Tim. That was just Miss Carter, who's painting Demoyte's portrait. And in fact I *would* have been with you this afternoon if it hadn't been that the car broke down.'

Tim was silent. All this isn't quite true, thought Mor. Oh God!

'Tim,' he said, 'I'm sorry. You've acted very kindly. There's been a horrible muddle today, all my fault.'

'You're not angry with me, Mor?' said Tim. 'You see, I *couldn't* just say you hadn't been there. I had to do my best. I had to try to think what to do.' He was still holding on to Mor's coat.

'That's all right, Tim,' said Mor. 'You acted very well, in fact. It's been all my fault. But there won't be anything like this again. We'd better just bury it quietly and not refer to it any more. I'm deeply sorry to have involved you in this. And thank you for what you did.' He touched Tim's shoulder lightly. Tim let go of his coat.

They looked at each other. Tim's look expressed curiosity, diffidence and affection. Mor's look expressed affection, exasperation and remorse. They began to walk back along the road.

When they got to the corner, Tim said, 'Have you talked to herself yet about that thing?'

'No,' said Mor, 'I will soon though.'

They stood for a moment.

'You're not angry?' said Tim. 'I tried to do the best for you.'

'How could I be angry?' said Mor. 'It is you who should pardon me. You did very well. And now we'll not speak of it again. Good-night, Tim.'

Mor turned and began to walk slowly along the road that led to his own house.

CHAPTER SEVEN

Already the light was leaving the earth and taking refuge in the sky. The big windows of Demoyte's drawing-room stood open upon the garden. A recruiting pattern of bird-song filled the room, not overlaid now by any human voices. In the last light of the evening Rain Carter was painting.

It was the day following the disaster with the Riley. The breakdown men had in fact managed to right the car fairly quickly, and towed it to the garage. The engine was badly jolted and drenched with water, but there was no serious damage to the car except for a certain buckling of the roof. The garage had promised to restore it, almost as good as new, in a short while.

Rain, however, was not thinking now about the Riley. Nor was she thinking about William Mor, although that was a subject which had preoccupied her for a while before she retired to bed the previous evening. She was completely absorbed in what she was doing. Early that morning Rain had found herself able to make a number of important decisions about the picture, and once her plan had become clear she started at once to put it into execution. A white sheet was laid down in the drawing-room on which the easel was placed, together with a kitchen table and a chair. Paints and brushes stood upon the table, and the large canvas had been screwed on to the easel. Enthroned opposite, beside one of the windows, sat Demoyte, his shoulder touching one of the rugs which hung behind him upon the wall. Through the window was visible a small piece of the garden, some trees, and above the trees in the far distance the tower of the school. In front of Demoyte stood a table spread with books and papers. Demoyte had been sitting there at Rain's request for a large part of the afternoon and was by this time rather irritable. During much of this period Rain had not been painting but simply walking up and down and looking at him, asking him to alter his position slightly, and bringing various objects and laying them upon the table.

Demoyte was dressed in a rather frayed corduroy coat and

was wearing a bow tie. This particular capitulation had taken place the previous morning after breakfast when Rain had said sharply, 'Don't think me eccentric, Mr Demoyte, but *these* are the clothes I want to paint you in' – and had laid the very garments on the chair beside him. Demoyte had made no comment, but had gone at once in quest of Miss Handforth to tell her exactly what he thought of this betrayal. Handy had informed him that needless to say she knew nothing about it and surely he knew her better than to imagine she would give information to that imp or make free with her employer's clothing. Demoyte had pondered the outrage for a short while, made a mental note to give Mor a rocket when he next saw him, changed into the clothes in question and felt immensely better and more comfortable.

Rain, surveying now at leisure the object placed before her, could hear her father's voice saying, 'Don't forget that a portrait must have depth, mass *and* decorative qualities. Don't be so fascinated by the head, or by the space, that you forget that a canvas is also a flat surface with edges which touch the frame. Part of your task is to cover that surface with a pattern.' What Rain had lacked was the motif of the pattern. But this had lately occurred to her, and with it came the definitive vision, which she had been seeking, of Demoyte's face. The old man's face, it now seemed to her, was of a withered golden colour, like an old apple, and marked with the repetition of a certain curve. Supremely this curve occurred in his lips, which Rain proposed to paint curling in a slightly sarcastic and amused manner which was highly characteristic of him. It appeared again, more subdued, in his eyebrows, which met bushily above his nose, and in the line made by his eyes and the deep wrinkles which led upwards from their corners. The multitudinous furrows of the forehead presented the same motif, tiny now and endlessly repeated, where the amusement was merged into tolerance and the sarcasm into sadness.

Rain had chosen as part of the background one of the rugs which, as it seemed to her, spoke the theme again. In some obscure way this patterned surface continued too to be expressive of the character of the sitter, with his passionate interest in all-over decoration. Rain selected a noble Shíraz, of a more intense golden shade, not unlike the colour in which she proposed to paint the old man's face, and wherein the curve occurred again, formalized into a recurrent flower. This rug, which was the same one which Rain had been studying when William Mor first beheld her, she had persuaded Demoyte to move, exchanging its position with another one so as to have it in the picture. He had done this with many complaints.

Rain was aware of the dangers of her plan. She was not especially worried at the possibility of depth and space being sacrificed to decoration. That was a risk which had to be run in any case and she found in practice that if she thought about decoration first, and then forgot it and thought about depth, the thing would usually work out. It was rather that this particular motif, combined with the colour scheme which seemed to be imposing itself, was a somewhat sweet one and might soften the picture too much. To counteract it she would rely upon the sheer mass and strength of the head – that would be her most difficult task – and upon the powerful thickness of the neck. The hands and the objects upon the table would have to play their part too, especially the hands. Rain did not yet see this very clearly. The treatment of the window was also to some extent problematic. She was tempted to paint the trees in a stylized and curly manner, but suspected that this was a false instinct. Something different must be done with the trees, something rather austere. What she could not bring herself to sacrifice was the idea of putting in the neo-Gothic tower of the school in the top left-hand corner, rising into the sky, with a fantastic flourish. The sky itself would be pallid, cooling down the rest of the picture, so far as was consistent with a strong light in the room. Demoyte himself would be looking back, away from the window, his glance not quite meeting that of the spectator.

'It's time you stopped that now, missie,' said Demoyte. 'There isn't anything like enough light to paint by.' He shifted restlessly about in his chair. He particularly resented being kept there when Rain was not painting him but painting a piece of the rug. Rain had told him when he complained that 'all the colours belong to each other, so the rug looks different when you are there.'

'I know,' said Rain abstractedly. She was wearing her black

95

trousers and a loose red overall on top, the sleeves well rolled up. 'It *is* too dark. My father would be cross seeing me painting now. I just want to finish this tiny square.'

She had filled in in very considerable detail one small segment of the rug in the top right hand half of the picture. The rest of the picture was vaguely sketched in with a small number of thin lines of paint. Rain, following her father, did not believe in under-painting. She painted directly on to the canvas with strokes of colour which were put on as if they were to stand and to modify the final result however much was subsequently laid on top of them. Rain also followed Sidney Carter's system of painting the background first and letting the main subject grow out of the background and dominate it and if necessary encroach upon it. In particular, she recalled her father's dictum: 'A little piece of *serious* paint upon the canvas will tell you a lot about the rest. Put it on and sleep on it.' Rain hoped that the following day she would be able to construct, from the small and finely worked segment of rug, a great deal more of the rest of her picture.

She laid the brush down. It was too dark now. Demoyte began to get up. 'Please wait a moment,' said Rain, 'just a moment more, please.' He subsided.

Rain came forward and studied him, leaning thoughtfully across the table. The hands. Much depended on that. The hands must be another mark of strength in the picture, shown solid and square, somehow. But how exactly?

'I don't know what to do with your hands,' said Rain. She reached across and took one of Demoyte's hands and laid it across the top of one of the books. No, that wouldn't do.

'I know what to do with your hands,' said Demoyte. He captured the one that was still straying about on the table and lifted it to his lips.

Rain smiled faintly. She looked down at Demoyte, not studying him this time. Now it was quite dark in the room, although the garden was glowing still.

'Have I given you a bad day?' she said. She did not try to free her hand. Demoyte clasped it in both of his, stroking it gently and conveying it frequently to his lips.

'You've kept me sitting here in one position and an agony of rheumatism for the whole afternoon, that's all,' said Demoyte. 'Let me see how much you've done by now.' He lumbered over to the easel. Rain followed him and sat down on a chair to look at the canvas. She felt exhausted.

'Good God!' said Demoyte. 'Is that all you've done, child, in the last two hours? You're still on that square inch of carpet. At this rate you'll be with us for years. But perhaps that's what you want – like Penelope, never finishing her work? I wouldn't complain. And I can think of one or two other people who wouldn't complain either.' Demoyte leaned on the back of Rain's chair and touched her dark hair. His enormous hand could cup the back of her head in its palm. He drew his hand slowly down on to her neck.

'The picture *will* be finished,' said Rain, 'and I shall go. I shall be sorry.' She spoke solemnly.

'Yes,' said Demoyte. He fetched another chair and placed it very close to her and sat down, his knee brushing hers. 'When the picture is finished,' he said, 'you will go, and I shall not see you again.'

He spoke in a factual voice, as if requiring no reply. Rain watched him gravely.

'When you go,' said Demoyte, 'you will leave behind a picture of me, whereas what I shall be wanting is a picture of you.'

'Every portrait is a self-portrait,' said Rain. 'In portraying you I portray myself.'

'Spiritual nonsense,' said Demoyte. 'I want to see your flesh, not your soul.'

'Artists do paint themselves in their sitters,' said Rain, 'often in quite material ways. Burne-Jones made all his people look thin and gloomy like himself. Romney always reproduced his own nose, Van Dyck his own hands.' She reached out and drew her hand in the half darkness along the rough cord of Demoyte's coat, seeking his wrist. She sighed.

'Your father, yes,' said Demoyte, 'he taught you many things, but you are yourself a different being and must live so. Here I prose on, an old man, and must be forgiven. You know how much at this moment I want to take you in my arms, and that I will not do so. Rain, Rain. Tell me instead, why do you think artists make their sitters resemble them? Will you paint me to resemble you? Would such a thing be possible?'

'I don't know,' said Rain, 'whether it shows a limitation, if we want to see ourselves in the world about us. Perhaps it is rather that we *feel* our own face, as a three-dimensional mass, from within – and when we try in a painting to realize what another person's face *is*, we come back to the experience of our own.'

'You think that we feel our faces as if they were masks?' said Demoyte. He reached out and touched Rain's face, drawing his finger gently down over the outline of her nose.

Miss Handforth came noisily into the room and switched the light on. Rain sat quite still, but Demoyte jerked awkwardly backwards, jarring his chair along the floor.

'Deary me!' said Miss Handforth. 'I had no idea you two were still in here, why you've been sitting in the dark! Mr Mor has just come, I sent him up to the library, because I thought you were upstairs.' Miss Handforth strode across the room and began lustily pulling the curtains. The garden was dark.

'I wish you wouldn't enter rooms like a battering ram, Handy,' said Demoyte. 'Leave all that and go and tell Mor to come down here.'

'Do you want all that stuff left here, or am I to clear it up every night?' asked Miss Handforth, indicating the white sheet, and easel, and the other paraphernalia.

'Please may it remain here for the moment?' said Rain.

'You propose to take possession of my drawing-room, do you?' said Demoyte. 'The whole house stinks of paint already. Go on, Handy, go away and fetch that man down from the library.'


When Mor had walked towards the front door of his house on the previous evening he had still not been sure whether or not he would tell his wife the whole story. The interference of Tim Burke seemed to complicate the picture. Frankness on Mor's part would now be an exposure not only of himself but of his friend. Yet it was not this that moved Mor so much as a feeling that Tim's lie, added to his own, made of the whole thing something far more considerable in appearance than it really was. There was something about the way in which Tim had said, 'I saw you in a car with a girl,' which made Mor suddenly see the situation from the outside; and seen from the outside it did look as if it were something, whereas seen from the inside it was of course nothing, nothing at all. So that, it seemed obscurely to Mor as he walked back, to tell Nan the truth would really be to mislead her. There was no way of telling the story which would not make Nan think that there was more to it than there was. So, in a way, it was more in accordance with the facts to let Nan think that nothing had occurred. For nothing *had* occurred and the whole thing would soon be buried in the past. Except for a few inevitable social meetings he would see no more of Miss Carter, and that would be that. Mor echoed again his words to Tim Burke: 'We won't speak of it again' – and this seemed to be the right note to strike. Mor knew he could trust Tim's tact and discretion absolutely. Whereas, if he told Nan, Mor knew that really, in one way or another, he would never hear the end of it, and that the incident, even against his will, would then be lent a permanent and indelible significance.

When he entered the house he had still not resolved the problem. He was met in the hall by Nan, who said, 'Well, dear, you're home at last, are you, I thought you were never coming. Look, your supper's in the oven, and I've made a cake, which is on the sideboard, if you want some. Felicity's had her supper and gone to the pictures, and I've got to go out this very minute to see Mrs Prewett. You can imagine how delightful that prospect is! It's Women's Institute tomorrow night and she wants to hear my views on how to get the women to come along other than by dances and film shows. I told her over the phone that there isn't any other way, but she still wants me to come over. I hope I won't be long, but you know how that woman pins one down!' And a minute later Nan had gone out of the front door.

Mor sat down to his supper. He felt that that, in effect, decided the matter. If he had been going to tell the truth that was the moment for telling it. But the moment had passed now. Nan had accepted the fiction, and it was better that he should not upset her view. If she had questioned him he would have owned up. As it was, he would leave things as they were. After he had cut the cake, however, it occurred to Mor that there was something else that needed doing, and that was to let Miss Carter know that he had changed his mind about telling his wife. If he did not do this, and do it soon, she might drop a brick. He paused to ponder over this. Then he began to wonder whether she would have told Demoyte about their outing. This notion made Mor uneasy. He thought, I must see her tomorrow, find out whether she's told Demoyte, and if necessary shut them both up. Mor knew that he could rely on Demoyte's discretion also; but he could not help hoping that the old man was not to be in the secret. He could imagine the sarcasms which he would have to suffer if he was. He thought it just possible that Miss Carter would not have told him. She was a curious independent sort of a girl and would know how to keep her own counsel.

On further reflection Mor decided that since the matter was of a certain delicacy it was quite likely that Miss Carter would not have told Demoyte about it. It also occurred to him that it might be difficult, in the nearer future, to procure a long enough interview alone with Miss Carter to make the matter decently clear. He was teaching most of tomorrow, and could only be sure of getting away at some time in the evening, when Miss Carter was likely to be in company, at least with De-moyte, and perhaps with other people too. He knew that it was hardly safe to ring her up, since with Handy as intermediary no embarrassment would be spared. Mor decided that the most sensible thing to do was to write a letter, to carry it in person over to Demoyte's house, to see Miss Carter alone if possible, and if not to find some opportunity of passing the letter to her unobserved.

Mor found these speculations extremely absorbing. Once the matter was settled, of course, he would have no more to do with the young lady, and would scarcely see her except at a party or two and at the ceremonial dinner. There was no prob-lem about that. All the same, when it seemed to him that it was necessary to write her a letter he found that this prospect was not unpleasant. He went upstairs to his bedroom, which also served as his study, collected plenty of paper, and settled down to draft the epistle. It was not a simple task. There were interesting problems about how to begin, and end it, how much to say, and how exactly to say what was said. Mor had several tries. What he wrote at first was:

Dear Miss Carter,
    When I arrived back last night I found that the friend whom I had intended to visit had officiously supported my false story. So in the circumstances I have decided not to tell the true one. I hope you will understand – and excuse me for having involved you in this deception.

I hope that the car is all right. It grieved me to leave you like that. I insist on being allowed to pay the bills.

Yours sincerely,

William Mor

Mor looked at this for a while, crossed out 'It grieved me, etc.', and finally tore the whole thing up and sat, brooding. He reflected that if he was indeed to pay the bills he would have to have further clandestine converse with Miss Carter. He could of course simply tell her to send him the bills. But would she? That girl, of course not. Alternatively he could send her a sum of money. This was difficult and embarrassing. To send too small a sum would be mean and disgraceful – whereas the idea of sending a sum large enough to be sure that it was not too small unnerved Mor, who was, if not exactly parsimonious, at any rate extremely careful with his money. He decided eventually not to say anything at all about paying the bills in the letter and to trust that he would have an opportunity in the ordinary course of events to discuss this with Miss Carter before she left. He then wrote a second letter as follows:

Dear Miss Carter,

This is just to tell you that I have decided, after all, for reasons which it would take too long to explain, to deceive my wife. I hasten to tell you this so that you may act accordingly; and I beg you humbly to excuse me for having involved you in this unpleasantness. I hope that the Riley survived its strange experience and will soon be on the road once more. I am sorry to have been, in that adventure, so inept and so useless.

Yours sincerely,

William Mor

P.S. – Have you told Mr Demoyte about our expedition? If you *have*, I should be grateful if you could signify as much to me, discreetly, as soon as possible. And please burn this letter.

There's no need to bring Tim Burke into it, thought Mor, and brevity and vagueness except on essential points, are what we need here. He studied this version for some time; then he destroyed it too. It was scarcely necessary, after all, to tell her to burn the letter. This request only made the thing seem more significant and conspiratorial. She would have enough sense not to leave such a document lying about. Mor started again. This time he would aim at being very brief and business-like, and in this way he would also be able, he felt, to strike a more sincere and serious note. He wrote as follows:

I am very sorry – I have decided after all *not* to tell my wife about our outing. So I beg you to keep silent about it. I apologize very humbly for all the trouble I've caused you, in this connection and about the car. I hated leaving you alone – and I hope the car will be all right.

W. M.

Mor looked at this for a while. It satisfied him, and he sealed it up in a plain envelope. He had left out any mention of Demoyte – and thought that he would rely on finding out somehow, from the girl or from Demoyte himself, whether anything had been told. If he found Miss Carter alone he could ask her, if he found her with Demoyte he could rely on the old man's making some mocking remark on the subject fairly quickly, if he knew anything about it. If he found company at Brayling's Close, that would be a problem – but one which he would deal with as he found it. Looking at his watch, Mor discovered that he had passed two hours in total absorption drafting the letters. Felicity had come home and had retired to her own room. Nan was still not back. Mor hid the envelope carefully and burnt the fragments of the earlier drafts. He felt as if he had accomplished a good evening's work. He went to bed and slept excellently.

When Mor awoke in the morning he found himself much less sanguine about the whole business than he had been the night before. He felt regret and distress at finding that not only had he decided to deceive Nan but he had even made complicated arrangements to do so. It also occurred to him now, and shocked him, that he had been entirely responsible for damaging a very expensive car – whereas yesterday evening the fate of the Riley had figured in his mind, absurdly as it now seemed, as part of an adventure. Mor sobered himself considerably by thinking about the bill. As for the course of action which he had chosen, he felt himself, for all his misgivings, to be committed to it, and indeed the tasks of the day left him little time for reflection; and as the afternoon wore on what more and more recurred to his mind, in the intervals of teaching, was the not unpleasant prospect of going over that evening to Brayling's Close and seeing Miss Carter again, and all this with a certain inevitability.

Mor had supper at home at seven-thirty, saw Nan off to her Women's Institute meeting, and then, at about a quarter past eight, left the house on foot. He told Nan, who was not particularly interested, that he was going to call on Demoyte, a thing which he often did on evenings when she was engaged. Mor usually cycled over to the Close, but this time he felt more like walking. It was a very clear warm evening. The good weather certainly seemed likely to last, thought Mor, and they could even hope for a fine day for the House Match. He walked along, wrapped in a pleasant pensive veil. The more disagreeable aspects of the task before him were not then in his mind. He seemed to enjoy the warmth and light of the evening with a simplicity which he had not known for many years; and he wondered why so much of his life was passed in fretfulness, and why moments such as these were so very rare. He walked a little way along the main road, and then struck off it across some fields by a path which led him eventually into Demoyte's garden. As the low stone wall and the mulberry trees came in sight, however, excitement, nervousness replaced his tranquillity. The conveying of a clandestine letter was something which Mor had not done before, and which he hoped he would not have to do again.

He entered the hall without ringing, and was greeted by Miss Handforth, who told him, 'His Lordship is in the library.' Mor mounted the stairs, but found the library empty. It was dark now, lowering with books, and melancholy. Its silence caught Mor, and half relieved he sat down for a moment beside one of the tables. Then Handy returned, and sticking her head round the door announced, 'Sorry, he's down in the drawing-room with Miss Thingumajite.'

Mor went down, knocked at the drawing-room door, and entered. The drawing-room was softly lit by many lamps and the curtains were drawn across. Demoyte was standing, leaning against the mantelpiece, and Miss Carter was sitting in a chair, enthroned upon a sort of white sheet beside an easel which was erected in one corner of the room. Mor was surprised and pleased to see the easel. It was the first time that he had had any material evidence that Miss Carter was a painter.

'Good-evening,' said Mor. 'Good-evening. I see the picture has begun.'

'Begun!' said Demoyte. 'I've been sitting all day for a portrait of one of my rugs. Come and look at this masterpiece!'

Miss Carter rose and stood aside. Mor came and looked at the canvas. It seemed to be empty, except for one small finely worked square of colour in the corner. A few faint lines were scattered about on the rest of the expanse. It looked odd to Mor, but he supposed Miss Carter knew what she was doing.

'Well, well,' said Mor.

Demoyte laughed explosively. 'He can't think of anything to say,' he said. 'Never mind, missie, they'll all be crawling to you later on.'

Mor was irritated. Demoyte was making it look as if he had been rude. 'Miss Carter knows I have complete faith in her talent,' said Mor. This sounded idiotic. He tried to help it out by giving Miss Carter a rather rueful and very friendly look. She smiled back with such warmth that Mor was quite consoled.

'That's cant,' said Demoyte. 'You know nothing whatever about Miss Carter's talent or anyone else's. This man doesn't know a Rubens from a Rembrandt. He lives in a monochrome world.'

Mor felt this was cruel, as well as being unjust. He tried to carry it off. 'I spoke of faith,' he said. 'Blessed is he who has not seen, but has believed! I believe in Miss Carter.' This was weak, but Miss Carter was still smiling at him in an encouraging way and that seemed to make the words stand up.

'Oh well,' said Demoyte, 'now you're talking about Miss Carter, not her talent. This conversation is degenerating into imbecility. Have you dined?'

'Thank you, sir, yes,' said Mor.

'So have we,' said Demoyte, 'and Miss Carter was painting until a few minutes ago. I suggest we all have some brandy. Miss Carter must be exhausted. She's been painting, or pretending to paint, for about six hours.'

'I *am* tired,' said Miss Carter. 'Mr Demoyte doesn't believe it, but I've done a great deal of work today.'

Mor was surprised to hear this. He had vaguely imagined that after the trials of yesterday Miss Carter would have spent today lying down in a state of collapse. He gave her a look of admiration, which he hoped she was able to interpret. Miss Carter was wearing her trousers, and had tossed off her overall soon after he entered to reveal a plain white cotton shirt. With her short dark hair and the strong dusky red of her cheeks she looked like Pierrot, and had, it suddenly seemed to Mor, something of his grotesque melancholy.

Mor and Miss Carter moved to chairs beside the hearth. Demoyte was fiddling in a corner cupboard. 'Where the hell are the brandy glasses?' he said. 'Handy will use them for drinking lemonade out of in the kitchen. I must go and find them. You two can amuse yourselves.' He turned and went out of the door, leaving it open.

Mor knew that now was his chance to give Miss Carter the letter. He was overcome with confusion and stood up, blushing violently. Miss Carter looked up at him, a trifle surprised. Mor fumbled in his pocket for the letter, and took a moment or two to find it. Then he drew it forth and threw it quickly on to her knee. It fell to the floor, and she picked it up with a puzzled look. As she did this, a movement caught Mor's eye and he looked over Miss Carter's head to see that Demoyte was standing at the open door and had witnessed the scene. Miss Carter, who had her back to the door, had not observed him. She put the letter quickly into her handbag, which lay beside her, and looked up again at Mor. Demoyte withdrew for a moment and then re-entered the room noisily bearing the glasses.

'They were on the dining-room table,' he said. 'Handy had got them that far on the way back. Now I must go and see about the brandy.' He left the room again, closing the door behind him with a bang.

Mor felt acute distress at Demoyte's having seen the passing of the letter. Everything seemed to be conspiring against him to make something which was really unimportant look like something important. Now both Tim Burke and Demoyte would be thinking that something was going on, whereas in reality nothing was going on. What Mor had hoped to terminate and bury was being lent a spurious significance by these witnesses. He looked at Miss Carter dumbly, almost angrily.

'The car is all right,' she said in a soft voice. She had risen too. They stood together near the mantelpiece.

'I'm very glad,' said Mor, 'and I'm so sorry I was so hopeless yesterday. Did you tell Mr Demoyte about it?'

'No, I didn't,' said Miss Carter. 'Perhaps it was silly of me, but I felt somehow I didn't want to. I just said the car had gone for repairs.'

'It's just as well,' said Mor. He spoke softly too. 'I haven't told my wife either. That note explains.'

'Then it's to be a secret between us,' said Miss Carter.

Mor didn't care for this phrase, but he nodded. 'I insist on paying the bills,' he said. 'You must let me know—'

'Of course not!' said Miss Carter. 'The insurance will pay, that's what they're for!'

At that moment Demoyte returned noisily into the room. 'Why,' he said, 'the brandy was in here all the time!'

Mor now felt a deep sadness that what were probably the last words which he would ever exchange tête-à-tête with Miss Carter had been such futile ones. He sat down gloomily and accepted a glass of brandy.

Miss Carter seemed to be in good spirits. She turned to Mor. 'Do you mind if I draw you,' she said 'as you sit drinking the cognac?'

Mor was surprised and flattered at this request. He blushed again, this time with pleasure. 'Please do!' he said. 'Am I all right as I am?'

'Exactly as you are,' said Miss Carter, 'is how I want you.' She picked up her sketch book, produced a pencil from her handbag, and began to draw, sipping brandy now and then as she did so.

Mor sat perfectly still, conscious on the one side of the gentle intent glances of Miss Carter, and on the other of the sardonic covertly amused attention of Demoyte. He felt like a man with one cheek exposed to the fragrant breezes of the spring, while upon the other is let loose an autumnal shower of chilling rain.

Demoyte seemed to have decided not to take any part in the conversation. He sat at his ease looking first at Mor and then at

Miss Carter. Mor thought, he wants to force us to talk so that he can observe us, the old fox.

Miss Carter said, 'What is your son's name, Mr Mor?'

'Donald,' said Mor.

'I was so sorry I didn't meet him the other day,' said Miss Carter, her eyes moving to and fro between Mor and her sketch book. 'Have you any other children?'

'I have a daughter,' said Mor, 'about fourteen. Her name is Felicity.' It gave him pain, somehow, to speak of his children to Miss Carter. She herself must be, he reckoned, no more than eight years older than Donald.

'What is Donald going to do?' said Miss Carter.

'He's taking College entrance in chemistry in a few weeks,' said Mor. 'I suppose he'll be some sort of chemist.' Mor wished he could have said something else about Donald.

'And your daughter,' said Miss Carter, 'what will she do?'

'I don't know,' said Mor. 'I expect she'll have another term or two at school and then do a secretarial course next year. She's not very clever.'

Demoyte could not let this pass. 'Oh, what rot, Mor!' he said. 'You don't seriously mean that you're going to let Felicity leave school? She's just slow at developing. After a year or two in the Sixth Form she'll be a different person. She ought to go to a university. Even if she couldn't get into Oxford or Cambridge, she could go to London. Give the girl a chance, for heaven's sake. Or would you rather see her as a little secretary reading the fashion magazines?'

Mor felt hurt and irritated. He turned towards Demoyte, but turned hastily back again as he saw Miss Carter's pencil poised. In fact, he was of Demoyte's opinion. But there was Nan, and the financial situation to be considered. Anyhow, nothing had been settled yet. He had only answered in that way so as to have something definite to say – and also, it suddenly occurred to him, because he had wanted, for some reason, to make everything look as dreary as possible.

He said to Miss Carter, 'Mr Demoyte has a rather exaggerated view of the benefits of education. He thinks that no one can stand up unless he's had the stuffing put in by his school and college.'

Demoyte said sharply, 'Don't attribute that cant to me, if

you please. Someone like Miss Carter, for instance, could stand up whatever her education had been. It's people like you and your daughter that need stuffing put into them.'

This was so spitefully uttered that Mor was silent. He felt quite unable to reply. Miss Carter's pencil was still.

Demoyte was sorry at once, and said, 'There now, Mor, I didn't really mean it, but you provoked me.'

'That's all right, sir,' said Mor.

There was a moment's silence. Miss Carter then said, 'If you'll both excuse me, I think I'll be off to bed. I really am very tired indeed, I can hardly keep my eyes open.'

Demoyte was obviously upset. He seemed to think that Miss Carter was retiring as a protest against his rudeness. She tried gently to convince him that it was not so. Mor looked on. He felt intense disappointment that Miss Carter was going away so soon. It was the last time he would really see her. He drained his glass.

'May I at least see the picture of myself,' he said, 'before you go?'

Miss Carter looked into the sketch book and then closed it. She looked rather oddly at Mor. Then she said, 'No, I don't think so. It's not very good. Sorry, I'd rather not show it to you, it really isn't anything.' She moved away towards the door. Mor stood by the mantelpiece while she lingered in the doorway, still disputing with Demoyte. Then she said 'Good-night' abruptly, and disappeared.

Demoyte came back to the hearth, shuffling his feet. Without a word he refilled Mor's glass. They both sat down and looked at each other irritably. Mor thought it quite likely that it *was* Demoyte's rudeness that had driven Miss Carter away, and he felt correspondingly annoyed with Demoyte. They sat for a while, glumly.

'You haven't got to rush away, have you?' said Demoyte.

Mor knew that, for all his irritation, the old man badly wanted him to stay.

'No, sir,' said Mor. 'This is Nan's Women's Institute night. I'm in no hurry.' They settled down to their brandy. Mor wondered if Demoyte would mention the incident of the letter. He was sure he was thinking about it.

'She is so small,' Demoyte began thoughtfully. 'What is she like? A small boy, of course, but what else, with her small hands and her big eyes, and the way she togs herself up in bright colours? She's rather like a clown or a performing dog – in fact, very like a performing dog, with a pretty check jacket on and a bow on its tail, so anxious to please, and doing everything as if it were not quite natural, and with those eyes.'

Mor thought this disrespectful. 'She seems very serious about her painting,' he said.

'You're a dull dull fellow, Mor,' Demoyte said suddenly.

'What's that one for, sir?' said Mor patiently.

Demoyte smiled. 'I saw you pass her a letter,' he said. 'I ask no more about that. I just wonder whether you can really *see* her.'

They looked at each other. Mor thought to himself, the old man is a little bit in love with her – and he wondered what Miss Carter would think if she knew of the tenderness she had inspired in this unexpected quarter. He felt he should disillusion Demoyte. 'The letter had no sentimental significance,' he said.

Demoyte looked at him critically, a little sceptically. 'Then so much the worse for you, my boy,' he said. 'Let's talk about something else – Felicity for instance. You didn't mean what you said just now about the secretarial course?'

'Not altogether,' said Mor, 'but it's not so easy to see what to do. An academic career would be a gamble for Felicity. She might develop – I believe she would – but she might just bungle it, and not be happier in the end. And there's the question of financing her. Even with a county grant, it'll cost a packet to put Donald through Cambridge. And I just don't know that I can manage it for both of them.'

'Mor,' said Demoyte, 'are you going to be an M.P.?'

'I'm going to be a candidate,' said Mor. 'Whether I'll be an M.P. depends on the electorate.'

'It's a safe seat,' said Demoyte. 'So you've decided at last. Nan came round, did she?'

'I haven't told her yet,' said Mor. He spoke tonelessly, swinging his brandy round in the glass and looking down into it.

'I take back what I said just now,' said Demoyte. 'I only said it to hurt you anyway, as you well know – and because I was for a moment – never mind that. I'm immensely glad that you've decided. My only sadness is that I may lose your friendship when you're an important man.'

This sounded so grotesque that Mor had to look up to see

whether the old man was serious. 'I'll never be important,' said Mor, 'so don't worry!' He felt too moved to reply seriously.

'I'm immensely glad,' said Demoyte. 'You'll get out of this hole, away from pious Evvy and dreary Prewett, and dotty Bledyard, up to London, where you'll meet all sorts of people. And women. Out of this hole, where all one can do is pass the hours until it's time to die.'

Nan had called Demoyte morbid. Mor himself knew something of the old man's moods, and of the melancholy which afflicted him when he was alone. He said briskly, 'Come, sir, none of that. I certainly don't despise this place. I only hope I'll be up to the other job. And by the way, please don't mention this to *anyone* just yet, not till it's officially made public.'

'With an M.P.'s salary,' said Demoyte doggedly, 'you can send Felicity to college.'

'That's just what I think I can't do,' said Mor. 'It's too risky. In my present situation at least I know exactly how much money I can reckon on. But in *that* job, with unpredictable expenses, it'll be a long time before I know where I stand. Anyhow, Nan would never agree. It'll be hard enough to get her to accept the M.P. plan at all – and she'd never agree if we were going to run this extra financial risk as well. I might get away with one of these things, but not with both.' As he put it thus, it occurred to Mor that in a way he was sacrificing Felicity's future to his own. This was an extremely unpleasant thought.

'Oh, Nan, Nan, Nan!' said Demoyte. 'I'm tired of that woman's name. Who is she that she has to be consulted about every damn thing that you do?'

'She's my wife,' said Mor.

'You're as timid as a water-snail,' said Demoyte, 'and a meaner man with money I never encountered. Pah! I despise this meanness. Felicity must have her chance. Listen, and don't turn down this proposal because I've been rude and you feel you have to put up a show of pride. Think of your daughter's future instead. I'll pay for Felicity to go to the university. She'll get a county grant anyway, so it won't be much. I've got a pile of money in the bank, and there's nothing to spend it on in this God-forsaken backwater, and as you know I hate travelling, and as you also know I'll very shortly be dead. So let's have no false reluctance or other posturing. I want that girl to go to college and there's an end to the matter. I shall be wretched if she doesn't. Don't cross me here.'

Mor sat rigid, leaning forward and still staring into his glass. He suddenly felt as if he wanted to weep. He didn't dare to look at Demoyte. 'You are immensely good, sir,' he said, 'and I am very moved indeed, I think you know how much, by your saying this. I won't pretend that I just couldn't accept the offer. But it needs some thinking over. I might be able to afford it myself. Also, quite honestly, I'm not sure that Nan would agree to our accepting money from you.'

'Oh, give me patience!' said Demoyte. 'Then deceive her, boy! Tell her it's a bonus from Evvy, tell her you found it in the street, tell her you won it on a horse race! Deceive her, deceive her! Only don't bother me with this nonsense.'

'I'll think it over, sir,' said Mor. Demoyte then filled up Mor's glass and they began to talk about something else.

It was about an hour later that, rather full of brandy, Mor decided that he must go home. Demoyte was already getting sleepy, and Mor saw him up the stairs to his bedroom. Then he came down again, put on his coat, and let himself quietly out of the front door.

He had to pause immediately when he got outside, so brilliant and heavily perfumed was the night. The moon was rising, and was visible as a great source of light behind the trees, and there was an immense concourse of stars, crowding up towards the Milky Way. It was one of those nights, so rare in England, when the stars give positive light to the earth. The garden was present on either side of him, clearly visible and, although he could feel no breeze, rustling softly. He looked up and could see the light on in Demoyte's room, above the door on the left. The right-hand window was the end window of the library, which stood above Handy's boudoir. It was dark. Mor walked across the gravel on to the grass and passed through the door which led to the big lawn at the side of the house, outside the drawing-room window. As he walked, the moon rose above the trees and cast his shadow before him. He paused, enjoying the sensation of walking quite silently upon the moonlit grass, and turned to see his footsteps left behind him, clearly marked in the dew and revealed by the moon. He felt an extreme lightness, as if he had become a spirit. Very distantly the traffic rumbled upon the main road. But here the silence hung in the air like an odour. He moved out into the middle of the lawn and looked up at the house.

The room at the end of the house to his right, which adjoined the library and had one window looking out at the back and one window looking on to the lawn, was the best guestroom. There was a light on in this room. The curtains were tightly drawn. That must be Miss Carter's room, thought Mor. She hasn't gone to bed after all. It must have been a fiction, about being tired. She must have been fed up with Demoyte. Or with me, he thought ruefully. Then quite unexpectedly Mor was struck with a dolorous pain. He was really unsure at first whether it was a physical pain or some sort of thought, so quickly did it come upon him. He realized in a moment that it was an agonizing wish to see Miss Carter again, to see her soon, to see her now. Mor stood quite still, breathing rather fast. I'm drunk, he said to himself. He never remembered feeling quite like this before. He wanted terribly, desperately, to see Miss Carter. I must be ill, thought Mor. He wondered what to do. It was all so inexplicable. He thought, it would be quite easy to go back into the house. The front door is still unlocked. And go up the stairs and along the corridor and knock at her bedroom door. At the thought that this was possible and that absolutely nothing stopped him from doing it if he wished Mor felt so amazed that he swayed and almost fell. The pain of knowing that it was possible was for a moment extreme.

As he recovered himself and turned slightly he saw that someone was watching him, standing in the shadow of one of the trees. Mor froze with fear and indecision. He took a step or two back. Then the figure began to move and come towards him, gliding forward noiselessly across the grass. For one wild moment Mor thought that it was Miss Carter. He tried to say something, but the silence stifled his voice. Then he saw that the figure was too tall. It was Miss Handforth.

'Why, it's Mr Mor!' said Miss Handforth in her sonorous voice, scattering the moonlit night about her in fragments. 'You gave me quite a turn, standing there so quiet.'

Mor turned about and began to walk quickly back towards the front of the house. He didn't, above all, want Miss Carter's attention drawn to the fact that he had been standing outside looking up at her window. The strange sensation had quite gone. Now he only wanted to get away, and not to have to hear

Miss Handforth's brassy voice echoing through the darkness.

She followed him, still talking. 'I saw you out of the drawing-room window as I was pulling back the curtains, and I said to myself, there's an intruder out there on the lawn. So I had to come out and see who it was.'

'That was very brave of you, Handy,' said Mor in a low voice. They had reached the front of the house now, and Mor had gone a little way down the drive, followed by Miss Handforth. He saw that Demoyte's light was out.

'You can't be too careful,' said Miss Handforth. 'There really are some odd characters about. There's someone been reported hanging around this vicinity lately, a vagabond man, a gipsy. Probably waiting to see who he can rob.'

'I hope you lock the house up well at night,' said Mor. He felt that he was being shown off the premises. They had almost reached the end of the drive.

'He won't steal anything from *our* house!' said Miss Handforth. 'Good-night, Mr Mor.'

'Good-night, Handy,' said Mor. He felt extremely disconsolate. He decided to walk back by the main road.

# CHAPTER EIGHT

'You can't behave *anyhow* to people and expect them to love you just the same!' said Nan to Felicity.

'That's just what I do expect,' said Felicity sulkily, and went back into her bedroom.

Mor, overhearing this exchange from downstairs, thought, she is right, that is just what we do expect. He looked at his watch. He was teaching at two-fifteen. It was time to go. He called good-bye, and as no one answered, left the house, banging the front door behind him.

Nan pursued Felicity into her bedroom. 'You have a *good look* in here,' she said, 'and you'll probably find it. It can't have gone very far. If you don't see it, you'd better look in my room again. I don't want to discover it in my slippers or in my bed.'

'It's no good,' said Felicity miserably, 'it must have crawled away into some crack in the floorboards and it'll die in there!' She began to cry.

Nan looked on exasperated. 'What possessed you to bring a nasty slug into the house, anyway?' she said.

'It wasn't nasty,' said Felicity. 'It was very sweet when it stretched itself out, it was so long and smooth, and its horns were so nice. I only left it for a moment. It was curled up into a ball, like a lump of jelly, and it kept moving to and fro, but wouldn't bring its horns out. I thought it was stuck, and I went for some water to wash it with, and when I came back it was gone.'

'Well, let's hope it went out of the window,' said Nan.

'I'm sure it didn't. It's just lost inside the house somewhere. I'll never find it now.' Felicity blew her nose.

'You've changed your room back again,' said Nan with disapproval.

'I like it better this way,' said Felicity. She threw herself on the bed and went on crying.

'Oh, stop it, dear,' said Nan, 'do stop it, there's absolutely nothing to cry about. Just pull yourself together and do something practical. I've told you several times to leave out your summer frocks for washing. If I don't do them today they won't be ready in time for going to Dorset.' She went away downstairs.

Felicity went on crying for a while. Then she dried her tears and began searching again for the slug. It was not to be found anywhere. A few more tears fell as she pictured its fate. It was all my fault, thought Felicity. It was so happy out there in the garden eating the plants – and I had to go and bring it indoors, away from its world. I won't ever do such a thing again.

Felicity went into the bathroom and examined her eyes. They were rather red. She washed her face in cold water. Then she decided that she would go into school and look for Don. This was something which was strictly forbidden by all the authorities concerned. Her presence in his room could bring quite dire penalties down upon Donald – and Felicity herself had frequently been told by her parents never to enter the precincts of St Bride's except when officially authorized to do so. Felicity, though strongly endowed with a sense of right and wrong, did not have any particularly reverential attitude towards authority, and her conscience functioned vigorously enough in complete detachment from the adult world of prohibition and exhortation which surrounded her, and which she often failed completely to make sense of. Felicity could not see that there was anything innately wrong in her going into St Bride's to see her brother – and this being so, the only remaining question was whether she could do so with impunity. She changed her dress, and combed her hair, making herself look as pleasant as possible. Then she ran downstairs and prepared to leave the house.

'Where are you off to, dear?' asked Nan from the kitchen.

'To the library,' said Felicity at random, and leaving the house she ran along towards the main road.

As she ran she whistled softly to Liffey, who soon came bounding up to run beside her, turning to look at her every now and then, and smiling as dogs do. She never came into the house now, or entered any human habitation. Since the dissolution of her material body Liffey had become rather larger, and now had black ears and a black tail, to signalize her infernal origin. There was as yet no sign of Angus, but Felicity knew, now that Liffey had come, that it would not be long before she saw him, in one or other of his disguises. Felicity passed the

115

main gate of St Bride's and began walking down the hill. A dried-up grass verge separated her from the dual carriageway. Up and down the hill the cars roared, going from London to the coast or from the coast back to London. They came savagely up like bulls and sped carelessly down like birds, and the swiftness of their passage made the air rock, so that as Felicity walked along her dress flapped in a perpetual breeze. Towards the top of the hill the school was shut in by a high wall, with broken glass on it, above which could be seen the upper windows of the Phys and Gym building. Half-way down the hill, the wall was changed for a high and well-made fence, above which could be seen the red-tiled roof of one of the houses, Prewett's in fact, where Donald lived, and then lower down the tree tops of the wood. After this, there was to be seen the green-glass roof of the squash court, and to be heard the frantic shouts and splashing from the swimming pool. Here the edge of the school domain began to swing a little farther away from the road, and a grass verge appeared on the inside of the pavement, and widened gradually as the arterial road and the grounds of the school parted company. By now the white walls and slated roof of Mr Everard's house were plainly visible at the bottom of the hill.

Felicity followed primly along the pavement, as if she had no interest at all in the school. Liffey, who had been amusing herself by passing spectrally through the bodies of several other dogs who were coming up the hill, was running along now by the fence, and in an instant had passed through it. Felicity paused and looked about her. Then she left the pavement and began to follow the fence, which was now turning sharply away from the road. At a certain point it met at right angles with another fence which was that of a private garden which belonged to a house in a side road. At the end of this garden, where the garden fence met the school fence, there was a shrubbery. Between the two fences at that point there was a very narrow place through which a slim body could squeeze itself. Felicity's body, though still of a material nature, was extremely slim, and in a moment she was kneeling among the bushes at the bottom of the private garden.

Here she could work at ease. The school fence was composed of slats of wood, each of them about two feet broad. One summer holiday she and Donald had been at pains to extract the nails which held one of these slats in place, and secure the slat again by means of nails which projected at an angle from the adjoining wood on both sides. Thus, by working the slat a little, it could be slipped out, leaving a gap through which a body similarly slim could pass. After pausing a moment to make sure that there was no one in the garden, Felicity began to tilt the slat until it cleared the nails on one side. The other side then slipped out easily and Felicity slithered through into the grounds of the school. She then reached back through the hole and drew the wood into place again.

She found herself in a dreary gardener's wilderness of rubbish heaps and abandoned bonfires behind some trees below Mr Everard's house. She began to walk along to her right so as to come up into the wood on the opposite side from the squash courts. This part of the grounds was less frequented, and if a neglected shrubbery which was part of Evvy's garden was taken into account, there was good cover all the way up the hill. Liffey, who had been waiting on the inside of the hole, glided noiselessly ahead of her, charming her footsteps to silence. Felicity wondered if she would see Angus now. She had only met him once within the precincts of the school, on an occasion when she had entered illicitly and he came upon her in the form of a man sitting in a tree, who observed her quietly without saying anything, and waited while she went past. That was eerie. Felicity preferred Angus disguised as a bricklayer or the driver of a police car. Remembering this occasion she felt frightened for a moment. Liffey disappeared, as she always did at such times. By now Felicity was in Evvy's shrubbery, making her way along, still close to the fence, by crawling under bushes and slinking behind clumps of greenery. The ground rose steeply here into the wood, and Felicity saw distantly between the trees the sunny open expanse of the playing fields. She moved on in the shadows at the edge of the wood. She would not strike dangerously across it until she was nearly level with Prewett's.

Suddenly she heard movements in the woodland not far in front of her, and then through the leaves she detected the flash of a white shirt. Felicity fell to the ground, and after lying still for a moment began to crawl forward. Liffey, who had appeared again, went before her, waving her black ears magically to silence any sounds which Felicity might make. This was just as well, as there was a good deal of bramble and crackly fern to be slithered through before Felicity could see what manner of creature she was stalking. At last a lucky vista gave her the view she wanted. Through a tunnel of green she could see, as in a crystal, a man sitting on the ground with his legs drawn up in front of him. He seemed to be alone. A book with wide white pages lay beside him. He had probably been sketching. He laid the book aside now and was staring straight ahead of him, his arms clasped round his knees. She watched him for a long time, nearly five minutes, during which his attitude did not vary. He was a strange-looking man with big hypnotic eyes and rather long hair. She thought that she had seen him before. After a while she remembered that he was the art master. She would have taken him for sure as a manifestation of Angus, except that Angus never appeared in the guise of people that she knew.

His extreme stillness began at last to frighten her. She was reminded of stories of yogis and magicians. She began to wriggle backwards out of the tunnel of fern; and when she was able to stand upright she ran away with careful silent strides diagonally across the middle of the wood, regardless of peril. She had managed by now to frighten herself thoroughly, and wanted only to get to Donald's room as quickly as possible. As she neared Prewett's, Liffey made off among the trees. In a moment Felicity emerged at speed from some sheltering bushes and shot in through a small green back door into Prewett's house. She paused a moment to listen. No pursuit and no sounds of imminent danger. She was in a disused cloakroom, which now served to store boys' trunks and cricket gear. Distant sounds of laughter and banging echoed through the house. There was a stale smell of wood and damp concrete and old perspiration and sports equipment. Felicity moved forward into a dark space out of which some wooden stairs rose into an equally dark region above. She fled up these – hid while voices near by became suddenly loud and then died away – then shot like a hare down the adjoining corridor and straight in through the door of Donald's room.

Donald was lying full length upon the table. The window was open, and one white clad foot was dangling somewhere outside. The other foot swung nonchalantly to and fro over the end of the table. His head was propped up on some books and a cricket pad. He was not alone. Underneath the table lay Jimmy Carde. Jimmy's head was flat upon the floor and his feet were propped up on the arm of a chair. One hand was dug behind the back of his neck, while the other hand had hold of Donald's ankle. At Felicity's violent entrance they both jumped, saw who it was, and resumed their former postures.

Felicity was very disappointed at not finding Donald alone. She had never been able to make out Jimmy Carde; and since he had become her brother's best friend a special hostility had existed between them.

'Fella,' said Donald, 'I have told you six times, and must I tell you again, that you should not come in here to see me.'

'No one spotted me,' said Felicity. 'I was very clever, the way I came through the wood. I spied on your art master. He was sitting there like a fakir in a sort of trance.'

'Bledyard will put the evil eye on you,' said Jimmy Carde. 'He stared at the school cat once all through chapel. It was sitting outside the window. And it died of convulsions three days later.'

Felicity shivered. 'He didn't look at me,' she said, 'though I looked at him.'

She began to wander round Donald's study to see if anything had changed. The room was small and papered with a flowery wallpaper which had faded to a universal colour of weak tea. A small mantelshelf was painted chocolate brown, and a matching brown cupboard contained Donald's bed, which was folded up during the day. A rickety bookcase with a chintz curtain contained Donald's chemistry books, a number of thrillers, some books on climbing, and *Three Men in a Boat*. A table, a chair and a carpet with a hole in it completed the room. Small pictures and photographs were dotted about at intervals on the walls, fixed by drawing-pins into the wallpaper. The position of these pictures was compulsory, since some previous inhabitant of the room had decorated it, shortly before he left, with a pungent and ingenious series of obscene drawings. In order to preserve these masterpieces for posterity it was the duty of each succeeding incumbent, enforced in case of need by the prefects of Prewett's house, to pin up pictures in the appropriate spots and see that they stayed in place.

Felicity studied Donald's pictures. She had not been told what lay behind them. She looked with interest, since she had not been in Donald's room since some time in the previous term. A photograph of Tensing on top of Everest. A small framed reproduction of the Snake Charmer of Henri Rousseau, donated by the parents. A coloured advertisement from the *New Yorker* showing some very fantastic-looking cars. A photo of the St Bride's second cricket eleven. That was new. Donald had only just made the second eleven. On the mantelpiece stood a photograph of the parents, with the glass cracked. Beside it was an enormous pocket-knife with several of its blades open, and a half-eaten doughnut.

'Can I eat the rest of this?' said Felicity. Permission was given. After all, there didn't seem to be much that was new.

'Have you anything else to eat?' said Felicity. 'I'm starving after that trek.'

Donald removed himself lazily from the table and began to dig in a black tin box which stood in the corner. Jimmy Carde got up, stretched, jumped on the table and squatted there, bumping up and down on his heels and drumming on the table top, in the rhythm of a recent dance tune. Felicity wished that he would go away.

'Here's a cake,' said Donald. 'We're not very flush at the moment.'

'That's an ancient British cake,' said Carde. 'It was part of Boadicea's rations for her troops.'

Felicity tried it. It tasted rather like that. She ate it all the same.

'How are the parents?' asked Donald.

'Mummy's in a fuss about going away,' said Felicity, her mouth full. 'I haven't seen much of Daddy.' She began to poke around in a coagulated mass of things on top of the bookcase. 'What's that?' She held up a long silvery object.

'That's a supersonic whistle,' said Donald.

'Supersonic!' said Felicity. 'What's it for, then?'

'People use it for calling dogs,' said Donald. 'It makes such a high note that only dogs can hear it and humans can't.'

'That's silly,' said Felicity. 'Why not call the dogs in the ordinary way? Of course, if it were a supersonic dog like—' She stopped, since the existence of the infernal Liffey was a secret between herself and her brother, and putting the whistle to her lips blew into it hard.

A thin piercing sound emerged. 'Oh, it's sonic!' said Felicity, disappointed.

'You have to blow harder,' said Jimmy Carde, 'and then the sound disappears.'

Felicity blew harder, the note rose higher and was succeeded by silence. 'How do I know it hasn't gone wrong?' she said suspiciously.

'It makes people neurotic,' said Carde. 'They hear it without knowing and it makes them feel queer. Chaps used to do it at the Nuremberg rallies, to demoralize the other chaps.'

'What are Nuremberg rallies?' asked Felicity.

'You're too young to know,' said Carde. 'Ask your big brother to tell you sometime.'

Felicity blushed, and said to Donald, 'Can I have it, please? You don't want it, do you?'

'Take it, Fella,' said Donald magnanimously, 'and come and blow it outside chapel during Evvy's sermon.'

'Have you seen Demoyters' glamour girl?' said Carde.

'No,' said Felicity, 'who's that?'

'Sleetie Carter,' said Carde. 'She's painting Demoyters' picture. Revvy Evvy wanted her in his house, but Demoyters pinched her instead. She's one of the rakish kind.' He burst into song. '*A nice girl, a day-cent gur-ril, but one of the rakish kind.*'

'Is that her real name?' said Felicity.

'She's called Rain Carter, for some obscure reason,' said Donald.

'I saw your dad showing her round,' said Carde. 'He didn't look as if he was fed up either. I wonder if Demoyters has made a pass at her yet?'

'I think it's a pretty name,' said Felicity. She felt extreme dislike for Jimmy Carde. Her eye roved round the room. She wanted to change the subject.

'Oh!' said Felicity. She had just seen something in the corner, peeping out from under a pile of coats and sweaters. She pounced upon it, and began to pull it out. It was an extremely long coil of fine nylon rope.

Felicity felt dizzy if she stood on a step-ladder, and she shared her mother's horror of the whole idea of climbing. 'Don,' she said, 'you *promised* you wouldn't!' She knelt down

121

with her arm thrust through the coil of rope, as if she were going to take it away.

'Oh, cut it out, Fella,' said Donald, 'why are you fussing about promises? You never keep any! Anyhow, this silly rope doesn't mean a thing.'

'Don,' said Felicity, 'you're going to *climb* something. What is it?'

'The school tower,' said Carde.

Felicity knelt there petrified. There was a moment's silence.

'Shut up, Jimmy, you fool,' said Donald, 'and now for Christ's sake go away, I mean you, Jim, not Felicity. I want to talk family policy with her, since she's bothered herself to come.'

'Ah well,' said Carde. 'Ah knows when Ah's not wanted. See you in the usual at the usual.' He sprang out of the door like a small panther and banged it behind him with his foot.

Felicity came over and seized the cuff of Donald's blazer. He was dressed for cricket. 'Don,' she said, 'Jimmy didn't mean it, did he, about the tower?'

'Of course not,' said Donald, not meeting her eye.

The school tower could be climbed, but it had been done only once in recorded history, by a man who was now an Under-Secretary in the Ministry of Town and Country Planning. He had placed upon the topmost pinnacle the traditional piece of porcelain, which had remained there for weeks until the games master had had the sporting idea of shooting it down.

'If you're going to climb it,' said Felicity, 'I'll tell the parents.'

'You won't do that,' said Donald easily. Felicity never told. 'And just be careful what you say in conversation. Any breath of this, and Carde and I would be expelled. You don't want to ruin my career, do you?' There was an inflexible rule at St Bride's that any sort of climbing on the school buildings was punished by immediate expulsion. This had been established after one or two of the easier climbs had tempted a few amateurs. The tower, however, was notoriously difficult, the chief problem being a fierce overhang which had to be negotiated a little way from its base.

'You'll kill yourself,' said Felicity. She was extremely upset.

'Please, please, *please* don't do it, Don. I'll give you my camera, the new one, if you won't do it.'

Donald detached his sleeve, and taking his sister's arm in a friendly grip, twisted it vigorously behind her back. 'Fella, darling,' he said, 'just don't make a fuss. If there's one thing I can *not* stand it's women making a fuss. Carde and I won't attempt it unless we're sure it's absolutely safe. We probably won't attempt it anyway.'

'You're hurting me, Don,' said Felicity. 'What are those drawings on the table?' She dragged her arm away and pulled several sheets of paper out from under a pile of books. They were sketches of the tower from different angles, showing its various profiles in detail.

'You see how business-like we are,' said Donald. 'Once we're past *here*,' he pointed to the overhang, 'it's child's play. And we have an ingenious plan for doing that. But we probably won't do it at all. It was just an idea. Carde said it partly to upset you.'

'Don,' said Felicity, '*please*! I'll do anything you like. I'll do any dare for you if you'll not do it. Dare me anything.' There was an old-established usage between them whereby if one wished the other to drop some cherished plan he would have in exchange to accept any dare that was named. This arrangement had not been invoked for some time.

'Well,' said Don laughing and lying back upon the table, 'what shall I tell you to do? What about making another raid for the Power Game?' The Power Game was an invention of Felicity's dating from long ago. It was a sort of eclectic witchcraft, which involved the purloining from the individuals who were to be bewitched of various intimate articles, such as socks, stockings, ties and handkerchiefs, which were subsequently to figure in the various rituals and ceremonies. The main point of the Power Game, however, as it turned out, had not been the actual magic but rather the preliminary raids. In the course of these raids a number of highly cherished prizes had been taken, including some underpants of Mr Prewett, Mr Hensman's braces, and an elegant sponge-bag belonging to Mr Everard, none of which had in fact been put to any magical use.

'All right!' said Felicity, tense and flushed, ready to dart away. 'Name anybody you like.'

'Oh, I don't know,' said Donald, waving a careless foot in the air, 'what about – oh, I don't know – what about – what about – Miss Thingummy Carter.'

'Fine!' said Felicity. 'I start now. Where did you say she was? Staying with Mr Demoyte?' She made for the door.

'My dear girl,' said Donald, shooting up like a jack-in-the-box. 'Stop! I'm not serious. You know we dropped all that long ago.'

'I haven't dropped it,' said Felicity. She was near to tears. 'Liffey is outside,' she said defiantly, 'and I nearly saw Angus on the road.' Angus had been a frequent ally in the Power Game raids. The translated and immaterial Liffey was Felicity's own private familiar.

'Oh, do leave all that old stuff,' said Donald, 'and for heaven's sake don't cry. You've been making a frightful row already. Anybody might have heard you.'

'Well, I'm going on that raid,' said Felicity, wiping her eyes. 'You agreed to it and you can't take it back now. And if I do that you'll have not to climb the tower.'

'Stop shouting, Fella,' said Donald. 'If Prewett passes, we're both for the high jump. Look, I'll see you out of this place. You're giving me the jitters. Now follow me and keep your mouth shut.'

Donald quietly opened the door of his room and looked both ways down the corridor. Distant sounds floated in, squeals of laughter, a gramophone playing jazz, a dull sound as of cricket stumps being rhythmically beaten together. Donald waited. Then seizing Felicity by the wrist he dragged her out of the room, took the stairs at a leap, and in an instant had her outside the back door. Here he let go of her and ran ahead into the wood, zigzagging rapidly between the trees. Fleet-footed Felicity sped after him. A moment later they had reached the wall and could hear the roar of traffic on the road just on the other side. Donald ran quickly along beside the wall until he came to a certain place. Here it could be seen that for a length of about eighteen inches the broken glass had been removed from the parapet.

Donald leaned crouching against the base of the wall. 'Jump on my back, Fella,' he said.

This was a familiar routine. Felicity jumped. Donald rose

slowly until he was standing upright, with Felicity standing upon his shoulders, her clambering hands now reaching the top of the wall, and her head well over the top. She began to pull herself up. Donald helped by putting his hands under her feet. She got into a sitting position on top of the wall and then gingerly transferred her legs over to the far side.

She looked down at Donald. 'Don,' she said, 'I'm going on that raid. I'm going *now*. And remember you promised.'

· 'I didn't promise anything!' said Donald, exasperated. 'Now shut up, Fella, and get down off that wall before someone sees you.'

'I *am* going!' said Felicity.

'I forbid you to go,' said Donald, 'and I won't pay you anything if you do. Now *get down off that wall*.'

'I'm going *now*,' said Felicity, 'and if you don't keep your promise I'll never speak to you again.' She addressed herself to the task of getting off the wall. It was a big jump. She let herself down as far as she could, and then closed her eyes. Next moment she was rolling over in the grass. She called, 'Goodbye, Don.'

'Wait a moment,' said Don's voice from the other side of the wall. There was a prolonged scrabbling sound. Then Donald appeared on top of the wall. He drew his feet up, half rose to a standing position, and then sprang down towards Felicity, staggered, and fell at her feet. He recovered himself quickly and then started walking, primly up the hill as if nothing had happened. Felicity ran beside him.

'Look here,' said Donald, and he sounded angry, 'you're going home now. I'm going to see you to the house and we won't hear any more of this awful rot.'

'You can see me home,' said Felicity easily, 'but you can't *keep* me at home. And as soon as you go I shall go off on the raid. Do look at Liffey. She's seen that big black dog and she's waving her tail. Can you see her tail? Shall I call her with the supersonic whistle?'

'Oh, shut up,' said Donald. 'Felicity, I will not be blackmailed by you.'

'How do people stop themselves being blackmailed?' asked Felicity.

'Listen,' said Donald, 'if you go on this silly raid I shall have to come too. And if we're caught, everyone will think it was my idea.' They had passed the school gates and turned into the green-shaded maze of roads near their own house.

'If Demoyters catches us,' said Felicity, 'he won't report you to Evvy. You know he never reports anyone to Evvy.'

'Maybe not,' said Donald, 'but Demoyters can be quite unpleasant enough on his own account.'

'I'm not afraid of him,' said Felicity. 'If you are, you needn't come.'

'I'll torture you when we get back, Fella,' said Donald. 'If anyone spots us, by the way, we met a few minutes ago by accident.'

They came down an overgrown gravel track between some garages and emerged on to the fields that lay between the housing estate and Brayling's Close. There was no shade here and the golden expanse was crackling in the heat. The hay had been cut for some time and the grass was sharp and stubbly and very dry. The footpath was crumbling and dusty. The hot weather had lasted a long time. Felicity led the way, and they walked on in silence until they could see distantly through the trees the rosy colour of the bricks and the glint of windows. They paused. Then Felicity saw Angus.

He had taken the form of a gipsy, and was sitting not far from the path on the edge of a dry weedy ditch. He sat with one leg down deep in the tall grasses of the ditch, and the other folded upon the shorter grass of the meadow. He sat in a dignified attitude with his head thrown back and his reddish brown neck and chest exposed. He looked straight at Felicity. His face had a sort of expressionless gravity. He was rather frightening. Felicity knew that it must be Angus because of the weird aura that surrounded him, and because of the strange unexpected manner of his appearance. This time it was certainly Angus. She wished that he would not take on these somewhat disconcerting forms, but she supposed that it was impossible for divine beings to manifest themselves without being alarming, even when they wished one well. He sat so still that he was almost invisible. Donald had not seen him, and Felicity decided not to reveal his presence. She took Donald by the sleeve and led him a few paces on until the gipsy was hidden by a hedge.

Felicity suddenly began to feel very uneasy. She wanted to

go back. She plucked Donald by the coat which he was carrying over his arm and said, 'Don, don't climb that tower. I know it will end badly. *Please* say now that you won't climb it, and then we can both go home.'

Donald looked down at her. He touched her freckled nose lightly with his finger. 'We won't turn back at this point, mister mate,' he said. 'As for the climb, I probably won't do it. It was all Carde's idea anyway.'

They walked on very slowly towards the house. In a minute the little path would reach the low crumbling stone wall at the end of Demoyte's garden and turn away to the left towards the road. It was the dead time of the afternoon. Donald and Felicity, who were familiar with the habits of the Demoyte household, knew that they could count on Demoyte and Miss Handforth being laid out in their bedrooms, with drawn curtains, taking their siesta. To enter the house should not be difficult. The only unknown quantity was Miss Carter herself.

While Donald was peering over the wall, Felicity looked about her. She was still unnerved by the manifestation of Angus. At the base of the wall a great many flowers were growing, and the freshness of their opening petals showed even through the brown dust which lay upon them: ragged robin, tansy, campion, valerian and charlock. The flowers that grow in waste places. Felicity looked down at them tenderly. Then she began to pick them.

'Christ!' said Donald. 'What a moment to pick flowers! Look, we'll get over the wall there, behind those bushes, and work our way along under cover of the yew hedge. Then come up close to the house, out of view of the windows, and walk round to the front door. If it's locked, we try the kitchen. If anyone sees us we say we're looking for Daddy, we thought he was here. Once inside the house, listen for sounds – then upstairs, and trust to our luck. The Carter will certainly be in the corner room at the back. All right? Follow me.'

Donald sounded eager. The excitement of the chase had taken hold of him. He dodged along by the wall and then climbed over it at a point where it was covered by a clump of tall syringa bushes growing in Demoyte's garden. Clutching her bunch of flowers Felicity followed. This wall was an easy one. They walked cautiously, keeping close to the hedge, and then passed through the archway into full view of the windows. In a quick stride Donald crossed the open piece of lawn and was against the wall of the house. Felicity followed. A moment later they were at the front door. It was open. They stepped inside the house.

Within there was complete silence. Both the children were breathing deeply, and it seemed to them that the sound must be audible on the landing above. They stood quite still until they had recovered their breath. They looked at each other with wide shining eyes, and Felicity took Donald's hand and pressèd it hard. Then with noiseless footsteps they crept across the hall and began to ascend the stairs. The house was sleepy with the heat. All the windows were wide open and the warm dusty atmosphere drifted cloudily in from the garden. The beams of the sun, falling directly upon the staircase, made a zone of hazy yellow light through which the children ascended on tiptoe. The stairs did not creak. Once on the landing they could lay their feet upon a long thick Baluchistan rug. They glided along it and stood poised outside the door of the guest room. No sound came from within.

The doorhandle was made of yellow crystalline glass and slippery to the touch. Donald took it very firmly in both hands and began to turn it. He opened the door sufficiently to put his head through. Its opening had made no sound. It seemed now as if no sound could be made in this silent and untenanted house. Donald was still for a moment, and then he leaned gently through the door and entered the room. With a breath of relief Felicity followed him. The room was empty.

Once they were inside with the door shut a wild glee overcame them, and they began to dance noiselessly about the room waving their arms. Felicity paused and drew the supersonic whistle from her pocket. She was about to blow a tremendous supersonic blast upon it when Donald stopped her.

'But it won't make a sound if I—' Felicity began to explain in a whisper. It was too much for them both. Convulsed with helpless silent giggling they fell in a heap upon the bed.

'But you said—' Felicity began again in a whisper. It was no good. They lay there writhing with smothered laughter.

At last Donald rose, pulled Felicity up and set the bed to rights. 'Now quick,' he whispered, 'find what we want and go. What shall we take?'

'Stockings,' said Felicity firmly. She suspected that Donald had other ideas, and felt a sudden feminine wish to protect Miss Carter against his depredations. They began to flit about the room, opening drawers.

'Here we are,' murmured Felicity. She drew a pair of nylon stockings out of a top drawer, waved them at Donald, and put them in her pocket. They turned to go. Felicity took a last look round the room. She picked up the flowers which she had left on a chair. The writing-desk beside the window stood open, littered with papers. Felicity went over to it and began turning them over.

'Come on!' hissed Donald.

Felicity said, 'Why, here's a letter from Daddy, I wonder what he says.'

'Never mind,' said Donald, 'better not look at it. Let's get out.'

'It doesn't matter, silly,' said Felicity, 'it's only Daddy!' She pulled the letter out of the envelope and read it. She stood quite still. Then she put the letter back on the desk and came away.

'What did it say?' said Donald.

'Nothing,' said Felicity. 'Let's go quickly.' She began to pull him to the door.

Donald looked at her face. Then he went back to the desk, found the letter, and read it.

'Come, come, come,' said Felicity. She opened the bedroom door and stepped out on to the landing. Donald followed. They walked with firm silent steps to the top of the stairs and began to descend.

Half-way down the lower flight Felicity stopped in her tracks. Donald paused, and then walked down to join her. Standing watching them from the drawing-room door was Miss Handforth. She looked at the children. They looked at her.

'Well, well, what a surprise!' said Miss Handforth, her voice echoing through the house. Miss Handforth was not a friend of the Mor children. 'This is a new way to pay visits!'

The Close seemed to shake at the sound and shiver into wakefulness. Donald and Felicity stood there paralysed.

'Come on,' said Miss Handforth, 'has the cat got your tongue? What have you two been up to up there, may I ask?'

Donald and Felicity were silent. At that moment the front door opened and Rain Carter came into the hall. All three turned towards her. She wore a white summer dress with an open neck, and for a moment as she entered the sun blazed behind her. She shut the door, and put her hand to her eyes, blinded for a moment by the change of light. She took in the little scene in front of her; and then turned questioningly to Miss Handforth.

Miss Handforth said, 'These are Mr Mor's children.' Her deep voice expressed incredulity and disgust.

Rain turned towards them. They stood, as in a group by Gainsborough, Felicity posed with her hand upon the banister, Donald more sulkily behind her.

'I am so glad to meet you at last,' said Rain. 'I think – Donald – I have at least seen before – but I am so glad to meet you properly. And I haven't ever met – Felicity. How are you?'

Donald said nothing. He looked straight at her unsmiling. Felicity came forward. She smiled at Rain. 'We just came over,' she said, 'to give you these flowers. They are wild flowers, but we hope you'll like them.' She handed her bouquet to Rain.

Rain took them with an exclamation of pleasure and held them to her face. She was a little shorter than Felicity and had to look up at her. 'They are *beautiful*,' she said. 'I love these English wild flowers. I really really cannot think of anything that would have pleased me more. How very kind of you to think of this. They are lovely flowers.' She held them close to her.

Donald came down the stairs and stood beside his sister. He took her arm.

'You aren't going already?' said Rain. 'Do stay and talk to me. Miss Handforth, I wonder if – some tea? It's about tea-time anyway, isn't it? I don't want to bother you. Or perhaps just some milk and cakes if there are any?'

Miss Handforth said nothing.

'I'm afraid we have to go at once,' said Felicity. 'I'm so sorry. We're expected at home and we're late already. We just called to bring the flowers.'

'How very dear of you,' said Rain. 'You *have* made me glad. Thank you so much. I hope we shall meet again soon.'

'I hope so too,' said Felicity. 'Well, good-bye. Good-bye, Miss Handforth.' The two children disappeared rapidly out of the front door.

They walked quickly through the front gates of Mr Demoyte's garden and then along the little path that led back again into the fields. Once Felicity was on the path she began to run, and Donald had to run hard to keep pace with her. As soon as they were well clear of the house Felicity turned off the path, ran across a field, and threw herself down in the stubble in the shadow of a hedge. Donald joined her and sat down beside her. They were silent for some time.

'Don,' said Felicity at last, 'you won't do that climb, will you?'

Donald did not answer for a moment. 'It hardly matters one way or the other,' he said, 'now.'

They sat looking down into the stubble. 'Tears of blood,' said Felicity. This was an ancient ritual.

Without a word Donald drew a razor blade from his pocket and handed it to her. Carefully she made a tiny slit beneath each eye. Both the Mor children could weep at will. A moment later mingled tears and blood were coursing down their cheeks.

# CHAPTER NINE

It was the day of Nan's departure. Mor viewed the prospect
with relief. For some time now their small house had been a
scene where washing, drying and ironing of clothes, discovery
and renovation of suitcases, unfolding of maps, and discussion
of trains and seat reservations and the weather, had gone on
without intermission until Mor had been obliged to invent
excuses for staying in school. End of term exams were just
beginning, and although this meant less teaching it meant
more correcting, and it was about this time too that Mor had
to settle down to the organization of reports and the solving of
various staff problems for next term with which Evvy was
patently unable to deal. His house became intolerable to him.
It was always too small, though usually it was better in
summer than in winter, since open windows could lend extra
space to the rooms. But Nan could be relied upon to turn the
place topsy-turvy before a holiday, and Felicity was being more
than usually tiresome and tearful. Mor's heart sank each evening as he came through the narrow front door, with its panel of
leaded glass, into the small hallway, filled now with suitcases,
tennis rackets and other paraphernalia. He would have liked to
have gone over to Demoyte's house to get away from it all. But
although the Close and its inhabitants were incessantly in
his mind, he did not go. A general sense of unrest and uneasiness filled him. It was now less than three weeks to
Donald's college entrance exam, and he was worried about
him. He had called on him twice lately to see how he was
getting on, but the boy had been very short with him, and Mor
had gone away hurt and puzzled.

On the previous day, Mor had at last made a serious attempt
to discuss with Nan the question of his becoming a Labour
candidate – or rather, as Mor put it to himself, to announce to
her his intention of becoming one; only it had not looked very
much like this when he actually came to opening his mouth.
Nan had simply refused to discuss the matter. She had used her
most exasperating technique. When Mor had settled down very

gravely to tell her of his hopes, his ambitions, his plans for how it would all turn out for the best, she had laughed her dry laughter, and sat there on the sofa, her feet drawn up and her eyes shining, mocking at him. At such moments she was invested with a terrible power which shook Mor down to the depths of his soul. She seemed to withdraw into a region of completely insulated serenity and superiority. Nothing which he said could touch her then, even when, as he now remembered with remorse, he was driven to making really spiteful rejoinders. It was not that she did not understand his arguments. In her presence, in the overwhelming atmosphere of her personality, his arguments simply did not begin to exist. Mor was astonished yet again at the tremendous strength of his wife. She was totally impervious to reasoning, relentlessly determined to get her own way, and calmly and even gaily certain that she would get it. Throughout the interview she kept her temper perfectly, laughing and jesting in a slightly patronizing way at her husband, whereas Mor by the end of it was reduced to almost speechless anger. He had left the room in the end saying, 'Well, whether you like this plan or not I propose to go ahead with it!'

Mor had said this at the time merely to annoy; but on the following morning he thought to himself that perhaps that was exactly what he would do. The deep wounds which Nan had inflicted on his pride tormented him without ceasing. He felt, with a deep spasm of anger, that she had provoked him once too often. She must learn that to trample upon the aspirations and self-respect of another is a crime which brings an almost automatic retribution. Mor thought to himself, when I see Tim Burke I shall tell him to go ahead. When the thing is made public Nan will have too much pride and too much concern for convention to try to make me go back on it. She will have to accept it then. Mor got a bitter, and he knew very unworthy satisfaction out of imagining Nan's fury when she found that he really meant for once to take what he wanted. What annoyed him perhaps most of all about her was the exquisite calmness of her assumption that when she had made it clear that he was not to do something he would not do it.

All these thoughts, however, with a talent born of years of married life, Mor buried deep within him, and behaved on the next day with a normal cheerfulness. Nan too seemed completely to have forgotten their quarrel and to be looking forward to the journey with unmixed delight. They were to catch the 10.30 train to Waterloo, have lunch in London, and then catch a fast afternoon train to Dorset. A taxi had been ordered to take them to the station, an expense which Mor disliked, but which Nan's colossal quantity of luggage seemed to make inevitable. The taxi was due in a few minutes, and Felicity was still not ready. She had been sulky and short-tempered all the morning, in spite of being promised lunch at the Royal Festival Hall, something which usually pleased her very much.

Nan and Mor had walked out into the front garden. The suitcases were piled on the step. Mor looked down at the ill-kept tangle of dahlias and asters which grew on each side of the concrete path. 'Look,' he said, 'Liffey's place is quite grown over this year. You remember how she used to lie there and sniff the plants?'

'That reminds me,' said Nan. 'A funny thing. I met that painter girl in the street, Miss Carter, and she said the children had given her some flowers.'

'What?' said Mor.

'Just that,' said Nan. 'They both went over to Demoyte's house, gave her a bunch of flowers and came away!'

'It *is* rather odd,' said Mor, 'but I don't see why they shouldn't just have taken it into their heads. Did Felicity say anything about it to you?'

'Of course not!' said Nan. 'You know how secretive she is. It's a delightful gesture, and Miss Carter, I may say, was tickled pink about it – but *really*, Bill, you know our charming little dears as well as I do. Would they have just thought of doing that? It must have been part of some joke.'

Mor was inclined to agree with Nan, and the whole story upset him considerably. He couldn't think what it could mean; and he feared his children especially when they brought gifts. He said, however, 'You're fussing about nothing, Nan. It was just a nice idea. I expect Felicity thought of it.'

'You're almost as naïve as Miss Carter,' said Nan, 'and that's saying something.'

Mor was disturbed at hearing Nan mention Miss Carter's name. He had by a curious chance seen Miss Carter twice in the last three days, once in the distance walking in the fields, and once passing through the housing estate in the direction of the shopping centre. On neither of these occasions had he spoken with her, but each occasion had given him a strange and deep shock.

The taxi drove up. Mor lifted the suitcases. Felicity appeared and got into the taxi without a word. Mor and Nan packed in and they drove in silence to the station. Mor paid the taxi-driver and stacked up the suitcases on the platform. They waited.

The sun shone from a clear blue sky upon the little station with its two platforms, each covered with a neatly peaked roof, like a toy station. On either side the glittering rails of the Southern Region curved away among pine trees between which here and there could be seen the red roofs of tall Victorian houses. Quite a lot of people were waiting for the London train, many of them known by sight to Mor. It was a scene which he usually found inexpressibly dreary. There was five minutes to wait.

Then it came over Mor like a sudden gust of warm fresh wind that Nan was going. *Nan was going.* She was going. And this time next year, thought Mor, perhaps everything will be different. Everything is going to be different. He lifted his head. How good a thing it was that he had made his decision. Obscurely in the instant he was aware of the future suddenly radiant with hope and possibility. At the same time he was filled with a great tenderness for Nan. He turned to look at her. She was glancing at her watch and tapping her high-heeled shoe on the platform. She smiled at him and said, 'Not long now!' She seemed quite excited. Felicity was standing some way off looking over the wooden palings of the station into the surrounding pine trees.

'Nan,' said Mor, 'are you really all right for the journey? Have you got something to read?'

'Yes,' said Nan, 'I have the day's paper and this magazine.'

'Let me get you something else,' said Mor, 'a Penguin book – and what about some nice chocolate?' He ran down the station as far as the little stall that sold papers and sweets. He bought a Penguin book of poetry, and a box of milk chocolates and two bananas. He came back and stuffed them into Nan's pockets.

'Bill, dear, you are sweet!' said Nan, taking the goods out of her pockets and putting them into a suitcase.

The neat green train sped into sight round the curve of the

line. The crowd surged forward. Mor found two corner seats for Nan and Felicity and packed the luggage in. There was not long for farewells. At these small stations the train waited only a minute. Mor kissed his wife and daughter, and then with breathtaking speed they were jerked away. Mor waved – and he saw Nan's face and her waving arm recede rapidly and disappear almost at once round the next curve and into the trees.

Mor walked very slowly back down the platform. He gave up his platform ticket. He came out into the sun and stood still in the dusty deserted station yard, which was quite silent now that the roar of the train had died away into the distance. Mor stood there, arrested by some obscure feeling of pleasure, and somehow in the quietness of the morning he apprehended that there were many many things to be glad about. He waited. Then from the very depths of his being the knowledge came to him, suddenly and with devastating certainty. He was in love with Miss Carter. He stood there looking at the dusty ground and the thought that had taken shape shook him so that he nearly fell. He took a step forward. He was in love. And if in love then not just a little in love, but terribly, desperately, needfully in love. With this there came an inexpressibly violent sense of joy. Mor still stood there quietly looking at the ground; but now he felt that the world had started to rotate about him with a gathering pace and he was at the centre of its movement.

Mor drew in a deep breath and smiled down at the dry earth below him, swaying slightly on his heels. I must be mad, he thought, smiling. The words formed, and were swept upward like leaves in a furnace. He walked slowly across the station yard to the wooden gate. He caressed the wood of the gate. It was dry flaky wood, warm in the sun, beautiful. Mor picked splinters off it. He could not stop smiling. I must be mad, he thought, whatever shall I do? Then he thought, I must see Miss Carter at once. When I see her I shall know what to do. Then I shall know what this state of mind is and what to do about it. I shall know then, when I see her. *When I see her.*

He left the station yard at a run and began to run along the road towards the school. It was a long way. The hot sun struck him on the brow with repeated blows, and the warm air refused to refresh his lungs. He ran on, panting and gasping. He must get to his bicycle, which was in the shed in the masters' garden. His desire to see Miss Carter was now so violent it was become an extra quite physical agony, apart from the straining of his lungs and the aching of his muscles. He kept on running. The school was in sight now. An agonizing stitch made him slow down to walking pace. The pain of his anxiety shaped his face into a cry and his breath came in an audible whine. He turned into the drive and managed to run again as far as the bicycle-shed.

He dragged his bicycle out, manhandling it as if it were a savage animal. It had a flat tyre. Mor threw it on the ground and kicked it, swearing aloud. He looked about and chose another bicycle at random. It occurred to him that the Classical Sixth would be waiting for him at eleven-fifteen, to have a history lesson. But he had no hesitation now. He had recovered his breath, but the other agony continued, biting him in the stomach so that he almost could have cried out with the pain of wanting to see her. He set off on the borrowed machine, bounced madly over the gravel, on to the main road, and started up the hill towards the railway bridge.

The hill was merciless, and his pedalling grew slower and slower, until the bicycle was tacking crazily upon the fierce slope. He got off and pushed it at a run to the top of the hill. Then as he sailed down the other side, seeing for a moment in the distance the glowing walls of Brayling's Close, he uttered to himself the word 'Rain'. At a tremendous pace, pedalling madly now to catch up with the speed of the wheels, he plunged onward. He turned the bicycle, without dismounting, across the grassy strip in the middle of the dual carriageway, and launched it like a thunderbolt into Demoyte's drive. The gravel flew to both sides like spray. He fell off the machine and threw it to the side of the house and then cannoned through the front door. The house was still and fragrant within. Mor crossed the hall and threw open the drawing-room door.

The easel was still in place and Demoyte was sitting in the sun near the window with his back turned towards the door, in an attitude of repose. There was no sign of Miss Carter.

'Hello, sir,' said Mor, swinging on the door, 'where's Miss Carter?'

'Accustomed as I am,' said Demoyte, without turning round, 'to being treated like an old useless piece of out-dated antediluvian junk, I—'

'Sorry, sir,' said Mor, and stepped into the room, 'forgive me. But I did want to see Miss Carter rather urgently. You don't happen to know where she is?'

'Suppose you come round to the front,' said Demoyte, 'if you have the time to spare, that is, so that I can at least see your face during this conversation.'

Mor came round and faced the old man, who looked up at him sombrely and waited for Mor to make another remark.

'I'm sorry,' said Mor. 'Do you know where she is?'

'If you had come at practically any other hour of any other day,' said Demoyte, 'you would have found the young lady here at work. She has been toiling like the proverbial black. But just at this hour of this day she has, unfortunately for you, gone out for a walk.' Demoyte spoke very slowly as if deliberately to torture his interlocutor.

Mor saw out of the corner of his eye that a great deal had happened to the canvas since he last saw it, but he did not turn to look. Making an effort to speak slowly too, he said, 'You don't happen to know, sir, in which direction she went or where I might have a chance of meeting her on the way?' The pain within him was continuing to bite.

'I don't, as you put it, *happen* to know this, I'm afraid,' said Demoyte. 'I wonder if you realize that your collar has come undone and is sticking up at the back of your neck in a rather ludicrous manner? I have never liked those detachable collars. They make you look like a country schoolmaster. And you seem to have got some oil or tar or something on to your face. May I suggest that you set your appearance to rights before you continue your search?'

Mor jabbed back at his collar, settled it somehow into the protective custody of his coat, and ran his hand vaguely over his face. He turned to go. 'I think I'll be off,' he said. 'Thank you all the same.'

As he got to the door, Demoyte said, 'She went by the path over the fields. Not that that will help you much.'

'Thank you,' said Mor. He ran out, seized his bicycle, and cycled out of the gate and sharply round on to the little footpath. The machine bucked wildly as he bounced over bumps and tufts of grass. He was riding now straight into the sun and had to keep one hand raised to shade his eyes. There was nobody to be seen on the path, and already the edge of the housing estate was well in view. Mor ran his bicycle through an alleyway and on to one of the roads of the estate. It was hopeless. He had much better go home now, put his face into some cold water, and think again about what he was supposed to be doing. But instead he rode past his house and up to the front gate of the school. It was just conceivable that Miss Carter might have gone into the school to call on Evvy.

At the front gate stood the tall white-clad figure of the games master, Hensman. He was lounging in an athletic way against one of the pillars of the gate.

'The good weather's keeping up,' said Hensman. 'Perhaps we shall have a fine day for the House Match for once.'

'Yes, it looks like it,' said Mor. He had got off his bicycle and was standing irresolutely at the gate.

'Your son's not shaping too badly,' said Hensman. 'We'll make a cricketer of him yet. He's quite the white hope of Prewett's team. Not that that's saying much, I'm afraid.' Cricket was not, in Hensman's view, taken quite seriously enough in Prewett's house.

'Yes, good,' said Mor. 'You haven't seen Miss Carter go past here, by any chance?'

'Why, yes,' said Hensman. 'I saw her on the playground about twenty minutes ago. She was going down the hill with old Bledyard.'

'Thanks,' said Mor. He forced his machine on rapidly down the drive. He felt a slight chill at the name of Bledyard. He left the bicycle at the corner of Main School in a place where bicycles were forbidden ever to be and began to run across the playground. He took the path beyond the Library which led down towards the wood. The path was a bit overgrown and he had to spring over brambles and long tongues of greenery as he ran. Two boys who were coming up the path stood aside and then stared after him in amazement. There was no sign of either Bledyard or Miss Carter. Mor ran into the wood. He stopped running then and listened. There was no sound except the soft continual pattering of the leaves. He walked quickly on, turning off the path and dragging his trouser-legs through the bracken.

Then quite suddenly he came to a clearing, and in the clearing he saw a strange sight which made him become rigid with mingled distress and joy. There was Miss Carter. But she had been transformed. She was a prisoner. She was dressed in a long flowing piece of sea-green silk which was draped about her body, leaving one shoulder bare. She was sitting in the midst of the clearing on top of a small step-ladder. Seated round about her on the ground with drawing-boards and pencils were about twenty boys. They were drawing her. Master of the scene and overlooking it with a powerful eye was Bledyard, who was leaning against a tree on the far side of the clearing. Before his attention was caught by Mor, he was looking fixedly at Miss Carter. He was in his shirt sleeves and had his hands in his pockets. His longish dark hair fell limply as far as his cheeks. He looked to Mor in that moment like Comus, like Lucifer.

Mor's sudden irruption into the clearing was noticed at once. Bledyard parted company with his tree, drew his hands out of his pockets and stood upright. He stopped looking surprised almost instantly and began to smile. His eyes and mouth thinned out into two long sardonic lines. The boys all turned to see who had come and stared at Mor with some astonishment. Mor saw that it was part of the Fifth Form. He reached back mechanically to see whether his collar had stayed in place. It had. Rain signified her awareness of his arrival by a very slight movement of her hand. She was posing like a child, rather stiffly and without making any motion. Bledyard was still smiling, his face stretched and immobile. Mor suddenly felt certain that Bledyard must be reading his mind. He began to walk round towards him, signalling to the boys to continue their work. He tried to make his presence seem more natural by making to Bledyard the first remark that came into his head which happened to be 'I wonder if I could see you some time about reports?' Bledyard looked into Mor's face, still smiling his infuriating smile. He nodded without speaking. The boys had returned to their drawing. Mor began to go round behind them looking at their work. He was intensely conscious of Rain's presence, but did not dare to look at her. He looked instead at the boys' drawings. He knew that it would not be very long before the twelve o'clock bell would ring and she would be set free.

One or two of the boys were working with water-colours, others were using ink and wash, others pencils only. Mor paused to look at Rigden's effort. Rigden was good at painting, which was just as well, since he was not a star at anything else. He had produced with pen and a brown wash a pleasing sketch, the head extremely well drawn and the drapery falling in a strong flourish. Rigden looked up at Mor. He could hardly believe his luck. Mor looked at the sketch and smiled approvingly. The smile made Rigden's day. Mor moved on, glancing surreptitiously at his watch. Jimmy Carde was sitting at his ease, his back against a tree, one leg raised in front and the other tucked under him. As Mor approached, Carde was whistling a little tune to himself, the same phrase over and over again. Mor looked at his sketch. Carde was no artist. He was working with a pencil and had a profile view of his subject. He had produced a squat figure, the drapery gracelessly drawn tight about the body, the breasts crudely exaggerated. As Mor observed the sketch, Carde looked up, and in spite of himself Mor exchanged a glance with him. He looked away at once. He hated Carde. He was glad that Carde was destined for Oxford, not Cambridge. He did not want him to go on being Donald's friend. At that moment the bell rang.

Everyone jumped. The boys shifted and some of them began to pack up their things and rise to their feet. Rain stirred upon her pedestal and began to hitch up the drapery. Mor saw this out of the corner of his eye. He looked at Bledyard and found that Bledyard was looking at him. Mor prayed that Bledyard was not blessed with a free period at twelve. Bledyard was not smiling now. He was moving his head gently to and fro in the way that was characteristic of him. The boys had now all risen and were making off into the wood in the direction of the studio to leave their paints and drawing-boards before going up to school for their next lesson. Mor and Bledyard and Rain were left alone in the clearing.

Rain was still sitting on top of the ladder. She seemed to enjoy being there, perhaps because it added to her height. She drew her legs up and turned towards Mor with a laugh. 'Mr Bledyard captured me, and see what a beautiful stuff he brought out of his store-room,' she said, unwrapping the green silk from her body and spreading it out. Mor saw that she was wearing a flowered cotton dress which left her shoulders bare.

'I really must try to buy it from you, Mr Bledyard,' she said, 'and hand it over to my dressmaker.' She stood up on the ladder, folded up the silk and held it out to Bledyard. Her legs were bare and very smooth. Both men averted their eyes and looked up into her face. She looked down upon them with the slightly prim slightly pleased expression of a Victorian little girl.

Bledyard took the material from her rather gloomily. He cast a look at Mor and seemed to hesitate. Mor stood his ground, trying to look like a man who was willing to stand there all day if necessary.

'Yes,' said Bledyard thoughtfully, 'yes, indeed, indeed.' His tone made it clear that he was not answering Rain's question. 'Well,' he said, 'I must I must go I'm afraid. I have boys boys waiting in the studio. You were most kind, Miss Carter, to favour favour us with this delightful—' His voice trailed away. He seemed to have more difficulty than usual in enunciating. He opened his mouth again, closed it, and turned away into the wood. His footsteps could be heard for some distance receding through the bracken. Mor and Rain were left alone.

She sat down again on top of the steps and laughed. She seemed a little uneasy. She said, 'I love posing for people—' and began to rub one of her ankles. 'Oh, I'm stiff though!'

Mor stood close beside her. His breath came quickly. He did not look at her yet. He said, '*Rain*'.

Rain saw at once that something had happened and she saw in the same moment what it was that had happened. She froze, her hand still holding her ankle, and looked down towards the ground. Then gradually she relaxed. She said very softly, almost thoughtfully, 'Mor', and again 'Mor'.

At the same instant they both turned to look at each other. Perched upon the ladder her face was level with Mor's. He leaned forward and very carefully enclosed her bare shoulders in his arms. Then he drew her towards him and kissed her gently but fully upon the lips. The experience of touching her was so shattering to him that he had now to hide his face. He let it fall first upon her shoulder, and then, as he felt the roughness of his chin touching her flesh, he bent down and laid his head against her breast. He could smell the fresh smell of her cotton dress and feel the warmth of her breast and the violent beating of her heart. His own heart was beating as if it would break. All this happened in a moment. Then Rain was gently pushing him away, and getting down from the ladder. She stood before him now, very small, looking up at him. 'No,' she said in a very quiet pensive voice, 'No, no, please, dear Mor, dear, no, no.' It was like the moaning of a dove.

She said, 'Would you mind taking the ladder back to the studio? You could leave it just outside in the yard.' She picked up the jacket of her dress, which had been lying on the grass, and drew it on.

Mor stood as she spoke, his hands hanging down, looking at her unsmiling as if his eyes would burn her. He had heard the beating of her heart.

She hesitated, looking down, her hand involuntarily held to her breast. Then she said, 'I'm so sorry—' Then she turned and ran away very quickly into the wood.

Mor did not attempt to follow her. He stood for a moment, leaning with one arm upon the step-ladder. Then, like one who is fainting, he sat upon the ground.

# CHAPTER TEN

The day of the House Match was, as everyone had predicted, a fine day. The heat wave had been lasting now for more than a month. The sun shone from a cloudless sky upon the cricket field, which was tanned to a pale brownish colour except where in the centre assiduous watering had kept the pitch a bright green. Mor was standing behind the double row of deck-chairs near the pavilion. He was in his shirt sleeves and suffering considerably from the heat. He would have liked to go away anywhere into the shade, preferably into the darkness. He would have liked to sleep. But he had to be there, to show himself, to walk and talk as if everything were perfectly ordinary.

Not that Mor was unmoved by the House Match. An irrational excitement always surrounded this ritual. Even the masters were touched by it; and this year Mor found himself almost excessively upset. He could hardly bear to watch the game. His own house were fielding. They had been batting in the morning and early afternoon and had put up a total of a hundred and sixty-eight. Prewett's were now batting, and one of the two batsmen who had been in now for some time was Donald Mor, who had gone in first wicket down. Donald was playing extremely well, with style and with force, and two fours which he had recently hit had won prolonged applause. He had made twenty-three, and looked as if he was settling in. Prewett's total stood at fifty-two for one.

Jimmy Carde had just come on to bowl. Carde was attached to Mor's house by an arrangement whereby the scholars were, for certain purposes, distributed among the other houses. In effect, this merely meant that they played games for these houses and sometimes travelled with them on expeditions. Carde was a rather ostentatious fast bowler, with a long run and a good deal of flourishing and bounding. The ball came down the pitch like a thunderbolt when launched by Carde, but not always very straight. Mor watched him bowl once to Donald. Then he turned away his head. He was moved by the spectacle of his son, and his identification with him was at that moment considerable.

Mor began to mooch along slowly behind the deck-chairs. He was feeling extremely unhappy. He looked across the field to where the housing estate lay spread out along the far boundary, a sprawling conglomeration of bright red boxes. He looked back over his shoulder towards the wood. It looked cool and dark. Mor wondered if he could decently escape, and decided that he couldn't. A burst of clapping arose, and he looked round to see that Donald had just driven the ball past cover point for another four. Donald's success was obviously pleasing to the school. He was standing now in the middle of the pitch, conferring with his fellow batsman. Carde came down and said something to them and they both laughed. Mor mooched onwards, watched as he passed by boys anxious to descry whether his loyalties at that moment were with his house or with his son.

The House Match, which was the final in a knock-out contest, normally lasted for two days, but it was the first day which was the great occasion; it ended with a dinner given by the Headmaster to the housemasters, a festival which under Evvy's consulship had reached an unprecedented degree of dreariness. Mr Baseford, who was a man who liked his bottle, had tried to coach Evvy into making something of this dinner, so far with little success, and now Baseford was away Mor did not care enough to try to continue his work. In the morning and afternoon, parents and other visitors were not encouraged to appear, although a few did sometimes turn up. The match was kept as a domestic occasion, the two lines of deck-chairs being occupied only by masters and by their families if any, and a few local friends. The School lounged along the edge of the wood, half in and half out of the shade, wearing the floppy canvas sun hats which St Bride's boys affected in the summer, or else crowded near the pavilion within talking distance of the batting side. Mor judged that almost everybody must be present. The crowd by the wood was especially dense. Occasionally a soft murmur arose from it, or the voice of a boy was heard far back under the trees, but mostly there was complete silence except for the intermittent patter of applause.

Mr Everard was sitting in one of the deck-chairs in the front row talking to Hensman, who was always the hero of this particular day. Prewett was just emerging from the pavilion. Tim Burke, who was present as usual on Mor's invitation, was also sitting in the front row. He seemed in good spirits, looking slightly bronzed and healthier than usual, and was talking over his shoulder to one of the Sixth Form boys. Tim always got on well with the boys. Mor decided that it was about time he went back to Tim or else sat down near the wood, but he did nothing about it. On this occasion no women were present. Nan, whom duty would have constrained to come, was away, and Mrs Prewett, who was an enthusiastic cricket fan, was at home suffering from a touch of sunstroke. Mor looked round the edge of the field and sighed. He wished the day was over.

It was now five days since Nan's departure and since the extraordinary scene in the wood. Since that time, Mor had not met Rain, nor had he made any attempt to meet her. She on her part had equally avoided him. He had caught not even a glimpse of her in the intervening days. Mor had gone to bed that night in a state of dazed and blissful happiness such as he could not remember having ever experienced before. He woke on the following morning in despair. He was ready then to attribute his outburst to a sudden relaxing of tension connected with Nan's disappearance, to a revengeful anger against Nan for her behaviour, to overworking, to the relentless continuance of the heat wave. Whatever the explanation, it was clear that nothing more must come of this. To have made the declaration at all was insane, he could not think how he could have been so foolish.

He was, in particular, astonished that he could have let himself be so moved and softened merely by putting to himself the idea that he was in love. It seemed almost as if this phrase in itself had done the damage. Yet he knew perfectly that the notion of being in love, which was all very well for boys in their twenties, could have no possible place in his life. Mor took seriously the obligations imposed by matrimony. At least he supposed he did. He had never really had occasion to reflect on the matter. He had always been scrupulously responsible and serious in everything that related to his wife and children. But it was not so much considerations such as these which made him feel that he had acted wrongly. It was simply the non-existence in his life, as it solidly and in reality was, of any place for an emotion or a drama of this kind. When he had imagined himself to be swayed by an overwhelming passion he had been a man in a dream. Now he had awakened from the dream.

It was not a happy awakening. Mor was tormented by the thought that he had startled Rain, perhaps shocked her, and might, for a while, be contributing to make her unhappy, or at least anxious. He had no idea what exactly her thoughts and feelings might be; but he was certain that her concern with him could not possibly extend farther than a mild and vaguely friendly interest. That being so, his outburst and subsequent withdrawal were not likely to cause her any serious suffering. At worst, there would be a certain amount of embarrassment at such few inevitable social encounters as might remain to be got through before she went away for good. All the same, it grieved Mor to think that he had subjected her to this unpleasant experience. Then he reflected also upon their previous *tête-à-tête*, and concluded that really Rain must have a very poor view of him indeed; and he was tempted to write her a note of apology. He resisted this temptation. The idea of writing to her was at once suspiciously attractive, and Mor had been made wary by his earlier experience of letter-writing. To write would merely be to add yet another act to a drama which had better simply terminate at once. He would just be silent and absent and hope that Rain would understand.

He had been anxious that morning in case she might take it into her head to come and watch the House Match. Evvy would have been certain to invite her to come. But she had not appeared, and would not be very likely to come at this late hour. Mor's attention returned abruptly to the pitch. Donald had hit a ball shortly to mid-on, had decided to run, and had been almost run out. The School gasped and relaxed. It was the last ball of the over, so now Donald had to face the bowling again. Mor wished half-heartedly that he would soon be out. The strain was too disagreeable. Anyhow, it was nearly time for the tea interval, thank heavens.

Just then a peculiar figure emerged from the wood. It was Bledyard. Bledyard seemed to think it incumbent on him on occasions such as this to make some sort of an effort to fit himself into the picture. His effort, in this case, consisted mostly of dressing himself in white flannels and wearing a blazer. It was through phenomena of this kind that Mor had become aware on purely sartorial evidence that Bledyard was an old Etonian. Bledyard came towards him, nodded, Mor thought a trifle coldly, and then went on to take a deck-chair in the second row by himself. Mor felt curiously wounded by Bledyard's coldness. Although he rarely reflected upon it, he valued Bledyard's good opinion. A gloomy guilty feeling crept through him, which changed into an exasperated misery. Everything was against him.

Then somewhere beyond the pavilion a patch of white shimmering light began to form itself. It quivered at the corner of Mor's field of attention as he was wandering slowly back again in the opposite direction. He stopped and took in what it was. It was Rain, who was approaching the scene across an expanse of open grass. She was dressed in a light-blue cotton dress with a wide skirt and a deep round neck, and she was carrying a frilly white parasol. She had rather a diffident air, and twirled the parasol nervously as she came forward. The moving pattern of shadows fell upon her face. Mor looked at her, and he felt as if an enormous vehicle had driven straight through him, leaving a blank hole to the edges of which he still raggedly adhered.

Rain's arrival created a stir. Someone tapped Mr Everard on the shoulder and pointed. All the incumbents of the deck-chairs began to jump up and to run backwards or forwards. Sixth Form boys began picking up chairs and moving them to what they took to be suitable places. Evvy struggled up, tried to squeeze backwards between the chairs, caught his foot in one, lost his balance, and was set upright again by Hensman. The eyes of the School were turned away from the cricket field. Everybody was looking at Rain, who was now walking along in front of the deck-chairs. Evvy was squeezing back again between the chairs so as to hand her to the seat next to his. Even some of the fielders were turning round to see what was happening, shading their eyes as they did so. 'Over!' shouted the umpire, waking up to his duties. The field began to change places. Donald, who had stolen another run, was still at the batting end. The ball was thrown to Carde.

As Carde crossed the field, he passed near to Donald. 'Your pappa's poppet!' he said – and he went away down the pitch dancing and whistling 'A nice girl, a decent girl, but one of the rakish kind!' and tossing the ball rhythmically up and down.

Donald coloured violently, looked towards the pavilion, then looked away and leaned over his bat, keeping his head down. He straightened up to face the bowling.

Carde took his usual long run and bounded up to the wicket like a performing panther. The ball left his hand like a bullet. Donald poked at it ineffectually; and turned to find that his middle stump was lying neatly upon the ground. There was a burst of applause. Donald turned at once and walked rapidly towards the pavilion. He did not look at Carde.

Mor turned about to see that his son had been clean bowled. Amidst the other shocks this shock was separately felt, palpably different in quality. Rain had seated herself beside Evvy, and the other spectators had settled back. Now they were clapping Donald into the pavilion. He had made thirty-one. The next batsman was walking out. Mor wondered whether he should go away. One of the junior masters came up to him and engaged him in conversation. He replied mechanically.

Two overs later it was time for the tea interval. Mor was still there, standing uneasily in the waste land between the deckchairs and the wood. He saw Tim Burke coming towards him, and together they set off in the direction of the marquee which had been set up at the far end of the field. Mor deliberately blinded himself to what Evvy's party was doing.

'A fine show young Don put up,' said Tim Burke.

'Yes, Don did well,' said Mor.

They entered the stifling marquee. There was a powerful smell of warm grass and canvas which brought back to Mor the long long series of past summer terms. A crowd of boys was already there fighting for their tea. A special buffet had been reserved for the masters, and here Mor and Tim were evidently the first to arrive. Mor pressed a tea-cup and a cucumber sandwich on his guest. With an effort he did not look back over his shoulder.

Tim Burke was saying something. He drew Mor away into a corner of the tent. 'We haven't had a moment to talk yet.'

Mor's heart sank, he hardly knew why.

'Look now, Mor,' said Tim, 'you said you'd give me the all clear today, and I'm asking you to give it now. The time's short enough, and we must get cracking. You have it agreed with your wife, have you not?'

Mor shook his head. He had simply not been thinking about this matter at all. But now he knew that he could not, or at any rate not just now, carry out what had been his firm resolve to go ahead regardless of Nan. 'You must give me a little more time, Tim,' he said. 'Nan is still terribly opposed. I *will* bring her round, but I don't want to act now while she's so obstinate.'

I seem to have changed my mind, Mor thought gloomily. Very lately he had been absolutely determined to go on. Now he was delaying again. It was only a delay, of course; but he didn't like giving Tim this answer all the same. The fact was that his rage against Nan had quite evaporated. He felt, rather, a sense of guilt which took away any pleasure or interest he might have had in reading the two letters which she had sent since her arrival in Dorset. This was no moment for punishing Nan. It was rather he himself who deserved punishment. He must wait, and patiently attempt to make her see his point of view. If he was firm enough in his resolve she would *have* to agree in the end. Moreover, he was still feeling very upset and disquieted by recent events. He could not afford, at this time in the summer term, to have two crises on his hands at once. The battle with Nan, when it came, and especially if it came as a result of aggressive action on his own part, would be violent and bloody. He could not undertake it while he was involved, however momentarily, in another struggle too. Of course, the other matter could safely be regarded as closed; but he had to be realistic enough to see that it would be some time before he regained any sort of peace of mind. He just could not face fighting Nan just now.

The crowd behind them thickened. Tim Burke thrust his neck forward and was looking into Mor's eyes as if he were about to remove a foreign body from them. 'I'm not sure,' he said, 'that I oughtn't just to beat you into it at this point. Haven't I spent a year and more coaxing you and petting you until you're willing to do what your plain reason should have told you to do from the start? And now you're still dithering!'

'I'm not dithering,' said Mor impatiently. 'I've decided definitely to stand. It's just a matter of getting Nan used to the idea. Give me another three weeks, and for Christ's sake, Tim, don't make a fuss. I really can't endure it.' He returned his cup and saucer to the table with a crash.

'All right, don't bite my head off!' said Tim.

Donald was coming towards them through the crowd. Mor

reflected that if Tim had not been there Donald would certainly have avoided him. The boy greeted them shyly and accepted their congratulations on his innings. He bent down to scrape ineffectually at the green patches upon his white flannel trousers where the grass had stained them. Mor noticed how his face was forming and hardening. But Donald always looked more grown-up in the context of something that he could do well. A little more confidence would do him a lot of good.

'What can I show you now?' said Tim. 'Let me see what I have in my pockets.' Tim had done this ever since Donald and Felicity were quite small children, and he did it now with exactly the same tone and gestures. He fiddled in his waistcoat pocket. Tim usually affected rather dandified velvet waistcoats, but today, in deference to the solemnity of the occasion, he had put on an ordinary grey suit, which he usually wore in his infrequent visits to church. What Tim drew out of his waistcoat pocket, and held between finger and thumb, was a gold cigarette lighter. It was made to resemble a 'hunter' watch case, and was marked in a complicated floral pattern on both sides. It came apart on a hinge in the middle, revealing itself to be a lighter. Tim flicked it and the flame appeared. Mor rapidly produced cigarettes for Tim and himself. Donald was under promise not to smoke until he was twenty-one.

Tim handed the lighter to Donald to look at. The boy turned it over admiringly. It was heavy, and the gold was warm and strangely soft-feeling to the touch. The work was intricate.

'Where did you get it?' said Mor.

'It's a little thing I made myself,' said Tim.

Mor never ceased to be surprised at what Tim Burke was able to do.

'Do you like it?' said Tim to Donald, who was flicking the flame into existence once more.

'*Yes!*' said Donald.

'Well, you keep it,' said Tim, 'and let it be a reward for a fine cricket player.'

Donald closed his hand round the lighter and held it, wide-eyed, looking at his father.

'Tim!' said Mor, 'you have no common sense at all. That thing's very valuable, it's gold. You can't give an expensive thing like that to the boy!'

'Just you tell me one sensible reason why I can't!' said Tim Burke.

'He'll only lose it,' said Mor, 'and anyway it'll encourage him to smoke.'

'Och, don't talk through your hat,' said Tim. 'He can use it to light camp-fires or look at the names of roads at night. You keep it, me boy.'

Donald still stood looking at Mor.

'Oh—' said Mor. He meant to say, 'It's all right,' but instead he said, 'What the hell does it matter?' He gave a jerky gesture which was interpreted by Donald as a gesture of dismissal. The boy turned away and disappeared into the crowd.

'You should be ashamed—' Tim Burke was beginning to say.

Mor became aware that Rain was standing two or three feet away from him. She must have witnessed the scene with Donald. Evvy was standing just beside his elbow and had evidently been waiting to get his word in.

'I just wanted to say,' said Evvy, 'that we're just going over now in Miss Carter's car to Mr Demoyte's house to look at the portrait. We won't stay long – we'll be back in time for start of play, or just after. Would you and Mr Burke care to come along, Bill?'

Mor had a second in which to decide his reply. 'Thank you,' he said, 'we'd love to come.'

Evvy led the way and they all trooped out of the marquee. Evvy went ahead with Rain, Prewett keeping up with them on the other side. Bledyard, who was also of the party, followed a pace or two behind. Mor and Tim Burke brought up the rear. Mor tried to remember where, on the edge of the wood, he had left his coat. There was not time to fetch it now. He rolled down the crumpled sleeves of his shirt. They reached the drive, where Rain's Riley was to be seen standing not far from the entrance to the masters' garden. When he saw the car, Mor's heart turned over. It looked perfectly sound, indeed better than before, since it had been repainted. The question of the bill returned to him painfully.

Tim Burke said, 'I'm afraid, after all, I must go. I didn't realize it was that late. No, I won't take a lift, thanks, I have my motor-bike just here.'

Evvy said, 'By the way, Mr Burke, do you know Miss Carter? This is Miss Carter.'

'Pleased to meet you,' said Tim, and with a wave of the hand to Mor he disappeared smiling. Mor felt both unnerved and relieved at his departure.

They crowded awkwardly round the car. Eventually, after a few minutes of polite muddle, they got in, Rain and Evvy sitting in the front, and Mor, Prewett and Bledyard sitting in the back. Mor still felt dazed at the suddenness of this development. He felt a little as if he were being kidnapped. Then he began to blame himself for having come. Rain had not wanted him to come. It had just been impossible not to ask him. The misery which had been with him all the afternoon returned with doubled intensity. By now the car was climbing the hill. As they neared the summit Tim Burke passed them on his Velocette, saluted, and roared straight ahead in the direction of Marsington. The Riley was soon level with Demoyte's gate, had run on to where a gap gave access to the other traffic lane, and had sped back and into the drive at full tilt. They began to unpack themselves from the car. Mor wondered whose idea the expedition was. He thought it must be Demoyte's, as neither Rain nor Evvy would dare to descend on the old man uninvited. They went into the house.

Demoyte was standing at the door of the drawing-room, and behind him could be seen a table with cups upon it, and Miss Handforth who was holding a tea-pot as if it were a hand grenade. Evvy was putting on the chubby, jovial conciliatory look which he always assumed when he saw Demoyte, and Demoyte had put on the grim, sarcastic, uncompromising look which he always assumed when he saw Evvy, and which made Evvy more nervous and chubby than before. They crowded into the drawing-room. During all this time Mor had contrived not to look directly at Rain. He now tried to occupy himself by talking in a distracted manner to Handy.

'Well, come on,' said Demoyte, 'come and look at the masterpiece, that's what you came for, then you can all have your tea and go.'

The picture was at the far end of the room. The easel had been turned round so that it faced the room. They all went forward towards it, leaving Rain and Demoyte standing behind them with Miss Handforth.

When Mor looked at the picture, everything else went out of his mind. He had thought about it very little earlier, and not at all of late, though he had known vaguely that it must exist. Now its presence assailed him with a shock that was almost physical. Mor had no idea whether it was a masterpiece; but it seemed to him at first sight a most impressive work. Its authority was indubitable. Mor scanned it. It looked as if it was finished. Fumbling he drew a chair close to him and sat down.

Rain had represented Demoyte sitting beside the window with one of the rugs behind him. Outside could be seen a piece of the garden and the tower of the school beyond, made slightly larger than life. On the table before him were some papers, held down by a glass paper-weight, and a book which the old man was holding with a characteristic gesture which the painter had observed very well. Demoyte had a way of holding a book with his fingers spread out across the two pages as if he were drawing the contents out of it with his hand. The other hand was clenched upon the table and the arm straightened above it. Demoyte was looking inwards across the room. It was the attitude of one who has been reading and who has now left the page to follow a thought of his own which the book has suggested. From the extremely decorative background Demoyte's head emerged with enormous force. The face was in repose, the curve of the lips expressing a sort of fastidious thoughtfulness rather than the sarcasm which was his more customary expression. He must look like that when he is alone, thought Mor, it must be so. I would never have known that. The features were meticulously represented, the innumerable wrinkles, the bright slightly bleary eye of the old man, the tufts of hair in the ears and nostrils. Mor felt that he was really seeing Demoyte for the first time; and with this a sudden compassion came over him. It was indeed the face of an old man. In spite of the bright colours of the rug, the picture as a whole was sombre. The sky was pale, with a flat melancholy pallor, and the trees outside the window were bunched into a dark and slightly menacing mass.

Mor let out a sigh. He became aware of his companions. They seemed all to have been equally struck to silence by the picture. Then Prewett began saying something. Mor did not listen. He got up. Rain was a considerable painter. Mor was astonished. It was not that he had not expected this; he had just not thought about it at all. And as he now let the thought hit him again and again like a returning pendulum he felt a deep pain of longing and regret.

Evvy said, 'Miss Carter, my expectations were high, but you have surpassed them. I congratulate you.'

'It's a remarkable picture,' said Mor, hearing his voice speaking from a great distance.

'Is it finished now?' asked Evvy.

Rain came towards the picture. 'Oh dear, no!' she said in a shocked voice. 'There are all sorts of things that still need doing.' She reached out her hand and smudged the line of the brow, drawing a long smear of paint into the golden brown of the rug in the background. Everybody winced. Mor felt an immediate sense of relief. Not yet, he thought, not yet.

Demoyte came forward. He said, 'I begin to feel that I am the shadow and this the substance. All the same, I can still talk, and would point out that everyone has now given his view except the only man whose view is of any importance or likely to be of any interest to Miss Carter.' He looked at Bledyard. Everyone else looked at Bledyard. Mor looked back at Rain. She looked intensely nervous, and it occurred to him with some surprise that she cared what Bledyard thought.

Bledyard took his time. He had been looking at the picture very intently. He opened his mouth several times in an experimental way before any sound came forth. Then he said, 'Miss Miss Carter, this is an interesting picture, it is nearly a good picture.' He was silent, but had clearly not finished. 'But,' said Bledyard. He held them in suspense again. 'You have made your picture too beautiful.'

'You mean I'm an ugly evil-looking old devil,' said Demoyte, 'and ought to appear so. You may be right.'

Bledyard was one of the few people capable of ignoring Demoyte. He went on, 'It is a question of the head head, Miss Carter. You have chosen to present it as a series of definitions, well executed in themselves, I don't deny. But as it is its strength depends upon the power of these definitions to appeal to a conception of character in the observer. One result of this is that while your sitter looks old he does not look *mortal*. It is the mass of the head that ought to impress us if the picture is to have the power of a masterpiece. The head should be seen as a coinherence coinherence of masses. The observation of character is very well. But this is a *painting*, Miss Miss Carter.'

155

There was a silence. 'You are absolutely right,' said Rain. She spoke in a slightly desolate voice. 'Yes, yes, yes, you are right.' Then she said with a sudden gesture, 'Oh dear, it's no good, it's no good,' and turned away.

Everyone except Demoyte and Bledyard looked embarrassed. Bledyard, having said his say, returned to a scrutiny of the picture.

Evvy said, 'I'm sure Mr Bledyard didn't mean—'

Demoyte looked at his watch and said, 'If you want to get back to that cricket game before it's all over you'd better gulp down some tea.'

Prewett and Evvy accepted tea from Miss Handforth. Mor refused. Rain was standing by the table, fingering a cup and looking gloomily towards the picture.

Mor went up to her. 'Bledyard may be right,' he said, 'I've no idea. But it's obviously a good picture – and if it has weaknesses, perhaps you can still mend them?'

He bent over her, aware of the crispness of her dress, and remembering the smell of the cotton as he had pressed his head against her. He felt very large and gross. He was sorry that he was still in his shirt sleeves. The perspiration was staining his shirt at the armpits and he felt in need of a shave. He drew back a little, sure that his proximity must be offensive to her.

'I must paint the head again,' said Rain. She put her cup down and turned to face Mor. He had the sense once more of being in her presence and with it a blessed relaxing of tension. A weight was taken off him. He said quietly, 'I was so glad to see the car on the road again.' The others were not within earshot.

Rain fingered the cup. She looked as if she wanted to say something, but remained silent.

'I shall have to go away in a moment,' said Mor, speaking very gently, 'and I should like to take this chance to say that I'm very sorry—'

Rain interrupted him. 'Could you have dinner this evening with me and Mr Demoyte at the Saracen's Head?'

Mor was surprised and moved. He could hardly think of anything he would like better. But he remembered at once that he was bound to dine with Evvy. 'I can't, I'm afraid,' he said. 'I'm dining with Mr Everard.'

A feeling of intense disappointment overcame him. This might be his last chance to see Rain. This very moment was perhaps his last opportunity of speaking to her alone. He looked into her face, and was astonished to see what an intense almost wild expression was in her eyes. He looked away. He must have been mistaken. He clutched the side of the table. He could hear Evvy saying, 'Well, we must be off now, I'm afraid.'

Mor said quickly, 'Why not drop in for a drink at my house tonight on your way back from dinner? Perhaps about nine, just for a little while?' He uttered the address.

Rain avoided his eye, but nodded her head. 'Thank you,' she said.

Evvy passed by, clucking. They went in procession after him to the Riley, and Rain drove them back to the school. She left them in the drive, and drove away, swinging the car violently round, its tyres grinding on the gravel. Evvy and Prewett began to hurry back towards the cricket field. The school grounds were empty and silent. The hollow ringing sound of bat upon ball could be heard in the distance. The game had started again. Bledyard mumbled something and set off in the direction of the studio.

Mor stood by himself in the drive. The sun was declining. Birds walked upon the grass verge, casting long long shadows upon the grass. Mor watched them. He knew that he had done wrong.

157

It was a quarter past nine. Mor had found the time on the way back from Evvy's dinner to buy a bottle of white wine and a bottle of brandy. He had tidied up the drawing-room carefully and set the bottles there with wine-glasses upon a tray. He had laid out a dish of biscuits. Now he ensconced himself in the dining-room window, which looked on to the road, to wait to see his visitor coming. At about dinner-time the sky had begun to be overcast, and by now it was entirely covered with thick black clouds. The heat was intense and quivering. A thunderstorm seemed imminent. But still the warmth and the oppressive silence continued, seeming endless. The light faded, and a lurid premature darkness came over the scene. 'It's like the end of the world,' a woman said in the road. Her voice echoed upon the thick atmosphere.

Mor sat in the window, shivering. He could not bring himself to turn the lights on. He felt no pleasure of anticipation, no joy at the thought of what he was bringing about. He did not know clearly what he was bringing about. He wished that he had not spoken. He would not have spoken if he had not seen that look upon her face. But what did the look signify? He knew that once again he had taken a step along a road that led nowhere. And he had made it that much more difficult for himself, and possibly for her, to dissolve this ambiguous thing that was taking shape between them. Was it something, or was it nothing? He must believe it to be nothing. At moments he could do so.

Earlier in the evening he had consoled himself with the thought that perhaps she would not come. She would realize that he ought not to have spoken, and she would know that he would have realized this too, and she would simply not come. After all, the meaning of his five days of silence could not have escaped her. He saw himself so clearly as contemptible: a middle-aged man deceiving his wife, inefficient, blundering and graceless. Surely she would not come. Now, however, although Mor had no expectation of joy from her coming, he was in an agony lest she should not come. He looked at his watch for the hundredth time. It was twenty minutes past nine. It was now almost totally dark outside.

There was a sound upon the path. She had come through the gate without his seeing her and had reached the front door. From the darkened window Mor watched her tensely. She stood on the step. She was wearing a mackintosh, in the pockets of which she fumbled for a moment. Then she drew out a letter, slipped it noiselessly through the letter-box, and turned and walked quickly away down the path.

Mor did not hesitate for a second. He sped out of the room and through the hall. He did not stop to pick up the letter. He swung the door open and left it wide behind him. He covered the garden path in three bounds. He saw the small figure some way down the road, running now. Mor shot after her. The pain in his heart turned into a fierce delight. He came up with her just at the corner of the road and caught her by the wrist. It was like catching a thief. He said nothing, but turned her about and began to pull her back towards his house. She scarcely resisted him. Together they ran back down the road, Mor still gripping her arm in a tight grip. As they ran it began to rain. They went in through the front door like a pair of birds. Mor closed it behind them.

In the darkness of the hall he turned towards her. They were both breathless from the running.

'Rain,' said Mor, 'Rain.' It did him good to utter her name. He picked up the letter from the floor. 'You brought a letter to say that you had decided not to come.'

'Yes,' said Rain. She was leaning back against the wall.

'Why did you do that?' said Mor gently, and did not wait for an answer. He suddenly felt calm. 'Take your coat off.'

She took it off and he hung it on a peg. She still stood there by the wall. Mor came to her and picked her up in his arms. She was exceedingly light. He carried her into the drawing-room, slammed the door behind him with his foot, and laid her down gently on the sofa. Then he drew the curtains and lighted one of the lamps.

'May I read your letter?' he said.

'Of course,' said Rain. She was not looking at him.

Mor opened the letter. It read:

I am sorry. I ought not to have asked you to dine or said yes to your invitation. No more need be said. Please pardon my part in all this.

He put the letter away in his pocket. Thoughtfully he took out a packet of cigarettes, offered one to Rain, which she took, and selected one himself. Mor now felt amazingly and unexpectedly at his ease. He was in a terrible fix. He had behaved wrongly and he had involved another person in his wrong behaviour. All this would have to be sorted out. But just at this very moment there was an oasis of calm. He had caught her, he had brought her back, she lay there before him, she was not going away at once, he would not let her. Then deep within he felt again the joy which he had felt in the first day when he had looked at the flaky wood of the station gate. He loved her.

Mor turned and looked at Rain. She was looking at him. He knew that there must be a sort of triumph in his face. He let her read it there. She began shaking her head. 'Mor,' she said, 'this is wrong.'

'Rain,' said Mor, 'did you *want* to come?'

'Of course I wanted to come,' she said. 'I wanted very very much to come. But I oughtn't to have done. If I'd really willed not to come, if I'd felt clearly enough how bad it was, I wouldn't have run the risk of delivering the letter – I would simply not have appeared. But I couldn't bear the thought of your waiting and waiting.'

'You wanted to come!' said Mor. He could hardly believe it. 'Will you have some brandy or some white wine?' he said. What he wanted now was a moment of quiet.

'I'll have brandy,' said Rain. She sat up on the sofa, running her hands nervously through her dark hair. It ruffled jaggedly around her face. The rain was coming down fast now. Its drumming increased in an alarming crescendo. Then there was a flash and a deafening crack of thunder. They remained immobile looking at each other.

'Yes,' said Mor, 'I think I'll have some brandy too. I feel a bit shaken after all this.' The air was growing perceptibly cooler. The drumming continued. Mor turned on an electric fire.

He came and knelt on the floor beside the sofa. 'Dear darling,' he said. He looked upon her with amazement, with incredulity. 'How is it,' he said, 'that you could possibly have wanted to come. That amazes me. How could *you* want to see *me*?' He touched her hair.

Rain took the glass from his hand and laid it upon the floor. Then she threw both arms about his neck and drew him down until his head lay upon her breast. She held him close, caressing his hair. Mor lay still. A deep peace and joy was in him. He could have died thus. For a long time they lay quiet. The thunder rumbled overhead and the rain came down steadily.

At last Mor lifted his head and began to kiss her. She returned his kisses with an equal fierceness, her hands locked behind his neck, drawing his head back towards her. When they were sated with kissing, they lay, their faces very close, regarding each other.

'When did you begin,' said Rain, 'to feel like this?'

Mor considered. 'I think the very beginning,' he said, 'was when you took my hand on the steps leading up to the rose garden. Do you remember? The very first evening we met. I was so terribly moved that you took my hand. But I didn't realize properly that I was in love till the day when I found you in the wood, when the boys were drawing you. Oh, Rain, I looked for you so hard that day, it was agony.'

She stroked his face, her eyes burning with tenderness. 'That was a marvel,' she said. 'You came and released me from a spell.'

'When did you first,' said Mor – he could not find the words – 'notice me at all?'

'Dear Mor,' said Rain, laughing at him, 'I think it was when I was drawing you at Demoyte's house that it first occurred to me that perhaps I was – falling in love.'

It stunned Mor to hear her utter these words. He looked at her open-mouthed. 'This is all beyond me!' he said.

Rain laughed again, a deep loose joyful laugh that was close to tears. 'That was why I went to bed early,' she said, 'and why I wouldn't show you the sketch. I thought you would certainly be able to read in it what I was beginning to feel.'

'Will you give me the sketch?' said Mor.

'I want to keep it!' she said, 'but I'll let you see it.'

'Rain,' said Mor, 'it was torment these last few days. I wanted to see you so much.' He realized as he spoke that the torment had only not been unendurable because he had suspected in his heart that he would see her again.

'I know,' said Rain, 'I too – I've thought of nothing else. I knew I oughtn't to go to that cricket match. I stayed away all the morning and the beginning of the afternoon. But then I couldn't bear it, I *had* to come.'

Mor felt, it is fate, it is not our will. We have both struggled against it. But it has been too strong. As he thought this, he answered himself. No, it is our will. And with this came a great sense of vigour and power. He took her triumphantly in his arms.

'Mor,' Rain said, murmuring into his ear, 'Mor, we cannot do this, we are behaving like mad people.'

Mor heard her, and her words moved in his head, becoming his own thought. It was a searingly painful thought. He continued to hold her close to him. Such pain could not be endured; and if it could not be endured, then there must be some way to avoid it.

'We have no future,' said Rain.

He felt her tears upon his cheek. She is brave, he thought. She says this so soon. I would have waited. He held her and went on thinking.

'Mor,' said Rain, 'please speak.'

'Dear heart,' said Mor. He sat back on his heels. The brandy was untasted beside him. He drank some of it. Rain sipped hers. He felt as if they were adrift together. A world of appalling desolation surrounded them. But at least at this moment they were together. The brandy was putting courage into him. He could not, he would not, let her go. Yet there was no way.

'I don't know what to do,' said Mor, 'but I want to go on seeing you.' Once he had said this clearly, he felt better.

Rain was silent. 'I know,' she said at last, 'that I ought to say no to that, but I can't. If you want to see me, I shall see you. But we are mad.'

Mor felt profound relief. 'It can't be,' he said, 'that you really love me. You must try to find out your real feelings. Let us have a little time at least for these things to become clear.' As he said this he felt much better. Here was something rational to hold on to. The situation was not yet quite clear. Perhaps Rain didn't really love him – and if not there was no problem, or at least not the same problem. They must wait a while to see what their real feelings were – and during that time they must quietly encounter each other, patiently waiting.

'Do not deceive yourself,' said Rain. 'If our feelings are not clear now, they will never be clear. If there is something called being in love, then we are in love.'

My God, what honesty, thought Mor. But he did not want her to lead him into a place from which there was no issue. He countered at once. 'All right, call it so – though how you can love me is still a mystery. But if it's granted that we do see each other again, then at least nothing can be decided at once. We must wait a while. I feel far too confused to make any decision – except the one that we've made.'

Rain was sitting up in his embrace. She had emptied her glass of brandy. 'Mor,' she said with a wail in her voice, 'what is there to be decided? You are married. You are not going to leave your wife – and really there is nothing more to be said. We may see each other again – but in the end I shall have to go.' She hid her face in his shoulder.

Mor sat there thoughtful, in a strange repose. He rocked her against him. Was it unthinkable that he should leave Nan? The thought was so colossal and came upon him so unexpectedly that he drew in his breath. His mind closed up at once. He would not think of this. At least he would not think of this now. He must have time – and meanwhile he must hold Rain and make her trust him and make her patient. 'Do not let us torment ourselves any more for the moment,' he said.

His tone impressed her. They remained for a while in silence. 'Have you been in love before?' said Mor. He was lying beside her now on the sofa, her head pillowed on his shoulder.

'Yes,' said Rain, 'do you mind? I was in love when I was nineteen with a young man in Paris, also a painter.' She sighed.

Mor felt a fierce pang of jealousy. Rain at nineteen. 'A Frenchman?' he said. 'What happened?'

'Yes,' said Rain. 'Nothing happened, really. My father didn't like him. He went away in the end. He got married since, I heard.' She sighed again, very deeply.

Mor held her violently to him. He wanted her.

'You know,' said Rain, 'like Mr Everard you probably think that I must have lived a very gay life in France – but it wasn't so. We lived very simply in the south, and we didn't often go to Paris or London. My father was so jealous of everyone.'

Mor tried to picture her life. It was difficult. 'You will tell me more,' he said, 'in time.' It was a consoling phrase.

Mor looked at his watch. Somehow it had got to be half past eleven. Now that he knew that he would see her again he was not anxious to detain her. He felt that enough had been said to bind them together – and he did not want to alarm Demoyte by keeping her out late. He said, 'You ought to go home, my child.'

Rain sat up and made a rueful face. 'I've been very silly,' she said. 'I told Mr Demoyte that I was going up to London and would spend the night there. I had to say that so as to get away from him – otherwise he would have kept me the whole evening. And I did intend when I'd delivered the note to get into my car and drive up to London. It's parked in the school grounds. But what shall I do now?'

'You could go back to Demoyte's and say you'd changed your mind,' said Mor, 'but it would sound rather odd. I think he'd guess the truth or something like it.'

'I should hate to hurt him,' she said.

They sat there avoiding each other's eyes. The rain was battering the house on all sides.

'There's no earthly reason,' said Mor, 'why you shouldn't stay here. It's idiotic anyway to go out on a night like this. You can sleep in Felicity's bed. I'll go and put some clean sheets on it now.'

She caught his coat as he got up to go. 'Mor,' she said, 'you're sure you don't mind my staying and not—'

Mor knelt down again beside her. 'I love you,' he said, 'will you get that into your head, I love you.' He kissed her.

As Mor went upstairs he felt how strange and wonderful it was after all to be keeping her in the house. He began to make up the bed. He wanted to sing.

Rain soon followed him up. 'I shall go to bed soon,' she said. 'I'm terribly tired.'

Mor felt exhausted too and knew that he would sleep well. He sat down for a moment on the edge of the bed and drew her on to his knee. She curled up, her arms about his neck.

'Mor,' said Rain, 'one thing – are you absolutely certain that your wife won't come back in the night and find me here?'

'It's impossible, my darling,' said Mor, 'she's in Dorset. Anyway, she wouldn't come back in the night. And I know she's in Dorset.'

'I feel frightened all the same,' said Rain. 'I think I should die if she came back.'

'She won't come back – and you wouldn't die if she did,' said Mor. 'But I tell you what I'll do. All the outer doors have bolts. I'll bolt them all, including the front hall door, and so no one could come in, even with a key. Then if my wife should come we'd hear her ring, and you could go out of the back door before I let her in. But these are just wild imaginings. No one will come.'

At last he left her to go to bed. He went downstairs and bolted all the doors. When he came up again her light was out. He called good-night softly, heard her reply, and then went to his own bed. The rain was still falling steadily. The thunder had passed over. Very soon he fell asleep.

Mor was awakened by a piercing and insistent sound. He sat up in bed and saw that it was just daylight. A cold white light filled the room. It was still raining. In an instant he remembered the events of last night. Rain was with him in the house.

Then the sound came again. Mor's blood froze. It was the front-door bell. It rang a long peal and then was silent. Who could be ringing at this hour? He got out of bed and stood there in his pyjamas, paralysed with alarm and indecision. Then the bell rang again, and then again, two short insistent peals. It must be Nan, he thought – no one else would ring like that, as if they had a right to come in. Horror and fear shook him. He crossed the room in the pale light and put on a dressing-gown and slippers. The bell rang again. Mor went out on to the landing.

At the same moment the door of Felicity's room opened and Rain came out. She had already dressed herself. She must have heard the bell before he did. She was carrying her stockings over her arm as she had done on the day of the Riley disaster. He read upon her face the same frozen horror as he felt upon his own. The bell began to ring again and went on ringing. The whole neighbourhood must be being wakened by the sound. It rang out with violence in the dreary pallid silence of the morning.

Mor took Rain's arm. Neither of them dared to speak. He began to lead her down the stairs. She was trembling so much that she could hardly walk. Mor was trembling too in fits which shook his body from top to bottom. The bell was still ringing. It stopped just as they reached the foot of the stairs. Here they were only a few paces from the front door. Mor drew in his breath. Their footsteps must be audible. He could hear the patter of the rain outside. He hoped that it would drown the sound they were making.

He drew Rain, half supporting her, through the kitchen, and unbolted the kitchen door. His shaking hands could scarcely control the bolt. The front-door bell rang again. Mor threw the kitchen door open and pointed to the gate in the fence beyond which was an alley which led away into the next road. For a moment he put his arms about her shoulders, and then he turned back towards the front door.

As he did so his heart sank utterly. He did not know what sort of demon of fury and suspicion might now confront him. He felt as if Nan would launch herself upon him like a tiger as soon as he let her in. Slowly he began to draw back the bolt. Then he opened the door.

Mor stood petrified with amazement. A man was standing on the step with his back to the door. Violently, amazement was followed by relief. The man turned his head slightly, then turned right round and looked at Mor with equal surprise. They stood for a moment staring at each other. Then Mor recognized the man. It was the gipsy-looking woodcutter whom they had seen in the wood, playing with the cards. A second later Mor realized the fantastic thing that had happened. The gipsy had been sheltering from the rain under the porch, and without noticing it he had been leaning his shoulder against the bell.

In a wild relief Mor put his hand to his face. At the same moment he felt anger against the gipsy for having given them such a fright. He said, 'You've wakened the whole house up. You were leaning against the bell. Didn't you hear it ringing?' The sound of his voice was strange, coming after the terror and the silence.

The gipsy said nothing. He had not taken his eyes off Mor's face. He turned and went away without hurry down the path. The rain fell relentlessly upon his black head.

Mor closed the door. He ran towards the kitchen. Heaven

only knew how far Rain might have got by this time. He ran out of the kitchen door and nearly fell over her. She had been waiting just outside the door. He pulled her back into the house and began embracing her like a mad thing.

'Mor, Mor,' said Rain, 'what was it?' Her face was still twisted with fear and her hair was plastered to her head, blackened by the rain.

'It's mad, mad,' said Mor. 'We must be haunted. It was that gipsy. The one we saw in the wood. He was sheltering at the door and leaning with his shoulder against the bell.' He began to laugh in a helpless desperate way, clutching her to him.

'Oh,' said Rain, closing her eyes, 'I was so frightened!'

'So was I!' said Mor. He was still laughing, almost hysterically, and holding her.

'Mor,' said Rain, 'did you give him any money?'

'No,' he said, 'of course not! I was very cross with him.'

Rain released herself from him. 'Please, please,' she said, 'you should have given him money. If we had given him money the last time he wouldn't have come this time!' She looked at him, her eyes still strained with terror.

Mor felt a chill at his back. 'My dear one,' he said, 'if you wish it I'll go after him now and give him some money. He can't have gone far.' They looked at each other.

'Go please,' said Rain. 'I know I'm stupid, but please go.'

Mor went into the hall and drew on a coat over his pyjamas and put on a pair of shoes. He found some silver. He left the house at a run.

The sudden chill silence of the morning appalled him. The rain was falling steadily from a white sky. It must be nearly six o'clock. He looked both ways along the road. There was no sign of the gipsy. He ran a little way and turned into the lane that led towards the fields. His damp footsteps resounded strangely. As he turned the corner he saw the man some thirty paces ahead. Mor ran after him, and as he came up to him he touched him on the shoulder. The gipsy stopped and turned to face him.

'Excuse me,' said Mor. He suddenly felt very apologetic to the man and a little nervous. 'I do hope you will accept this. I'm sorry I turned you away so harshly.' He held out the money.

The man looked at him silently. He was wearing an old mackintosh which reached well below his knees. From out of

167

the upturned collar his streaming head, carved by the rain into something more unmistakably Oriental, was turned in Mor's direction. There was no comprehension in his face; but neither was there questioning or any alarm. He looked at Mor as one might look at a momentary obstruction. In that instant it occurred to Mor that the man might be deaf. That would explain this strange stare and why he hadn't heard the bell ringing. When he had thought this he was certain that he was right, and with the thought came a certain awe and distress.

The man turned away, ignoring Mor's outstretched hand, and continued to walk at the same steady pace towards the fields. His soaking mackintosh flapped at his heels as he walked.

Mor stood still and watched him till he was out of sight. Then he began to walk slowly back. He was very shaken, both by the ringing of the bell, the horror of which was still with him, and by the gipsy's silence. He decided that he would not reveal what had happened. He walked back through the abominable rain and stillness. The light was increasing, but always with the same dead pallor. The rain fell steadily, steadily. But for his footsteps there was no other sound. The sleeping houses lay about him. He turned into the garden and came through the door to find Rain waiting in the hall.

'Did you give it to him?' she asked anxiously.

'Yes,' said Mor, 'I did.'

'What did he say?' said Rain.

'Oh, he mumbled some sort of thanks,' said Mor, 'and walked on.'

Rain sighed with relief and let him embrace her.

He took her into the drawing-room, pulled back the curtains, and poured out a glass of brandy. 'Dear child,' he said, 'you've had a terrible hour. I'm deeply sorry. It was somehow my fault. Drink this.'

Rain sat on the sofa, holding the glass, while Mor sat on the floor and laid his head upon her knees. They stayed in this way for a long time.

So that this was the spectacle which greeted the eyes of Nan when twenty minutes later she came in through the drawing-room door. She had entered by the front door, which Mor had left unbolted after his return. The patter of the rain had prevented the lovers from hearing the sound of her approach. The first they knew of her presence was when they looked up and saw her standing in the doorway and looking at them.

Mor was the first to recover. He gently and quite slowly disengaged himself from Rain and stood up. He was about to say something when Nan turned, and rushing away across the hall ran out of the front door.

Mor was about to follow her when Rain said, 'Do not go.' She had risen too. Now that the real horror had come she was much calmer. Her hand upon his arm was chill but only slightly trembling.

'I must go,' said Mor. 'You wait here for me. Do not go away. Wait here.' He spoke with authority.

Then for the second time that morning he ran out of the door in pursuit. He looked up and down. There was no sign of Nan. He began to run towards the main road, looking down all the side roads as he passed them. She was not to be seen. The rain fell, blinding him, and making a grey curtain through which it was impossible to see where Nan had gone. He came up to the main road. Already a few cars were passing and a man on a bicycle was doggedly pedalling up the hill. Mor looked and looked. He could not see Nan. He turned back into the maze of suburban roads, and for a long time he ran to and fro searching for her. But he did not find her. She had disappeared into the rain and the whiteness of the morning.

# CHAPTER TWELVE

Nan had had her first shock of discovery when she overheard
Felicity talking by long-distance telephone with her brother.
The villa which the Mors rented every year near Swanage was
equipped with two telephones, one in the drawing-room and
one in the main bedroom. Donald had rung up, and imagining
that her mother, who had not hastened to answer the call, was
still out shopping, Felicity had spoken frankly with him. Nan,
who did not think that children should have secrets from their
parents, had lifted the receiver in the bedroom and was disquieted indeed at what she heard.

Nothing emerged very clearly from the conversation, but
enough emerged to make Nan suspect that more must lie
behind. She sat for some time in the bedroom, thinking hard.
Nan's first emotion was extreme surprise. What followed it was
anger. This was mingled with what was almost a feeling of
satisfaction at the prospect of being able to find her husband so
palpably in the wrong. After the quarrel which preceded her
departure Nan had had a small twinge of conscience. She was
quite sure that she was right to oppose Bill's foolish and unsuitable plan; but she felt that perhaps she had been unduly
unpleasant in her manner of doing so. The information which
she had gained from Felicity, vague as it was, was sufficient to
dispel her sense of guilt, and also to put her in possession of a
weapon which it was certainly at this time convenient to have.
Not that Nan imagined that Bill would persist much longer
with his Labour Party scheme. She had never in the past, in any
major issue, failed to persuade him eventually to see things as
she did. But deep in her heart she was pleased all the same to
have this unexpected access of strength, although the source of
it was so extremely disagreeable.

Very soon, however, the disagreeable aspect predominated.
Nan found herself exceedingly disturbed. She was deeply certain both of her husband's correctness and of his common
sense, and it was a measure of this certainty that the matter
had appeared to her at first sight in terms of a momentary

lapse on his part which gave her, in her struggle with him, a momentary advantage. But now her mind began to dwell on Miss Carter. Running over every meeting she had had with the girl, she now saw her as the sly insinuating creature that she was. How could she have thought her naïve? Yet in a way she was naïve. That sort of girl was able to mature the most infamous plans behind a mask of naïvety which deceived even herself, living in an atmosphere of hypocrisy so total that she was unable any more to distinguish the true from the false. Was it possible that Bill really liked her? Presumably this soft cat-like nature must appeal to some desire to be soothed and comforted which existed in all men, especially middle-aged ones.

Nan had never reflected on this sort of matter before. She had never in her life for a single second doubted of Bill's absolute fidelity to her. She did not propose to start doubting it now. Surely the children must have exaggerated or misunderstood. At the very most, all that was involved was some moment of infatuation, something which even by now was over, dissolved into the air. There was almost certainly nothing to it.

Or was there? Nan continued to be extremely uneasy and restless. What ought she to do? She thought of writing a letter to Miss Carter, and even began in her mind to compose one whose venom amazed her. But that was foolish. She had no vestige of evidence, and with that sort of girl one never knew, she might have the insolence to invoke legal proceedings. Nan had extremely vague ideas about libel and slander, and a corresponding nervousness at the idea of putting anything down on paper. And in any case, as she kept telling herself, it was all probably a misunderstanding, there was surely nothing to it.

She wandered about the house and got through the afternoon somehow. She managed to conceal her distress from Felicity. By six o'clock in the evening she had reduced herself to a condition of mental turmoil such as she never remembered having experienced before. She decided that the only thing to be done was to go home at once, explain the whole thing to Bill, and get it definitely once and for all cleared up. Then she would be able to enjoy her holiday in peace. She was surprised at her inability to behave with normal calmness. She decided to go on the following morning. Then she tried to settle down to a book. It was impossible. She told a story to Felicity about having to go to London to see someone who was ill; she packed a bag and boarded the night train.

What Nan beheld when she entered her house surprised her very much indeed. She had arrived home at this hour, not with any intention of discovering a guilty pair, but simply because of her own impatience and the working of the train timetable. It had never occurred to Nan to imagine Bill capable of bringing the girl into the house. In a second she saw that she had been wrong throughout. Things had certainly gone very far. She turned and ran, partly as an effect of sheer shock, and partly because she needed to think again before she confronted her husband.

As she ran away through the rain she could hear his steps pursuing her in the gloomy stillness of the early morning, and she ran down a side road and into an alley that led to some garages. There she stood quite still for some time after the sound of his footsteps had disappeared. She leaned back against the fence, clutching her small handbag, her feet deep in a clump of weeds which was growing out of the gravel. She stared fixedly at the side of the house opposite. The curtains were drawn. The people in the houses all about were still sleeping. By now the rain had soaked through the scarf which she was wearing about her head and was beginning to trickle down her neck inside the collar of her raincoat.

As she stood there Nan felt, for the first time since she had found out that something was wrong, overwhelmed with sheer misery. She had felt amazement, fury and extreme disquiet, she had even experienced a curious exhilaration, something of the instinct of the hunter. But it had not occurred to her to feel exactly unhappy. She had never in her life allowed Bill to cause her real unhappiness. There had been, there could be, no occasion for this. In her situation, that of a successfully married woman, unhappiness of that sort would have been merely neurotic. Nan despised the neurotic. But now she felt real grief – which her husband had caused. Gradually the conception that he was interested in another woman began to reach not only her mind but her emotions. As she stood there, her back against the fence, chilled and soaked by the rain, she felt that she had suddenly been dragged into some awful nightmare: she had been driven out of her own house. Her hand went to her mouth. She shook with the grief and the horror of it. The hot tears warmed her cheek, mingling with the rain.

After a while Nan began to walk along the road. She walked through the housing estate and out at the other end, through the shopping centre. The shops were not open yet, but the day was beginning. People were passing on their way to work. The rain was abating a little. Nan went into a public lavatory and adjusted her appearance as best she could. Then she went out and boarded a bus that would take her to Marsington. She wanted to see Tim Burke.

Nan's relations with Tim Burke were curious. She had known Tim for more than ten years, ever since her husband, who was teaching at that time in a Grammar School in south London, had first made his acquaintance through the Labour Party. She had always liked him. He had, it seemed to her, a sort of absurd grace and elegance of character which had occasionally, on particular evenings which she still remembered, shown her husband to her by contrast as a rather dour, rather dull and clumsy man. Nan had not, however, made much of these thoughts, and would not even have kept them in her mind had it not been that, at a certain moment, she noticed that Tim Burke's attentions to her were becoming very marked.

Tim had always treated her with a slightly ludicrous sort of gallantry which Nan had put down to his racial origin, and which she had often laughed at with Bill, but which had pleased her very much all the same. Her husband was never gallant. But now she began to feel, with a mixture of distress and pleasure, that it was possible that Tim Burke was the tiniest bit in love with her. She had said nothing to Bill about it, had made no effort either to see or to avoid Tim, but had watched him closely. One evening about nine o'clock she had been alone with him in the shop. Bill had gone down the street to make a phone call, since Tim kept no telephone. Tim had been putting a necklace round Nan's neck, something which he often did when Bill was there. He was facing her and his hands met behind her head to fasten the clasp. The clasp was fastened. But Tim did not withdraw his hands. Then he kissed her on the lips.

Nan had been shocked and upset; yet in the very same instant she had been delighted. She had pushed him away from her. Bill came back almost at once and cut off any possible discussion between them of what had taken place. Nor did either of them ever refer to it again. For some time after this Nan avoided Tim, and saw him, if it were inevitable, only in the company of Bill. Tim behaved in what seemed to Nan a very transparent manner, trying by his whole bearing to indicate to her his regret for what had passed, combined with his continued respect and affection. But Bill noticed nothing, and Nan said nothing. That was four years ago. Gradually relations between them became more natural, and Nan began to remember the incident not with any pain but with a sort of sad gratification. She could not help hoping that Tim Burke remembered it in this way too. It was packed away forever. But the distant thought of it gave a special fragrance to the infrequent occasions on which, always in the company of her husband, Nan permitted herself to see the Irishman.

As Nan sat on the bus, her tearful face turned towards the glass of the window, she did not experience any doubts or hesitation concerning the propriety of visiting Tim in this crisis. She was *in extremis*. She must have help. She did not know what to do. The idea of confiding in one of her women friends, such as Mrs Prewett, was inconceivable. Her need to see Tim, once the notion had occurred to her, was extreme. She sat there and suffered – and more and more the feeling that bit into her, appearing as a physical pang, was something which she began to recognize as pure jealousy. She breathed in quickly through her mouth and found that she had uttered an audible sob. She buried her mouth in her handkerchief.

Nan got off the bus and hurried down the street towards Tim's shop. She saw him far off, outside on the pavement. He was taking down the wooden shutters, although it was not yet nine o'clock. Nan ran up to him, touched him on the shoulder, and went at once into the shop. Tim followed her in. He had seen her face. He shut the shop door and locked it. The room was darkened, as half the shutters were still up.

'What is it?' said Tim Burke.

Nan said, 'I'm sorry, Tim, to come like this. Something awful has happened.' She kept her handkerchief pressed to her mouth.

'Is Mor all right?' he said. 'Or is it the boy?'

'No, not an accident,' said Nan. 'I've found out that Bill is having a love-affair with that girl Miss Carter. I came back and found them in our house embracing at six o'clock in the morning!' Her voice trailed away into a wail, and she sobbed without restraint into the handkerchief.

'Oh God!' said Tim. He led her back through the shop and into his workshop. The rain had stopped, and the sun was shining into the tiny whitewashed yard where the small sycamore tree was growing. Nan went through into the yard. Here they were in private. The yard was not overlooked. She put her hand on the slim trunk of the tree.

'Let me take away your coat,' said Tim, 'it's drenched you are.'

Nan gave up her coat and accepted a towel to rub her hair with. She sat down on a little bench beside the tree, her back against the wet white wall. She felt the dampness through her dress, but it didn't matter now. The world had exploded into a lot of little senseless pieces. Sensations of the body and small pictures of her surroundings moved around by themselves, now blurred and now extremely clear. She saw with immense clarity the leaves of the sycamore tree, still drooping with water. She reached out and plucked one off. She had almost forgotten Tim Burke by the time he came to sit beside her.

'When did this happen,' he said, 'that you found the pair of them?'

'What? Oh, this morning about six,' said Nan. As she saw again in her mind the scene with Bill sitting beside the girl on the floor, his head resting on her knee, her tears were renewed, and she reached out and plucked another leaf from the tree.

'I tell you what,' said Tim Burke, 'I'll give you a sup of whisky, it'll stave off the shock from you.' He came back with two glasses. Nan took hers automatically and began to sip the golden stuff. At first she coughed, but then she felt it warm and violent inside. She felt a little better.

Tim had swallowed his at a gulp. He sat down again. Someone was knocking at the door of the shop. He paid no attention. Through her grief Nan became aware that Tim was at a loss. He did not know what to do. Nan hated it when other people did not know how to conduct themselves. She was used to taking control of situations. She would have preferred not to have to control this one.

'Did you know what was happening?' said Nan, drying her

eyes. The effort made her feel better. 'Did you ever see them together?'

'No,' said Tim, 'I didn't. I'm sorry. But you know it's likely not anything important at all. Whatever it is, it'll soon be done. Don't be too angry with Mor.'

'Oh, *don't*!' said Nan. Somehow to talk of being or not being angry with Bill had nothing to do with it. That was not what it was like.

'What did you do?' said Tim.

'I ran straight out of the house,' said Nan, 'and came here.' She drank some more whisky and Tim filled up her glass. She reached out again to the tree.

'You'd better go back again,' said Tim. 'Mor will be waiting, and he'll be in an agony.'

Go back, yes, thought Nan. The real pain after all was not that the world had fallen into little pieces. That was a relief from pain. It was rather that the world remained, whole, ordinary and relentlessly to be lived in.

'Don't be too hard on Mor,' said Tim again. 'He'll have a bad time of it. And anyway you are the stronger one. Yes,' he said, 'you *are* the strong one, you know.'

Nan knew. She would have to hold this situation as she had held all other situations, controlling Bill, easing the effects of his clumsiness, guiding them both through. *She* would have to cope with this. The thought was melancholy but there was a little comfort in it.

'I'll go out in a minute,' said Tim, 'and order you a taxi. But just now relax yourself and don't be thinking what you'll say. Let *him* do the talking.'

Nan thought, he wants me to go, he wants to be rid of me, to move this awful thing away to another place. She felt no animosity against Tim. In the intense rainy sunlight of the yard she saw his face close to hers, pale, unhealthy, puckered up with distress and indecision. She reached out and found his hand. They sat so for a while, rather awkwardly side by side, as if posing for an old-fashioned photograph. Nan laid her glass down and with her other hand plucked some more leaves from the tree. The sun was beginning to warm them. It was a strange interval.

After a while Nan raised her eyes to Tim. He was looking at her intensely. She sustained his gaze.

'Come inside,' he said, rising suddenly, and reaching a strong arm to pull her to her feet. 'Come inside now, and rest in the big armchair.'

Nan got up. The yard began to rotate quietly round her. The whisky must have gone to her head. She sat down again. The nightmare feeling returned. The objects in the yard were present to her with an appalling precision. She made an effort and stood up on her own. The yard was looking very strange, as if it were growing brilliant and slightly larger. She saw that she had picked nearly all the leaves off the sycamore tree. It stood there rather wretchedly gaunt with a premature autumn, its shadow stretching up the bumpy wall which was steaming in the sun. A curious light was shining. Nan looked up and saw directly above her a rainbow displayed against a pewter-coloured sky. She shuddered, and went back through the door which Tim Burke was holding open for her.

In the little workroom it was very dark. Tim worked there usually by neon light. Nan stumbled against the thick leg of the work bench. The big armchair stood in the farthest darkest corner, a large decrepit thing, banished some time ago from Tim's small sitting-room upstairs.

Awkwardly Tim led her towards the corner. Nan began to say something and turned to face him. A moment later, half pushed by Tim and half collapsing of her own accord she had fallen back into the grinding springs of the chair. She lay there spread-eagled, suddenly helpless, her legs outstretched, her shoes propped at the high heel. She saw through the small square window a section of the rainbow. Tim was leaning over her now, his hands upon the two arms of the chair. He was leaning closer, and the window was blotted out. Then, placing one knee upon the edge, he lay upon her, his arms struggling to meet behind her back while his heavy body crushed her into the depths of the chair.

Nan lay there limply, her hands upon his back and upon the sleeve of his coat, not grasping, but dropped there like two exhausted birds. His shoulder was pressing her chin back and her head sank into the deep dusty upholstery, releasing a musty smell. For a moment or two Nan lay still, looking thoughtfully over his shoulder through the half-open door of the workroom and into the darkened shop. Then she wriggled slightly, trying to release her chin from the pressure. She became aware that the weight of Tim's body upon her was comforting, was more than that. She began in a half-hearted way to struggle.

At once Tim moved, taking his weight off her and endeavouring to shift her to one side so that he could lie beside her in the chair. For a minute they jostled, Nan withdrawing her arms and awkwardly edging away, her heels braced and slipping on the floor, and Tim burrowing beside her, his big hands underneath her body. Then they lay still again, facing each other. Nan found that her heart was beating very fast. She felt a little fear and a little disgust at finding Tim's white face so close to hers, his lips moist and parted. Then she threw her arms about his neck and drew him up against her, partly so as not to see any longer the staring look that was in his eyes.

'Nan,' said Tim, 'I do love you, you know that, don't you? I wish I could do something for you, some good thing.'

'Yes,' said Nan. She knew that the strange comfort that she felt would last only a few seconds longer.

'Dear, I've so often wanted to tell you things,' Tim went on, his voice burring in her ear.

'What things?' said Nan. Distantly she could hear the voices of people passing in the street.

'Oh, foolish things,' said Tim. 'Things about Ireland, about when I was a child there, things I couldn't tell to anybody else.'

Nan thought, now Tim is going to tell me about his childhood. She had an instantaneous vision of herself spending the morning lying in the armchair and hearing about Tim's childhood. I must be drunk, she thought. She began to struggle again.

This time Tim braced his hand against the back of the chair and pulled himself out until he was kneeling beside her. Nan dragged herself up to a sitting position. A light dust surrounded them and a smell of the past.

Now that she could see his face again Nan felt her despair returning. After all, it was nothing but a senseless pause. Another minute and they would both be feeling embarrassment. 'Please call me a taxi, Tim,' she said.

Bowing his head, Tim rose and went out into the shop, closing the door behind him. She heard him pass into the street. She sat up and began to search for her handbag. She examined herself in the pocket mirror. As she saw her dishevelled head in the half-light she started quite quietly to cry again. But by the time Tim had returned she had combed her hair and applied some powder to her nose.

When she heard his steps she got up and they met at the door of the shop. He put his two hands at her waist.

'Oh God!' said Tim Burke. Words failed him.

'Is the taxi coming?' said Nan.

'It'll be here in half a minute.'

Nan looked into his face. Now that she was erect it no longer appalled her; and suddenly she wished desperately that she could stay with Tim Burke that morning and talk to him, talk to him about anything at all, about Ireland, about his past life of which she knew nothing, about his hopes and fears, about when he had begun to love her. For an instant she apprehended him there, pale, awkward, strong, with his two large palms seeming to enclose her body. In that instant she saw him close, mysterious, other than herself, full to the brim of his own particular history.

There was a loud knock at the door.

'It's the taxi,' said Tim.

They looked at each other.

'Shall we send it away?' he said.

Nan was silent. She wanted, very much she wanted to know him now, this person that confronted her. She could not think how she had endured to have so little knowledge of him. In the privacy and difference of his past, in all that had brought him, by ways that he had never told, to the present moment, there lay for her a promise of consolation and a long long solace of discovery.

'If you could only come to me,' said Tim, 'be with me some-how—'

Nan turned from him. With coldness, with violence, the reality of her situation touched her, the irresponsible silliness of her present conduct. She shook her head. She saw the glass of whisky standing near by upon the counter and she drank the rest of it in a single gulp. The knocking on the door was resumed.

'Open the door,' said Nan.

Tim fumbled at the latch, and then the pale sunlight was falling in a broad shaft into the shop, as far as where Nan was standing. The taxi-man was waiting in the road.

Nan came forward.

'Don't forget me,' said Tim, as she passed him.

'Yes,' said Nan. She steadied herself out on to the pavement.

'Don't forget me,' he repeated, standing behind her in the doorway of the shop.

Nan got into the taxi. A moment or two later it was speeding away. Her grief was restored to her.

As the taxi rolled along, Nan wondered what on earth she was going to say to Bill. She had never been in a situation remotely resembling this with Bill before. In ordinary life all her talk with Bill was planed down into simple familiar regularly recurring units. Any conversation which she might have with him was of so familiar a type that they might have talked it in their sleep. This was one of the things that made marriage so restful. But from now on all speech between them would have to be invented. The words spoken would be new things, composing a new world. Nan did not know what she would say – but in spite of Tim Burke's warning she was determined that it was she who would talk and not Bill. She wondered if Bill would say he was sorry. What did people say at a time like this?

Nan stepped out of the taxi. Tim had already paid the fare. The taxi-man helped her out. He was wearing an odd expression on his face which made Nan realize that her breath must be smelling strongly of alcohol. When she thought this she staggered, and the gatepost came rushing to meet her at an unexpected angle. She was beginning to feel a slight nausea which was just distinguishable from the rest of her distress. As the taxi drove away she began to search through her handbag for her latchkey. It didn't seem to be there. It had gone. She stood in the front garden wondering what to do.

She was very anxious that Bill should not know that she had been drinking whisky. So in what was to come she must keep him at a distance from her. She decided not to ring the bell, but to go in through the drawing-room doors at the back of the house, which were normally unlatched, and interview Bill in the drawing-room with the doors open. These thoughts came rather slowly. In the picture as she now saw it there was only Bill; it was a matter of managing him. It was something between herself and Bill.

Nan began to walk round the side of the house, supporting

herself against the wall. She felt mortally tired. But when she reached the drawing-room doors she found that they were closed and evidently bolted on the inside. This was unusual. She pulled at them helplessly for a while. Then she decided that she would get in instead by the low window which was beside the doors. It seemed to be undone. She stepped on to the flower-bed. The earth was soft and muddy after the rain. She pulled the window open and managed to put one foot through the opening.

'Nan, what in heaven's name are you doing?' said Bill's voice from behind her. He had just come into the garden by the side gate. Nan could see him out of the corner of her eye.

She said nothing, but made desperate efforts to get through the window. She had now got half-way, and was straddled across the sill, her skirt drawn tight, with one leg well into the drawing-room and the other one still outside. She could see the mud falling off her shoe on to the cushions of the sofa. Her other shoe had come off, embedded somewhere in the earth behind her.

'Nan!' said Bill's voice again. He was coming towards her.

'Keep away!' said Nan. She was pulling furiously on the frame of the window. She could hear Bill stepping on to the flower-bed. He put one hand on her shoulder and one underneath her and propelled her forward into the drawing-room. Nan collapsed on to the sofa. She had to restrain a strong desire just to lie there and whimper at the idiocy of everything.

She sat up. Bill was still standing at the window looking in. He was holding her shoe in one hand and was feebly trying to brush the mud off it.

'Bill,' said Nan loudly and clearly, 'how long has this business being going on?'

'What a minute,' said Bill, 'I'll come round the front way.'

As soon as he disappeared, Nan jumped up and opened the doors wide. Then she drew the sofa a little nearer to them and lay down upon it, propping herself up with cushions and facing into the room. She found a rug and drew it over her feet. Behind her lay the garden, drenched with rain and dazzling now with pearls of light as the strong sun shone upon it, and the plants gradually lifted themselves up, murmuring as they did so. The fresh air blew into the room, dissipating, so Nan hoped, the remaining smell of the whisky. Bill entered by the drawing-room door.

'Sit down, Bill,' said Nan. She indicated a chair near the door.

Bill did not sit down, but stood by the wall kicking his feet. He looked very like Donald.

'Let me explain,' began Bill, 'about last night. Miss Carter stayed here all night because of the storm, and because she'd made an excuse to Demoyte and couldn't go back there. It was the first time she was in this house. I'd only seen her alone twice before that – or three times, if you count the first night. And I've never made love to her.' He hated saying these things. He stood, pawing with his foot and looking down.

Nan believed him. 'All right, Bill,' she said. 'You are obviously what they call a fast worker. How little I knew you! Anyhow, I'm not interested in this sentimental catalogue. You talk as if you were confessing the secrets of your heart to someone who wanted to hear them.'

At this moment Nan realized with dismay that she was developing hiccups. The only hope was to check them at once by holding her breath. She breathed in very deeply.

Bill waited for her to go on, and as she continued to be silent he said after a moment or two, 'I should not like you to think that I regard this as anything trivial.'

Nan was still holding her breath.

After another moment of waiting Bill began to say, 'I realize that I have acted—'

Nan gasped and drew in another breath. It felt as if she had defeated the hiccups. She interrupted him. 'Listen, Bill,' she said, 'I'm not going to make a scene about this. I believe all you say. I've trusted you all my life, and I trust you now not to act in a way that will make us both ludicrous.'

'You don't quite understand—' said Bill. He was leaning back against the wall and looking with a frown at a particular place in the carpet as if he were trying to decipher the pattern. He beat the wall lightly as he spoke with the heel of Nan's shoe.

'Don't do that,' said Nan. 'You're making marks on the wallpaper. I think I do understand. You've got yourself into a sentimental state about this girl. All right. There's nothing very terrible about that. But whatever there is to it, now you must just stop. Your own good sense must tell you what to do here and how to do it.' Nan found to her surprise that the words were not new after all. The pattern of her former conversations with her husband was not lost. This thing could be dealt with as she had dealt with all crises in the past. She felt with a sense of relief her protective power over him. The nightmare was at an end.

'I can't stop,' said Bill in a dull voice, still looking at the carpet.

'None of that, please,' said Nan. 'You made this mess and you must get out of it. Be rational, Bill! Wake up and see the real world again. Even if you have no consideration for me or for that wretched girl who's scarcely older than Felicity, think a little about your reputation, your position as a schoolmaster. Think about the precious Labour Party. This flirtation is bound to end pretty soon. If you let it drag on you'll merely do yourself a lot of harm.'

'I love this girl, Nan,' said Bill. He tried to look at her, but could not face her stare.

'If you only knew,' said Nan, 'how pathetic you are! Just see yourself, Bill, for a moment. Just look at yourself in a mirror. Do you seriously imagine that you could make anything out of a love affair with an attractive, flighty little gipsy with a French upbringing who might be your daughter? Don't make yourself more ridiculous than you already are! If the silly child seems attached to you at the moment, and isn't just being kind so as not to hurt your feelings, it's probably because she's just lost her father.'

'I've thought of that too,' said Bill.

'Well, I'm glad you see the point,' said Nan. She hiccuped violently and disguised it as a cough. 'Now you get yourself sorted out and stop seeing this girl – and we'll say no more about it. You know I don't want to make a fuss.'

'I can't stop seeing her,' said Bill. He was still leaning against the wall with a sort of exhausted lassitude.

'Oh, don't be so unutterably spineless and dreary!' said Nan. 'You know perfectly well you've got no choice.'

'Nan,' said Bill, trying to look up again, 'how did you find out?'

'I overheard the children talking on the telephone,' said Nan.

Bill jerked himself upright. He said, 'The children know, do they— Oh, Christ!' He turned to face the wall and leaned his head against it. The shoe hung limply from his hand behind him.

'Don't use that language, Bill,' said Nan. 'It's not a very nice thing to inflict on them, is it? At least the children won't tell anybody. I only hope the gossip hasn't started already. Does anybody else know about this little caper?'

'I don't think so,' said Bill, 'no one who'd talk, that is. I think Demoyte has probably guessed. And Tim Burke knows.'

'Tim Burke knows?' said Nan. She leaned back among the cushions. A feeling of extreme tiredness came over her, and with it the nausea was renewed. The strength which had carried her through the interview faded from her limbs, leaving them heavy and restless. She knew that the misery was still there, after all, waiting for her. She wanted to end the conversation.

'Oh, go away, Bill,' she said. 'You know what you ought to do, just go and do it.'

Bill stood irresolutely at the door. 'Are you going to stay here now?' he said. 'Can I get you anything?'

'No, go away,' said Nan. 'Go away into school and don't come back for a long time. When I've had a rest I'm going back to Dorset.'

'Going to Dorset?' said Bill. He seemed alarmed. 'Wouldn't it be better if you stayed here?'

'To keep an eye on you?' said Nan. 'No, Bill, I trust you completely. I don't want to spoil Felicity's holiday – and I don't want to make people talk by suddenly reappearing here. I leave you to finish this thing off by yourself.'

'But, Nan—' Bill began to say.

'Oh, get out!' said Nan. 'I'm tired, tired of you. Get out. I'll write to you from Dorset.' She turned over on the sofa, hiding her face in the cushions.

She heard Bill take a few steps across the room as if he were going to come to her. Then he stopped, turned back and went out of the door. A minute later she heard the front door close behind him. Nan waited another minute, and then she got up, went into the kitchen, and was extremely sick.

# CHAPTER THIRTEEN

It was Sunday. Mor was sitting in his place in the school chapel. Although it was well known that he had no religious faith, he felt bound, as a housemaster, to attend Mr Everard's Sunday afternoon services. These functions were attended by all the boys whatever their denomination – although in fact most of the boys at St Bride's were Anglicans. The chapel was a high oblong building with cream-washed walls, somewhat resembling a parish hall. The congregation sat on rather comfortable modern wooden chairs. The altar was a large table, decorated with flowers, not unlike the sort of object that would be found in the waiting-room of a progressive country doctor. The tall neo-Gothic windows on either side of it were of glass, and outside in a tree birds could be seen tumbling about and chirruping. A plain cross hung above the altar, and a low wooden stockade, folded up by one of the senior boys when not in use, divided the chancel from the nave. A sort of crow's nest of light oak, to which access was had by a pair of rickety detachable steps, stood at the side, and served Evvy as a pulpit, from which at this moment he was preaching.

The chapel was consecrated as a church in the Anglican communion and every morning something which Evvy insisted, to the manifest irritation of Mr Prewett, in calling, Mass was celebrated at seven on ordinary days and eight on Sundays, either by Evvy himself or by the local parson or his minion. On Sundays a large number of boys usually attended this ceremony; but on weekdays, except just before confirmation, very few turned up. Often, as Mor knew, there was nobody present except Evvy and Bledyard. His mind dwelt upon this gloomy rite. His nonconformist upbringing, still strong in him, gave him a general distaste for such goings-on. In addition, the thought of Evvy dispensing the body and blood of Christ to the solitary Bledyard was faintly ludicrous and, in some obscure way, appalling.

Mor spread out his legs. He felt stiff and restless. Evvy had been going on now for some considerable time and showed no sign of stopping. He had taken it into his head lately to preach a series of sermons on popular sayings. They had already had 'It's an ill wind that blows nobody good', and 'Too many cooks spoil the broth', while 'You may lead a horse to the water but you can't make him drink' was rumoured to be still to come. Today it was 'God helps those who help themselves'. Evvy had started, as usual, with a little joke. When he had been a child, he explained, he had understood the phrase 'help themselves' in the sense of the colloquial invitation 'Help yourself!' and so had thought that the saying meant that God helped thieves or people who just took what they wanted. Evvy explained this point rather elaborately. The juniors, such of them as were listening, or understood what he was talking about, giggled. The senior boys wore the expression of embarrassed blankness which they always put on when Evvy made jokes in chapel.

Mor was not attending now. He was thinking about Rain. It was four days since the drama of Nan's return. Nan had carried out her intention of going back at once to Dorset. Since then Mor had received a letter from her in which she repeated what she had said to him. It was a rational, even a kind letter. Everything had happened that might overturn his love for Rain: the sheer shock of being found out, from which he had still not recovered, and which he had thought at first could not but kill his love by its violence, and now in addition the reasonableness of Nan and the manifest sense of what she urged. Yet when Mor had found himself able once again to consider where he stood he found that his love for Rain was still fiercely and impenitently intact. This was no dream. The vision of beauty and happiness and fulfilment with which he had been blessed, so briefly, in Rain's presence, had come again and with unfaded power. What he rather feared was that the shock which had so much confounded him would have destroyed her.

In fear and trembling he sought her out at Demoyte's house in the evening of Nan's second departure, and they had walked round the garden together. He had found her extremely shaken and sobered. She had then reassured him by saying that her feelings were quite unchanged by what had happened — and that the fact that this was so proved to her, what indeed she had scarcely doubted before, that she truly and seriously loved him. But she went on to say that there was no issue. There was, after all, no issue. They had walked through the gate in the yew

186

hedge and across the second garden towards the stone steps. Mor had said in his heart, there *must* be an issue. To save himself he would have to impose upon her simplicity his own complexity. Only so could he win what he wanted with the desperation of a perishing man, a little more time. He talked with eloquence and subtlety, he argued, he used what he could of his authority – and after he had at last drawn her into discussing the matter he knew with a deep relief that they would not have to part. At any rate, not just yet. And as they walked through the rose garden in the direction of the avenue of mulberries the intense joy which they felt at being together overwhelmed everything.

Mor had felt extreme relief at the discovery that the shock which they had undergone had not dislocated their love. Now when they began to talk he was surprised to find himself able quietly to unravel so many deep and obscure thoughts about himself and about his marriage, things which he had in the past but half understood, but which as he drew them out at last in Rain's presence emerged clear and intelligible and no longer terrifying. He talked and talked, and as he did so his heart was lightened as never before. He was able, a little, to explain how in the long years Nan had frustrated him, breaking within him piece by piece the structure of his own desires. He was able to explain how and why it was that he no longer loved his wife.

As he spoke of this Mor felt suddenly present to him the anger which was the tremendous counterpart of so long and so minute an oppression, and which, because in the end he had been afraid of Nan, he had always concealed even from himself. It was a great anger as it rose within him, complete, as if the memory were by some miracle retained within it of every smallest slight and every mockery. It was upon this strength, he knew, that he would have to rely to carry him through to what he must believe to be possible, an issue. Rain listened to him silently throughout, with bent head, until he had told her everything – except for one thing. In all his outpouring he made no mention of his political ambitions. Demoyte had obviously not spoken of this matter to Rain, and Mor saw no reason to confuse things still further by introducing it. This question stood apart from his immediate problems and there would be time to decide how it should relate to them. Later, much much later, he might try to explain this also. Meanwhile he and Rain had quite enough to think about.

Sitting now in the chapel, and watching through the window the birds spreading their wings in the tree, and hearing the distant drone of Evvy's voice, Mor was rehearsing what he had said to Rain and wondering if it was strictly true. He had said that he no longer loved Nan. Of course he no longer loved her. But somehow to say this was not to say anything at all. He had lived with Nan for twenty years. That living together was a reality which made it frivolous, or so it seemed to him for a moment, even to ask whether or not he loved her. On the other hand, while his not loving her might not be important, it *would* be a matter of importance if it turned out that he hated her. Certainly there were times when he hated her. He could see her, as he thought about it, sitting there insulated by calm and mocking superiority, announcing to him decisively that one or other of his dearly cherished plans was merely laughable and out of the question. Mor said to himself, of course there are faults on both sides. I am a clumsy oaf and I've given her a dull life. Yet, he thought, I may have failed to understand her, but I have at least tried. I've never inflicted on her that terrible crushing certainty of being always right. When I've disagreed with her I've always been willing to listen, always been ready to come as far as I can to meet her. Indeed, he thought to himself, I have come so far that I have almost invariably ended by doing exactly what she wanted. His anger blazed up, terminating the reverie.

Evvy was still prosing on. When Evvy preached, he puffed up his chest like a pigeon, grasped his vestments firmly in each hand just below shoulder level, and swayed rhythmically to and fro upon his heels. His earnest boyish face, shining with a benevolent zeal, was bent upon the congregation. Mor began to listen to what he was saying.

'And so we see,' said Evvy, 'that God is to be thought of as a distant point of unification: that point where all conflicts are reconciled and all that is partial and, to our finite eyes, contradictory, is integrated and bound up. There is no situation of which we as Christians can truly say it is insoluble. There is always a solution, and Love knows that solution. *Love knows!* There is always, if we ponder deeply enough and are ready in

188

the end to crucify our selfish desires, some one thing which we can do which is truly for the best and truly for the good of all concerned. If we will truly gear our lives on to God, and keep moving always towards that distant point, we shall be able, when the scene otherwise would seem dark indeed, to perceive clearly what is that one good thing that is to be done. And indifferent as we shall at such moments be to all worldly vanities and satisfactions we shall know the priceless joy of duty faithfully performed – for "not as the world giveth give I unto you". Often throughout our lives will the darkness fall – but if we are ready, through prayer and through the ever fresh renewal of our efforts, to "help ourselves", the grace of God will not be found wanting. And now to God the Father, God the Son, and God the bla bla bla bla . . .'

The School woke abruptly from its coma and staggered sleepily to its feet, drowning Evvy's concluding words in a clatter of chairs. There was a white flutter of hymn-books. The organ began to play the introduction to the final hymn. It was *Praise, my soul, the King of heaven*. This hymn was a great favourite with the School. It had a jolly swinging tune and was good for singing loudly. The boys began to look more animated. Then they burst into song. Evvy had found his way back to the place in the right-hand side of the chapel which he usually occupied at Sunday afternoon services. He stood there sideways on to the congregation, with the other masters in two rows parallel with him, facing each other. The boys faced the altar. Evvy had a serene and satisfied look, as if the tremendous burst of singing were a tribute to the power of his exhortations.

> *Ransomed, healed, restored, forgiven,*
> *Who like me His praise should sing?*
> *Praise Him! Praise Him!*
> *Praise Him! Praise Him!*
> *Praise the everlasting King.*

sang the School with abandon. As they sang, bent to hymn-books or looking upward in the joyful freedom of knowing the words by heart, their faces glowed with hope and joy. Mor reflected that in most cases it was joy at the termination of

189

Evvy's sermon and hope of a jolly good tea to follow shortly, but he was moved all the same. It was at such moments that the School *en masse* was most affecting. He thought to himself, what a sod I am, what a poor confused sod.

The voices rose above him in two layers. The hoarse breaking voices of the older boys were surmounted by the bird-like treble of the younger boys, roughened a little at the edges like unworked silver. Amid the concert it was usually possible for Mor to discern the voice of his son. Donald's voice was breaking, and from its present raucous clamour a pleasant baritone seemed likely to emerge. Mor listened, but he could not hear his son singing. Perhaps today Donald did not feel like crying 'Praise Him!' Mor turned his head cautiously towards the rows of faces, seeking Donald. For a moment he could not find him. Then he saw him standing at the end of a row, his hymn-book closed in his hand. Donald was looking at him. Their eyes met with a shock, and they both looked away.

Mor stared at the floor. He felt himself exposed. His face was suddenly hot and he knew that he must be blushing. The hymn ended. Evvy's voice was raised, and with an enormous crash the congregation flopped to its knees. Mor knelt gloomily, his eyes wide open in a fixed obsessive stare. Opposite to him he could see Bledyard kneeling. His eyes were shut very tightly as if against a violent light, his face was contorted and his lips were moving. Mor supposed that Bledyard must be praying. Evvy concluded whatever requests he had been making, and everybody got up. Mor stood waiting for the words of dismissal, his eyes glazed lest he should anywhere encounter the glance of Evvy, Bledyard or his son.

The thought that he would very shortly see Rain came to him now gently and insistently, warm and calming. He had a rendezvous with her in twenty minutes' time. He had asked her to meet him at the squash courts after the service was over. This was a convenient and secluded meeting place. The courts were strictly out of bounds to the School on Sundays – indeed, by reason no doubt of their peculiar seclusion they were out of bounds at all times except for the actual playing of squash. All games were forbidden on Sundays at St Bride's, although swimming was permitted, which for some reason did not count as a game. The squash courts were thickly surrounded by trees and could easily be reached by a woody path which led down through the masters' garden. They were situated close to the school fence wherein, near to that point, there was an unobtrusive gate to which Mor possessed the key. He intended to pick up Rain at the courts and then take her out through the gate and away. He had suggested the initial meeting place so that he could be sure of a moment of complete privacy in which to kiss her. He felt embarrassed now to meet her at Demoyte's house – and he was not yet in a state of mind where he could invite her to his own.

The organ was playing a cheerful march and the boys were filing out of the chapel. Mor looked up, but he was too late to see Donald go. The truth, had he told Rain the truth? He had not spoken about the children. But what was there to say? Mor turned and began to shamble along towards the other door, close behind Prewett's back. The music ended abruptly, and he heard his own footsteps shuffling unrhythmically in the direction of the exit. He got outside. He would give the others a little while to disperse and then he would make unobtrusively for the place of meeting. He wandered a short way down the hill and hung about on the edge of the wood.

He had deliberately given Rain the impression that his marriage was a complete failure, a wash-out, something that was already breaking up, quite independently of her arrival. He had, he knew, been anxious, very anxious, that she should think this, lest she should suddenly decide to go away. He wanted to ease her mind and to relieve her scruples. Had he in doing so exaggerated the situation? It was true that Nan had often said to him in the past – why do we go on? And he had always brushed this cry aside. But he had believed that Nan was not serious. Then it had suited him to believe that Nan was not serious. Now it suited him to believe that she was serious. Where was the truth?

Perhaps, indeed, Nan is not serious, Mor thought. But that isn't the point. As far as Nan is concerned our marriage may be solid enough. But why shouldn't it be, for her – since it's always been an arrangement devised for her convenience? Possibly I too am one who is to decide whether our marriage is solid. And it will not be solid – if I decide to break it. He leaned against a tree, disturbing the ferns with his foot. For the hundredth time he conjured up memories from the past, memories of the long long quarrels with his wife, from which he would emerge feeling as if every bone in his body had been broken, and she would emerge fresh and smiling, with the familiar mockery upon her lips. But this time the memories would not perform their task. Mor no longer felt any anger. Instead he saw again, clear as in a photograph, the look which he had received from Donald in the chapel. He closed his eyes. Oh God, what a mess he had made of it all. Only one thing was clear. He would not surrender Rain. The prospect of doing this, when he came to contemplate it, as many times in every day as he forced himself to do so, was like the prospect of cutting off his own arm at the shoulder with a blunt knife.

A long time had passed. Mor looked at his watch. He was almost late. He turned and began to walk through the wood in the direction of the squash courts. Now that the heat wave had broken, the weather was pleasantly warm and cloudy. A scent of moist sand and moss was rising from the crisp path beneath his feet and small white clouds, seen for a moment between coniferous branches, were tumbling down in the direction of the valley. Mor began to wonder where he would go with Rain that afternoon. They could go away somewhere in the car, somewhere a long way off, London perhaps, or perhaps over the top of the downs to the coast, to the sea. So slowly and reassuringly the idea of her took possession of his mind. She drew him. He quickened his pace.

As he went, his path crossed another path which led down the hill from Prewett's house. Here some of the younger boys were padding along, dressed in bathing wraps and rubber shoes, bound for the swimming pool. When they saw Mor they shouted 'Good afternoon, sir!' and stood aside to let him pass. With a hasty salute he hurried across and plunged into the deeper wood, leaving the path now, and ran down the hill through the dragging bracken and the brambles until he saw close to him through the trees the pale rough-cast walls of the squash courts. The building was plain and oblong with an entrance at each end and a pointed glass roof. Within, it consisted simply of the six adjacent courts with the corridor which joined them, and a narrow overhanging gallery for spectators. Mor came running across the open grass, swung in through the door and straight into the first court.

A person was standing there; but it was not Rain. It was Bledyard. It took Mor a second to recognize him and another to conclude that he was not there by chance. They looked at each other in silence. Mor waited for Bledyard to speak. Bledyard was dressed in his Sunday clothes, a black suit and an unusually clean shirt. He looked at Mor from under his eyebrows. He seemed a little embarrassed. Mor was panting from his run and leaned back against the dirty green wall of the court. Once the first shock was over he felt strangely little surprise at seeing Bledyard there. It was all part of the madness of the present time.

Bledyard said at last, 'I sent her away.'

'*You sent her away?*' said Mor. He almost laughed at the impudence of it. 'How dare you do that? She's not a child.'

'Well, you know you know she *is* a child,' said Bledyard.

'Which way did she go?' said Mor. 'I regret that I can't stay to tell you just what I think of this perfectly idiotic interference.'

'I have things to say to you,' said Bledyard.

'I have no time to listen to you,' said Mor. They stood for a moment, Mor glaring and Bledyard squinting at the floor. Mor made another impatient movement. He was extremely angry and upset and anxious to go to find Rain, wherever she might be, distressed no doubt by the unspeakable Bledyard. However, he was also rather curious about what Bledyard was up to. He still hesitated.

'I want to talk to you about the things you are doing now,' said Bledyard, 'to your wife and Miss Carter.'

'Suppose you mind your own goddamn business!' said Mor. He was trembling. Bledyard's impertinence was almost beyond belief. Yet it was not as impertinence that Mor felt these words.

'I think that you should reflect reflect carefully,' said Bledyard, 'before you proceed any further.' He was looking directly at Mor now. He was no longer embarrassed.

'I know it's Sunday, Bledyard,' said Mor, 'but one sermon is enough. You speak of matters of which you know nothing whatever.'

Over their heads, upon the green glass roof of the court, birds were moving to and fro, their shadows flickering, scratching on the glass. A sudden din of shouts and splashes from near at hand announced that the juniors had hurled themselves into the swimming pool. The birds flew away.

'I have to bear witness,' said Bledyard, 'and say that I think you are acting wrongly.' He stood very straight, his hands hanging down, his eyes wide open and bulging, looking at Mor.

Mor knew now that he could not go away. He regretted it deeply. He knew too that he could not fend Bledyard off with anger and indignation. 'I seem to remember your saying not so long ago,' he said, 'that human beings should not judge one another.'

'Sometimes,' said Bledyard, 'it is unavoidably our duty to attempt to attempt some sort of judgment – and then the suspension of judgment is not charity but the fear of being judged in return.'

'All right, all right,' said Mor. 'Your interference is absurdly impudent and self-righteous. But I'm insane enough at the moment to be willing to hear what you have to tell me.' Something in the seriousness of Bledyard's manner, combined with the extremity in which he now continuously felt himself to be, made him engage the discussion on Bledyard's own terms. He added, 'Let me say at once that I doubt if my conduct is defensible on any front.'

The latter showed no surprise. He replied, 'That is a very strong position, Mr Mor! The point is not to lament or cry out *mea maxima culpa*, but rather to do the thing the thing that is right.'

'Well, you tell me what that is, Bledyard,' said Mor. 'I can see you're going to in any case.' He squatted back against the wall. The lower part of the wall was covered on all three sides with black footmarks where boys had sprung up against it in the course of play. Above him hung the face of Bledyard in the fading greenish light. The roof was darkened. It must be clouding over. A few drops of rain pattered on the glass. Mor shivered. The screams were still rising unabated from the swimming pool.

'You know what it is,' said Bledyard. 'You are deeply bound to your wife and to your children, and deeply rooted in your own life. Perhaps that life will hold you in spite of yourself. But if you break break these bonds you destroy a part of the world.'

'Possibly,' said Mor, 'but I might then build another part.' What he said sounded empty and trivial in his own ears. 'And how can you, an outsider, assess the value of these bonds, as you call them, in terms of human happiness?'

'Happiness?' said Bledyard, making a face of non-comprehension. 'What has happiness got to do with it? Do you imagine that you, or anyone, has some sort of right to happiness? That idea is a poor guide.'

'It may be a poor guide,' said Mor, 'but it's the only one I've got!' He spoke with bitterness.

'That is not true, Mr Mor,' said Bledyard. He leaned forward, stooping over Mor, his long hair flapping. 'There is such a thing as respect for reality. You are living on dreams now, dreams of happiness, dreams of freedom. But in all this you consider only yourself. You do not truly apprehend the distinct being of either your wife or Miss Carter.'

'I don't understand you, Bledyard,' said Mor. He spoke wearily. He felt himself strangely cornered in the bare monochrome square of the squash court which seemed suddenly like a cell.

'You imagine,' said Bledyard, 'that to live in a state of extremity is necessarily to discover the truth about yourself. What you discover then is violence and emptiness. And of this you make a virtue. But look rather upon the others – and make yourself nothing in your awareness of them.'

'Look here, Bledyard,' said Mor, 'even if it were the case that I could set aside all consideration of my own happiness and my own satisfaction I should still not know what to do.'

'You lie,' said Bledyard. He spoke quite evenly and quietly. 'You do not know even remotely what it would be like to set aside all consideration of your own satisfaction. You think of nothing else. You live in a world of imagined things. But if you were to concern yourself truly with others and lay yourself open to any hurt that might come to you, you would be enriched in a way of which you cannot now even conceive. The gifts of the spirit do not appeal to the imagination.'

A burst of ear-splitting screams arose from the swimming pool. It sounded as if hell's gate had been opened.

Mor was silent. He did not know how to answer Bledyard. He said, 'I am probably not capable of what you speak of. Such an austerity would be beyond me. I am too deeply involved now even to attempt it. Perhaps too I don't think as highly as you do of these "bonds" and "roots". All I can say is that this is my situation and my life and I shall decide what to do about it.'

195

'You speak as if this were a sort of virtue,' said Bledyard, 'you speak as if to be a free man was just to get what you want regardless of convention. But real freedom is a total absence of concern about yourself.' Bledyard was speaking earnestly and quickly and was now scarcely stammering at all.

Mor stood up. Bledyard's didactic tone was beginning to anger him. He had humbled himself quite sufficiently before the man. 'I don't despise what you say, Bledyard,' he said. 'I'm sure it's very wise. It just doesn't manage to connect itself with my problems. And now, could I ask just one thing, and that is that you don't go bothering Miss Carter with any talk of this sort.'

His utterance of the name altered the atmosphere. Bledyard thrust his head forward and said in an excited tone, 'You know you are damaging damaging her. You are diminishing her by involving her in this. A painter can only paint what he is. You will prevent her from being a great painter.'

He is raving, thought Mor. But the words wounded him deeply all the same. Why had he been so patient with this maniac? The screaming in the background was rising to a crescendo. He had to raise his voice to be sure that Bledyard could hear him. 'Leave that to me and to her!' he said. 'You are not our keeper. And now enough of this.'

Bledyard went on excitedly, 'She is young, her life is only beginning beginning, she will have many things—'

'Oh, shut up, Bledyard!' said Mor. 'You only say this because you're jealous, because you're in love with her yourself!'

The whistle blew shrilly in the swimming pool. There was an immediate silence. The splashing diminished and ceased. The rain had stopped too, and there was a sudden and startling stillness. Mor bitterly regretted what he had said. Bledyard stood looking at the wall, blinking his eyes, a slightly puzzled and patient expression on his face.

Then Mor heard, very near to him, the sound of voices. The sound came from the other side of the wall. It must have been drowned till now by the din from the swimming pool. There was somebody talking in the next court. Mor and Bledyard looked at one another. For a moment they listened. Then Mor strode back to the corridor and stepped into the second squash court, followed by Bledyard.

The tableau which confronted them was this. Sprawled with

his back against the wall, one long leg spread out and the other crooked up at the knee, lay Donald Mor. Lying upon the floor with his shoulders supported by Donald's lifted leg, his own legs crossed and one foot swinging was Jimmy Carde.

The four regarded each other. Then as if jerked from above by pieces of wire the two boys sprang to their feet. They stood erect and attentive, waiting for whatever storm should break.

Mor looked at them and all his pent-up anger broke through. *'Clear out!'* he said in a low and savage voice. He and Bledyard stood aside. The boys passed between them without a word.

The distant bell could be heard ringing for evening prep. Mor and Bledyard began in silence to climb the path that led towards the school.

# CHAPTER FOURTEEN

Felicity began to swim back again towards the shore with long slow strokes. The sea was dead calm. She swam breast stroke, very steadily, trying to break the surface as little as possible. The water kissed her chin like oil. The sun warmed her forehead and dried the drops of moisture from her cheeks. It was a declining sun, but still triumphantly in possession of the sky. The coast was deserted. Felicity was in a rocky bay where at low tide there was revealed a great expanse of rounded boulders heaped at the base of the cliff. At high tide the water covered them and there was no way. Beyond the headland on either side were stretches of sand and there the holiday-makers had congregated. But here there was no one. This was very important just at the moment as Felicity was about to perform a magic ceremony.

Felicity had realized at an early age that she must be psychic. She had discovered a witch mark upon her body. This was a very small protuberance a little below the nipple of her left breast which was not at all like an ordinary mole. It rather resembled an extra nipple. Felicity knew that witches were provided with these so that they could be sucked by their familiars; and although she was not altogether attracted by the idea of furnishing this sort of hospitality to some being from the other world she was pleased to discover that she was undoubtedly gifted in this special way and she waited with interest for further manifestations.

So far nothing very remarkable had happened. Felicity was without information about the moment at which witches properly came of age. There had been, it was true, the advent of Angus – but Angus, although he could at times be very strange and startling to Felicity, manifested himself always, with a sort of modesty which she realized to be characteristic of him, in some form which would not shock the sensibilities of the other non-psychic people with whom Felicity was surrounded. Her brother, she had at last to conclude reluctantly, was not psychic. He had pretended for a long time to be aware of Angus, but it was now clear to Felicity that it had been only a pretence. He had also taken part with her in various magic rites – but Felicity had noticed with regret that Donald's attitude to these ceremonies had been distinctly frivolous. Donald did not possess the patient and meticulous nature required for a magician. He would always forget some detail, and then say that it didn't matter, or start laughing in the middle. In fact, because of Donald's non-psychic carelessness, the magic rituals had never yet been carried out with completeness; and lack of completeness in magic is fatal.

Felicity had made a careful study of magic from as many original texts as she could lay her hands on. She was distressed to find, however, that almost every magical ceremony that was likely to be any use at all involved the shedding of blood. Felicity was anxious to fulfil her destiny. On the other hand, the notion of, for instance, holding an immaculate white cock between her knees, decapitating it, and drinking the blood from her right hand did not attract her in the least. Eventually she decided that since she was patently under a taboo concerning the shedding of blood, she was at liberty to invent her own ceremonies. This, she felt sure, would be pleasing to Angus, who would be deeply offended at any shedding of blood, particularly animal blood. Angus was very fond of animals. Whether Angus would have liked a human sacrifice Felicity for practical reasons did not specially consider. She had therefore begun to compose her own rites – and on one New Year's Eve had written, under inspiration, a small compendium of various rituals some of which she had vainly attempted with Donald's assistance to perform.

Now for the first time Felicity intended to carry out one of these rituals by herself and to carry it out in its entirety. She had decided to wait, before putting her plan into operation, for a manifestation of Angus. Angus had been some time in turning up. That morning, however, she had seen him. He had taken the form of a man on stilts, with very long blue and white check trousers and a top hat. She had met him quite suddenly round the corner of a lane. He was making his way towards a fair which was being held in some fields half a mile farther on. He said nothing, but raised his hat solemnly to Felicity. It was quite early and no one else was about. The sudden appearance of this very tall figure startled Felicity very much for a moment.

But then she guessed its identity and immediately ran home to start making her preparations.

This was one of the direst of the rites and also one of the more complicated ones. The paraphernalia had all been collected beforehand and now lay spread out on top of a large flat rock which was just at the water's edge. For this particular ceremony it was necessary to choose a place beside water and a time when the sun and the moon were both in the sky at once. Fortunately the moon was rising early and its appearance coincided roughly with low tide. All this Felicity took as a good omen. It was nearly eight o'clock and there was still a strong light from the sun which was now low down over the headland. The moon was large and pallid, the colour and consistency of cream cheese, risen just above the sea. Felicity climbed out on to the rock, keeping her dripping body well away from the magical apparatus. Her swim had not been recreational. It formed part of the rite. A purificatory wash was essential; also the wearing of a seamless and sleeveless garment. Felicity's bathing-costume did duty as the latter. She dried herself thoroughly with a new and hitherto unused towel which she had bought that morning.

When she was dry and warm she began to prepare the scene. The water lapped just below the rock, extremely still. It was the dead moment of low tide. Upon the top of the rock Felicity drew a large circle of sand, and within the circle she drew a triangle of salt. In the arcs of the circle which lay outside the area of the triangle she laid small heaps of poppies and dog roses. At the peak of the triangle, which pointed out to sea, she laid her electric torch which had been bound round with St John's wort. This faced towards the centre of the triangle and was to be illuminated when the ceremony started. In the right-hand apex of the triangle stood a copper cup containing white wine, a new penknife, also purchased that day, some camphor and aloes in a packet, a large bottle of lighter-fuel, a live beetle in a matchbox, the supersonic whistle which Felicity had taken from her brother, and a pack of Tarot cards. In the centre of the triangle stood a tripod under which lay some laurel twigs mingled with wood shavings. Perched in the tripod was a handle-less aluminium saucepan containing milk and olive oil. In the left-hand apex of the triangle lay an image of a human figure about eight inches high which had been made out of

Miss Carter's nylon stockings stuffed with paper. Beside the image lay a fork made of a single hazel twig, since the image must not be touched by hand during the ceremony. There was also a box of matches which Felicity had stuck into the bosom of her bathing-costume.

Now everything was ready. Felicity began to feel nervous and a bit frightened. She looked up and down the coast. There was no one in sight. Only the randomly piled up boulders, shapeless and brown, stretched away in both directions. She looked out to sea. The declining sun was striking its last beams upon the sea. The moon was higher and smaller and less pale. Out of the hazy light a black shape came slowly and steadily towards her, moving very close above the surface of the water. It was a cormorant. It came straight in towards the coast and perched upon a rock a short distance away. Felicity switched on the electric torch. The light shining through a wreath of leaves illumined the uneven surface of the rock.

Felicity opened the ceremony with two silent invocations. The first was the invocation of the Spirit who was to be bound by the rites to perform for her what she desired. This Spirit was not Angus, but a greater than Angus to whom Felicity had not given a name and towards whom she rarely allowed her thoughts to turn. The invocation was wordless. Felicity had written down various spells for use on such occasions, but they had all sounded so silly that she had decided to abandon the vulgar medium of words. She had also decided that it was neither necessary nor desirable to specify exactly what it was that she wanted done. The general nature of the ceremony made that clear enough and the details could safely be left to the Spirit. The second invocation, also wordless, was one which Felicity appended to all her magical activities. It was to the effect that whatever else the Spirit, or spirits, should decide to do as a result of her rites, they should not reveal the future. Felicity had a horror of knowing the future. She feared very much that this might turn out to be one of the penalties of being psychic, and she was uneasily aware that unless they are carefully controlled spirits have a tendency to blurt out things to come.

After that, Felicity took the new penknife and made a small incision in her arm. This was for use later, but she felt, guided here she was sure by Angus, that it was advisable to make the incision before she used the knife for various other purposes. She then cut up the laurel twigs and set light to them. This was not enormously successful. The wooden shavings burnt quite merrily, but the laurels, which were rather green, merely became black at the edges. After several attempts they began to burn a little and the milk and oil in the saucepan became warm. Felicity threw on to the fire first the camphor and then the aloes. The flames began to burn yellow and green and a strange pungent smell arose from under the tripod. After some of the laurel had at last got burnt Felicity allowed the fire to die down and very carefully scraped up some of the ash which she was sure was laurel ash and dropped it into the copper cup of white wine. She stirred it and then lifted it to her lips. It tasted far from pleasant. Felicity took a sip or two and put it down. No more was demanded by the ritual, and she feared to poison herself. She then took the Tarot pack in her hand.

This was a crucial moment, since if the draw from the pack was contrary, or non-significant, the ceremony could not go on. Felicity knew from experience that she was able to interpret almost any draw in a way favourable to her designs. This was one of her psychic gifts. She was nervous all the same about what the pack might tell her. In relation to the Tarot Felicity had developed her own private symbolism. She had identified various figures in the pack with people that she knew, the more important people in her world appearing usually in two roles. Her father was the Emperor, and also the King of Swords. Her mother was the Empress and the Queen of Swords. Donald was the Juggler and also the Fool. She herself was the Queen of Cups. The mystic figure of the Pope represented the unknown person who was to appear one day to transform her life. The figure of the Papessa or High Priestess was her own transfigured personality, still distant from her and covered by a veil. For the purposes of the present ceremony Miss Carter was represented by the Moon Card and the Queen of Pentacles.

Felicity held in her hand only the cards of the Major Arcana and the court cards of the four suits. This reduced the chances of a meaningless draw. She cut the pack and then drew out five cards which she laid face downwards upon the rock. She paused solemnly, breathless. Then she began to turn the cards over one by one. She looked – and could scarcely believe her eyes. From left to right the cards she had drawn were these:

the Empress, the King of Swords, the Broken Tower, the Hanged Man, and the Moon. This was extremely easy to interpret and very favourable to her ceremony. The centre card was always crucial. Here, Felicity took the Tower struck by lightning to symbolize the magical rite itself which was to divide her father from Miss Carter. Her father's card and Miss Carter's card were placed on different sides of the Tower. Her father appeared in his material guise as King of Swords, not in his spiritual guise as Emperor. The two women appeared in their spiritual guises. But her mother was placed next to her father, while Miss Carter was at the far end next to the Hanged Man. Felicity was not able to interpret the Hanged Man – but she decided that he didn't matter. The omen was in any case extremely favourable.

She proceeded with the ceremony. The next act was to blow a long blast upon the supersonic whistle. This was the summons to the Spirit. The whistle was disconcertingly sonic at first, but as Felicity blew harder the note rose higher and higher and disappeared. She looked round to see if she had frightened the cormorant. He was still there. She then very carefully took the matchbox which contained the beetle. He was a shiny black beetle, vigorous and healthy. She moved to the end of the triangle where the lamp lay, its light seeming brighter now that the sun had disappeared behind the headland, and she upended the box upon the rock. She then turned the beetle so that his head was towards the centre of the triangle and let him go. He started to walk. He was to determine the exact place where the rite was to reach its consummation. As if he knew what was required of him the beetle ambled along the rock and then stopped in a small depression not far from the image. Immediately Felicity began to squeeze her arm. A little blood emerged from the cut which she had made with the penknife. She mingled this upon her finger tip with a little of the milky brew and put a drop of it on the rock in front of the beetle. As he showed no interest in the offering Felicity very gently pushed his nose into it and put him carefully back into the match box. Then upon the place where the blood and milk were smeared she placed the warm saucepan of milk and oil.

Seizing the bottle of lighter-fuel, she poured a good quantity of it into the saucepan and then tried to set light to the contents. It refused to light. The match just went down sizzling into the greyish mixture. Felicity was frantic. The whole thing was going to go wrong at the last moment. She tried match after match. She was nearly in tears. Whatever happened, she must not ignite the image directly. At last she picked up one of the blackened laurel leaves and floated it in the saucepan. At the same time she picked up the image with the hazelrod fork. She applied a final match to the laurel. There was a quick flare, during which Felicity brought the image forward and held it full in the leaping flame. The flame died down at once; but the image had caught. Felicity had taken the precaution be- forehand of soaking it thoroughly in lighter-fuel.

The image was burning fast. Felicity stepped quickly round the circle, keeping her feet inside the triangle, picking up the poppies and the wild roses which she then threw into the sea. The tide was coming in. Already the water was gurgling to and fro on three sides of the rock. The sun was almost hidden now and the outline of the land was purple and heavy. The moon was beginning to shine. It had become very small, a button of bright silver in a patch of greenish sky. It shone balefully down on Felicity. She stood, her eyes starting from her head, watch- ing the image burn. A chill breeze blew from the sea, fanning the flames.

Nan was standing with her feet in the water. At low tide a layer of small pebbles was uncovered which lay beyond the sand. When they were wet they were multicoloured and beauti- ful, but when they dried they all became grey. They hurt her feet a little, but she walked along, the very still water caressing her ankles. It came to the shore with scarcely a ripple. The tide must be on the turn. She looked out to sea. The sun was going down and covering its expanse with a spacious and tender light. The moon had just risen, with a big pale melancholy pock-marked face. There were not many people left on the beach now. She had hoped to find Felicity there, but there was no sign of the child. She seemed to be avoiding her.

Since her return to Dorset Nan had passed in her thoughts through a number of different phases. She had never reflected so much in her life. Her normal existence had not demanded, had even excluded, reflection. It had contained her firmly like a shell with every cranny filled. There had been problems, of course, and moments of decision, but Nan did not remember having felt any doubt ever upon an issue of importance. She had always understood, she had always known what to do – and when it came to persuading her husband to share her opinion, the pattern of argument had been reassuringly familiar, as if it were continually the same discussion.

Now the pressure of reality upon her had been withdrawn, and she was left alone in the centre of a void where she had suddenly to determine afresh the form and direction of her being. It was only within the last two days, however, that Nan had really become aware of this aloofness of the world. She had come back from Surrey in a state of mind far from cheerful, but at least energetic and confident. She had occupied herself upon the journey with intermittent thoughts of Tim Burke. She had been deeply hurt to learn from Bill that Tim had known all about it – was perhaps even an accomplice as well as a confidant. Reflecting on this, Nan had a feeling in which she rarely indulged. She felt sorry for herself. Only once in all these years, years which had often been discouraging and dreary enough, had she stretched out her hand a little way towards another person – and she had been betrayed. She was sad, too, because she knew that with this a sort of fragrance, a streak of colour, was gone from her life. The thought that, although nothing passed between them, Tim Burke still cherished her in his heart had been, but now would be no longer, a refreshment to her. Later, however, Nan began to feel less extreme, more ready to forgive Tim for his knowledge, and less anxious to interpret it as a betrayal. It was then that she allowed the memory of how they had lain together in the armchair to come back fully to her consciousness. She remembered the scene in detail, and everything that Tim had said. She dwelt upon it. Already it was like remembering the remote past, something tender and sad and utterly cut off. Perhaps after all it was best for Tim to play his old part and for everything to be as before. Everything must be as before. The thought that it must and would be so was reassuring. She realized soberly how much she would have missed him.

Her thoughts reverted to Bill. The sense of relief which Nan had felt during her interview with Bill, when she found herself once more in control of the situation, did not leave her for several days. During that time, when she thought of the interview, she filled in the details of her own powerful and vigorous attack. What Bill's replies had been she could scarcely remember. She felt complete confidence that her instructions would be carried out. How exactly they would be carried out she did not care to know. But she would come back to Bill to find that it had been done – and then she would endeavour to carry out her promise of not referring to the matter again. She was pleased that she had maintained throughout a civilized and rational demeanour. Fundamentally, Nan grasped the situation at this time as a drama, and one which she was able to fashion to her own pattern. She felt the satisfaction of one who is in the right, able to impose his will, and doing so mercifully.

Almost at once, however, certain other and quite irrational feelings came to plague her. She was not able to forget what she had seen when she came in through the drawing-room door. Gradually the notion that Bill had actually embraced and kissed this girl, certainly more than once, became a reality to Nan. From there it was only a little way to the notion that possibly Bill was still embracing and kissing her. Nan did not make the transition immediately. She had never experienced jealous feelings before – she knew that they were the sort of feelings which it is neurotic and irrational to indulge. So she put them away. But they would not be put away.

Nan began to have bad dreams. This was new to her as well. Usually she was not aware of having dreamed at all. Now the figure of her husband haunted her continually throughout the night. She did not dream of the girl. Nan began to think about her husband. In those few days she thought about him more intensely than she had ever done since she had first been in love with him. His face haunted her. One vision of it especially she had, seeing it as she had so often seen it in the early mornings beside her, in the days when they had shared a bed, when she had woken first, the tired unshaven sleeping face of a man. She began to miss him. She began, though she did not let this become clear to herself, almost to desire him.

It was a day later that she began to be afraid. She started to wonder what, at that very moment, was going on. She began to doubt whether after all her instructions would be carried out. A letter came from Bill in answer to hers. It was very vague. It was not at all reassuring. It was the more alarming because Bill was usually so direct and not fond of ambiguities. Then she began to wake in the night and speculate about what Bill was doing. She began to rehearse detailed and catastrophic fantasies. She wished then very much that she had not come back to Dorset – but she could not yet make up her mind to return to Surrey. She began to remember what Bill had said during their interview. Now it was her own words which appeared in memory hazy and unimportant, while Bill's words were filled in sharply. It came to her as a real possibility that she might lose her husband.

During these days Nan spoke to no one except Felicity, and she spoke to Felicity only of ordinary things. Felicity avoided her in any case, leaving the house immediately after every meal and disappearing along the coast or into the country. Nan had no wish to speak frankly with her daughter. But she wanted more and more to have the girl's company, as it became less and less agreeable to be alone. She had come to look for her now along the beach, but without success. The sandy bay was almost deserted. The setting sun and the cool wind had sent hurrying home the few families that still lingered there. Nan's feet were chilled. She dried them on her handkerchief and put her shoes on.

Her wandering had brought her close to the headland beyond which the coast became jagged and rocky. In that desolate bay of rocks she knew that Felicity liked often to sit alone. She thought that she would look round the headland before she went back to the villa. She did not want to go back just yet to the empty villa. She started to walk along the shingle. Already the rocks were beginning. It was hard to climb upon them with high-heeled shoes. These loose rocks appalled Nan. Round, random, detachable, they were strewn at the foot of the cliff and the sea moved them a little every time it came in to cover them. They were terrible and without sense. As Nan stood balanced, about to step from one boulder to the next, she heard a thin piercing wail, which grew higher and higher and then died away. It was not like the cry of a bird. She stood a moment, shivered, and then went on, awkwardly stepping from one smooth tilting surface on to the next one. It was a little while before she had got sufficiently round the headland to be able to see into the next bay. Near to her a great black thing suddenly rose and went slowly away, out towards the horizon, black in the final brilliance of the sun. It frightened Nan for a moment. But it was only a cormorant.

The sky was a rich darkening blue at the zenith, but the golden light, still lying in sheets upon the water, dazzled Nan for a moment. As she paused it was already fading. Then as her eyes became more accustomed to the scene she saw a strange flame leaping upon a rock not far away. A figure was standing upright upon the rock, which was now surrounded by the incoming tide. It was Felicity. Nan called out, and began to hurry across the rocks, stepping as quickly as she could towards her daughter. As soon as Felicity saw her mother coming she began in desperate haste to pick up a lot of things which were lying about on top of the rock. Then she began to sweep the rock with her hand, sweeping everything that remained upon it off into the sea. The little fire which had been burning on the rock was swept off too, and lay upon the surface of the water, where amid a wide scattering of leaves and flowers which were already floating there it continued to burn.

Amazed, Nan arrived close to the rock, and stood there looking out at Felicity. In spite of the chill of the evening Felicity was dressed only in a bathing-costume. A number of odd tins and bottles stood upon the rock. It looked as if she had been having a picnic. But it must have been a strange picnic. The flare continued upon the surface of the water and the incoming tide carried it almost to Nan's feet where it burnt uncannily. Felicity now stood paralysed, staring down at the flames.

'Darling,' said Nan, 'have you gone quite mad? You'll catch your death of cold standing there with nothing on. There's quite a cold wind now that the sun's gone down. And if you don't hurry you'll be stranded on that rock. Where are your clothes?'

'Here,' said Felicity dully. She produced them from a shelf on the other side of the rock.

'Throw them across to me,' said Nan, 'and you'd better pass me those other things as well, whatever they are, and then come across yourself at once. I think as it is you'll have to wade.'

A wide channel now flowed between Felicity's rock and the mainland. Afloat upon it the flame was still alight.

'Whatever were you burning?' said Nan. 'It smells very funny, and it's odd the way it hasn't gone out.'

The flame rose from the glassy surface of the gently flowing tide and was reflected in it. The sun was down now and the air was denser with the twilight. Then quite suddenly the fire was out, and there was nothing but a little blackened lump, floating near to the edge of the rock.

Fascinated, Nan leaned down and was about to pick it out of the water.

'Don't touch it!' said Felicity. 'Here, catch!' She bundled her clothes up into the towel and threw them. Nan stepped back hurriedly and caught them. Then in a fever of haste Felicity began to pack all the remaining objects into a bag. She took it in her hand and gently tossed it across the channel. It landed neatly upon a rock. Then Felicity jumped down into the sea. She gasped at its coldness. She began to wade across to where Nan was standing. On the way she beat with her hands at the charred black thing which still floated there. It disintegrated completely.

Nan had the towel ready for her. She began to rub her down vigorously as she had so often done when she was a small child.

'Don't, you're hurting me!' said Felicity. Then, with snuffling sobs, she began to cry.

'Dear me, dear me!' said Nan, 'What a cry baby! You're always wailing. Now then put your vest on quick – and tell me what's the matter.'

Felicity was trembling with cold. She got her vest on and began to fumble with her dress. She said, 'I saw a butterfly flying out to sea. It will get lost out there and die.' She pulled the dress on over her head. Her tears were still falling.

'What nonsense, child!' said Nan. 'It could fly back again, couldn't it? Anyway, they can fly for miles, they often fly over to France. That's nothing to cry about.'

Felicity sat down. It was quite dark now. The moon shone out of a cloudless sky of dark blue, revealing on either side of them the tumbled heaps of rock. Felicity was trying to dry her feet. Nan felt them. They were limp and cold as ice.

'I saw a fish,' said Felicity, 'that a man had caught. It was a big fish. It was lying all by itself on the sand, and struggling and gasping. I wanted to pick it up and throw it back into the sea. But I wasn't brave enough to.' Her voice broke in renewed sobs.

Nan bent forward, chafing one white foot between her hands. She felt the tears rising. She could not control them any more. She took a deep breath and her weeping began. Sitting there, her hand still clasped about her daughter's foot, she wept without restraint. The moon shone brightly down upon them both,

During those days Mor learnt what it was to have a mind diseased. There was no longer any point at which his thoughts could find rest. They fled tortured from place to place. Only by absorbing himself in the routine duties of the school was he able to find, not peace, but the means simply of continuing to exist. He felt as if he were under an intolerable physical strain, as if his body were likely at any moment to fly to pieces. Other strange physical symptoms came to trouble him. An unpleasant odour lingered in his nostrils, as if he could literally smell the sulphur of the pit; and he had from time to time the curious illusion that his flesh was turning black. He had to look continually at his hands to be sure that it was not so. Nightmares troubled him, waking and sleeping – and one bad dream conjured up another, running from box to box to release its fellows. The world around him seemed to have become equally mad and hateful. The newspapers were full of stories of grotesque violence and unnatural crimes. He knew neither how to go on nor what to do to bring these horrors to an end.

Part of his torment was the knowledge that Rain was tormented equally. She had stopped painting, and had told Mr Everard that the picture was finished. The date for the appalling presentation dinner had even been fixed. Her decision distressed Mor, not because he imagined that it mattered now whether the official date of her departure was late or early, but because he felt responsible for having ruined the picture. Although he did not think that in the long run he either would or could do harm to her art, he could not forget what Bledyard had said. Rain had intended to improve the picture, to paint the head over again. She had not done so, because he had reduced her to the same frenzy that he was in himself.

Mor was standing in Waterloo station. He was waiting for Rain to arrive by train. He had had some school business in London, and they had agreed that she should meet him after lunch when it was done and they should spend the rest of the day in town. Mor noted, desperately, that to be together was not now quite enough of a salve for their unhappiness – they had to have novelties and distractions. He thought, this is what it is to be one of the damned.

There was still fifteen minutes to wait before the train arrived. Music began to play through a loud-speaker. Mor looked at the people hurrying to and fro in the wide echoing hall between the booking-offices and the platforms. The music drew the scene together until it had the look of an insane ballet, eerie, desolate and sinister. The performers glided to and fro across the stage, weaving in and out with an inscrutable precision. Mor turned his head away. He bought a paper and opened it quickly. Dreadful headlines stared him in the face. *Bridegroom Kills Bride in Car Crash. Possible Contamination of Earth's Atmosphere: Scientists' Grave Warning.* Mor crumpled the newspaper up and threw it into a wastepaper basket. He sat down on a seat and lighted a cigarette. He would have liked a drink, only it was the middle of the afternoon. He had taken to drinking quite a lot lately.

His thoughts began again upon the old round. Had he misled Rain totally concerning the nature of his marriage? Did Rain really love him anyway? Would her attachment to him endure? Supposing he were to destroy everything in order to be with her, would it turn out in the end to be a disaster? Was he not simply criminal to contemplate a union with so young a girl? Perhaps he was no more to her than an ephemeral father figure, endowed by the pain of her recent bereavement with a size larger than life? All this he had discussed with Rain herself in considerable detail for hours and hours and hours, without coming to any satisfactory conclusion. These talks went on now so far into every night that Mor was exhausted, waking tired and headache-ridden, scarcely able to stagger through the minimum of necessary tasks. She had tried to convince him, oh she had tried to convince him, at least that she loved him. He knew that she was convinced herself. At times, the spectacle of this love moved him so much that it seemed that nothing else mattered. But Mor knew now, and it was both a torment and a consolation, that in this damned condition no state of mind lasted for very long. Certainty and uncertainty chased each other through him at intervals, and it seemed that it would be a matter of chance in which phase exactly he should decide irrevocably to act.

One decision at least had been definitely put off. Rain had not yet become his mistress. She herself had wished to. But Mor had decided that it was better to wait a little while until the situation had become clearer. Time passed, the situation did not become clearer, and Mor began to conjecture that just this delay might be his fatal error. But it was some lingering puritanism out of his rejected childhood which still made him hesitate to become in the final and technical sense unfaithful to his wife. He knew that, in almost every way that mattered, his unfaithfulness was now complete. He had written to Nan hinting as much – but he had not dared to speak clearly to her, for he feared that she might return while he was still in a state of indecision. He saw that he had now definitely and irrevocably parted company with the truth. In the country where he lived now, truth could not decide his choices. Neither could happiness. He had told Bledyard that this would guide him – but now even this light was gone. He no longer conceived, as measurable entities capable of being weighed against each other, his own happiness, Rain's, or Nan's. He scarcely conceived that he could ever be happy again – nor did this especially matter.

What remained real and composed his agony was his intense, and it seemed to him increasing, love for Rain; combined with doubts about whether it was not wrong to thrust this love upon her, and complete paralysis at the thought of having to announce to Nan and the children that he was going to leave them. If only his love for Rain could drive him a little madder, or, on the other hand, his sense of belonging to his previous life become a little stronger, he would be able to decide. As it was, he was perfectly balanced in the midst of all these forces and quite unable to move. Only from time to time, consoling in itself and carrying the promise of a possible decision, there came to him a vision of himself and Rain together, far away from the present agony, beyond it, having forgotten it, enriching each other by love. This vision, he felt, if he could only hold it steady in his imagination for long enough, would draw him to a decision. Yet even this would not be sufficient. He realized, with a spasm of pain, that in order to come to his beloved he would have to summon up not his good qualities but his bad ones: his anger, his hatred of Nan, his capacity for sheer irresponsible violence. Between him and Rain lay this appalling wilderness; and how changed by it would he be before he could finally reach her? He must keep his look upon her very steady if he was to go across.

Mor threw away his cigarette. It was nearly time for the train to arrive. He went to the end of the platform to wait. His longing to see her drove away all other thoughts. He stood staring down the line. A few minutes passed. Surely the train was late. Mor began to walk up and down, biting his nails. Perhaps something terrible had happened, perhaps there had been an accident. He had a momentary but very detailed vision of Rain lying bleeding in the midst of some piled and twisted wreck. He looked at his watch again. Oh, let the train come! Now at last the train was appearing, there it was after all. It slid smoothly round the curving platform, stopped quickly, and immediately disgorged hundreds of people. They surged towards the barrier. There was no sign of Rain. Perhaps she had been taken ill. Perhaps she had decided not to come. Perhaps she had been offended at something he had said yesterday. Perhaps she had decided to go away altogether. No, there she was, thank God, so small he hadn't seen her behind that porter. She had seen him and was waving. She was almost at the barrier now. She was here.

'Oh, Rain—' said Mor. He enveloped her in a great embrace. He no longer cared if anyone saw him, he no longer cared about concealment and gossip.

Rain struggled out of his clutches, laughing. She drew him across towards the exit, looking up at him. 'You've been crying, Mor,' she said. 'You have a way of crying inside your eyes which is terrible. I would rather you shed tears.'

Mor realized that he had, after his fashion, been crying. 'Well, you see how feeble I am!' he said. 'But it's all right now.' They came out of the station and began to walk towards the river.

'Where shall we go?' said Mor. He had discovered that Rain knew London far better than he did.

'First we cross the bridge,' said Rain, 'and then I take you and show you something.' She was pulling him along, as a child pulls an adult. They came on to Waterloo Bridge.

The enormous curving expanse of the Thames opened about them girdled with its pale domes and towers. Above it was a great sky of white bundled clouds. The day was chill, and there

214

was a promise of rain. The river glittered, thrown up into small foam-flecked waves that set the anchored barges rocking. Yet above the tossing water the air was light, and the familiar skyline receded into a luminous haze. They both paused to look, and Mor felt within him the quick stir of excitement which came with the first sight of London, always for him, as in his country childhood, the beautiful and slightly sinister city of possibilities and promises. The wind blew upon them coldly. They looked eastward in silence.

Rain shivered. 'You know,' she said, 'in this place it's autumn already. I thought the leaves fell in September. But here they begin to fall in July. I don't think I could live in England all the year.'

Mor shivered too, but not at the wind. He was reminded yet again that Rain was free. Also, he had not been able to keep it out of his consciousness, she was wealthy. She could wonder to herself whether she would spend the winter in England, or go back to the Mediterranean, to Majorca perhaps, or Marrakesh. At this thought Mor felt a mixture of attraction and revulsion.

Rain read his thoughts. She did not want him to know that she had read them. She wanted somehow to make it clear that she did not envisage any going away that did not include him. She said, 'I wonder if we shall work together one day, I at my painting and you at your books—'

Mor had told Rain about the half-finished work in political concepts. He had still not said anything to her about the possible candidature. This was all the less necessary since he had almost finally decided now that he would not stand. Whatever happened, probably, he would not stand. He could not bring himself even to think about the Labour Party at the moment. Compared with his present preoccupations, everything to do with the Labour Party paled into triviality. He was surprised to find how little he cared. He must settle the more pressing problem first – and other problems could just look after themselves.

'You would always be working hard,' said Mor, 'but I don't know how I would make out in a state of—' he searched for the word – 'freedom.' He pictured himself for a moment living in a hotel in Majorca on Rain's money. He did not find the picture nauseating, merely ludicrous. Of course, there would be nothing like that. When the scandal was over, he would start a school of his own. They had envisaged this and even discussed

215

it. Mor tried to fasten his thoughts upon a possible future. It was not easy. Instead, he kept seeing in his mind's eye the face of his son. He remembered with a jolt that it was less than ten days to Donald's chemistry exam.

They reached the other side of the bridge. It was beginning to rain.

'We go the rest of the way by taxi,' Rain announced. She seemed unusually cheerful today. The storms of doubt and guilt seemed to have passed over for the moment. Mor thought, if only she were, even for a short while, absolutely certain, I could make my decision; and this thought seemed to bring it nearer. He hailed a taxi, and once inside he held the girl violently in his arms and forgot everything else.

The taxi stopped, at Rain's request, just off Bond Street, and they got out. Mor looked round vaguely. Rain's presence made him live so completely from moment to moment that he had not even wondered where they were going. Then he saw a poster beside a door near by. It read: FATHER AND DAUGHTER. *An Exhibition of Works by* SIDNEY *and* RAIN CARTER.

Rain watched him, delighted at his surprise, and began to lead him in. Mor felt considerable emotion. Except for the portrait of Demoyte, he had seen no paintings by Rain, or her father, in original or reproduction. He felt both excited and nervous. He began to think at once that he might hate the exhibition. They climbed the stairs.

Rain's appearance created a mild sensation in the room above. She was known to the girl who sold the catalogues and to two art dealers and the owner of the gallery, who were chatting in the middle of the room. One or two other people, who were looking at the pictures, turned to watch. Mor felt himself for the first time in Rain's world. He felt intimidated. She introduced him without embarrassment as a friend of Demoyte's. The art dealers knew about the Demoyte portrait, inquired after it, and said that they would make a point of going down to St Bride's in the autumn to see it. The notion that connoisseurs would now be making pilgrimages to St Bride's was strange to Mor. In any ordinary state of mind it would have pleased him. But now to speak of the autumn was like speaking of some time after he would be dead. He listened as a condemned man might listen to his warders chatting.

Rain seemed in no hurry. She exchanged news and gossip

with the three experts. They spoke a little of her father's work, mentioned the recent sale of one of his pictures, and the price. The price astonished Mor. He stood aside in silence, looking at Rain. She seemed now so utterly at her ease, quite unlike the weeping ragamuffin he had seen two nights ago when they had talked for hours about their situation. She could step out of *that* into *this*. He marvelled again that she had not gone away altogether. She was dressed today in a dress which he had not seen before, a clinging dress of light grey wool, which made her look taller. As she talked, he watched her bright thrown-back boy's face, and the extreme roundness of her breasts, displayed now by the close-fitting wool. He noticed that she was wearing high-heeled shoes, instead of the canvas slippers which she usually wore down at St Bride's. He noticed her handbag and a long black-polished heel tapping rhythmically. He coveted her, and his need for her was suddenly so extreme that he had to turn away.

He wondered for the hundredth time what it was that he wanted from her. It was not just to be the owner of that small and exotic being. He wanted to be the new person that she made of him, the free and creative and joyful and loving person that she had conjured up, striking this miraculous thing out of his dullness. He recalled Bledyard's words: you think of nothing else but your own satisfaction. All right, if two people can satisfy each other, and make each other new, why not? After all, he thought, I *can* be guided by this. Let me only make clear what I gain, and what I destroy. With relief he felt his mood shifting. The cloud of nightmare which had hung over his head while he was waiting at Waterloo was lifted. In a world without a redeemer only clarity was the answer to guilt. He would make it all clear to himself, shirking nothing, and then he would decide.

Rain had finished with the connoisseurs. They said good-day, and all departed together. She turned to Mor. 'You haven't been looking!'

'I *have*,' said Mor, smiling. 'Now you show me the pictures.'

They began to walk round. Mor was not used to looking at pictures, and these ones startled him. They were very various. Some were meticulous and decorative, like the portrait of Demoyte, others very much more impressionistic, with the paint plastered heavily upon the canvas. After making one or two wrong guesses, Mor gave up pretending to know which were Rain's and which were her father's. There seemed to be no way of deciding on grounds of style.

'How do the experts know?' he asked Rain.

'My father's pictures are better!' she replied.

The pictures all showed a great intensity, even violence, of colour, and a bold harsh disposition of forms. Everything was very large and seemed to have more colours and more surfaces than nature possessed. Compared to these works, the portrait of Demoyte seemed more harmonious and sombre.

When Mor said this, Rain said, 'I am only just beginning to develop my own style. My father was such a powerful painter, and such a strong personality, I was practically made in his image. It will be a long time before I know what I have in myself.'

Mor thought, even at this moment she knows that there is a future. He wished that she could communicate this sense of futurity to him. He said, 'Is there a picture of your father here?'

'Several,' said Rain. She stopped him in front of a portrait.

Mor saw at first the jagged mountains and valleys of the paint, and then he saw a thin-faced man, looking suspiciously sideways towards the spectator, his face turning the other way, a thin wig-like crop of straight black hair, grey at the temples, big rather moist eyes with many wrinkles about them, and a slightly pursed thoughtful mouth.

'Did you paint that?' asked Mor.

'No, my father did,' said Rain, 'a little while before he died. It's a very good painting. See the authority of that head. Mr Bledyard would not have criticized *that*.'

Mor felt unable to make any judgment on the painting. He had a dream-like sensation of being translated into Rain's world, as if she had laid him under a spell in order to show him the past. How objective she is, all the same, he thought. They moved on.

There was a portrait of a young girl with long black plaits, leaning over the keyboard of a piano. Out of a haze of colour her presence emerged with great vividness, bathed in the light and atmosphere of a southern room.

'Who is that?' said Mor, although he already knew.

'Me,' said Rain.

'Did your father paint it?'

'No, I did.'

'But you were a child then!' said Mor.

'Not so young as I look,' said Rain. 'I was nineteen. It's not very good, I'm afraid.'

To Mor it looked marvellous. 'And you had long hair!' he said. 'When did you cut it?'

'After— In Paris, when I was studying there.'

They moved on quickly to the next picture. Rain's father stood in a doorway, leaning against the jamb of the door. He was dressed in a loose-fitting white suit, and his face was in shadow. Beyond him through the door could be seen a dazzling expanse of sea.

'I painted that too,' said Rain. 'That's a more recent one, not quite so awful. That's through the door of our house.'

'Your house!' said Mor. He must have supposed that Rain and her father lived in a house – but somehow his imagination had never tried to provide him with any details of how she must have lived in the past, before he knew her.

'Here's our house again,' she said. 'You see more of it here.'

Mor saw the façade of a white villa, powdery with sun and scored with blue shadows, with pinkish patches on the walls where the plaster was falling off, and decrepit grey shutters disposed in various positions. A ragged cypress tree partly obscured one of the windows.

'Where is the sea?' said Mor.

'Here,' she said, indicating a point beyond the foreground of the picture.

'Which was your room?' said Mor.

'You can't see it here,' she said. 'That was my father's room. Mine looked out at the back. You can see the window here.' She pointed to another picture. It was evening, and the back of the house was glowing in a soft diffused light. A wilderness of flowering shrubs, with grotesque shapes and violent purple shadows, crawled right up to the wall.

'There's no path!' said Mor.

'No, you have to push your way through.'

'And the view from the window?' said Mor.

'Here,' she said. It was mid-afternoon, and line behind line a drowsy landscape, crumbling with dryness, receded into mountain slopes spotted with vines and mauve distances of dry vegetation and rock.

'Who—' he began.

'I painted this one,' she said. 'The other ones are by my father. He never tired of painting the house.'

'Who has the house now?' asked Mor.

She looked surprised. 'I have it,' she said.

They moved from picture to picture. Almost all were either pictures of the house, or of the landscape near it, or self-portraits, or portraits of each other, by the father and daughter. There were two or three pictures of Paris, and about five portraits of other people. Mor looked with bewilderment and a kind of deeply pleasurable distress upon this vivid southern world, where the sun scattered the sea at noon-day with jagged and dazzling patches of light, or drew it upward limpidly light blue into the sky at morning, where the white house with the patchy plaster walls was stunned and dry at noon, or shimmering with life in the granulous air of the evening, as it looked one way into the sea, and the other way across the dusty flowers and into the mountains. He looked, and he could smell the southern air. And here at last in the room that he had come to recognize as the drawing-room sat a black-haired girl in a flowered summer dress. It was midday, but the shutters were drawn against the sun. The room was full of the very bright and clear but shadowed light of a southern interior. The girl had tossed back her very short hair and turned towards the spectator with a smile, one hand poised upon a small table, the other touching her cheek. The picture had something of the fresh primness of a Victorian photo. This was a Rain whom Mor recognized, the Rain of today.

'One of my father's last pictures,' said Rain.

Mor was moved. How he must have treasured her. In this sudden movement of sympathy towards her father it occurred to him for the first time that his general attitude to this person was one of hostility.

'Who possesses that picture?' Mor asked.

'The Honourable Mrs Leamington Stephens,' said Rain.

Mor frowned. What right had the Honourable Mrs Leamington Stephens to possess such a picture of Rain? 'I want it!' he said.

'I will paint one for you, dearest,' said Rain. 'I will paint

220

many, many. I will paint pictures of you. I will paint you over and over again.'

Mor saw the years ahead. The room was full of pictures of himself and Rain. Himself reading upon the terrace at evening, working in the drawing-room in the noon light, walking in the wilderness between the dusty leaves of the bushes where there was no path. Rain, slowly losing her boyish looks, the tense and precious simplicity of her childhood changing into the serenity of middle age, and so picture behind picture away into the farthest future. Rain with her brush in her hand, looking through a thousand canvases towards the end of life.

He said nothing. Rain was looking up at him. He met her eyes without smiling, yearning for her to decide his fate.

'Is there no picture here of your mother?' Mor said at last.

'No,' said Rain. 'My father hardly ever painted her.'

They moved a pace or two and Mor wondered to himself how much that missing face would have told him. He wanted to ask a question, but Rain interrupted.

'This is rather a curiosity,' she said, pointing to a large canvas which hung at the end of the room. Here both the faces appeared. Rain's father sat behind a table which was strewn with books and papers, facing the spectator. Upon the left side of the table, propped up upon it, was a large gilt mirror, in which could be seen the reflection of Rain and of the canvas which she was painting, whereon the same picture appeared again, severely foreshortened. Rain's father was wearing an open-necked shirt. His close-cropped dark hair fell in a silky fringe along his brow, his narrow brooding face looked intently upward towards his daughter, and one hand rested upon the frame of the mirror wherein was seen the reflection of her face, equally intently looking down on him. The heads were close together and the resemblance between them was marked and touching.

'That's extraordinary!' said Mor.

'Not very successful, I'm afraid,' said Rain. 'I must try again sometime with you.' She spoke in the most ordinary tone, her attention still upon the picture.

Mor thought: she has decided. *She* has decided. He began to want to get away from the pictures. Without words they turned and went slowly down the stairs. As his heels bit into the thick carpet Mor felt the pain of the transition, back to the cold rainy autumnal afternoon and the roaring traffic outside the door. Here all was the same as before, chilly, noisy, ugly, without space, without leisure, without peace. He looked sideways at Rain as they came out of the door. No, she was not quite the same; a new light fell upon her from the pictures, she was strengthened and made radiant by her past. All the different faces that he had seen, from the young girl with the plaits to the posed beauty in the flowering dress dwelt in her face now, giving it suddenly a new authority and a new age. He thought too how much at this moment she resembled her father, except that what in him appeared as a sort of self-contained moroseness appeared in her as a pedantic and dignified serenity, which combined with her rounded head and fresh face of a child was absurd and affecting. Mor was overcome with emotion. It was raining steadily. Mor had no overcoat. Rain had a small umbrella swinging over her arm. She handed it to him in silence and he opened it above them both. Arm in arm they made their way back to Bond Street.

'Tea at Fortnum and Mason,' Rain decreed.

Tea at Fortnum and Mason! Mor was suddenly filled with a deep and driving joy which furrowed through his body with such force that he did not at first know that it was indeed joy that shook him so. She had decided. He had decided too. He could do no other. 'Rain—' he said.

She looked up, squeezing his arm, bright-eyed and confident. 'I know,' she said.

The rain began to fall faster. 'I tell you something,' said Mor. 'I'm not sure that I could really live outside England, not all the time, not even most of the time.'

'Dear Mor, then we'll live in England!' said Rain.

She clutched his arm more tightly. The rain began to pelt down with spitting violence. They started to run as quickly as they could in the direction of Fortnum's.

# CHAPTER SIXTEEN

It was the following day. That evening Bledyard was to give his famous art lecture, and Rain had been persuaded by Mr Everard that she really must be present – especially as the lecture, on this occasion, was to be on the topical subject of portrait painting. Mor usually cut Bledyard's lecture, but this time, as Rain was coming, of course he would come too. Since he had finally and definitely made up his mind, the world had been completely altered. A tremendous energy, which had previously consumed itself in perpetuating his indecision and conjuring up all kinds of catastrophic fantasy, was transformed into the purest joy. Mor now felt an intense benevolence towards his colleagues, including Bledyard, and he found himself positively looking forward to the lecture as if it were to be the most enormous treat. He would be sitting in the same room as Rain, and as Bledyard talked he could think about her, and see again the extraordinary and moving images of the previous day which still hovered for him about her head, like a cloud of angels surrounding the madonna.

Mor had had a bad hour during the afternoon when he had drafted a very frank letter to Nan. Even this task had been lightened, however, by the extreme relief which he felt at finally knowing what the truth was and being able to tell it. When he had completed the draft he roughly sketched a letter to Tim Burke explaining briefly that after all he would not be able to stand as a Labour candidate. Concerning this, Mor felt another quite separate and deep regret. But he gave himself the same answer. He had won a great prize. He was willing to pay for it. When he had done, there was no time left to copy the drafts, so he put them away in a drawer. They would go on the morrow.

The one matter to which he had not yet let his thoughts fully turn was the matter of the children. When he felt himself inclined to think about them he told himself: whichever way I move, something must be destroyed – and the destruction may well be less than I fear. After all,

223

the children are nearly grown-up now. We cannot lose each other altogether. But so far as he could he prevented himself from considering the children. He had made up his mind, and there was no point in indulging in painful self-laceration which had no longer any relevance to the making of a decision. He had suggested in the draft letter to Nan that nothing be said to Donald or Felicity until after Donald's exam. He had considered the possibility of delaying his letter to Nan until after this date – but his anxiety to tell her what he had decided was too intense. He felt, still, that his achievement was precarious and must be fixed and established at once. Towards Nan he felt no more of his former anger, only a dull feeling of hostility, mixed with pity and regret. He knew that she would be very surprised. She would hardly be able to imagine that he would turn against her decisively at last. At the thought of her surprise he felt a very slight satisfaction which faded into a sense of shame. Then pity began to take possession of his mind – and as soon as he was able to he brought the full focus of his attention back towards Rain.

Bledyard's lecture took place after supper and was to be given, as usual, in the Gymnasium, which was easier to black out than the hall. In fact, it would be dark soon after the lecture started, but it was worth blocking out the twilight for the sake of the first few slides. It was to be hoped that the epidiascope would not go wrong again, and that the number of slides inserted upside-down would be kept to a minimum. Somehow these things always seemed to happen at Bledyard's lecture, when their tendency to bring about total chaos was especially strong. The most trivial incident, which on any other occasion would pass unnoticed by the School, on this one was a cue for hysterics. The School came to Bledyard's lecture as to a festival or orgy, in the highest of spirits and ready to be set off by anything. The atmosphere was infectious. Mor found himself caught by it and looking forward in a crazy way to the enlivening of proceedings by all kinds of absurdities.

He met Mr Everard crossing the playground. His face wore an anxious expression. 'I hope you're coming this time, Bill?' he said.

'Most certainly!' said Mor. He felt like embracing Evvy. He wondered if he was looking as wild as he felt.

224

'It's rather a relief that you'll be there,' said Evvy, shaking his head. 'I hope things won't get out of hand.'

The School was already trooping into the Gym. The dark curtains had been drawn, and the lights were on inside. Outside, the evening was warm and the air was penetrated with smells, conjured up by the recent rain, which lay in heavy layers, earth and leaves and flowers. A pleasant hazy twilight enveloped the school, softening the bleakness of the red brick and turning the neo-Gothic into Gothic. Opposite to the Gym the tower soared up magnificently into the curling rings of evening mist and darkness, and here and there a few lighted windows made by their gold the surrounding air more dusk. One by one the lights went out. It was customary for everyone at St Bride's to attend Bledyard's lecture.

A violent and increasing din of high-pitched voices and clattering chairs issued from the Gymnasium. Already the slightly hysterical note was to be heard. Then someone clapped his hands and some voice, probably Hensman's, said, 'Stop that noise, you'll bring the roof down! If you all talk in your ordinary voices you'll all hear each other perfectly well.' An instant later the din was renewed, louder than before. Mor reflected that he probably ought to be inside supporting Hensman. It was on the latter that the task of working the epidiascope had now devolved. Usually this task was performed by Mr Baseford – but in his absence popular vote had given it to Hensman. Mor reflected that Hensman could hardly do it worse than Baseford, and was likely to do it better, since he was totally imperturbable and impervious to any kind of ragging. Mor was rather glad that he had not himself been detailed for this tiresome, and on this occasion rather nerve-rending, duty. Still leaving Hensman to control the increasingly rowdy scene within, he stood looking towards the far end of the playground. He hoped to see Rain arriving, and if possible to sit near her, even next to her.

It was growing darker. A stream of juniors went by, carrying additional chairs. They sped past in a mad race for the Gymnasium door. Three of them, reaching the door simultaneously, locked themselves together into a thick yelling tangle of small boys and upturned furniture in the doorway. A struggle developed, someone pretended to have been knocked out. Mor took a few steps towards the scene. The barricade of chairs and squirming bodies dissolved instantly and the children vanished into the Gym, to dispute with their friends for the best places. As Mor turned round again he saw Rain coming across the playground escorted by Mr and Mrs Prewett. It seemed to Mor as if she glowed in the twilight and came towards him carried by a gentle but infinitely powerful wind. Even the Prewetts, who were walking on each side of her, had caught some of the radiance from her triumphal course. How exceedingly nice the Prewetts are! Mor thought. They were both smiling at him. Rain's face he could hardly see. As he stepped forward, Evvy suddenly appeared out of the evening air and intercepted Rain. He had been lurking in the doorway of the Library building, shirking the scene in the Gym. He took charge of Rain and began to escort her towards the door. Mor followed with Mr and Mrs Prewett.

As he entered, Mor blinked at the bright light within, and at the noise which had now settled to a sort of continuous high-pitched rumbling scream, not unlike a jet engine. He saw Evvy's back ahead of him, and then his profile. Evvy was visibly shaken by the scene. The small boys in the very front, once it had become clear that some people would have to sit on the floor, had taken it into their heads to lay several rows of chairs on their sides, and by this method to seat three boys on each chair, one sitting on the back, one on the seat, and one on the legs. Round each of the prostrated chairs a small squabble was going on as the occupants attempted to reach a suitable equilibrium. Beyond this riot area the older boys were massed, eager, chattering, wildly animated, right to the back of the hall, some standing up, some kneeling on their chairs, some sitting astride talking to people behind them. Already the rows were so crooked in some places that it was impossible to discern whether there was a row at all. The chairs were placed higgledy-piggledy in a great clattering undulating sea.

Evvy, who seemed to be, no doubt because of the presence of Rain, more than usually paralysed, picked his way without a word between the juniors down a ragged aisle which had been left clear in the middle, at the far end of which stood the epidiascope. Mor followed closely, nipping in in front of the Prewetts, determined if possible to sit next to Rain. He felt at that moment as light-hearted as a Fifth-Former. As he passed

through the shrieking barrage of juniors he said in a pen-
etrating voice, 'Put those chairs upright!' He hoped this would
not offend Evvy. But in fact when it came to it nothing ever
offended Evvy, dear old Evvy. And to permit this sort of an-
archy right from the start was really asking for trouble. The
juniors scrambled to right the chairs, and further battles then
developed between the different trios as to who should be the
single occupant of each. Mor left them to it, passing on close
behind Rain and the Head.

In front of the epidiascope, on either side of the aisle, there
were a number of chairs which had been kept free by Hensman.
Several masters had already settled themselves in this region of
comparative safety. With a sigh of relief Evvy ushered Rain in
and flopped down beside her. Mor was able quickly to instal
himself on her other side, and the Prewetts sat next to him. He
looked round to see who was behind him and to see if he could
locate Donald in the throng, but his son was not to be seen.

Bledyard had already arrived. He was usually in fact the first
man in the Gym on the evening of his lecture. He stood now in
the open space in front of the junior boys, leaning upon the
long rod which he was to use to draw attention to features of
the various pictures and to tap the ground for the next slide.
Behind him a great white sheet had been suspended on the wall
of the Gym. He leaned there, looking into the pullulating
crowd of boys, his face twisted into a sort of bland and pensive
expression, as if he were rehearsing what he was about to say
and finding it extremely interesting. Bledyard never needed to
speak from notes. When once set off, on any subject on which
he chose to hold forth, he could continue indefinitely in his
stumbling but unhurried manner, with sustained coherence and
even elegance. Bledyard was in his way a good speaker and
could have impressed almost any audience but an audience of
schoolboys.

It was customary for lecturers, if they belonged to the school
and were not outsiders, to begin their lectures without introduction once the Headmaster had arrived. Bledyard therefore
watched to see Mr Everard seated, and then rapped sharply
upon the ground with his rod. He looked completely unruffled
and reminded Mor suddenly of a representation of a pilgrim,
leaning on his staff, patient and full of hope. Bledyard must
surely know what he was in for. But he seemed each year to be,

on the occasion of the lecture, full simply of the subject in hand, and he accepted the storms that so often broke over him without surprise but also without interest. On one occasion when Demoyte had had to stop the lecture in the middle because the School had become totally hysterical, Bledyard would have been quite willing to continue, although not a single word would have been audible. He stood now, head slightly bowed, as the hubbub gradually died down and was reduced to a low mirthful murmur. He had pushed his long limp strands of dark hair back behind each ear, revealing a large area of very pale cheek, which now grew concave, sucked thoughtfully into his mouth. The lights went out.

The murmur from the School increased in the sudden darkness and then died down. Audaciously Mor thrust out his hand and found Rain's hand near by. He squeezed it violently. She returned the pressure and then gently disengaged hers. Mor tried to catch it again. It eluded him, and alighted like a bird upon his wrist, to give an admonitory pat and then vanish, to be locked away, chaperoned by her other hand, on the far side of her knee.

The juniors were already giggling in anticipation. Bledyard said, 'Quiet please, boys.' A sort of silence fell at last.

The epidiascope came into action, casting a white square of light on to the screen. By this illumination Mor turned to look at Rain's profile. She was looking sternly forward. He realized that, if he was not careful, she would very shortly burst out laughing. He hurriedly transferred his attention elsewhere, concentrated on remaining reasonably solemn himself.

Bledyard had started talking. He began, 'The human face has been described as the most interesting surface in the world.' An explosion of laughter, quickly muffled, came from the younger boys. 'By a mathematician a mathematician,' said Bledyard. He did not find the word easy. A silent shudder of mirth went backward through the room. 'Now shall we ask ourselves ourselves the question,' Bledyard went on, 'why we are always interested in faces, and why when we meet our friends we look we look at their faces and not at their knees or elbows? The answer is simple. Thoughts and emotions are more often expressed by movements of the face than by movements of the knee or elbow.'

A guffaw, which the School had been holding in with

difficulty until the end of this period, broke out explosively. Mor glanced sideways again and saw that Rain was hiding her face in her handkerchief. Her chair trembled slightly. Beyond her Mor caught a glimpse of Evvy, wide-eyed and serious above his dog-collar. He began to feel that he could not hold out much longer. He started to search for his own handkerchief.

'Let us now go on to ask go on to ask another question,' said Bledyard. 'Why do painters represent in pictures the faces of their fellow fellow men? To this it may be answered that painters represent things that are to be found in the world, and human faces are things that are to be found in the world.' Another ripple of mirth, quiet but deep, shook the room. The School was still holding back, with the delighted expectation of someone waiting for the conclusion of a long but undoubtedly very funny story.

'This answer is hardly sufficient sufficient,' said Bledyard. He spoke throughout with total solemnity and with the slow deliberation of one announcing a declaration of war or the death of royalty. 'There have been at different times in history different reasons why painters have painted people and why people have wanted to be painted by painters painters painters.'

When Bledyard repeated a word three times the glee of his audience knew no bounds. A joyful roar went up, which drowned the noise of Bledyard rapping for the first slide. A long silence followed. Hensman had not heard the rap, and Bledyard was waiting patiently for the first picture. Mor, who immediately guessed what had happened, leaned across Rain to whisper to Evvy to nudge Hensman. At that moment, however, Evvy turned away, looking back over his shoulder disapprovingly at some scuffling that was going on at the back. Mor swayed back into his seat. As he did so, his cheek lightly touched Rain's. He cast another sideways glance and saw that she now had herself sufficiently under control to turn towards him, her bright eyes slightly tearful with mirth, looking out from above her handkerchief, which she still held pressed tightly to her mouth. The silence continued.

'Sound track's broken down,' said a clear voice from the back of the hall. The School let itself go and rocked hysterically in a great surge of laughter. Rain threw her head forward with a wail, her shoulders shaking. Mor began to laugh silently. He felt an extreme crazy happiness.

'Could we have the first slide, please, Mis-ter Hens-man?' said Bledyard.

The first slide appeared at last. It represented the Laughing Cavalier of Frans Hals. The School gurgled into silence.

'Now this gentleman,' said Bledyard, 'is of course well known to all of you. And if we ask what is the bond here that holds the sitter the sitter and the painter together the answer is – charm. The sitter wishes to be depicted as charming, and the painter obliges him without difficulty.' Bledyard rapped the floor.

The School had subsided for the moment, and were listening to Bledyard. A soft murmur arose from them, however, as from a hive of bees about to swarm.

The next slide represented the head of the Emperor Theodoric, taken from a mosaic at Ravenna. 'Now, what have we here?' said Bledyard. 'Not the portrait of an individual by an individual, but an abstract abstract conception of power and magnificence created in the form of a man.' He rapped the floor again. The School was restive, baulked of its prey.

'Now this noble portrait–' A shout of laughter went up. The next slide represented the digestive tract of the frog. Bledyard could be seen moving hastily back from the screen in order to see what had happened and falling over some small boys.

'Someone's been tampering with the slides!' Mor said into Rain's ear. This had happened once before. Now anything might be expected. He moved his chair a fraction closer to hers and looked at her. She turned her head slowly and gave him a look of joyful tenderness. Mor turned back towards the screen, bringing his foot cautiously into contact with hers. The frog was still there. Bledyard's voice was saying, 'I think that one must be a mis-take.' Mor felt that he was in paradise.

Hensman blotted out the frog by putting his hand over the front of the projector, but then found that he was unable to insert the next slide. It was a minute before things were reorganized and the next picture appeared. It was one of the later self-portraits of Rembrandt.

'Now here,' said Bledyard, 'if we ask what relates the painter to the sitter, if we ask what the painter is after, it is difficult to avoid answering – the truth.' The audience was now totally silent. Bledyard paused, looking up at the picture. The enormous Socratic head of the aged Rembrandt, swathed in a rather dirty-looking cloth, emerged in light and shade from the screen. At the edge of the lighted area Bledyard could be seen regarding it. He seemed for a moment to have forgotten where he was.

'Mmmm, yes,' said Bledyard, and stepped back into the shadow. He rapped the floor with his rod.

The next slide was a coloured photograph of the Queen, dressed in a blue coat and skirt, standing on the steps at Balmoral. A well-organized group at the side of the room immediately began to intone the national anthem. The audience rose automatically to its feet. A bedlam of laughter followed immediately. A few people still tried to sing, but soon gave it up. Mor tumbled weakly back into his chair. Evvy was saying to Hensman, 'I hardly think Mr Bledyard could have intended—' Hensman, with greater presence of mind, blotted the offending slide by superimposing another one. Rain said, 'I don't know how much longer I can bear it!' Mor discovered that he was clasping her hand. They both leaned forward, moaning and holding their sides. 'I love you madly!' said Mor under cover of the undiminishing din. 'Sssh!' said Rain.

Hensman managed to remove the Queen and reveal the next slide, which was a Tintoretto portrait of Vincenzo Morosini. The School groaned and wailed itself into silence at last.

Bledyard seemed unperturbed. 'Now this picture,' he was saying, 'which is also in London—'

Rain murmured to Mor, 'Terribly good! I wish I—'

A loud whispering was going on at the back of the Gym. There was a scraping of chairs and one or two people seemed to be going out of the door at the farther end. The boys in front were turning round to see what was happening. Evvy looked over his shoulder and said, 'Silence, please!' Bledyard was saying – 'to draw some moral moral from these preliminary examples.'

'What's the excitement back there?' said Mrs Prewett to Mor. Mor didn't know. He turned in his chair, bringing his knee into contact with Rain's thigh. A number of boys were standing up and exchanging whispers. Then several of them began making for the door. '—being as Shakespeare Shakespeare put it, the lords and owners of our faces,' said Bledyard. Mr Prewett got up and began to make his way down the side of the Gym towards the centre of disaffection at the back.

'Where is that picture?' Mor whispered to Rain.

'National Gallery,' she whispered back. 'We'll go—'

Bledyard was standing full in the light of the screen pointing upward with his rod. He looked like an alchemist dealing with an apparition. The noise at the back was becoming considerable. More boys were now looking to the back of the Gym than to the front. A whisper of excitement went through the audience. 'What's up?' said someone audibly in the front row.

Prewett had come back down the aisle and was leaning towards Evvy. He said in an agitated voice, 'You'd better come out, sir. Two boys are climbing the tower.'

Mor's blood turned to ice. The scene about him was annihilated. He sprang up from his seat and got out into the aisle, stumbling in front of Evvy, who was also rising. He made for the nearest door at the back of the Gym. But a stampede had already started. The boys in the back rows had got up and were pushing towards the door. Their excited voices grew louder and louder. Mor was caught in the midst. As he fought his way through he caught a last glimpse of the scene in the Gym. Bledyard was still standing in the light of the screen, his rod lifted, looking back now towards the audience – while throughout the Gym boys were standing up, pushing, climbing over the chairs, and the smaller boys in the front, who still did not know what it was all about, were asking to be told in tones which rose, with excitement and panic, higher and higher. Evvy was stuck somewhere in the middle of this. His face was visible for a moment in the light reflected from the screen, open-mouthed and stricken with alarm. As he struggled through and finally passed out of the Gym, Mor turned all the lights on.

He ran into the centre of the playground. It was now completely dark outside. A large crowd of boys had already collected, and others were joining them, streaming out of the two doors of the Gymnasium. Mor looked up. After the brightness of the screen he could see nothing at first, not even the tower itself. A dark haze fell in front of his eyes. He tried to look through it. He did not need to be told the identity of the two boys on the tower.

'There they are, sir,' said someone at his elbow. It was Rigden. He was pointing upward. Mor tried to see. He could still discern nothing. He felt as if he had become blind. A terrible blockage in his throat nearly stopped him from breathing.

Then gradually he began to make out the shape of the tower, rising up sheer into the night sky above him. He stepped back a little.

There was no moon, and the tower emerged blackly against a black sky. It was in two segments: a lower square part which rose out of the roof of Main School, and was used as a book store – there were two small windows in this segment – and above this an extremely tall spire, ornamented with a great deal of grotesque tracery, and ending in a bronze pinnacle. Between the square part of the tower and the Gothic spire there was a jutting parapet, which reached out for a distance of two or three feet, overhanging the lower segment. On the upper side the spire reached almost to the edges of the parapet, which was wide below and narrow above, so that the whole tower had a top-heavy spear-like appearance.

'There, sir, at the parapet,' said Rigden, still beside him. Then Mor, craning his neck backwards, saw two dark shapes clinging to the tower. One seemed to be on the parapet, the other just below it, adhering somehow to the side of the wall. They didn't appear to be moving. A claw of fear contracted slowly about Mor's heart. He could see better now.

Someone said, 'They must be stuck.' A great crowd had by now collected in the centre of the playground, almost the whole School must be there. Glancing back, Mor saw row after row of heads outlined against the light which streamed from the doors of the Gym. Everyone was talking and pointing. The noise rose in a cloud through the warm night air. Mor thought, this will scare them out of their wits and they'll lose their nerve. He turned, half resolved to clear the boys from the playground. But it was impossible. To do so would create even more noise and chaos than there was already. He looked up again. The pair on the tower were still motionless. It looked as if they were able to get neither up nor down.

Prewett came up to him, pushing through the throng. It was too dark to see his face. He said to Mor, 'Bill, I'm afraid it's your son and young Carde.'

'I know,' said Mor. He was still looking up. *What could be done?* He realized that he was shaking all over with violent tremors. 'Has anyone sent for the fire-brigade?' he asked Prewett. A long ladder. Why hadn't he thought of that instantly?

'Everard is telephoning,' said Prewett.

'Oh God,' said Mor, 'Oh God! They're obviously paralysed and can't move.'

Prewett put a hand on his shoulder. 'There's the ladder that's kept behind the pavilion—'

'It's too short,' said Mor.

'Shall I go and get it, sir?' said Rigden, who was standing in a group of boys just behind them.

'Yes, go,' said Mor, 'but it's too short.' Several boys ran away to accompany Rigden.

Mor bit his hand. *Was there nothing he could do?* He feared that at any moment Donald or Carde would lose his nerve completely. Still, neither of them appeared to be moving. The agony of the fear nearly broke his body in two.

A steady murmur of excitement was rising from the watching crowd. 'Turn on the floodlights!' cried a voice from the back.

'No!' cried Mor, turning towards the speaker. 'You'll startle them!'

It was too late. A stampede had started in the direction of the boiler-room, where the master switches were. A moment later the façade of Main School sprang violently out of the darkness, mercilessly illuminated by the powerful floodlights. Carefully adjusted beams lit up the tower from top to bottom, picking out every detail. A gasp arose from the crowd and everyone covered his eyes, dazzled. Mor gave a moan of fear and tried to look upward. His eyes closed against the violent light. When he opened them he saw, very clearly revealed, the figures of the two boys clinging to the tower. Donald was above, lying full length upon the extremely narrow top of the parapet. Carde was below the overhang. He was clinging like a fly to the edge of the tower. He had one arm over the parapet, and the other curiously flattened against the wall. Then Mor saw that he was holding on to the wire of the lightning conductor which ran down from the top of the tower. His feet were turned sideways, finding a precarious foothold on a tiny decorative ledge, an inch or two wide, which girdled the tower a few feet below the parapet. A rope, which the boys had somehow managed to fix to the base of the spire, dangled some distance away, out of Carde's reach; and even if he could otherwise have hoisted himself out, past the overhang and on to the parapet, helped perhaps by the lightning conductor which went snaking on upwards above his head, it was impossible for him to do so since Donald was in the way.

Donald lay full length along the extremely narrow upper side of the parapet, his face turned inward towards the stone, and one long arm extended above his head to grasp a projecting piece of decoration. His other arm was hidden. His legs were oddly twisted under him. He had obviously got himself into an awkward position and now dared not move for fear of rolling off the narrow ledge, which could not be more than about ten inches across. On the ledge close to Donald's outstretched arm was balanced a white shining object which it took Mor a moment to recognize as a chamber-pot. This had evidently been destined to be placed on the topmost pinnacle as evidence of the climb.

Alarmed by the sudden illumination, Donald had moved slightly and shifted the chamber-pot. It oscillated for a moment, and then came toppling over the edge of the parapet, flashed downward, and broke into a thousand small pieces on the asphalt of the playground. A terrible shudder went through the crowd. Mor could hear one or two of the smaller boys beginning to cry.

Mor studied the tower. If only there were anything, any plan, which could help. Clearly something had gone wrong about the rope. Mor surmised quickly that the boys might have ascended from the roof of Main School on the adjacent side of the tower, helped by a drainpipe which went part way up at that point, far enough in all probability for them to get their feet on to the tiny ledge, while holding on to the parapet with their hands. Here they must have managed to reach over the overhang and fix the rope on to some projection on the base of the spire. They had then edged their way round to the front, drawing the rope with them, in order perhaps to get the extra help provided by the lightning conductor in getting past the overhang. At some point, however, perhaps when Donald was almost on to the parapet, the rope, which was drawn across the corner from the farther side of the spire, must have escaped and swung back again to its former position, out of the boys' reach.

Was there any way of getting the rope back to them so that they could hold on to it? Unfortunately they had used only a very short section of the rope, some three feet of it, and even assuming that it was still securely fixed, it hung now on the blind side of the tower where there was no window and no way of getting at it. Someone might reach it by climbing the drainpipe as the boys had done – but then it would be impossible to bring it round again to the front of the tower without edging round the corner on the ledge – and the position of the two boys made any such move impossible. In fact, it was clear that to try to reach them by climbing, even if anyone was willing to attempt it, would be useless, and more likely to dislodge them than to bring them help.

Mor turned about to look for Mr Everard. He found that he was still gasping for breath. He ran into him almost at once, forcing his way through the mass of fascinated and now almost silent boys.

'Is the fire-brigade—?' Mor began.

'They can't come,' said Evvy. 'They've all been called to a big fire on the railway. We rang through to Marsington, and the Marsington fire brigade are coming – but they'll be about another twenty minutes.' Evvy was white, and his lower lip trembled. He held on to Mor as if to support himself.

Rigden appeared, pushing through frenziedly to Mor's side. 'The ladder from the pavilion,' he said.

The boys laid it on the ground, the top of it lying at Mor's feet. It was obviously far too short, that could be seen at a glance.

'It's no use,' said Mor. He wrung his hands. Could the boys hang on for twenty minutes? It was a miracle that Carde had not fallen already. And if Carde fell, Donald would be panic stricken, would try to move, and would fall too. Carde could be seen shifting slightly, trying to get his arm, which must be taking a great part of the weight of his body, a little farther on to the upper side of the parapet.

'A sheet,' said Mor. 'Oh God, if only there was something for them to fall on to.' He spoke aloud, and fell to tearing at his fingers with his teeth. He knew that the school possessed nothing like the professional fireman's sheet.

'Bedclothes!' said Evvy. He was still holding on to Mor's shoulder.

Mor did not understand him. But Rigden did. 'School House!' said Rigden, and turning about led his crew of followers at a run through the staring crowd.

As Mor looked round after them he saw that in the excitement the floodlights had been switched on to all the other buildings as well. The entire school was floodlit. It was as bright as day in the playground. As he looked he saw a commotion near the opening that led out to the drive, and then an ambulance came backing in. The boys were scuffling and pushing to make way for it. A number of people seemed to have arrived with the ambulance, and a crowd of outsiders, attracted by the unusual spectacle of the lights, had come in from the road. One man was taking photographs. Mor turned his head away.

Below the tower a strange scene was developing. Rigden and his friends had rushed into School House and were now staggering out with piles of sheets, blankets and pillows in their arms. They ran, with warning shouts, through the crowd and deposited these at the base of the tower. Then they ran back for more. Mor understood Evvy's idea. He shook his head. It was no use. The drop was colossal. A few blankets on the ground would hardly help. Other boys were now rushing to assist Rigden. They crowded in a struggling mass into School House. Those who could not get in through the doors went in through the windows. Others could be seen running down the paths that led to the other houses. Small detachments set off in the direction of the hall and the Gym and could be seen returning bearing the curtains from the windows and from the stage which they had ripped down. The pile of stuff at the base of the tower grew higher and higher. Almost all the boys were now running to and fro, cannoning into each other, falling, getting entangled in the textiles, and finally struggling forward to climb on to the mounting heap in order to put their burden on the top, slipping, and rolling down again upon those that followed them. They ran now in silence, breathlessly, in their hundreds, vividly revealed, each with several shadows from the opposing lights of the four illuminated façades.

Mor still stood looking up, as if with the very force of his will he could keep his son from falling. The fire-brigade should be arriving now very soon. Only let their ladder be long enough! Suppose it were not? Or suppose — So intently was his gaze now fixed upon the motionless extended form of Donald, that it was not until he heard a gasp of horror from the crowd who had now stopped their racing to and fro, and were staring upward, that he transferred his attention to Carde. Carde was swaying. His head had dropped forward and his arm was very very slowly sliding off the parapet. As this arm supported gradually less and less of his weight, he gripped more and more frantically on to the lightning conductor, trying to pass the hand by which he held it through between the conductor and the stone. He had been spreadeagled against the wall. Now he began to swing slowly round, as one arm moved from the parapet and the other attempted to twine itself about the wire of the conductor. His feet, which had been perched sideways upon the tiny ledge, turned until he was gripping the ledge with his toes. Then Mor saw something terrible. The lightning conductor, now beginning to take most of Carde's weight, was slowly parting company with the wall. But this was not what was, for Mor, the most dreadful. He saw that the conductor passed upward, over the parapet, across the wider ledge and under his son's body. If the wire were ripped right away it would dislodge Donald from the ledge.

Mor had not time even to draw a breath at this discovery before Carde fell. The lightning conductor, with a tearing sound which was audible in the tense silence, came away from the wall, and with a sudden and heart-rending cry Carde fell backwards, turning over in the air, and landed with a terrible sound somewhere upon the heap of blankets. A number of boys had run forward in an attempt to break his fall. Confused cries arose, and a strange wailing sound as of a number of people crying. The crowd closed in upon the place where Carde had fallen. The ambulance was backing across the playground. People who were presumably doctors and nurses were clearing a way, helped by Mr Everard and Prewett.

Mor did not look at this. Nor did most of the boys. They were watching Donald. What Mor feared had happened. The lightning conductor, pulled violently from below by Carde, had been jerked upward from the place where it passed under Donald's legs. Convulsively Donald's body moved, and for a moment it looked as if he would be swept off the ledge. But his hand-hold upon the tracery was strong enough to prevent this. His legs slithered for a moment over the edge, but holding on fiercely with both hands he managed to clamber partly back, his shoulders now raised a little above the ledge, his head pressed against the backward-sloping stone of the spire, both hands clinging to the masonry, one leg bent and braced against the edge of the parapet, and the other leg dangling in space. In this position he immobilized himself. A groan went up from the crowd. It was not a position which could be held for more than a few minutes. The strain on his arms would be too extreme – and he was patently too tired or too terrified to make the effort, almost impossible in any case, of hoisting himself back on to the ledge.

Mor knew that now it was no use to think of the fire-brigade. If there was anything that could be done it must be done in the next minutes. He looked about him wildly. He saw the ladder which the boys had fetched from the pavilion still lying at his feet. It was a tool. Was there anything he could do with it? Then an idea came to him. It was almost hopeless, but it was something to try. He turned to look for helpers. Rigden was still standing beside him. Mor opened his mouth, and found it almost impossible to articulate in order to explain what he wanted to Rigden. In a sort of snapshot he saw Bledyard standing a few feet away, his face screwed up, his mouth open.

'Is there a rope,' Mor said to Rigden, 'which would be long enough to draw this ladder up to the top window in the tower?'

'There's a fire escape rope in one of the upper classrooms,' said Rigden, 'which reaches to the ground from there. If we dropped it from the tower it would certainly reach the top of the ladder, if we put the ladder up against the building.' He spoke quickly and calmly.

Mor said, 'If we drew the ladder up to the window of the stack room and then stretched it outward it might be possible to rest the other end of it somewhere on the Library building.'

Rigden understood at once. The Library jutted out into the playground, overlapping the front of Main School, but not coming as far forward as the tower. From the top window of the tower, however, it might be possible to slope the ladder not too steeply downward and rest it either on one of the Library windows, where it could be held in place at that end, or upon the roof. In his new position Donald was more or less above the tower window, and the ladder would then be roughly below him.

'You come and show me where the rope is,' said Mor. 'The others can deal with the ladder.'

Rigden explained quickly to two of his friends, who then

began explaining to Prewett. The ambulance bearing Carde was driving slowly out of the playground. The smaller boys were reassembling the tall mound of blankets in a new place. Several of Rigden's friends began to run towards Library building, while others seized the ladder and began to erect it against the wall of Main School. Mor, tearing up the many flights of stairs, could hear Rigden running behind him. They reached the top classroom.

'There it is,' said Rigden. The rope was fixed by an enormous iron staple to the ceiling, and coiled neatly on top of a cupboard. Mor looked at it with despair. There seemed to be no way of detaching it. To cut or burn through it would take minutes and minutes. With a pickaxe one might have dislodged the staple. As it was—

Rigden had placed a chair on one of the desks and was climbing on to the top of the cupboard. Several of the older boys who had followed them stood in the doorway.

'We can't undo it!' said Mor.

'No need to, sir,' said Rigden. 'We'll throw it out of the window here, haul the ladder up, and then we can just push it on up from here to the stack room outside the building.'

Mor did not pause to think how stupid he had been. He caught the coil of rope from Rigden, and opened the window and threw it out. Looking down, he saw the playground far below, brilliantly lit up and covered with upturned faces. It was already a long way down. At every moment he expected to hear the terrible cry as Donald fell, and he felt in his own bones the frailty of his son's body. The ladder was leaning against the wall. A boy who had been mounting it caught the rope as it came flying down, tied it to one of the higher rungs, and slithered to the ground. Mor and Rigden began to pull on the rope.

As Mor saw the ladder rising he turned, and let one of the boys take his place. He ran back out of the door and up the two remaining flights of stairs towards the stack room. Two boys ran after him. One had already gone ahead. As he ran an alternative plan occurred to him. It might be possible to push the ladder straight up vertically to Donald, holding it from the windows and resting its base on one of the lower window sills. But as soon as he had thought this he realized that the overhang was too wide – for the ladder to get to Donald it would have to lean out farther from the building than their arms would reach, and this would mean supporting it precariously with the rope. Could they control it then, even without Donald's weight upon it, and would he be able to turn round and get himself even partly on to it without falling? The swaying ladder, moving about somewhere above their heads, would be as likely to knock the boy off as to bring him down to safety. It was altogether too dangerous. His mind reverted to the first plan. But the first plan was terribly dangerous too. If only he could think clearly!

Mor was now inside the lower segment of the tower, mounting a narrow zigzag iron staircase. His footsteps clattered and echoed. He thought, before I reach the top he will have fallen. His breath came in violent gasps and it felt as if blood were flooding into his lungs. Outside the door of the stack room there was an iron platform. Here a boy was standing, pulling at the handle of the door. Mor reached the top with a rush and began to drag at the door too. He gave a cry of despair. It was locked.

'Where is the key kept?' said someone below.

Rigden was now fighting his way up, past several boys on the iron stairs. 'No time for that,' he cried, 'we must break the door!'

Mor stood aside. He saw as in a dream that Bledyard, Hensman and several other people were standing below him on the next landing. He noticed the curling details of the ironwork and the green paint of the walls and the naked electric-light bulb. Rigden and three others were hurling themselves against the door. It withstood them. They began to kick the lower panels. With a loud splintering sound the door was beginning to crack. In a moment Rigden and his friends had kicked a hole in the bottom large enough for them to crawl through. With some difficulty Mor followed them.

Framed in the small square window and clearly seen in the brightness of the floodlights which fell directly upon it was the top of the ladder, which was being held up by the boys in the upper classroom. Mor threw the window open and tried to lean out. It was too high. He dragged a chair into position and Rigden mounted another one beside him. Mor looked down. The crowd was there as before, now much farther away below him, still looking up. He thought, in a detached way, Carde can hardly have survived. Above him in the air, as he leaned out to grasp the ladder, something was hanging, some six feet above him. He knew that it was his son's foot. He did not look there. He and Rigden began to draw the top of the ladder backward into the room. It was still being held from below. He thought, when we take the full weight of it, it will drop. 'More hands here,' he said.

The boys crowded round the window and began to pull the ladder in. The people below, whom Mor could vaguely see leaning out of the upper classroom, let go, and the ladder hung in the air swaying, a small section of it inside the stack room, and most of it outside, tilting away into space. Diagonally opposite in the Library building faces were at several of the upper windows and hands outstretched to catch the ladder. But it was still swinging, a long way beyond and below them.

Mor looked back into the room. It was now crowded with boys, who were stumbling about among the books, trying to move a set of steel shelves that stood in the centre. A steady stream of volumes was falling to the floor, and other books which had been piled against the walls were collapsing towards the middle of the room and being trampled under foot. More boys were crawling in through the hole in the door. Someone who had got hold of an axe was aiming blows at the lock.

The difficulty was that there was not enough space inside the room to draw enough of the ladder in through the window to give the leverage necessary to lift it up towards the top of the Library. And even if we could lift it, thought Mor – it may just fall to the ground when we begin to pay it out of the window again. He moaned to himself. He began to wonder, is it long enough in any case?

The end of the ladder now reached across the room and was jammed against the angle of the ceiling. 'Pull it down,' he said to the boys behind him.

They began to drag on the ladder, swinging on it, and clambering on to piles of books to get on top of it. Under their weight the near end swung down abruptly. The longer section, which was outside the window, swung upward. It was now well above the level of the Library roof. The boys clung on desperately, and the ladder swung erratically to and fro, pivoting on the edge of the window. It was very hard to control it.

'We'll have to rest it on the roof,' said Rigden. This was already clear to Mor. The Library windows were too far below, and the ladder, once the weight on the near end was released, would probably fall too quickly for the people at the other end to catch it. This meant, since there was no access to that part of the Library roof, that no one would be able to hold it at the far end. But nothing could be done about that.

'Let it go out slowly,' said Mor, 'keeping this end down as long as you can.'

The ladder began to ease outwards through the window. Mor guided it as best he could. Eight or ten boys were still hanging on to the end, crowding and climbing on top of each other in the small room, and swinging with all their weight from the last rungs. As more and more of the ladder came to be on the outside of the window, it began to incline downward at an increasing pace. There was a final tumbling flurry inside the room, the near end of the ladder went flying upward, and the far end met the Library roof with a clatter. Mor saw that the ladder had landed in the gutter. He hoped it was secure. It was not possible to lift it again now.

Mor looked upward. He could see Donald's foot, clad in a white gym shoe, still dangling several feet above him. It was not directly over the ladder. Helped by Rigden Mor began to push the ladder into a more diagonal position, one end of it in the corner of the window. This made the far end more precarious, but it still looked as if it were firm, provided the gutter held. The ladder was now placed as nearly as possible underneath where Donald was hanging.

Mor began to lean far out of the window, putting one hand on the ladder. Rigden was holding on to his coat. He could now see most of Donald's leg, and his other foot drawn up just under the edge of the parapet. The rest was out of sight above. As Mor saw the body still perched there over the sharp edge, and as he felt the terrible drop opening beneath him, he was in such an agony of fear that he almost fell himself. Then he began to try to speak. That Donald could be spoken to was in itself something fantastic. Mor hardly expected that the boy would be able to understand him. He took a quick glance to his right. The arterial road was visible, marked by the flashing lights of cars, for several miles in both directions. There was neither sight nor sound of the fire-engine.

Mor spoke, his voice coming out strangely into the empty air above him. 'Don,' he said, in a loud clear voice, 'Don—' He had to choose his words carefully. 'Listen. A fire-engine is coming with a long ladder – it'll arrive soon, but we don't know exactly when. If you feel that you can hang on securely till it comes, then do that. But if you feel that you're slipping, then listen to me. We've stretched a ladder across from here to the Library building, passing just underneath you – it's about five feet below. If you feel you can't hang on, then drop on to the ladder and clutch on to it hard, and we'll pull you in through the window. So – if you're secure, stay where you are – if you're not, drop on to the ladder. We'll just be waiting here.'

There was silence. Mor swayed back into the window. He leaned his head against the frame of the window and looked straight out into the night. In the pit of darkness before him he could see, after a moment or two, a few dim stars. He began to pray. He was muttering words half aloud. He heard a faint movement above him. Donald's foot was moving. It swung a little and was still. There was a scraping sound from the parapet. Then with the violence of a missile Donald's body struck the ladder. He flung his arms out, clutching on to it. The ladder rocked, and sagged in the middle. But it stayed in place, Rigden and several others holding firmly on to the near end of it.

A second later all was still again, the ladder suspended between the two buildings and Donald lying upon it lengthways, his head towards the window, his arms and legs twined into the rungs. He lay there quite still, his face turned sideways. He seemed to be scarcely conscious. Mor began to lean out again. Donald's extended hand was within reach of his.

'No, leave this to us,' said a voice behind him, and someone was dragging at his coat. It was Hensman. Mor stepped, or fell, back into the room. He saw that someone had got the door open and there was a crowd upon the stairs. He saw Bledyard climbing past him towards the window. Hensman and Rigden were leaning far out, being held from behind by those inside. Mor could see that they had each secured hold of one of Donald's arms, and were trying to draw him towards them. This was difficult, because his legs were entwined in the ladder. As he felt the pressure on his arms Donald began feebly to try to get his legs free. His head was moving upward towards the window. More hands were stretched out. Then the ladder began to tilt. One side of it seemed to have come clear of the guttering at the Library end. It swayed. Then, as Donald's head and shoulders were to be seen at last appearing at the window of the stack room, the ladder tilted right over and fell into the gap between Main School and the Library, landing on the asphalt with a resounding clatter. Donald was pulled head first into the room.

Mor found that he was sitting on the floor, sitting somewhere in the sea of books, and leaning his back against more books. The body of Donald, breathing and unbroken, lay somewhere near him. He stretched out a hand and touched his son's leg. People were leaning over them both. Someone was offering him brandy. Mor drank a little. His relief was so intense that he was stunned by it. He could see Donald being raised and propped up against the other wall. The boy's eyes were open and he seemed to be taking in his surroundings. He turned his head and accepted some of the brandy. Bledyard was kneeling somewhere between them and trying to say something.

Donald was sitting more upright now. He drank some more and looked about him. He put his hand to his head. Then after a little while he tried to get up. People were saying soothing things to him. He pushed them aside, and began to stumble to his feet. He stood for a moment, staring about the room, his feet spread wide apart upon the sea of books. Then without warning he made a dive for the door. The boys scattered before him. His recent peril had made him numinous and alarming. He could be heard clattering away down the staircase.

Mor got up. He rubbed his hands over his face. He did not try to follow. Several boys were running down the stairs after Donald. A minute later Rigden, who had stayed beside Mor, and had now mounted one of the chairs by the window, said in an astonished tone, 'There he goes!'

Mor mounted the other chair and looked out. He saw once again far below the lighted expanse of the playground, scattered with groups of people. Then he saw a running figure. Donald had issued at speed from the door of Main School and was streaking across the asphalt towards the darkness of the river. The crowd of boys stood there and stared at him. It was a moment before they realized who it was. By then Donald had almost reached the drive. A cry arose from the School. Donald disappeared into the darkness, running fast. Like a pack of hounds, the other boys began to stream after him, shouting incoherently as they ran.

Mor got down from the window. He subsided again on to the floor. Two figures were leaning over him. They were Rigden and Bledyard, who were the only people left in the room. They were saying something. Mor did not know what they were saying. He leaned his head back wearily against the wall and lost his consciousness, half fainting and half falling into an exhausted sleep. In the far far distance now he began to hear the clanging bell of the fire-engine.

# CHAPTER SEVENTEEN

Nan thrust her arm through Mor's as they began to walk slowly back up the hill, taking the little path that led from the Headmaster's garden into the wood. It was the end of term. They had just been talking with Mr Everard. It was now four days since the climbing of the tower, and nothing had been seen or heard of Donald since the moment when he ran away across the playground and disappeared into the darkness. The boys who had pursued him as far as the main road had lost him there in the wilderness of fields and waste land on the other side. He had vanished and there had been no news of him since. After two days of waiting, Mor had asked the help of the police, but without much hope of results. Nan and Felicity had of course returned home at once, and now one of them was always in the house in case the telephone rang. But it did not ring, and Donald's absence and silence continued.

Jimmy Carde had had a miraculous escape from death. He was saved largely by Mr Everard's pile of blankets; and was now in hospital with broken ribs, two broken legs, and a fractured skull. He was declared to be in no immediate danger, and likely to recover. Two of the boys who had tried to break his fall were also in hospital with concussion.

Against both Carde and Donald Mor Mr Everard had reluctantly invoked the law that decreed instant expulsion for climbers. He had been so apologetic to Mor about this that the latter had virtually had to make up his mind for him, pointing out that he had no choice but to expel them both. This was grave. What was in a way more grave was that it was now two days before Donald's chemistry exam was due to start. Everard had told Mor that there would of course be no objection to Donald's taking the exam at St Bride's and using the laboratories as he would normally have done. But Mor knew that now his son would not take the examination, and was perhaps deliberately staying in hiding until the date was past. This was very grievous to him; but to think of it in this way a little relieved his more profound anxieties concerning Donald's well-being.

On the night of the catastrophe Rain and Demoyte came to see Mor at a very late hour in Rain's car, and wanted to take him back then and there to Brayling's Close. Mor had refused, since he felt he must stay in his own home in case of telephone messages or in case Donald came back. Rain had cooked him a meal, which he was unable to eat, and had administered a sedative. She and Demoyte persuaded him to go to bed, and then they went away. Since then Mor had seen her frequently, now always at the Close. He had convinced her of what he himself hoped was the truth, that Donald was perfectly well but simply hiding so as to miss his exam. Mor had not yet spoken to Nan about what he and Rain intended to do. He knew that Rain was by now intensely anxious that he should speak; but she had not yet attempted to discuss the matter with him again. Mor found meanwhile that his resolution was unshaken, indeed the stronger for these new troubles. But he had not yet found the moment at which, in the midst of such distresses, he could decently tell his wife that he proposed to leave her.

Mor's anxiety about Donald was intense. But his anxiety about Rain was equally intense; and he might, even then, have been able to speak decisively to Nan if the latter had given him the slightest chance. Mor knew that what he needed, in order to be able to speak with finality, was a moment of violence. If Nan, by provoking him, or by visiting almost any extreme of emotion, had given him the gift of anger or the sense of extremity, he would have spoken the words which would be fatal. But Nan, as if once more to cross him, had been since her return enormously calm, reasonable and compliant, doing her best to generate once more that atmosphere of homely *ennui* which Mor could still remember that he had once found reassuring.

Nan was very worried too about Donald, but she had reasoned it out with Mor that the boy had almost certainly come to no harm, and would reappear after the opening date of the examination. As far as the exam was concerned, Nan was obviously more glad than otherwise that Don would miss it, but she refrained from irritating Mor by saying so. The person who was most genuinely afraid about what might have happened to Donald was Felicity, who busied herself with imagining the worst possible and was continually in tears. Nan vented some of her nervousness upon her daughter, but whether intentionally or not did nothing to upset her husband or to provide the great storm for which he was waiting and on which alone he would have felt himself able to ride.

'Evvy has been awfully nice, hasn't he?' said Nan, still clinging on to Mor's arm.

The wood was silent and empty. Many of the boys had already gone away on early buses and the rest were hanging about in the playground or the upper drive, waiting to be picked up. Some more charabancs were due at eleven o'clock to take the West Country contingent to the station.

'He's very decent,' said Mor. 'Did he say anything special to you before I came?'

Last year's leaves, and a few that had already floated down from the branches after the recent storm, drifted about under the trees or blew sharply to and fro across the path, striking their ankles. It was a dark windy morning.

'He said they're going ahead with the presentation dinner for Demoyte's picture,' said Nan. 'It's happening on Tuesday.'

'Of course they're going ahead!' said Mor. 'Or does Evvy think the school ought to be in mourning? Yes, I know it's Tuesday. Will you come – or shall we send an excuse? It's perfectly easy to get out of it now.'

They came to an open glade where the trees drew back to circle an expanse of mossy earth and short grasses. Mor recognized the place, with the dull revolving sadness that he now felt continually when he was in the presence of his wife.

'I shall come, I think,' said Nan. 'We'd better go on making life as normal as possible – it'll keep us from fretting too much. I even let Evvy persuade me into saying a few words. I just hadn't the strength to say no. He said something very short would do.'

'You'll answer the toast!' said Mor. 'I'm so glad.' But he was not glad, he thought, any more about anything connected with Nan. He felt as if he were talking to someone who was already dead, but who didn't yet know it. He felt such intense sadness at this thought that he would have liked to ask Nan to comfort him in some way, but with the impulse he remembered that this too was impossible. Nan was the one person who could not ever give him ease for the pain that was in him now.

They passed by Prewett's house. It had an empty abandoned air, doors and windows left open, silent of boys.

'I wish Felicity would cheer up a bit and not be so wretched,' said Mor. He had to talk to stop himself from thinking.

'She got a bad cold down at the sea,' said Nan. 'I found her wandering about in her bathing suit late one evening. She hasn't been well since.'

As they reached the gravel path behind the Library a sound was to be heard of cheerful voices, laughter and singing, and when they emerged on to the playground they saw the crowd of boys waiting with their hand luggage near the entrance to the drive. A charabanc had drawn up and some of the boys were climbing in. In the background, beyond School House, a few private cars could be seen drawn up on the grass, their doors wide open, being loaded with suitcases, tennis rackets, cricket bats and other paraphernalia. The mass of those who were not yet called for stood by in a joyful chanting crowd to wave away the departing ones. On this day all feuds were forgotten, and the most puny and unpopular boy in the form would get a warm unanimous shout of farewell, heartening and misleading to his parents, especially if the latter arrived to fetch him in the latest Bentley or the oldest Rolls.

The charabanc had filled up, and began to move away amid shouting and waving. A dozen boys ran after it down the drive, pushing it while it crawled slowly from the asphalt to the gravel, and then pursuing it as it gathered pace, to escort it as far as the gates. Hands were flapping out of every window. The charbanc disappeared into a cloud of dust and cheering. Meanwhile the crowd in the playground were dancing a Highland reel, accompanied by human voices imitating bagpipes, while through the windows of echoing and empty classrooms a few late lingerers leaned out to shout to their friends or to unwind, contrary to Mr Everard's most explicit wishes, long rolls of lavatory paper which undulated in the wind like streamers.

'Let's go round the other way,' said Mor. He looked on the scene with revulsion.

'Don't be silly, Bill,' said Nan. She drew him firmly on across the playground towards the drive, keeping close to the wall of

Main School. A group of reelers removed their capering for a few steps to let them pass.

'Good-bye, sir, happy holidays!' called one or two voices.

'Good-bye, good-bye, happy holidays!' came the echoing cry from the rest of the crowd.

Mor felt that he was anonymous. He was just one of the masters. He felt almost annihilated by the presence of so much happiness. 'Good-bye,' he said, 'happy holidays to you too.'

They turned along the drive. As they neared the gates a car passed them slowly. The window came down and the small head of Rigden came out, bobbing violently as if it were on a spring.

'Good-bye, sir,' cried Rigden. 'Good luck – and see you next term!'

Rigden's parents, who knew Mor slightly, could be seen waving within, anxious now to escape and to avoid any last-minute courtesies. The car reached the main road and joined the endless procession of fast-moving traffic, London-bound, flying away into the world that lay outside St Bride's at an increasing pace as Rigden's father, who was a very successful barrister, stepped hard on the accelerator.

Mor and Nan turned into the suburban roads of the housing estate. In a minute or two they had reached their own house. Felicity met them at the door.

'Any news?' she said. Her eyes had grown big and bloodshot with intermittent weeping and continual expectation.

'No,' said Mor. 'Did anyone ring?'

'No,' she said, and went back to sit at the foot of the stairs.

Nan said, 'I'll make some coffee. Then I really must do that ironing. What are you going to do, Bill?'

Mor was going to see Rain at Brayling's Close. He said, 'I'll go down to the Public Library on my bike – and then I'd better go back into school and do various jobs.'

'Must you really work today?' said Nan, staring at him from the kitchen door. 'I thought holidays had started.'

'I've told you a hundred times,' said Mor, 'holidays don't start for *me* at the end of term.' He went into the drawing-room. Now that the weather was cool it seemed a tiny room, hideously crowded with objects and jumbled with colours and designs. He loathed himself.

'Don't sit in that draughty place, darling,' Nan was saying to Felicity. 'Come and have your coffee.'

Felicity said, 'I don't want any coffee. I'm going to lie down for a while.'

'Don't be silly,' said Nan, 'you'll only start crying again if you lie down. Why not wash all your underclothes now while the water's hot? I'll leave out the ironing board, and I can iron them for you this afternoon.'

Felicity made no reply, but walked upstairs with a heavy tread and closed the door of her room.

Nan brought in a tray with coffee and biscuits. They sat looking out of the window. The garden was damp, and tousled by the wind.

'The autumn is coming,' she said. 'It's strange how early you can see it. As soon as the phlox comes out you know that the best part of the summer is over. Then you can soon expect the falling leaves. You remember how pleased Liffey used to be when the leaves began to fall? She would go on and on chasing them about the lawn in such an idiotic way. Then when you had raked them together in a heap she would charge into it and scatter it and you would be so cross.'

'Yes,' said Mor, 'I remember.' He finished his coffee quickly. 'I must be off now,' he said. 'I'll be back for lunch.'

Nan got up and followed him into the hall. 'I think I'll just look in on Felicity,' she said. 'The child will make herself ill with this grieving.'

Mor left the house. He took his bicycle, started off in the direction of the Library, turned sharply back down another road, and joined the dual carriageway near the brow of the hill. Then he sailed swiftly down the other side towards Demoyte's house, the wind pressing upon his cheeks and jerking at his hair. The clouds came low over the road ahead of him, which went straight on into the far distance, an arrow pointing towards London. The wind was fresh and carried a smell of the countryside. Mor threw back his head. He existed still, he, Mor, and could do what he would. In a minute he would see his dear one, whose presence would dispel all horror and all grief. Already the splendour of it touched him, driving the blackness out of his flesh – and all things began to fall into place again as preliminaries to a life of renewed truthfulness and love. By the time he reached the door of the Close his heart was light.

He went straight into the drawing-room, where he found Rain sitting with Demoyte. They were a great deal together in these days. When Mor came in, Rain jumped up and ran to seize the sleeve of his coat, while Demoyte looked on with a sombre expression.

'This place is turning into a madhouse,' said Demoyte. He began to gather up his books preparatory to leaving the room.

'Don't go, sir,' said Mor.

'Don't give me that stuff,' said Demoyte. 'I'll be in the library, if either of you wants to see me, which is unlikely.'

As soon as the door closed, Mor picked Rain up violently in his arms and held her as if to crush their two bodies into one. It seemed as if such an embrace must surely mend all. He set her down at last, protesting and laughing a little.

She led him to a chair, in a way that was now familiar to him, and sat on the ground before him to interrogate him. He had little to tell her.

'How was it this morning?' asked Rain.

How could he tell her how it was? This morning he had suffered to extremity. This morning he had been a liar and a traitor. But now he could scarcely remember these things – as perhaps the blessed spirits when they enter paradise very soon forget the horrors of purgatory which seem to have been a dream until they vanish altogether from the memory.

'This morning was all right,' said Mor. He had already told her that there was no news of Donald.

'Mor,' said Rain, tugging at his knees, 'you haven't – said anything to Nan yet?'

This was the question which Mor had been dreading. 'No,' he said.

'Will you – soon?' she asked. Her look of tender anxiety made Mor cover his face.

'Rain,' he said, 'I can't give this blow to Nan just now, just when we're so worried about Donald. We must wait a little longer.'

'Mor,' said Rain, 'I *cannot* wait. I know this impatience may be very tiresome or wicked. If it's wicked, it hardly adds much to the sum of what we've already done wrong. But I think we should tell Nan the truth now, even if it is a bad moment.'

'Why now?' said Mor. 'Or are you afraid I'll change my mind?' He held her by the chin, and looked into her eyes. He had never known before what it was to converse with someone, reading their eyes the whole time. Angels must know each other in this way, without a barrier.

'Not that!' said Rain. 'Yet I am afraid of something, I don't know what. I want to bind you to me.' Her small hands gripped his wrists and tried to shake him.

When Mor saw her intensity and her determination, he felt deep gratitude. He drew her towards him. 'So you shall, my dearest,' he said. 'But you must leave this other matter to me. Now tell me about something else. Have you worked on the picture again?'

'No,' said Rain, 'I haven't touched it. I feel far too rotten to paint. It's no good, but it'll have to stay like that.'

The picture had been taken from the easel and was leaning against the wall in the far corner of the room. They both looked at it. It seemed now to Mor a little less good. He even thought he saw dimly what Bledyard had meant. The colossal strength of Demoyte's over-sized tyrannical head was not really present in the picture – though many of his traits were present, especially a musing thoughtfulness which Mor had not often seen in him, but which he was ready now to believe to be one of his most fundamental moods. It was a gentler and more pensive Demoyte that the picture showed – but also one that was less strong. However, there was no doubt that it was a good portrait.

'I'm sorry,' said Mor. 'I hate having stopped you from painting.'

'Nothing could stop me,' said Rain, 'except for a moment!'

'You know this awful dinner is on Tuesday?' said Mor.

Rain shuddered. 'Your wife won't be there, will she?' she asked.

'Yes,' said Mor, 'but that won't matter.'

Rain jumped to her feet. 'I can't come to the dinner if your wife is there,' she said, 'I *can't*.' She was almost crying.

'Darling,' said Mor, 'don't be foolish. It'll be awful, but it's just something we must get through. It's no madder than everything else is at the moment.'

'You must tell her at once!' she said.

'Rain,' said Mor, 'leave it to me, will you?'

Rain was suddenly in tears. He embraced her. 'I can't,' she kept saying, 'I can't go to that dinner, I can't.'

'Stop this nonsense,' said Mor, 'you must come to the dinner, of course.' He added, 'Anything may have happened by then. I may have told Nan everything. As for the dinner, if she doesn't know the worst she won't attack you, and if she does she won't come. So stop crying.' But somehow Mar did not believe that he would have told Nan by next Tuesday. There was some date by which he would have told her. But it was not next Tuesday.

Rain sat down on the floor again and went on crying. Mor stroked her hair. He felt a strange diminution of sympathy. He loved her. Now he made her grief. But soon he would make her happiness. Meanwhile, it was he who was to be pitied, he who had to act the murderer and the traitor. Her grief was that of a temporary deprivation. His was a grief for things which would never mend again once they were broken. There would be a new life and a new world. But that which he was about to break would never mend, and he now knew he would never cease to feel the pain of it. Inside all his happiness this pain would remain always intact until his life's end. He continued to caress her hair.

# CHAPTER EIGHTEEN

It was Tuesday. The opening date of the chemistry exam had come and gone, but Donald Mor had not come home, nor had any news been received which might provide the slightest clue to his whereabouts. Mor had not told Nan that he intended to leave her. It was the day of the presentation dinner. Rain was to be present, of course; and Nan had not changed her mind either about coming or about replying to the toast.

The dinner was to take place in the masters' dining-room at St Bride's, and its organization had for some time now been producing alarm and confusion among the school staff who were rarely called upon to stage manage anything more magnificent than a stand-up tea for Speech Day. The masters' dining-room, like so many things at St Bride's, was misnamed. No one at that institution ever *dined*, in that room or else-where, since the relevant meal was known, not at all inap-propriately, as supper – and in fact the room in question was not normally used for eating in at all, but had become the meeting place of the Board of Governors, the Sixth Form Essay Society and the Games Committee. To transform this grim chamber into the setting for a festive scene was not likely to be easy. Great efforts had however been made, inspired largely by the ubiquitous Hensman, whose enthusiasm was the more touching as he was not to be present at the dinner, since after much discussion it had been decided that only senior masters were to be invited in addition to the Governors.

Mor was in evening-dress. This was, for him, an extremely rare experience, and he felt very odd. He had bought himself, especially for the occasion, a soft white evening-shirt to re-place the errant carapace by which he had been tortured in the past; but he still felt at wearing these unusual clothes an in-tense discomfort which was caused partly by general embar-rassment and partly by the discovery that he must have grown stouter since the last occasion. The trousers met, but only just. Fortunately the old-fashioned jacket could be left unbuttoned. For all that, he thought that he looked well, and sadly that it would, if things had been different, have been a pleasant jest to show himself to Rain in this disguise. This thought shocked him by its lightness, and he turned quickly back to his griefs. He was in a state of increasing disquiet about the fate of his son. His imagination had begun at last to be busy with visions of Donald bitterly resolving never to return, Donald suffering from loss of memory, Donald suffering from hunger and despair, Donald derelict, Donald dead. These fears, by a strange chemistry of the afflicted spirit, slightly eased his other tensions by making it the more obvious that nothing could be told to Nan until after the reappearance of the boy.

The company was supposed to assemble at seven-thirty in the Common Room which adjoined the masters' dining-room. Dinner was to be at eight. Mor had made arrangements for a taxi to call for Nan just before half-past seven, and to go on to fetch Mrs Prewett. Rain was going to bring Demoyte over in her car. Mor himself had intended to get dressed much earlier and go over to school to offer his assistance to the staff and make sure that everything was quite ready in the dining-room. However, his dressing had taken longer than he expected, and it was nearly seven before he reached the scene. He peered in through the dining-room door; and then entered, whistling with amazement for the benefit of Hensman, who was standing by hoping to see signs of shock.

The room had certainly been transformed. The green leather armchairs were nowhere to be seen, and neither was the ponderous roll-top desk which was usually slanted across one of the corners, nor the massive deal cupboard whose contents were unknown since the key had been lost some years ago. Instead of these, three slim Regency tables, which Mor recognized as belonging to Prewett, decked the side of the room, adorned with flowers, and a fine sideboard had appeared to fill the space on one side of the mantelpiece. Of the upright chairs, the more deplorable ones had vanished, to be replaced by some imitation Chippendale, also Prewett's, which did not harmonize too badly with the set of Victorian chairs which were the normal inhabitants of the room. The long oval table, usually covered with a length of green baize, was draped now in a silvery damask cloth which reached almost to the ground, and upon it a thick array of silver and glass glittered in the light of some of the candles which Hensman had experimentally lighted. From the mantelpiece the bulbous and inexplicable brass ornaments had vanished, to be replaced by flowers – and above the mantel, surmounting all, was hung the portrait of Demoyte.

'Marvellous!' said Mor. 'It's unrecognizable.'

'You relieve my mind,' said Hensman. 'I feared some traces might remain! You know Evvy's motto – if a thing's worth doing it's worth just blundering through somehow. I thought I'd better take things in hand. I'm afraid the walls are rather discoloured where we've taken the monstrosities away, but when it gets dark and you've got nothing but candlelight that won't show.'

'I'm sorry you won't be here,' said Mor.

'Don't you worry,' said Hensman. 'There's another party below stairs! The man I'm sorry for is Baseford – he'll never get over missing this spread. Two kinds of wine, and all! By the way, did I tell you how the sherry battle ended? Evvy has now demanded the very best Spanish and nothing else will do!' Evvy had previously been of the opinion that South African sherry, if served from decanters, would be quite good enough for his guests, especially as, in his view, it was mere snobbery to pretend that there was any difference in taste.

Mor laughed. 'You'd better go and change,' he said. 'It's after seven.' Hensman was still dressed for tennis. Junior masters had been invited to the brief sherry-drinking before the dinner; for this they had been let off with lounge suits.

'I'm not coming,' said Hensman. 'I bequeath to you the company of Sir Somebody Something-Something, Bart., and other such late joys. I must start organizing my own party. I'm just off to fetch my guitar. Cheerio! Happy drinking.'

Mor was left alone. He blew out the candles which Hensman had left burning, and began to look up at the picture of Demoyte which was hung up, Rain was sure to think too high, above the ornate Victorian fireplace. It was a sunny evening, and the light was still good. The masters' dining-room was situated at the end of the upper floor of the Phys and Gym building and was served by a kitchen which was now incorporated in Mr Baseford's flat. It faced west, so that the sun was shining in past the heavy rep curtains, the colour of an old inky desk top, which Mor reflected must not be drawn together on any account. The picture of Demoyte looked different again.

Bledyard had said that the man in the picture did not look mortal. To Mor then it seemed a very mortal face. But he knew that he was touched by the occasion, and by memories of the almost incredulous regret he had felt at the thought that the old tyrant, who had been used to an almost complete authority over hundreds of souls that feared him, was to be reft of his power and sent into exile, able now only to oppress and punish those who loved him. The number of those, Mor thought sadly, was few enough. This evening's gathering would number more of Demoyte's enemies than of his friends.

At that moment an efficient-looking butler, hired for the occasion, appeared and ushered Mor away into the adjoining Common Room. The butler then returned to put the finishing touches to Hensman's masterpiece. As Mor entered the Common Room, Evvy came in the door, followed by Prewett. Another butler materialized with a large silver tray covered with sherry-glasses which had already been filled. Mor suddenly began to feel extremely nervous and apprehensive. Rain's terrors had not left him untouched. He tried to calm himself by picturing the relief which he would feel when this absurd and hateful evening was over.

'Ah, my dear fellow,' said Evvy, 'I'm so glad you're here early. Yes, yes, I've seen the dining-room. Hensman's done a fine job of work. I hope he'll be able to be with us for the sherry – but he said he had a meeting of Scouts this evening and mightn't manage to come.'

'He's gone off to Scouts, I'm afraid,' said Mor. He was too depressed to take any pleasure in Hensman's little joke.

'Too bad!' said Evvy. 'I wanted his opinion on the sherry. Spanish, you know!' Evvy made a face like a choirboy acting a French *roué* in a parish play. 'No point in spoiling the ship for a ha'porth of tar, is there? That's my text for first School Service of next term, so I thought I'd better be guided by it! I only hope the Governors won't think we're indulging in unnecessary expense.'

'No,' said Mor, 'they'll be delighted.' The irresponsible reactionary old sybarites, he added to himself. Demoyte had always been quite right about the Governors.

'It's only once in a while, isn't it?' said Evvy. 'Do you think one might just sip some sherry before our guests arrive, to try it? I must confess, I need some Dutch courage. "Unaccustomed as I am to public speaking" is the simple truth for me, a sermon isn't the same thing at all, and the prospect will quite spoil my dinner. By the way, Bill, I'm so glad your wife has agreed to speak, it's terribly kind of her to take it on. She really was my last hope. I'd asked at least twelve people before I got to her.'

Mor noted this instance of Evvy's tact, saw Prewett note it, and forgot it at once. 'I'm glad too,' he said. 'It'll be good for her.' The words were empty. The future in which Nan would enjoy the benefit of her daring did not belong to him.

The door opened to admit Sir Leopold Tinsley-Williams, the man with whose company Hensman was so ready to dispense, followed by Bledyard and two other masters. Evvy, who had just taken a glass of sherry from the tray, turned with inarticulate cries of embarrassment and welcome, and spilt the sherry with one hand, while the other sawed to and fro, undecided whether it should shake hands with Sir Leopold or offer him a drink. The butler took charge of the situation, spreading social calm by the very bend of his head.

Mor retired a step or two with Prewett, and was glad to find a drink in his hand. Prewett looked rather odd in evening-dress too. Mor was relieved to be with him for a moment. He replied briefly to his inquiries about Don. Some more Governors arrived. Mor and Prewett backed farther away, and surveyed the scene, making comments. It was notable that Bledyard's evening-dress fitted him extremely well, and made him look handsome and slightly wicked. He looked like a man who was used to these garments, and in this respect resembled the Governors rather than the masters. He was talking now in an animated way to several of the former, amongst whom he appeared to have a number of steady acquaintances.

'The old school tie does its stuff!' said Prewett. Prewett had been at Bradford Grammar School.

'I don't think so,' said Mor. 'They take him for a person of distinction. And they are right,' he added.

'What I hate,' said Prewett, 'is to see Evvy crawling to those swine. He doesn't seem to realize he's worth ten of each of them.'

Nan and Mrs Prewett came in, causing a stir. Mor turned towards his wife and felt the accustomed shock at seeing her in party array. She was wearing an extremely *décolleté* black nylon evening-dress, with a very full skirt and sort of bustle at the back. About her shoulders she wore a cloudy yellow stole, made of some gauzy material and run through with golden threads. She also had on the ear-rings which Mor had accepted for her from Tim Burke, although they didn't quite go with the severe smartness of the dress. Her fine bosom, extensively revealed, was rounded and powdery smooth. Her hair was sleekly curled about her face, in a fashion reminiscent of the nineteen-twenties, which showed off very well the strong shape of her head and the slenderness and pallor of her neck. She surveyed the room without nervousness. Her eyes flamed towards her husband.

After her came Mrs Prewett. Mrs Prewett was a tall stout woman, with a broad tranquil face and very large hands. She had elected to don a dinner-gown made of coffee-coloured lace, with a coffee-coloured slip to match. A serrated line crossed her enormous front from east to west, above it the generous contour of her breasts, below it a flicker of underclothes and an expanse of flesh mottled by the sun to a deep reddish brown. Her arms, which were white and rather plump, swung energetically from the short puffy sleeves of the lace gown as she looked about for Mr Prewett. She saw him and swept forward with a shout. Prewett was obviously delighted to see her. He began complimenting her on her appearance. With a strange pang of sadness Mor turned away to join Nan. Nan meanwhile had been presented to Sir Leopold, and was making herself extremely charming to him. Mor stood by watching, not included and feeling awkward.

Then Rain and Demoyte arrived. A curious synthetic cheer greeted their appearance, and a number of people hastened to surround them and make the pretence of a festive welcome. Sir Leopold, who had always detested Demoyte, made no move, but went on talking to Nan, his eyes riveted to the point at which her dress indicated, but just failed to reveal, the division between her breasts. Sir Leopold was well placed and he made the best of his height. Mor stepped back a little, so that he could observe the newcomers without being anywhere in Nan's field of vision.

Demoyte looked splendid. He wore his evening-dress like a soldier, and confronted his foes with the familiar front, as shameless as brass and as hard as steel. He cast a belligerent look round the room, his lips already trembling with scorn.

Beside him Rain was tiny. She wore a long white cotton evening-dress, very simply covered with blue flowers with black outlines, drawn well in to her small waist. A long twining string of black carved beads seemed to make her neck longer and her black-capped head smaller. Her hair was slightly untidy. She looked like a boy actor. Mor felt his heart twist and turn within him for sheer tenderness. He looked towards them with a love which embraced them both, the old man and the girl.

One of the Governors was being polite to Rain, and cutting out Evvy, who was also trying to talk to her. Demoyte was talking to Bledyard, and conspicuously indicating by his behaviour that this was one of the few people in the room that he could tolerate. Sir Leopold was still concentrating. Nan had turned a little so that she could see Mor. Mor looked away. He tried to attend to the problem of how to be rude enough to Sir Leopold for the latter to realize that the rudeness was intentional without being so rude as to be boorish.

Dinner was announced. Evvy had of course given no thought to the question of precedence. There was a courteous scrimmage in the doorway. The women were pushed forward. Besides Rain, Nan and Mrs Prewett, there was a Mrs Kingsley, the wife of one of the Governors who had arrived rather late and was patently the oldest woman present. Evvy was now attempting to urge Rain through the door while Rain was trying to give way to Mrs Kingsley. Eventually, after an embarrassed silence had fallen and the protagonists had all started to say something and stopped, alarmed by the pause, Sir Leopold passed through the door first, with Mrs Kingsley on one arm and Nan on the other. Evvy followed with Rain and Mrs Prewett. Demoyte and Bledyard, still talking, went through next, and everyone else came after in a hurly-burly.

Fortunately the places at the table were all clearly labelled, so that the confusion was not repeated in the dining-room. Everyone found his position and Evvy said grace at some length. The company then sat down with relief and immediately received their soup. The place of honour was in the centre of the table facing the picture. Here sat Evvy in the middle place, with Rain on his right and Mrs Kingsley on his left. Demoyte sat next to Rain, and Sir Leopold next to Demoyte. Nan was on the other side of Sir Leopold. Another Governor was next to Mrs Kingsley, and Mrs Prewett sat at the end of the table next to Bledyard, with whom to everyone's continually renewed surprise she seemed to get on very well. The rest of the company were disposed round the ends of the table and along the side nearest to the fireplace. Here Mor sat, opposite to Sir Leopold, so that both the women were facing him, Nan to his left and Rain to his right farther away. The fish had by now arrived, and with it the welcome glass of white wine. Mor hoped that Hensman had briefed Evvy about quantity as well as quality of wine. He felt an extreme need of alcohol, and spent a vain moment wishing that he were altogether elsewhere with Hensman and the guitar.

The soup and fish were good. The meat was only middling, but it mattered less as there was a good deal of red wine to wash it down with. Mor heard one of the Governors asking the name and year of the wine and approving of the answer. Evvy had evidently been well schooled by someone, doubtless Hensman. Mor emptied another glass. He began to feel a little less anxious. The evening was now half over and the women had so far not had occasion to notice each other. At this moment they could not even see one another, since they were on the same side of the table, and he could keep them both under his eye. Demoyte and Sir Leopold ignored each other. Sir Leopold talked to Nan, while Demoyte talked to Rain, across Rain to Evvy, or across the table to Mor. When not actually addressed, Mor sat silent, watching his wife and his beloved, turning over in his heart the grievous things that he knew, and waiting for the evening to end.

At last came the toast to the Queen, and the meditative glow of cigars was to be seen appearing here and there along the table. It was quite dark outside by now and the candles gave a bright but soft light to the room, in which gentle illumination the stained walls were, as Hensman had predicted, not conspicuous. Fortunately nobody so far seemed anxious to draw the curtains. Mor discovered to his relief that Madeira was to be served with the fruit. The waiter was not insensitive to his needs, and his glass was filled again. The candlelight touched the wine-glasses and scattered silver. He looked through a maze of reflections towards Rain, and managed to catch her attention. She flashed him a quick look, humorous and loving, and made as if to close one eye. Mor, with a surreptitious and ambiguous movement, raised his glass towards her. She looked away. He now felt impelled to look at Nan. She was gazing towards him, though in lively and gesturing conversation with Sir Leopold. Mor noticed that she had drunk a little wine.

The first of the official toasts was the toast to Demoyte, which was to be proposed by Sir Leopold and answered by Evvy. The second toast was the toast to the School, to be proposed by Demoyte and answered by Nan. Sir Leopold rose to his feet and a serene silence fell, rich with the harmony which a large quantity of alcohol had introduced into the conscious and unconscious minds of the company. They looked up benevolently at Sir Leopold. Even Mor controlled his nausea. Sir Leopold, it would seem, was faced with the almost impossible task of proposing a toast to Demoyte without saying anything pleasant about him. But Sir Leopold's ingenuity turned out to be equal to the occasion. He contrived to say nothing pleasant about Demoyte by saying nothing about him at all. He spoke at length about St Bride's, its history, its high traditions, and the great line of its headmasters, all dedicated, at least those of them who were worthy of their trust, to the task which Mr Everard had so aptly described as 'the full development of the good seed of the personality', regardless of intellectual excellence. Hatred of Demoyte had triumphed, in Sir Leopold's bosom, over contempt for Evvy. He was prepared even to exalt Evvy in order to annoy Demoyte. The latter listened unmoved, showing in lip and eye how impossible he considered it that he could be belittled by such a person. Sir Leopold sat down amid lukewarm applause. He was not, in any quarter, a popular figure.

Mor was wishing that Nan's speech was not the last one. He was anxious for it to be over, as he was feeling a good deal of nervous apprehension on his wife's behalf. He imagined how scared Nan must be feeling. He knew that there was a special absurdity in his identifying himself, at this hour, with Nan; but it was the habit of half a lifetime and it was the absurdity which at present composed his whole being. He felt fairly sure that Nan would acquit herself well. She would certainly have something decent to say – only her delivery of it might be nervous and halting.

Evvy was now talking. Long practice in Hall and Chapel had made Mor able to switch off Evvy's voice completely. With an effort he switched it on again. '—whom we know and love,' said

Evvy. Accustomed as Evvy was to think the best of everybody, it had not quite escaped his attention that Sir Leopold had been rude to Demoyte; and he tried to make amends, laying it on, it seemed to Mor, rather thick. 'Under whose able and inspiring leadership,' Evvy was saying, 'St Bride's rose from the deplorable slough in which it formerly lay, and became, dare we say it, a sound and reputable public school of the second class.'

Evvy was here excelling himself, having forgotten that one of the Governors present was the younger son of the Headmaster who had preceded Demoyte. Mor looked along the table at this gentleman, whose eyebrows had flown up into furious triangles, and then looked to see how Demoyte liked Evvy's description of his achievement. Demoyte seemed amused. This was probably due to the proximity of Rain, who looked as if she might burst into wild laughter at any moment. When Mor saw her so gay, although he knew that it was largely the effect of the wine, he felt irritation and sadness. Nothing today could have moved him to gaiety or laughter. Agonizing thoughts about Donald came back into his mind. Where was his son now? He did not believe that any bodily harm could have come to Donald. But to what other demons might he not now be the prey? He pictured Donald sitting at this moment in some dreary café, staring at a stained tablecloth, while the waitress looked on, contemptuous and curious, or else in a public house, trying to look several years older, and avoiding the eye of the barmaid, or walking along a country road in the dark, caught in the headlights of cars, trying to beg a lift to – where? Afraid to come home. Afraid.

'—that I did not find it easy to be the successor to such a man,' Evvy was saying. His speech was turning out to be far too long, as usual. Sir Leopold had set the decanter circulating, and a whispered conversation was going on at the far end of the table. Each man protected himself from boredom after his own fashion: Sir Leopold by drinking and looking sideways into the top of Nan's dress, Rain by suppressed laughter, Demoyte by amused contempt. Mr Prewett by talking to his neighbour, and Bledyard by talking to himself.

Evvy continued, 'And it has been my constant study to resemble him in every way possible.' This was almost too much for Rain. It became clear from Demoyte's expression that she had kicked him under the table. They looked at each other. What a spring of life she has within her, Mor thought, to be able to laugh at such a time. But the secret of this is simple. She is young.

Evvy's voice was now taking on the elevated and lilting quality which it displayed in Chapel when he was nearing the end of a sermon. '—that in future years, when time and mortality shall have taken from us the great original, we shall be privileged to possess, for the admiration of the boys and the wonder of our visitors, this painting, the representation by so distinguished a painter of so distinguished a man.' Polite clapping broke out. Evvy sat down, and everyone looked at Demoyte.

Demoyte rose to his feet. 'Ladies and gentlemen,' he said, 'this is for me a moving and a sad occasion. It is the first time since my retirement that I have set foot inside the school which was for so many years my creation and my home. Needless to say, my absence from this scene has been at my own wish, unwilling as I am to play, within these walls which are so dear to me, the rôle merely of an ancestral ghost whose days of productivity are past and who can now only unnerve and terrify the beholder. This would in itself be a theme for sadness. Add to this, however, the fact that what has called up this apparition is the presence in the world of something new – a work of art: the extremely fine picture which we now have before us.'

Demoyte looked up at the picture. So did everyone else, the guests nearest to the fireplace leaning backwards across the table in order to see it. Nobody was bored now.

'The reverend speaker who preceded me,' said Demoyte, 'spoke, as it is his especial right to do, of mortality. And what indeed could be more calculated to impress upon one a sense of finitude than the dedication, to the place where one has passed, such as it was, one's life, of an image of oneself, to be left as a memorial for future generations? This is to give a palpable body to the sad truth that we can enjoy immortality only in the thoughts of others – a place in which during our lives we have not always been cherished and in which after our death we shall be without defence. I speak, of course, *sub specie temporis*.'

A polite smile spread round the table. Demoyte had transformed the scene. The look of condescension which the Governors had been wearing all the evening had faded now from their faces. They no longer felt themselves to be conferring, by their presence, a favour upon a bunch of simpleminded provincial schoolmasters.

'This truth,' said Demoyte, 'may trouble us or it may merely wound us. My situation is, however, more complex – since I am so fortunate as to have my image passed on to posterity by the brilliant brush of Miss Carter, whom we are so glad and so privileged to have with us tonight.' Applause followed. About time, thought Mor. He looked at Rain. He felt proud.

'Such an experience,' Demoyte went on, 'cannot but induce humility. How well we know the faces and how little we are concerned with the obscure careers of so many of the men and women whom the great painters of the past have made to live forever amongst us. Who was Dr Peral? Who was Jacob Trip? Who were Mr and Mrs Arnolfini? In a way we know, with a supreme knowledge, since we may look upon their faces through the eye of a genius. In a way we do not know, nor do we care, what were their talents, their hopes and their fears, or how they must have appeared to themselves. And so he too will live on, this obscure schoolmaster, held in the profound, and if I may say so, charitable, vision of Miss Carter – and it is a consolation to think that if St Bride's is in the years to come distinguished for nothing else, it will at least be a place of pilgrimage for those who are interested in the early work of one who – can we doubt it in the face of such evidence – is destined to be one of the more remarkable painters of her age.'

Mor was watching Rain. Demoyte continued to speak. She was fingering her glass, looking down, frowning. She was moved by his words. Mor returned his glance to the tablecloth, and then after a suitable interval looked at Nan.

Nan was looking, for the first time that evening, thoroughly nervous and disturbed. She was looking straight ahead of her with an unseeing stare, and her hand which lay upon the table was visibly trembling. She had drawn out of her handbag and clutched in her other hand a small piece of paper with notes upon it. A deep blush had spread downward from her cheeks to her neck. Her lips moved slightly. Poor Nan, thought Mor. He tried to catch her eye. She turned towards him – and he was startled by the scared and wide-eyed expression with which she looked at him. He smiled and made an encouraging gesture with his hand. Mad, mad, he thought to himself, all is mad. But at least this evening will soon be done. After Nan's speech they would adjourn to the Common Room, and soon after that one could decently go. The evening was almost over. Nan was still giving him a look of distress and fear, and he could see now that her lower jaw was trembling. He had to look away. He was beginning to tremble himself. He hoped that she would not blunder too much. It was certainly hard on her, following after so accomplished a speaker as Demoyte.

By now Demoyte's speech was almost done. He was speaking of the school. He was even being gracious to Evvy. At last the toast was being proposed: St Bride's! They lifted their glasses. Sir Leopold was laying an encouraging hand upon Nan's bare arm. Nan rose to her feet. Mor averted his eyes and tried to think how splendid it would be in a few minutes when they had all escaped into the Common Room and could relax.

'Ladies and gentlemen,' said Nan, her voice pitched higher than usual and quivering with the uncanny refinement of the nervous woman, 'I am privileged and pleased that such a gathering as this should be the occasion of my very first public speech.' Everyone was leaning forward, looking upon her sympathetically. 'And it is fitting too that the person who answers the toast that we have just had should be an outsider, a mere wife, someone who, while living in the shadow of this great institution, does not really form part of it.'

Mor began to feel some relief. Nan had caught the absurd tone of the evening's proceedings quite well. Her voice was becoming steadier. Now she was going on to say suitably banal and complimentary things about St Bride's. She was acquitting herself quite respectably. Another sentence or two, thought Mor, and she will have said enough and can decently sit down. He looked up approvingly, hoping that she was about to make an end. But Nan went on.

'St Bride's,' she was saying, 'has always been distinguished for its tradition of public service. Our great democracy has not looked towards St Bride's in vain – and public servants in all ranks of honourable employment are numbered among our old boys.' Mor smiled inwardly. He knew just how much Nan cared about traditions of public service. He was amazed at her capacity to put on this act. He would not have suspected her capable of such a masquerade.

'I trust then,' Nan was saying – her voice was trembling

again now, 'that you will not think it unsuitable if, before ending my speech, I strike a more personal note. The windows of St Bride's have never, as we know, been closed upon the world of commerce and of politics. Enriched by contact with the School, many have gone out, boys and masters alike, into the world beyond the classroom and the library. And here I am sure you will pardon me if I speak to you of something which has long been known to many of you – the ambitions of my husband.'

Mor jumped, and upset what remained of his glass of wine. He looked up quickly at Nan. She was looking at the ceiling, her mouth open to speak again. Mor's heart began to twist within him like a corkscrew. But still he did not realize what was coming.

'It has been for many years,' Nan went on, 'the dear wish and ambition of my husband, myself and our children that he should serve his country in the highest role to which a democratic society can call its citizens – that of a Member of Parliament. After a long period of patient work, my husband has now the great happiness of being able to realize his life-long ambition. The nearby borough of Marsington have decided to adopt him as their Labour candidate – and as we know, Marsington, with all respect to those present who are of the other party, is a safe Labour seat.'

Amazement, horror and anger struggled within him; Mor could scarcely believe his ears. He turned his head to where Demoyte and Rain were sitting. Demoyte looked completely stunned; he was half turned towards Nan, his haid raised to his mouth. Then he turned sharply back towards Mor, a look of surprise, dismay and accusation. But it was the face of Rain that made Mor almost cry out aloud. He had told her nothing of his political plans. She was hearing of them now for the first time. She looked towards him, her lips parting as if to question him, her eyes expressing astonishment and sheer horror, her whole face working in an agony of interrogation. Mor shook his head violently.

Nan was going on. 'As Shakespeare says, there is a tide in the affairs of men that taken at the flood leads on to fortune. This tide now runs for my husband, and for myself and for our children. We have discussed the matter and we are at last agreed that there is no other bond or tie which can prevent us from adventuring forward together. Courage is needed to make the great step. To delay would be fatal. Such a chance comes but once in a lifetime. Courage he has never lacked – nor is it likely that he will hesitate now when all his deepest and most cherished wishes are about to find so complete a fulfilment.'

Mor was breathing deeply. He was still almost deprived of breath by the shock. Who would have thought that Nan would be so ingenious – or so desperate? He knew that something vital, perhaps final, was happening to him, but he did not fully see what it was. He tried to keep Rain's eyes, but she turned away from him, grimacing with distress. Mor told himself that what he ought to do now, now this very minute, was to get up from his seat and lead Rain out of the room. Nan had attempted to corner him by a public gesture. She should be answered in the same way. To rise now and go out with Rain would set the seal on all his intentions. At last Nan had raised the storm. It was for him to ride it. But Rain had turned away her eyes – and although Mor struggled in his seat he could not bring himself to get up. A lifetime of conformity was too much for him. He stayed where he was.

'To you, therefore, my husband's friends and colleagues,' Nan continued, 'I turn at this crucial moment of choice, and ask for your blessing and your good wishes for an enterprise worthy indeed of the traditions of St Bride's, and of the great talents of my husband. In the end, no destiny could satisfy him but this one, which he has always so ardently desired and which is now so unexpectedly placed within his reach.'

Nan was speaking slowly and precisely, making every word count. Once more the tremor had gone from her voice. She was masterly. She paused for breath.

Quite quietly Rain rose to her feet. She turned towards Demoyte as if to speak to him, but did not. She turned about, gathering up her evening-bag, and went soft-footed out of the room. Everyone shifted uneasily, stared at her as she departed, and then looked back to Nan, puzzled but still spellbound. The candles were burning low.

Nan prolonged her pause. From the corner of his eye Mor could see her figure relax. She threw her page of notes down on the table. She began to say, 'But you will have heard enough now of my personal hopes and fears – it remains for me to conclude my remarks by—' Her voice became inaudible to Mor. He half rose from his seat, and then slumped back again, helpless. He became aware that everyone in the room was looking at him. He thought at first it must be because of Rain's departure, but then realized that it was because of Nan's speech. He knew he ought to follow Rain out – but again, he could not. The scene held him prisoner, his wife's presence and her words pinned him to his chair, his whole previous life contained him like a strait-jacket. He turned to face Demoyte and flinched away from the expression of blazing fury in the old man's eyes that bade him get up and go. He could not.

Nan sat down amid applause, and an immediate buzz of excited talk. Everyone knew that something odd was happening, nobody knew what it was. Curious stares were directed at Mor. Sir Leopold was filling Nan's glass. She sat there with her elbow on the table, her face hidden by her hand. Evvy was saying to Demoyte that he hoped Miss Carter had not been taken ill, and oughtn't they – Demoyte got up and left the room, slamming the door behind him. Mor closed his eyes.

Some ten or fifteen minutes passed during which Evvy made some rather lengthy concluding remarks and the bottle circulated again. Then the company began to rise to their feet to adjourn to the Common Room. Several people converged on Mor, to make sympathetic remarks and offer good wishes. He walked with them through the door into the Common Room. Then he excused himself and ran out into the corridor.

He ran down the steps and out into the playground. It was an exceedingly dark night, and apart from the blaze from the windows above him no lights were on in the school. Only a lamp burning at the corner of School House lit up an expanse of asphalt and gravel and the edges of the grass. He looked about. Where had Rain gone to? Where could he find her now? He began to run down the drive. He saw the Riley parked upon the grass verge. But there was no sign of Rain. He called her name, cautiously at first and then more loudly. He turned and ran back to the main buildings, hoping to see some trace of her or of Demoyte. There was nobody. He ran up as far as the school gates. It was in vain. He came back, panting with exhaustion, and fell down, hiding his face in the grass near to the wheels of the car.

# CHAPTER NINETEEN

Mor waited beside the car for a long time. Now and then voices were to be heard and footsteps on the gravel, but it was only the departing guests. No one came near the Riley. At last he got up and searched for a while in the grounds, more or less aimlessly. Then he ran to find his bicycle. It was not in the shed in the masters' garden. It must be at home. He began to run as fast as he could towards his house. He wondered how long a time had passed. He could not judge. Why had he let her go away? If only he had held her *then*, taking her hand before the whole company, none of the forces which Nan had tried to drive between them would have been of any avail.

As he came near his house he saw that there was a light on in Nan's room. She had evidently returned. He forced his way through the gate, kicking it violently open, and ran down the side way into the garden to find his bicycle. As he dragged the machine towards the road he could hear the curtains being drawn back. Light fell upon the path and on the flowers which he had kicked aside. Nan was looking out. He paid no attention and did not look round. He mounted the machine, bounced noisily off the pavement, and began to pedal as hard as he could in the direction of Brayling's Close.

There was a light on in the hall of the Close and another in the drawing-room. The bicycle came bucking across the gravel, and Mor dismounted it at speed. As he ran the last few steps he saw that the front door was ajar. Demoyte was standing in the hall. Their bodies came into violent collision. Demoyte seized Mor by the shoulder in a grip that hurt. For a second he thought that the old man was going to strike him. Mor wrenched himself free. The power which he had lacked when he sat at the dinner table now flowed in him with such abundance that he could have torn a wall down to reach Rain.

'Where is she?' he said to Demoyte.

'I don't know!' said Demoyte. He began to say something else, but Mor had already turned and shot out of the door again. He seized the bicycle, which seemed to have got entangled in a rose bush, shook it free, and began to pedal back in the direction of the school. He moaned aloud now, partly with breathlessness and partly with the agony of suspense. For he still did not know what had happened.

The bicycle came hurtling down the drive. The Riley was still there. Mor braked violently and dismounted beside the car. What could he do now? Where could he look? It was impossible to find her, yet impossible too to endure her disappearance. It came to him that this was the first time for many weeks that he had not known where Rain was. He threw the bicycle on the grass verge and began to walk towards the playground. She might still be here, somewhere inside the school. The lamp had been extinguished at the corner of School House and the drive was in total darkness. Hours had passed. It must now be well after midnight. Everyone would have gone home. Yet perhaps she was still here. The Riley had not gone. She must be somewhere here.

He walked into the playground and looked about him. All was dark. Except for one light. Looking up, Mor saw that a light was still burning in the masters' dining-room. They were probably clearing up the remains of the dinner. But at that hour? He stood looking at the light. Then he began to run towards the door of the building, his feet clattering on the asphalt and his footsteps echoing from the dark façades. The main door was unlocked. He mounted the stairs two at a time and blundered into the Common Room which was in darkness. He switched the lights on, sprang across the room, and threw open the door of the dining-room.

A bright electric bulb now lit the room, which looked exceedingly strange. The remnants of the feast had been removed. It seemed at first as if there was no one there. Then Mor saw Rain. She was high above his head. She had found a very tall step ladder and had set it up, standing it upon the tiles of the fireplace. She was sitting now upon the very top, level with the portrait which still hung in its place high aloft above the mantelshelf. She was applying paint to the canvas. She held the enormous palette upon her left hand and her lap was full of paints. Paint marks of all colours streaked her white evening-dress which fell in a great fan about her, hanging down over the side of the ladder. As the door opened she did not look

273

round but continued carefully with what she was doing. She was working on the head.

'Rain!' said Mor. He ran to the foot of the ladder and shook it violently as if he wanted to hurl her to the ground.

She steadied herself, and then turned back to the picture. He saw that as she worked the tears were streaming slowly down her face, steadily one after the other.

'Rain!' said Mor, 'that was not true. It was simply a trick of Nan's. Surely you weren't taken in?'

'It is true,' said Rain, in a dull voice. 'I asked Mr Demoyte.'

'Well, it was an idea I had once,' said Mor, 'but Nan misrepresented the whole thing. And we never discussed it or agreed anything like she said. You can't possibly have believed that!'

'It doesn't matter,' said Rain, 'it's what you want to do.' She was still staring through her falling tears at the picture.

'That isn't so,' said Mor. 'I swear it isn't so! I'd quite given up any plans of that kind.'

'Yes,' said Rain, 'because of me.' She took the brush away and turned to look down at him. Her small feet were neatly together upon a high step of the ladder, the toes of her shoes just visible under the white dress. Mor reached up to touch her.

'No, no,' said Mor. Holding her feet he leaned his head against the ladder. How could he convince her?

'Look,' he said, 'this makes no difference at all. Why should it? I ought to have told you long ago, only I didn't want to complicate things. If I'd told you myself you wouldn't have made this into a difficulty, would you? You're just upset because it came from Nan. Well, don't be such a fool. I love you, and nothing else is of any importance. This other thing is empty in comparison, it's nothing. I love you, I should perish without you. *Will* you understand that?' He spoke savagely, trying to force the ideas into her mind.

'Don't, you're hurting my leg,' said Rain. 'I do understand. I had just not realized that I was wrecking your whole life. I see it all quite differently now. I see your children, I see your ambitions. You love me, yes. But you wouldn't really forgive me for having deprived you of so much. And I would not forgive myself for doing so.' She spoke in a monotonous slightly whining voice, and her tears were very slow but ceaseless.

'No, no, no, it's not like that!' cried Mor. How could he bear it, that Nan had bewitched her so? She saw it all exactly as Nan had intended. How could she be so stupid? 'No!' he cried. 'I shall not let you do this thing to both of us!'

'It's useless, Mor,' said Rain. 'What am I doing in your life? I've often wondered this, you know, only I never told my doubts. You are a growing tree. I am only a bird. You cannot break your roots and fly away with me. Where could we go where you wouldn't always be wanting the deep things that belong to you, your children, and this work which you know is your work? I know how I would feel if I were prevented from painting. I should die if I were prevented from painting. I should die.' For a moment she shook with sobs and the ladder trembled under her.

'I love you, Rain,' said Mor, 'what else can I say? I haven't cared for these other things at all since I've known you. I shall never be an M.P. now, whatever happens. I no longer want this. I want you. Don't kill me, Rain.' He leaned against the ladder, embracing the lower steps.

'You would be happy with me for a short while,' said Rain, 'but then what would happen? It's all dry sand running through the fingers. I can wander about the world and wherever I go I can paint. If we were together my work would continue. But what about yours? Would it in the end satisfy you just to be with me? Would you be able to write and go on writing? If you had really wanted to write as much as I want to paint you would have written by now, you would have found the time somehow, nothing would have stopped you.'

'I could write,' said Mor, 'or I could start a school. I'm not an idiot. I've thought of these things too. I could make my life with you. What sort of life do you think I have now, or would have even if I were an M.P.? You've made me exist for the first time. I began to be when I loved you, I saw the world for the first time, the beautiful world full of things and animals that I'd never seen before. What do you think will happen to me if you leave me now? Don't abandon me. Don't do such a wicked thing. Don't!'

He reached up his hand towards her. She leaned forward and took it in a strong grip. They paused for a moment, pressing each other's hands. But all the comfort was gone out of the contact. They both knew it and felt despair. Rain withdrew her hand.

'Rain, do you love me?' said Mor. He stood squarely at the foot of the ladder gazing up at her. 'If you've just changed your mind about me, say it, and don't wrap it up in this torturing way.'

'I love you,' said Rain, 'I do love you, I do. But what does that mean? Perhaps, after all, it has all been because of – father.' She laid the palette down on her lap and rubbed her face violently with both hands. Patches of red and blue paint appeared on her cheeks and forehead.

'Oh, for Christ's sake,' said Mor, 'don't give me that. I shall not allow you to leave me, Rain, I shall just not allow it. Nothing has happened tonight which can alter anything between us. Don't be tricked by my wife. Don't look anywhere but to me.'

'Oh, Mor, Mor,' said Rain, her voice wailing, 'if you only knew how I do look to you! I've got nobody but you at all. But now I can see. I see that it was you that tricked me – and I too that deceived myself. I saw it all so simply, with nothing to it but you leaving your wife whom you didn't love and who didn't love you. But a life has so much more in it than that. I had not seen that I would break so many many things.'

'If you love me—' he said.

'That word cannot guide us any more.' She spoke wearily, with finality.

'Make it all right,' said Mor. 'Sweep away what has happened tonight, do not remember it.'

'Oh, my dear,' said Rain, 'my dear—' She turned her eyes, red and hazy with tears, towards the face in the picture which was level with her own.

'Make it all right,' said Mor.

'Oh, my dear—' said Rain.

It was the final negative. Mor stepped away from the foot of the ladder. He stood silent for a moment. The pain in his heart was almost beyond bearing. Then he said, 'I accept nothing of what you say. We shall speak of this again.'

Rain said nothing. She took up the palette and began to mix some paint, but could not see for her tears.

Mor took two steps towards the door. He said, 'You should stop that now, and go to bed. You're far too upset to paint. Shall I fetch your car and bring it round into the playground?'

Rain shook her head violently. It was a moment before she

could speak. 'No,' she said, 'I must finish this. I want to repaint the head. I see what to do now. I must go on working. Don't wait up.'

Mor hesitated. He had a terrible feeling that if he left her now he might never see her again. But he had to see her again. They would speak tomorrow. He would force her to agree with him. It could not be otherwise.

'We are both too overwrought,' he said. 'We will speak of this again tomorrow.'

'Yes, yes,' said Rain, 'please go. I must work now. Please go.'

Mor got as far as the door. He stood watching her. She had begun to paint again, dashing the tears from her eyes.

'Rain,' he said.

She did not answer.

'Tomorrow,' he said.

'Yes,' said Rain, 'yes.'

She went on painting. Mor stayed for a minute or two watching her, and then he went out and closed the door behind him.

# CHAPTER TWENTY

When Mor awoke it was cold. He turned in bed and looked towards the window. A very white dim light. It was early morning. No need to get up yet. Then as he turned again to settle down, the memory of last night spread through his mind like a crack. He sat up in bed and held his hand to his face as if to prevent great cries from issuing forth. He must see Rain very soon, immediately after breakfast, sooner. Last night she had been mad. If he had been less drunk himself he would have realized it and would have left her alone at once. He looked at his watch. Ten to six. He lay back on the pillow. There were still hours to wait. Then he found out that he could not stay in bed. He was in too great an agony. He began to get up and to dress, stumbling about searching for his clothes. He had a violent headache.

When he was dressed, he wondered what to do. It occurred to him that Rain might have been painting all night and might still be there in the masters' dining-room. But on reflection this seemed very unlikely. He sat for a while on the edge of his bed. The time was now five past six. He swung his legs and lit a cigarette. The time opened in front of him like an appalling steam-filled abyss. How could he wait so long? He walked about the room, keeping his footsteps silent. He began to think about his wife.

Then a thought came to him, a thought which he had had last night, but which had been overwhelmed by the violence of the events. He crept downstairs, carrying his shoes with him, and went into the dining-room, where his writing-desk was. He opened the drawer of the desk where he had hidden the two draft letters which he had written, the one to Nan and the other to Tim Burke, announcing his intentions. The letters were there, but Mor could see at once that they had been moved from their original place. He stood for some time in a melancholy daze looking into the drawer. Nan must have found them. That explained the desperation which had driven her to make such a dramatic sacrifice of her own wishes.

Mor closed the drawer and sat down on one of the chairs beside the dining-room table. The house was cold and very silent with the death-like abandoned silence of the early morning. He felt sick in his whole body as if ripped by innumerable wounds. He sat for a few minutes listening for a sound, but there was nothing to be heard. Then he decided he must go out into the road. He crept into the hall. At the front door he put his shoes on, donned an overcoat, and went out, closing the door quietly.

He began to walk along the pavement. The morning was exceedingly still and pale. He was reminded of the day of Nan's return when he had come out into this appalling morning air, and such a feeling of catastrophe overwhelmed him that he had to bite his hands. Today there was no rain, but the sky was pure white, covered over absolutely with an even sheet of cloud. When he reached the main road he wondered what to do. A car went by, desolate and portentous upon the empty road. He decided that he would go to Brayling's Close and wait outside until they were stirring. If he did not at least come near to where Rain was he would fall down faint at the pains that were eating his heart.

He remembered that his bicycle was in the school. In his agitation of last night he had left it there, and had come home on foot. He walked through the school gates, his feet crunching loudly on the damp gravel in the midst of the empty gardens. He found his bicycle lying on the grass where he had thrown it. The Riley was gone. He wheeled the machine as far as the entrance to the drive. There was no point in making haste. No one would be up yet at the Close. He might as well spin out the time between into some sort of motion and activity. He began to wheel the machine up the hill, and then turned into one of the suburban roads which led past his own house to the fields. He thought he would go by way of the fields. He wanted to be in the open and in that kinder solitude to collect himself.

As he came down the road he saw a figure approaching him. It seemed familiar. Then as it came nearer he saw that it was the gipsy whom he and Rain had first seen in the wood, and who had come to shelter under his porch with such strange results. Mor felt an immediate thrill of fear at seeing the man. The gipsy was walking on the opposite pavement with a slow loping stride, and carrying on his shoulder a bundle wrapped in a sheet. He was making for the main road. Mor thought at once: he is going. The man did not look across at him, though he could hardly have been unaware of the appearance in so empty a scene of another human figure. Mor wondered about him, wondering if he was right in thinking that he was deaf. The man passed, and disappeared from view, turning to the left into the main road. Mor walked on pushing his bicycle.

He passed his own house. Then suddenly a sense of great urgency came over him. Why had he been dawdling like this? He must hurry. How could he have endured to delay? Why had he ever left Rain at all on the previous night? He was by now at the beginning of the path across the fields. He jumped on to his bicycle and began pedalling vigorously along the path; and as he rode the blanched coldness of the morning was becoming softer, and a slight almost imperceptible glow was spread through the air, to show that behind the thick expanse of cloud the sun was rising higher.

Demoyte's house, as Mor saw it from the fields, looked dead, surrounded still by silence and sleep. He turned sharply where the path came up to the wall, and rode along the narrower track beside it until he could turn into the drive. He dropped his machine near the gate, and walked forward on to the circle of grass which lay before the front door. The curtains were pulled in Demoyte's bedroom. Their faded colourless lining closed the window like a dead eyelid. Mor stood for a while looking up. Then he went forward and tried the front door. It was locked. He looked at his watch again. It was only six-thirty. Rain must be sleeping. She would surely want to sleep late after her exertions of last night. If he could have got into the house he would have lain down outside her door.

He began to walk round to the garden at the side of the house. He wanted to look up at her window. The lawn was covered with a glistening sheet of dew in which his steps left clear footprints behind. He walked silently across the lawn, looking up at the corner window. Here too the curtains were still drawn. The house was asleep. He must wait. Now that he was so near to her he felt more tranquil. All would yet be well. He would make it so. The strength which all along he had lacked was in him at last, as if he had been touched by a wand and made invincible. He stood there, and his gaze wandered into the sky where a rift had appeared in the clouds and a streak of very pale blue was to be seen. A sharp breeze was blowing. He drew his overcoat more closely about him. He would have liked to lie down on the grass, only the dew was too thick.

Several minutes passed. To warm himself a little he turned to walk a few steps along the lawn, his chilled hands thrust deep into his pockets. Then his eye was caught by a movement in the house. He looked up and saw that in one of the library windows Miss Handforth was standing and watching him. She stood very erect and motionless. It seemed to Mor that she must have been there a long time. She seemed like an apparition. He stopped and looked up at her. He hardly expected that there could be any communication between them, so far away did she seem. So they looked at each other for a moment without any sign.

Then Miss Handforth undid the window and pushed up the sash. In a loud clear voice, without leaning out, she said, 'She is gone.'

Mor looked down at the grass, at the dew, and at the marks in the dew of his own footsteps. With bent head he began to walk very slowly back towards the front door. When he reached the door he found it open and came into the hall. Miss Handforth was standing on the stairs.

'Is Mr Demoyte up yet?' Mor asked.

'He's in the library,' she said, and came down the stairs and disappeared in the direction of the kitchen.

Mor mounted the stairs very slowly. It seemed an effort to lift each foot. He opened the library door, and saw Demoyte sitting at the round table near the window. He was in his dressing-gown. The curtains were all pulled well back and the morning light filled the room, warmer now, turning to a weak sunshine.

Mor took a chair and sat down on the opposite side of the table. He did not look at Demoyte. There was silence for a moment.

'Oh, you fool, you fool, you fool,' said Demoyte in a tired voice.

Mor said nothing. He leaned his elbows on the table and began rubbing his eyes and passing his two hands over his brow.

'What happened?' said Mor at last.

'Nothing happened,' said Demoyte. 'She went on painting for two or three hours after you left her. Then she came back here and packed all her things, and went away in the car.'

Mor turned towards Demoyte. The old man looked ashy grey with his sleepless night. Behind him near the wall Mor saw a square of colour. It was the portrait, which stood on the floor, propped against one of the bookcases. Mor did not let himself look at it. 'Is she coming back?' he asked Demoyte.

'No, of course not,' said Demoyte. 'She said she was going straight to France, but not to her own house. Then probably to America.'

Mor nodded slowly. He was looking down again, at the floor between his two feet. One foot tapped rhythmically without his will.

'When did she go?' he asked.

'About two hours ago,' said Demoyte. He turned suddenly on Mor, and his anger shook him so that he had to hold on to the table. 'Why did you leave her? Why did you leave her for a single moment? You must have willed to lose her!'

Mor did not look up. He could feel the table trembling between them. 'It was inevitable,' he said dully.

'Coward and fool!' said Demoyte. 'Nothing was inevitable here. You have made your own future.'

Mor put his head down upon the table for a moment. He raised it to say, 'Will we see her – again?' His voice did not have the cadence of a question.

'Do not deceive yourself,' said Demoyte. 'I shall never see her again. You may meet her once more by accident in ten years' time at a party when you are fat and bald and she is married. Would you like some coffee? I'll get Handy to make us some.' He rang the bell.

'Did she leave any messages for me?' Mor asked.

'She left something,' said Demoyte. He got up and went to the desk at the far window. 'Here it is.'

He brought a large plain envelope and put it into Mor's hand. The envelope was unsealed. In an agony of apprehension and insane hope Mor drew out its contents. It was a sketch. He saw at once what it was. It was the sketch which she had made of him on the first evening when he had come and found her painting, and had sat with her and Demoyte, the evening when she had begun to fall in love with him. She had never remembered to show him the sketch. He looked at it now. She had said that it might have betrayed that she was beginning to love him. He saw upon the paper a young man with a strong twisted humorous face and curly hair, head thrown back in a rather proud attitude, a thick pillar of neck, a hand raised as if in dispute. It bore some resemblance to himself. He laid the sketch down on the table. Nothing was written upon it.

'Was this all?' he asked Demoyte.

'Yes.'

Miss Handforth knocked and came in. She had interpreted the bell and carried a tray with black coffee and a bottle of brandy. She laid it down between them and went away without a word.

Mor mixed some brandy with the black coffee and drank it. He turned now to look at the portrait. He got up and walked across the room to study it more closely. Demoyte followed him. They looked at it a while in silence. Rain had changed the head a great deal. At first sight it seemed as if she had spoilt it. The fine sensitive lines which had built up the quiet musing expression which Mor had liked so much had been covered over with layer after layer of tiny patches of paint. The head stood out now solider, uglier, the expression no longer conveyed by the fine details, but seeming to emerge from the deep structure of the face. Mor was not sure whether he liked it better. He turned away. They both went back to sit at the table.

'Well,' said Demoyte, 'we've each of us received a picture of ourselves.' He poured out some more coffee.

'I suppose I ought to go back,' said Mor. 'Nan will be wondering where I am.' He said this without thought, automatically.

Demoyte pushed the bottle of brandy towards him. 'You will take on the candidature, of course?' he said.

'Yes,' said Mor, 'I will do that now. Nan won't resist it any more. She'll abide by what she said last night.'

'If you drop this plan,' said Demoyte, 'if you let her cheat you out of that too, I'll never receive you in this house again. Never. I mean that.'

'Don't worry, sir,' said Mor. 'I shall go ahead. I shall go ahead now.' He drank some more brandy. He got up to go. He found that he still had his coat on with the collar turned up.

Demoyte rose. 'Aren't you going to take this?' He indicated the sketch which still lay on the table.

'No,' said Mor, 'you keep it for me. I should like it to be kept here.' He turned away from it.

He got as far as the door. 'By the way, sir,' he said, 'could I ask one thing?'

'Yes,' said Demoyte.

'You remember you offered to help us to send Felicity to college if it were necessary? Does the offer still stand?'

'Of course,' said Demoyte.

'Thank you,' said Mor. 'I may be glad to accept it. Perhaps I could discuss this with you later.'

'Do as you like,' said Demoyte. 'Good-bye.'

'Good-bye,' said Mor. He felt a desire to say 'I'm sorry,' but kept silent, lingering at the door.

'Come and see me in a few days,' said Demoyte.

'Yes,' said Mor. He left the room. The last he saw of Demoyte, the old man was leaning on the edge of the table, looking gloomily towards the portrait.

Mor went out of the front door and found his bicycle. The sun was shining now, pale yellow, through a white haze. A steady stream of traffic was passing both ways along the main road. Mor decided to return home by the road and not by the fields. He got on to his machine and began to pedal slowly towards the hill. He felt extreme weariness. His headache had not left him. There was a buzzing in his ears and the brandy which he had drunk seemed to make his limbs weighty. The wind was against him.

As he neared the foot of the hill, pedalling with his head down, he heard through the noise of the traffic a strange cry. He looked up. Then he saw Felicity, who was coming flying down the hill on her bicycle, across on the other carriage way. She had seen him and was calling out. She came whirling towards him, dismounted at a high speed, and hurled herself and the bicycle across the grass which divided the two sections of the road. Mor came rapidly in towards the centre to meet her, and rode his bicycle on to the grass. As she came up to him, tumbling off her machine, Felicity called out something which at first Mor understood as 'Rain's come back!' Then he realized that what Felicity must have said was 'Don's come back!' They met with an impact, cannoning into each other, their bicycles colliding.

'Oh, Daddy,' cried Felicity, 'I'm so glad I found you!' She clung on to him.

'Did you say Don had come back?' said Mor.

'Yes,' said Felicity, 'at least he's not actually back yet. He came very late last night to Tim Burke's house, and Tim rang up about half an hour ago to say that he was going to bring Don over on his motor bike. He says Don is quite all right. They ought to be arriving any moment now. We might see them on the way.'

'Well, thank God for that,' said Mor. He picked up Felicity's bicycle and his own, and they got back on to the road and began to push their machines up the hill. Felicity still clung on to his arm.

'How did you know where to look for me?' said Mor.

'I saw you go out,' said Felicity, 'and then I saw you go by again towards the fields. So I thought you might be down at Mr Demoyte's house.'

Mor was silent. Arm in arm they plodded up the hill.

'Daddy,' said Felicity, 'will you be an M.P. now?'

'I suppose so, darling,' said Mor, 'if I get elected.' He put his hand into hers.

'Will we move to London?' said Felicity.

'Yes,' said Mor, 'we'll move to London.'

'I'm so glad,' said Felicity. 'I shall like that. I'm tired of living here. Daddy—'

'Yes?' said Mor.

'Need I go on that secretarial course?' said Felicity. 'I wasn't sure before, but now I think I'd much rather stay at school for the present.'

'You shall stay at school then,' said Mor, 'and later on perhaps you'll go to a university.'

'Daddy,' said Felicity, 'don't be too cross with Don.'

'I won't be cross with him,' said Mor.

'Do you think Don could work with Tim Burke now?' said Felicity. 'He'd much rather do that than chemistry, only he was always afraid to tell you. He's missed his silly exam anyway.'

'We'll see about that, darling,' said Mor. 'Perhaps it may be the best thing. But we'll see.'

285

They were nearly at the top of the hill.

'Daddy,' said Felicity, 'when we go to London do you think we could have another dog?'

Mor was very near to tears. Not the tears that he cried, as Rain had told him, inside his eyes, but visible tears that would stream down and wet his cheeks. 'Yes,' he said, 'I expect we might have a dog when we go to London, if you'd like that.'

They had reached the top of the hill. They mounted their bicycles and began to free-wheel down the other side towards Mor's house. The tears came to him now, coursing down his cheeks and blown away by the wind. He put one hand to his eyes. By the time he had reached his own front gate they were no longer flowing.

Nan was standing at the door. Mor leaned his bicycle against the fence and came up the path, followed by Felicity. He looked at Nan. He felt that his shoulders were bowed. She looked at him. She looked very tired and like an old woman. Before they could exchange any words a sound was heard which Mor recognized. It was the note of Tim Burke's Velocette. They all three turned back to the road.

Tim Burke appeared round the corner, riding very slowly now. Donald was sitting behind him on the pillion, his arms clasped round Tim's waist. The machine stopped outside the house and the two riders dismounted. Donald was still dressed in the flannels and gym shoes which he had worn on the day of the climb. He was also wearing an old mackintosh. His face was pale and withdrawn. Tim held him by the shoulder and turned towards the group at the gate. He seemed as nervous about his own reception as about Donald's. He said in a defiant voice, 'The prodigal's return!'

'Come inside,' said Mor. He led the way into the house. Donald followed directly after him, pushed forward by Tim Burke. They all crowded into the hall. Mor turned to Donald. The boy looked at him, raising his eyebrows in a half humorous half desperate appeal. Mor embraced him, holding him fast for a minute in his arms. Then he said, 'I expect you're dead tired.'

Felicity was hugging him now and Nan was kissing him on the cheek. 'I'm exhausted,' said Donald. 'I'm afraid I gave Tim an awful night too. We've hardly slept.'

'You'd better go straight to bed,' said Nan. 'Your clothes look as if they're sticking to your body. Off with you now, and I'll bring you up some hot coffee and an egg in bed.'

Donald began to mount the stairs. Mor followed after him and went with him into his bedroom. The door closed behind them.

Nan went into the kitchen. She nodded to Tim Burke to come with her. She put the kettle on the stove, and a saucepan to boil the egg. She lit the gas. Then she looked towards Tim Burke. He was sitting beside the table in an attitude of dejection. He would not meet her eye.

Felicity was sitting by herself on the stairs, half-way up. From the kitchen she could hear the noise of crockery and of the hissing gas. From up above she could hear the quiet sound of voices as Mor and Donald were talking in the bedroom. Everything was all right now. Why was it then that she was starting to cry? She fumbled in her clothes until she found a handkerchief. Her eyes were filled with tears and soon they were streaming down her face. She gave a little sob into her handkerchief. Everything was all right now. It was all right. It was all right.